Milo
and the
Dragon Cross

This is for Barbara who was such an important contributor to the existance of this book. Thanks, Barbara, and may Milo and his friends travel with you!

MILO
and the
DRAGON
CROSS

A Novel

Robert Jesten Upton

SUNSTONE
PRESS

SANTA FE

Sunstone books may be purchased for educational, business, or sales promotional use.
For information please write: Special Markets Department, Sunstone Press,
P.O. Box 2321, Santa Fe, New Mexico 87504-2321.
Body typeface › Bookman Old Style
Printed on acid-free paper
∞
eBook 978-1-61139-510-5

Library of Congress Cataloging-in-Publication Data

Names: Upton, Robert Jesten, author.
Title: Milo and the Dragon Cross : a novel / by Robert Jesten Upton.
Description: Santa Fe : Sunstone Press, 2017. | Summary: "A curious
    fifteen-year-old boy, a cultured talking cat, and a Magical Scavenger Hunt
    lead the reader into a world of sorcerers, wizards, and witches in this
    tale about the struggle of good over evil, loyalty, life lessons, and
    friendship"-- Provided by publisher.
Identifiers: LCCN 2017006291 (print) | LCCN 2017026074 (ebook) | ISBN
    9781611395105 | ISBN 9781632931771 (softcover : alk. paper)
Subjects: | CYAC: Good and evil--Fiction. | Magic--Fiction. | Treasure hunt
    (Game)--Fiction. | Friendship--Fiction. | Grail--Fiction.
Classification: LCC PZ7.1.U69 (ebook) | LCC PZ7.1.U69 Mi 2017 (print) | DDC
    [Fic]--dc23
LC record available at https

SUNSTONE PRESS IS COMMITTED TO MINIMIZING OUR ENVIRONMENTAL IMPACT ON THE PLANET. THE PAPER USED IN THIS BOOK IS FROM RESPONSIBLY MANAGED FORESTS. OUR PRINTER HAS RECEIVED CHAIN OF CUSTODY (COC) CERTIFICATION FROM: THE FOREST STEWARDSHIP COUNCIL™ (FSC®), PROGRAMME FOR THE ENDORSEMENT OF FOREST CERTIFICATION™ (PEFC™), AND THE SUSTAINABLE FORESTRY INITIATIVE® (SFI®). THE FSC® COUNCIL IS A NON-PROFIT ORGANIZATION, PROMOTING THE ENVIRONMENTALLY APPROPRIATE, SOCIALLY BENEFICIAL AND ECONOMICALLY VIABLE MANAGEMENT OF THE WORLD'S FORESTS. FSC® CERTIFICATION IS RECOGNIZED INTERNATIONALLY AS A RIGOROUS ENVIRONMENTAL AND SOCIAL STANDARD FOR RESPONSIBLE FOREST MANAGEMENT.

WWW.SUNSTONEPRESS.COM

SUNSTONE PRESS / POST OFFICE BOX 2321 / SANTA FE, NM 87504-2321 /USA
(505) 988-4418 / ORDERS ONLY (800) 243-5644 / FAX (505) 988-1025

Dedicated to my sister,
Joan Upton Hall,
who read to me before I could
read on my own.

The Grail contains that which is precious to the human heart.
It holds the Spirit and the hopes, dreams, fantasies, and the Truth
Which nurtures the best of the human condition.

What is the Grail?
Our stories.
Whom does the Grail serve?
The Grail serves us all.

Preface

I was on the top of a high mountain pass. In the Pyrenees. Spain stretched out beneath me. History surrounded me. At that time I knew nothing about Bori and Milo, who you will meet as you begin to read this book. Our paths had yet to converge. But I would soon discover that the pilgrim's path, the one I was beginning that day, has a way of tying the present and the past together into a sensation of timelessness. The physical present—very physical, walking mile after mile after mile—becomes saturated in the awareness of those who have come that way before through ages of history and before history when only the faintest trace of them remains. As you walk, you feel them as though they were walking shoulder to shoulder with you in the moment.

Twelve centuries before my own arrival on this spot, Roland and his companions had made their last—and heroic—stand protecting Charlemagne's extraction from Moorish Spain. That was long ago. Since then, this pass has been the cross-over point for thousands and thousands of pilgrims on their way, as I was that day, to Santiago de Compostela, the sacred interment place of Saint James, who was one of Jesus's twelve disciples, the patron saint of Catholic Spain, and its Reconquista from Moorish domination. But even before that, and well before Roland, this had been a pilgrimage for much earlier travelers who called it the Milky Way, the earthly Path of the Stars. They followed it all the way to Finisterre, land's end, at the westernmost point of Europe where the Atlantic Ocean puts an end to the earth. It was their pilgrimage to the End of the World.

Standing there I was overwhelmed by so much history, the vast landscape, and the layered traditions threaded through the centuries of evolving culture that had guided all those pilgrims from the rest of the continent into Iberia. As I gazed over the leagues I had to cover, by foot as pilgrims must and as so many have, my anxiety struggled with the thrill of adventure, for I was setting off into a land where I knew not a single soul, did not speak the language, and knew nothing about what lay beyond my immediate line of sight. In short, I was a pilgrim.

Milo and Bori introduced themselves to me several years later. I was noodling around with paper and pen, and I began to describe a town like the many I had walked through during my trip across Spain. I knew how this town I was conjuring up looked, and smelled, and sounded. I knew that it was called the Kingdom of Odalese. Then I ran into Milo and Boriboreau. Milo had that day become a contestant in an event called the Magical Scavenger Hunt and I soon was, too.

Although I had not set out to write a fantasy novel for young people— and not so young people who appreciate the imaginary—Milo and Bori insisted in taking me with them. It was an undertaking which, frankly, I found to be intimidating. Many of my favorite books and authors have appealed to the same readers but I wasn't sure that I was ready to enter their league. Besides, I was working on a science fiction novel at the time, expanding a novella I had written which had won a writing contest (and is still awaiting my attention). But Milo was persuasive. He had a story to tell and it was my job to give it a voice. So, off I went.

It was a pilgrimage. I followed the Road of Stars that took me into ages of myth where I met fascinating fellow pilgrims and puzzled my way through intriguing plot twists. Like my descent from the pass in the Pyrenees, I had no more than a vague idea that somewhere ahead lay a final destination. Day by day and page for page I had little more than line-of-sight to guide my steps. But Milo and Bori gave excellent companionship and encouragement.

Not that it was easy. Halfway through the novel I realized that I had taken a wrong turn. We had to backtrack. I threw out all the pages I had written, down to the first half dozen or so, and took the trail that would eventually lead us back to the Kingdom of Odalese and Thomas Jefferson.

How does one recognize the right path if the signs are down and no butterflies appear to show the way? I recall a quote from Don Juan (years ago I was an avid reader of the Carlos Castañeda books about his experiences with the old Yaqui sorcerer) who was a traveler of paths. He advised which ones to choose. "Does this path have a heart?" he asked. "If it does, the path is good; if it doesn't, it is of no use. Both paths lead nowhere; but one has a heart, the other doesn't. One makes for a joyful journey; as long as you follow it, you are one with it."

What wonders might you come across as you travel a path with a heart! Milo was my guide; he knew instinctively which way had the heart. Because of that, he could feel the draw of what lay beyond the line of sight, and he took me there.

It was a lesson I had discovered as a pilgrim. Like the day after climbing higher and higher into the mountains of western Spain and arriving at yet another pilgrim's chapel built centuries before. And there, inside the cool, dim, and incense-scented interior, bathed in the glow of smoky candles, was the Grail. THE Grail! The most precious relic of the Arthurian Mysteries, and I was standing before it! A mythical heirloom passed down through the stories from that time lost in the mists of legends of King Arthur and his Knights.

It was beautiful, but a simple cup, nothing really so very special. The local tradition explained how it had come to be there after disappearing from the environs of ancient Logres and brought for safekeeping to this remote corner of Iberia where it was secreted in plain view in this humble little chapel.

The question is not, however, if that chalice is authentic or not; the question is, as always, "Whom does it serve?" That is the Grail Question.

Milo, following the mysteries of the Magical Scavenger Hunt, was not the first seeker to be baffled by this question. It is a quest, a question about bafflement. And it has been a question that has haunted me ever since my sister—older and wiser than I—read me the tales of King Arthur, Lancelot, Perceval and so on, as they wrestled with the illusive meaning of the Grail.

So, okay; what is the Grail Answer?

Generations of storytellers, artists, and mystics, each of whom has confronted the enigma in his own way, have been haunted by what that answer might be. At least part of the problem comes out of the frustration of what the Grail *is*. Is it an actual vessel, like the one I encountered in the pilgrim's chapel? Or is it a profound religious truth? Is it Celtic, is it Romantic; is it an invention of the medieval troubadours? What does it do?

As I confronted the Grail in the tales from the Arthurian legends or the more recent mystics of esoteric lore, or even the surprise encounter of facing it in the factual every-day world, it remained ever-elusive. Something not unlike the question of the pilgrim: why pilgrimage?

Everyone who takes up the pilgrim road does it for her own reasons, but everyone who completes the task has a similar experience. Whatever the reason for starting the pilgrimage, it becomes trivial compared to the accomplishment of entering into the fellowship at the finish. It is not where the path leads that counts, it is the process of getting there. It is the Quest that defines the Grail. The Grail is for the seeker, the pilgrim, to find. To find something you must first seek it, and then recognize it when you find it. You must first ask the Grail Question before you can know the Grail Answer. The purpose of my long walk across Spain was not to arrive in Santiago de Compostela or Finisterre, it was the walk, day by day. Milo's return to the castle of the Fisher King was the result of his quest, the Question, as the culmination of all he had encountered to get there—his recognition of what he had done.

I found my Grail in a pilgrim's chapel. Milo faced it by looking into his own heart. Don Juan said, "For me there is only the traveling on the paths that have a heart, on any path that may have a heart. There I travel, and the only worthwhile challenge for me is to traverse its full length. And there I travel—looking, looking breathlessly."

Milo and I want to share what we found. So now, it's up to you, the reader, to follow your path in your own way. We hope we may find ourselves to be companions on your journey. As you stand at the top of the pass, deciding if you wish to step down into the landscape, we know you will travel, looking, looking breathlessly.

What is the Grail? Our stories. Whom does the Grail serve? The Grail serves us all.

Oh, and by the way, check your pockets; do you have a Jefferson/Buffalo nickel?

1

Milo in the Kingdom Of Odalese

Milo sketched out the shape of the cat, a tall, almost vase-like pose with its tail looped over the ledge where it sat. Its whiskers sprayed out across the page in his history notebook and he drew its ears to turn at an angle so it could hear two directions at once. He took extra care with its green eyes. Their slant suggested an otherworldly origin, challenging him to puzzle out their secrets. And then, just as he adjusted the second one, to his amazement, the cat winked at him.

"Milo!"

History class jerked him back into the present, vaporizing the image of the cat.

"Can you answer the question, please?" Ms. Mayfield demanded, arms folded in impatience.

"Uhh...what was the question again?" Milo stammered. It was a rotten answer. The scowl that his American History teacher wore deepened and snickers rippled through the tenth grade class. Milo wondered if Ms. Mayfield had ever thought about anything more...engaging...than attentive students. Ms. Mayfield drove down the snickers with a stern look. Milo stared into his notebook as if the question she'd asked might be located there somewhere. It wasn't.

"Milo?" Though peeved, Ms. Mayfield's tone took a slightly sympathetic tone. "What are we going to do with you?" Though her exasperation overlay her tone, this was a somewhat kinder comment than usual. Would she send him to the principal's office—again—or would it be the counselor this time? The counselor had diagnosed Milo's wandering mind as a "learning disability" while the principal preferred to identify it as a "behavioral problem." His mother tried to persuade them that Milo had a "very active imagination," pointing out that he was really very bright. Milo considered the whole thing unfair because his teachers always asked him questions when they knew he wasn't listening.

This time, apparently, Ms. Mayfield decided not to waste more time on him. She opened the question up to the class. "Who was it that sent Lewis and Clark out to explore the West?"

Crystal's hand went up. It had black polished nails today. "Thomas Jefferson," she stated. "He was the third President of the United States." Her hair was blue. Milo thought she was interesting even if she pushed the goth thing kind of hard. And her general hostility to just about everything and the withering glance she threw him, told him that she considered him a doof.

"That's right, Crystal," Ms. Mayfield said, her tone sweetened. Milo winced. Crystal was usually as distracted as Milo. "They were hoping to find a Northwest Passage, the Grail of western exploration." It was an exact quote from the text book. He remembered it because stories about the grail were among his favorite.

As she took Lewis and Clark off on their grand adventure, Milo settled down again into the sketches in his notebook. The cat had come up during his day-dreaming about an imaginary place called the Kingdom of Odalese.

The Kingdom of Odalese wasn't really a kingdom at all, Milo considered, because it didn't have a king. It had a mayor. If that made its name odd, it was okay because towns have all sorts of names. Milo knew of a town right in his own state called Truth or Consequences. An odd name for a town in Milo's opinion since there was nothing unusually truthful about it, and as far as Milo could tell there were no consequences, either. It was just a name. So it was for the Kingdom of Odalese.

He imagined that the Odalesians didn't think the name of their town was odd at all. They liked their town and the way it was, built on a hill above the River Dulcy—he was drawing that in now—with stone houses two or three stories tall lining narrow streets. It had shops for the butcher, the baker, and the candlestick maker where people could shop, meet, and visit each other. Right down at the foot of the hill there was a broad, grassy park with lots of old oak, sycamore, and chestnut trees. The grass was worn in places, because the Odalesians used their park a lot. The younger ones played games like hide-and-seek or chase while their parents and grandparents took strolls on nice sunny afternoons, catching up on the latest with their friends and neighbors.

But just now, it was a place with a number of campsites set up, because the Kingdom of Odalese was hosting its big event. It was held only every ten years, and was called the Magical Scavenger Hunt.

Milo puzzled over this for a while, wondering what that really was. He knew it had something to do with an odd feature of the Kingdom of Odalese, because of the magic part.

He speculated that the Kingdom of Odalese wasn't the sort of place you could find on a map, and if you didn't know how to get there, you'd never just come across it, like you can other towns. That's because it was a place of the imagination. Or a place where imagination *is* the map. Any direction you take away from the town, you can go on and on, from one adventure to the next, meeting any kind of person in any sort of landscape.

That's not to say it wasn't real, it was simply that it belonged in an imaginary, magical realm. If you didn't use your imagination, you couldn't get there, and if you reject magic, there would be no point. Furthermore, to be a contestant in the Magical Scavenger Hunt, you would have to use your imagination, so the requirement of using your fantasy to get there in the first place would automatically weed out anyone who wouldn't be any good at the MSH. Milo thought that was really a clever qualification.

He checked in with Ms. Mayfield's lecture to see if she might be setting him up again, but she wasn't. She had Lewis and Clark taking flat boats up the Missouri River and wasn't asking questions, so Milo felt fairly safe in returning to the Kingdom of Odalese.

To be a contestant in the Magical Scavenger Hunt, first you'd have to get to the Kingdom of Odalese. He thought about that real hard, trying to envision how it could be done and picturing every detail of the place so he could draw it. It would look like some places you can visit even today, with cobblestone streets closed in by houses built wall to wall the way medieval towns were built and can still be visited in places that have yet to be plundered by the requirements of automobiles. He imagined the scents from the flowerboxes hanging in windows from the second floors where the shopkeepers lived, of fresh hot bread in the bakery, and the fainter smell on the breeze from the woods behind the hill. He pictured himself arriving for the hunt, fantasizing more and more vividly, in ever greater detail what the town would be like. He imagined the streets just before dawn, empty since the villagers would still be in bed. He could see only a cat slinking alone in the shadows of the empty streets, and a pink and gold light brushing the clouds above with the first touch of a new day.

As he conjured all this, he could actually smell the scents and feel the cool, fresh morning air touch his skin. He blinked, then blinked again. Sixth period History class had vanished. The houses were there all around him and he could feel the worn cobblestones of the street beneath his feet. To his shock and surprise, he had arrived in The Kingdom of Odalese.

Milo stood there dumbstruck. Surely this illusion would pass and be replaced by the teacher's question and he'd have no idea how to answer. No matter how real it seemed, this had to be an illusion. But it didn't pass. This is really getting out of hand, he warned himself, starting to agree for the first time with his teacher. But it didn't pass.

At first, Milo didn't even know he had begun to move, but his body must have known he was really in a new place and was eager to find out more even if his mind was paralyzed.

It was probably good that he'd come at an early hour before the Odalesians were out and about, because it gave him time to adjust before having to act like he was a normal, rational person. He had no idea about how things worked here, what its customs were, and what people might ask a wandering teenager.

Milo poked down a street of uneven cobblestones, so unlike the smooth asphalt of the streets in his own home town. It was very narrow, much too narrow for cars. There were houses on both sides that snaked first to the right, then back to the left. Closed shops verified the early hour and Milo could see shuttered windows with flowers blooming in flower boxes. But there were no doors.

Milo was trying to figure out how the people could get into or out of their houses when he spotted a large, gray cat hiding under a stairway. This cat watched him with huge green eyes as if trying to predict if Milo might throw something at him.

Milo wasn't thinking that sort of thing at all, because Milo liked cats. He had a cat named Gracie, who was gray just like this cat, only much smaller. So Milo offered this cat part of a sandwich he had stuffed into his pocket after lunch, thinking that it might be hungry.

The cat *was* hungry. He came out very slowly, very carefully, as if he thought Milo could just be using the sandwich as bait. Milo used patience and calm tone to speak to the cat, wanting to show him that he couldn't really be the kind of boy who would offer food just as a ruse. Sidling along on his stomach the way cats do when they want to move cautiously and make of themselves a smaller target, he stretched out to sniff the offering. Milo didn't pull the sandwich away. Instead he opened it up so the cat could see the bologna. He put it down, took his hand away, and then just sat still.

"It's all right," Milo told the cat. "You don't have to worry. I won't hurt you."

This encouraged the cat and he crouched down on his belly to very delicately eat the bologna without eating any of the lettuce. Then he said, "Thank you. I haven't had anything to eat for a long time."

Milo said, "Wha...! What did you say?"

"I said I haven't eaten for a long time. That was very kind of you to share your food with me."

Milo was thunderstruck. "No! I mean...I mean...You talked!"

"Of course I talked," the cat replied. "It wouldn't be polite to accept a kindness without thanking the giver. You must be one of the contestants for the Magical Scavenger Hunt," the cat commented as he licked the mayonnaise off his chops, then washed his paws clean.

"I...what's...Well, I was *thinking* about a scavenger hunt, a very odd one in a magical place, and...well, I found myself here."

"That's as good a way to arrive as any," the cat agreed. "It's not as if the Magical Scavenger Hunt is advertised in newspapers all over the place. The Mayor just expects the contestants to show up. They always do. So you must be the right sort to be a contestant. Are you a wizard? You look a bit young to be a wizard. Maybe you're an exceptionally gifted apprentice. Ambitious, then, for your age?"

"What? No, I'm...I'm just Milo."

"And I'm Boriboreau, at your service."

"Where am I?" Milo asked.

"Why, The Kingdom of Odalese," the cat answered. "It's not really a kingdom, you see..."

He went on to explain the rest, which Milo had already figured out. Then he gave Milo some important information.

"If you want to be a contestant in the Magical Scavenger Hunt, you'll have to register with the Mayor," Boriboreau explained. "You *have* registered, haven't you?"

"No, I didn't know I needed to," Milo replied. He went on. "I didn't know I was a contestant, or that I was coming here. I didn't even know there was a here *here*. This is all very puzzling, and I...I don't know anything."

Boriboreau looked Milo over carefully. "You're a very honest young man if you admit that. Very few humans I've met would admit to a cat that their knowledge is in the least bit limited. You are unusual indeed."

"Would you...help me?" Milo asked the cat. "You seem pretty unusual yourself."

"Well," Boriboreau considered. "I like you, and you gave me your sandwich. One good turn deserves another. I'll take you to the Mayor's office."

By this time, people began coming out of their houses. The shop-keepers opened their shops, and men and women came and went to buy the morning's groceries or to stop at their favorite cafés on the way to work.

Milo was surprised to see plenty of doors to the houses now, when only a little earlier he had been confounded to see none. He asked the cat about it.

"Oh, but of course! They're open now, because their owners are going out. By the way," he put it, "you can call me Bori."

"Oh, okay. Bori. But back to the doors. A little while ago, I didn't see *any* doors."

"That's because they hadn't opened them yet."

"But...there were no doors *at all*. There were windows, but no doors."

"There were windows because people like to be able to look out, but there weren't any doors because people didn't want to go out yet. As soon as they wanted to go out, they opened them," Bori explained with a great deal of patience.

"But where *were* the doors?" Milo asked in exasperation. "There weren't any doors at all. Now there are. Where were the doors before people opened them?"

Boriboreau looked at Milo closely. "You are a very odd, very percep-tive boy. I see you *are* an original thinker. You may do very well in the MSH. Come this way now, the Mayor's office is just up the next street, in the Courthouse on the Square."

It was a very fine Square, although it was really more a rectangle. The two longer sides had shops and cafés, the cafés with tables out in the open air, with white tablecloths and neatly ironed napkins rolled into rings of silver or horn. People already sat at many of the tables, drinking coffee or tea from china cups and smearing butter and jam on fresh, flaky croissants. The aroma reminded Milo that he was hungry, but he didn't regret giving his sandwich to his new friend.

There were shops with groceries, shops with cheeses and milk, wine shops, bakeries, butcher shops, and so on. There were dress shops, housewares shops, shops specializing in metal products, porcelain, soap—pretty much any sort of product that a town needs to make it an agreeable place to live.

Big, shady trees sheltered benches where people could sit on the Square, and a bandstand in the middle suggested evenings with music. But since the whole town was built on a hill, the Square sloped, with buildings of different kinds on the two ends. At the upper end stood an imposing edifice built of cut stone, with arched buttresses and all sorts of figures carved in relief. A tower rose even above that with bells to ring the hour.

On the lower side where Bori and Milo had entered was another kind of building more massive than tall, with at least two or three more floors than the regular houses. Sculptures suggested figures of municipal pride and banners spanned from just beneath the roof overhangs in long strips, adding color. They were tied off well above the heads of people and billowed nicely in the breeze. At the center, steps ascended to tall bronze doors, high enough to let in giants, but as far as Milo could tell, the people using them were of ordinary proportions. These doors were flanked on either side by two bronze lions, lying on their sides and looking regally out over the Square to observe whoever passed through the doors.

"Those lions were the familiars of Count Abracadabracus," Bori explained. "He was the founder of the Kingdom of Odalese centuries ago. The story is that they're here to guard our town. I've heard it said that they prowl the streets at night, on the lookout for spies and rogues, but I've lived in these streets my whole life and never run into them during my own prowling. But then, you never know...."

Bori led as he and Milo climbed the steps of the Courthouse. Passing into the galleried foyer with its floor of polished and patterned marble, Milo expected...well, something unexpected. Perhaps moving staircases like the ones in the Harry Potter movies, or portraits on the walls that watched you when you walked by. The paintings on these walls were huge, but they remained inanimate.

As they walked down a marble corridor, Milo's footfalls echoed and he could hear muted voices from unseen places. Still, there was nothing you would call magical.

Milo asked Bori about it. "Magical?" Bori replied. "Why, if the Courthouse were magical, that would make magical things an everyday sort of condition, and then it wouldn't be magical anymore. That's why we have the Magical Scavenger Hunt, and celebrate it only once a decade. It highlights how Magic makes it...well, magical. Come this way; the Mayor's office is up here."

They climbed a stair of white marble with black onyx risers and balustrades, quite impressive in a regular sort of way, and at the top of the stairs, they entered an office. It had thick carpets with intricate patterns. A receptionist with a pinched-looking face sat at a huge walnut desk. Bori hopped up with his tail lifted in his friendliest manner.

"My young friend here would like to register as a contestant in the Magical Scavenger Hunt," he announced.

"Are you his cat or is he your boy?" asked the receptionist in a bureaucratic, bored sort of way.

Milo thought he should answer for himself. "No, I just met him and he agreed to show me where to register as a contestant. May I register, please?"

The receptionist pushed a form across the desk at Milo. "Fill this out and pay the court treasurer the entry fee downstairs."

"Entry fee?" Milo asked apprehensively. "How much is that?" He knew how little of his weekly allowance he had left in his pocket.

"Fifty kuzurians," she said without taking her eyes off the papers in front of her, ignoring the boy and the cat.

Milo didn't know what a kuzurian was, but he knew he didn't have fifty of them or anything else.

"I...I think I'll have to come back later," he told her, pushing the entry form back across the desk.

"All right," she said as she retrieved the blank form, "but don't wait too long. The deadline for entering the Hunt is this afternoon when this office closes."

Milo turned away, feeling just a bit crestfallen. He hadn't realized how enthused he had become about being in the Magical Scavenger Hunt. "What should I do?" he asked Bori.

"I would loan you the fifty kuzurians if I had them. But I don't, seeing as how I have no pockets to put them in," Bori replied. "We'll just have to find you a sponsor."

"How will I do that?" Milo protested, trying not to sound whiny. "I don't know anybody here, and no one knows me."

"Then you'll just have to be imaginative. I'm sure you can do it. Let's go out and see what we can come up with."

It seemed like a better plan than just standing there, so Milo went along with the cat.

As they walked away from the courthouse and past the cafés, Milo remembered how hungry he was. Just then, breakfast was more appealing than fifty kuzurians. He took a fist full of change and a wadded dollar bill out of his pocket and showed it to Bori.

"Do you think this might be enough to buy us a breakfast?"

Bori looked it over. "No, its not kuzurians, but I have an idea. Let's go down that side street."

Bori led him into a small shop several houses away with a sign that said "Numismateria." Although Milo didn't know what that meant, displays of coins suggested that the shop was for coin collecting.

"You're on your own here," Bori whispered to him. "I don't have...a very good history with Dame Constance. I think I'll just slip off to the side. See if she might be interested in your coins."

A woman who looked like a character out of a French movie sat at the counter, polishing coins.

"Ahh...good morning," Milo said as he moved up to her counter. The woman looked up without replying. One eye peered and the other squinted at him, presumably from looking at the tiny marks on coins for so long.

"I...ahh...wondered if you might be interested in any of the coins I have here," Milo said as he pulled the handful out of his pocket. He laid out six pennies, two quarters, a dime, and three nickels on the counter, taking care not to disturb the ones she was cleaning.

"Hmm," she said, suggesting an ability to speak. Then very carefully she picked them up one by one, studying them minutely, using that well-practiced squint.

"Nothing particularly interesting here," she said at last. "Nothing truly ancient, and that's my specialty at this shop. But this one is interesting, and well minted."

She held up one of the nickels. "I've never seen a portrait of Count Abracadabracus on a coin in semi-profile before."

Milo decided not to correct her by telling her that the face on that nickel was Thomas Jefferson's.

"And what sort of magical beast is this on the reverse?" she asked.

"Why, that's just a"—he checked himself. "That's an American buffalo—a bison," he corrected, deciding that bison was a more impressive word. "It's sacred to the American Indians."

"Hmm," she said. "I might be interested in that. What do you want for it?"

"What might you offer me for it?"

"I'll give you two kuzurians."

"Can I get breakfast for two kuzurians?"

She looked him over as if he were a coin. "You must be a Hunt contestant. Yes, that would get you a breakfast. I'll give you three kuzurians for the lot."

That seemed a fair price to Milo. Eighty-one cents for a breakfast was a pretty good deal.

"Okay, I'll take it." He pulled out the dollar bill. "How much would you give me for this?"

"I don't buy certificates," she replied without even looking. "They have no value."

Milo poked the bill back into his pocket as she pushed three coins across the counter at him, raked his coins into her palm, and dumped them into a drawer.

The kuzurians were about the size of quarters and apparently made of silver. On one side was a head that in profile looked like Thomas Jefferson, and on the other a symbol of some sort. He turned and left the shop.

Bori was sitting just outside the door. Milo showed him the three kuzurians.

"Did I get a good price?" he asked the cat.

"How should I know," Bori replied. "I told you I don't have pockets, so I don't have any coins."

"I suppose we should see about breakfast, then," Milo suggested. "If we can get a breakfast, it doesn't matter, does it?"

Bori agreed and led away, tail held high with purpose.

They went to a café of Bori's choosing. "The woman proprietor sometimes sets me a saucer of milk out back," he explained about his choice. He indicated the café across the square with a lift of his chin and a flattening of his ears. "The best I get from that one over there is to have a wilted carrot thrown at me from time to time. Usually while I'm serenading a lady friend. Very disrespectful."

They sat at a table with a pale blue table cloth and a vase of tiny daisies in the middle. Milo ordered tea with milk, croissants with butter and fresh jam, and two poached eggs. Boriboreau asked for a saucer of warmed milk and a strip of bacon, which he nibbled like a cultured gentlecat while sitting on the table, his paws neatly wrapped about with his tail.

By the time they were both down toward the last crumbs of their breakfasts, the necessity of the entry fee had begun to reassert its importance. Milo was at a total loss about how to raise the money.

"Everything I have with me only bought three kuzurians, and we ate two of them. I won't even be able to afford lunch, and I've got to come up with forty-nine more kuzurians by this afternoon," Milo lamented. "There's no way."

"There must be a way, or you wouldn't be a contestant," Bori pointed out, his confidence in Milo unwaivering.

"But I won't be a contestant if I don't pay the entry fee!" he told Bori in exasperation.

"Then we must find you a sponsor, as I suggested earlier. There's an old woman who lives not far from here who has a kind heart. She always gives me her kitchen scraps. On the other hand, judging from the scraps and the tiny amount I see her eat, which looks exactly like what she feeds me, I don't think it's likely that she has fifty kuzurians, either, although she does have pockets. No, I think we need to approach a merchant, someone who has piles of kuzurians."

"You know, where I come from, contestants are often sponsored by businesses. The businesses see it as advertising," Milo told the cat.

"What's advertising?" asked Bori.

"The contestants wear a shirt or something with the name of the business on it. People see it and then want to go to that business. The better the contestant does, the more people are likely to buy things from that business."

"We'll try that, then," Bori said between licks, washing his paws properly after finishing the last nibble of bacon. "I can think of someone to try first." And off they went.

The person Bori had in mind was a banker, and he indeed had piles of kuzurians. Milo explained to him his situation and his idea that the bank could sponsor him as advertising in the Magical Scavenger Hunt. The banker looked him over.

"Since it's obvious that you have no collateral," the banker said, "I must ask you this: are you a qualified magician?"

This was a difficult question for Milo, because he wasn't, but he wanted the banker to *believe* he was so he would be willing to give him the kuzurians he needed.

"I can make things disappear and reappear," he assured the banker. He took his last remaining kuzurian out of his pocket. He was thinking of a trick he had learned from his Uncle Johnny. It had been very impressive to him when he was about five years old. He held a coin up in his left hand before the banker's face, supported by its edges between his thumb and forefinger. He made several impressive passes over it with his right hand, coming up behind it and then driving his right hand straight in at it, and "Voilá!" it vanished before the banker's eyes. Actually, he let the coin drop flat into the palm of his left hand just as the right seemed to engulf it. With the "voilá" part, he held his right hand up, palm open, as if it had done all the work, while taking his left hand away, the kuzurian secretly tucked in the palm.

"And now to make it reappear," Milo said, thinking that a man in his position might get nervous about seeing kuzurians disappear, unless they reappeared pretty quickly. Bori was sitting on the desk beside him, watching the display with great interest.

"Now, where might that coin have gotten to?" Milo said with dramatic effect, while he secretly transferred the kuzurian from his left hand to his right. "There!" he announced, reaching toward Bori, and 'drawing' the coin out of the cat's ear. He held it up triumphantly for the banker to see.

Bori was amazed. The banker not so much. "I don't think I'll be needing any advertising," he said.

"I thought it was a great trick," Bori said when they were back in the street. "I didn't even notice that I had the coin in my ear. Perhaps I don't even need pockets."

Next they tried some other prospects. The butcher. The baker. Even the candlestick maker. Actually, the candlestick maker might have been interested if the strong scents of lavender, patchouli, cinnamon, mint, pine, sandalwood, etc. hadn't started Bori sneezing. First once, then twice, then in a stream of explosions that sounded like he might be choking to death or something. The candle lady became distracted, then frenzied. She wanted Bori out of her shop. Milo took him out, got him settled down again, and went back in. By then, the woman had soured on the idea, and didn't want to talk about it anymore.

"Okay, what do we do now?" he asked Bori. They were sitting on the stone wall along the side of the park, overlooking the River Dulcy. The day was getting late, and the mayor's office would close in about an hour.

The park was teaming with other contestants setting up their camps. At the nearest one a man with a full black beard and wearing a fine, silk turban sharpened a long, curved scimitar. He had a servant who was trying to put up a black-and-white striped tent and at the same time stir a thick stew that steamed with the aroma of curry. Tethered alongside was a magnificent black stallion cropping grass. He would have been a remarkable horse even without the huge wings folded alongside his body.

"That's Ali-Sembeck, of Qutan," Bori explained.

The aroma of cooking made Milo's stomach growl. He hadn't eaten since breakfast. To make matters worse, food aromas from other camps wafted through the park. To the other side of Milo and Bori was a camper who looked more like a wild man. His hair and beard were tangled and he was almost naked, with a tattered rag wrapped haphazardly around his middle. The only thing he had was a staff that looked like something he had picked up in the forest, but he was using it to conjure morsels of food out of thin air. His name, Bori told Milo, was Tivik. Milo looked away from him, finding the whole thing rather disturbing.

The contestant beyond Tivik was disturbing too, but for a very different reason. She was as alluring as the wild man was repulsive, and nearly as undressed. Milo felt embarrassed even to be looking at her, but compelled to glance just the same. Her costume—or its lack—was made elegant by ornate jewelry that gleamed through gossamer fabric of a color Milo could not ascertain, because it shifted constantly with her motion. He tore his eyes away from her, thinking that she really was nothing like the ladies he was accustomed to seeing around his own neighborhood.

About then another person approached the spot where he sat with Bori. She was rather normal looking—thank goodness—in corduroy pants, sweater, and one of those many pocketed vests bulging with small notebooks, pencils, and pens.

"Hi!" she said. "I'm from the *Odalese Observer*. You must be one of the contestants. May I ask you a few questions?"

"Well," Milo said uncomfortably, "I don't know if I should. I mean, I'd be happy to, but I guess I'm not really a contestant."

"Why?" she retorted. "You look like a contestant."

Milo looked at the man in the turban, then to the wild man, and next over to...and skipped back to the newspaper reporter, wondering what made a contestant look like a contestant.

"I got here to be a contestant, but I don't have fifty kuzurians to enter. All I have is one."

"Really?" the woman said, scribbling into her notebook. "But you came to be a contestant?"

"Yes, I guess so. I'm here, and earlier today I wasn't. So I guess I did."

She scribbled furiously.

"And this"—she indicated Bori with a flick of the eraser end of her pencil—"is your familiar?"

"My...familiar?" Milo asked, unsure of the term. "He's more like my guide. He's helping me figure out the Kingdom of Odalese, because it's not very much like where I come from."

"And just where is that?"

"I don't think I have the faintest idea," Milo replied.

At this point Bori broke in. "As you can see, Milo is a very clever young man. He's generous and forthright, but he keeps his own counsel. I expect him to do very well in this competition if his entry is assured."

A laugh from another quarter followed Bori's pronouncement and interrupted the reporter's scribbling. "Clever? Cleverly said, at least. Perhaps this cat should be the contestant. If his tongue is tricky enough to make magic for this young pup, he should be able to compete with real sorcerers and sorceresses like Ali-Sembeck, Tivik, Aulairess, or, for that matter, myself."

"So you would go on record," the reporter said, turning to address the intruder, "that this contestant, because of his youth, should not be allowed to compete?" Her pencil was moving as fast as her tongue.

"He's a baby!" the man exclaimed. "What can he know of the demands of a high-level competition like this? Look around you. The contestants assembled here are the cream of the wizarding trade. Each of them is a master of his or her craft. Otherwise they wouldn't be here."

"This boy *is* here, just as you are, Count Yeroen" the reporter pointed out, identifying the critic in the process. "Isn't that the core qualification for joining the Magical Scavenger Hunt? In fact, isn't it the only requirement?"

Count Yeroen threw up his hands. "Yes, that and having fifty kuzurians as an entry fee. Which the boy does not have."

"But that could be provided by anyone," Bori put in. "Even yourself, if you chose to do so."

"Ahh, you *are* a clever cat. Yes, I could pay his entry fee—if I chose to do so. But if I chose not to do so, he wouldn't compete, would he? The office closes in about half an hour."

"Why would you wish to prevent this young man from competing?" the reporter asked. Her pencil scratched swiftly as the Count answered.

"I have no personal reason to bar this young man from the competition," the Count stated. "I do, however, believe it would be very risky for him and the other contestants due to his inexperience. The Hunt is a serious, even a deadly, undertaking. But since I believe that poverty as a single condition and a factor certainly unaddressed in the rules of competition, should not prevent an otherwise—as our feline friend here has astutely stated—*qualified...*" Yeroen edged the word with such a smear of sarcasm that the reporter's pencil seemed to get stuck in it. "...competitor from joining the Hunt, I will pay his fee and allow him to fail on his own merits."

Off they all went: Count Yeroen, Milo, Bori, and the reporter. As they entered the treasurer's office at the Courthouse, the clerk was clearly closing for the night.

"I would like to pay the entry fee for this young man," the Count stated.

"Oh my goodness," said the clerk. "I've just closed my lock box, and Hilda upstairs will be shutting her office before I can make out the receipt."

"I'll run up and stop her," the reporter offered, and dashed away.

"I hope you have the correct change," the clerk said, peeved. "I'll have to redo the bookkeeping record as it is."

Yeroen counted out the appropriate number of kuzurians and the clerk wrote out the receipt and marked it with the seal.

"There you go, young man," the clerk said, handing it over to Milo. "Next time you should consider being better prepared. Good luck in the contest."

Up they went to the Mayor's office where the reporter stood talking to Hilda, the receptionist. "Here they come," the reporter said, and the two turned back into the office just ahead of Milo, the Count, and Bori.

"Very close, cutting it like that," Hilda said. "In the next two minutes I would have been locked up and gone."

A sixth person burst into the room. "I would like to register for the Hunt," she announced breathlessly and waving her receipt from the clerk.

"Oh for Pete's sake!" exclaimed the receptionist, taking the sealed receipt.

The reporter was scribbling madly. "And who are you?" she asked the newcomer.

"My name is Analisa, and I'm a fully trained witch, the best in my class!" she insisted, as if someone had contested it.

"A witch?" exclaimed the receptionist in dismay. "Even if you are here in time to register, I can't possibly allow you to register as the thirteenth contestant. Not a witch!"

The girl was about Milo's age and even reminded him of Crystal, the girl in his class at his school. Like her, Analisa was dressed all in black:

black pants, black boots, and a black tunic (instead of a heavy metal band tee shirt). But instead of blue, her hair was midnight black, which he liked better. In a word, Milo thought she was very pretty, with green eyes. That went a long way with Milo.

"I haven't registered yet," he said. "What if you register her first, and then I'll register as the thirteenth? I'm not a witch or anything. I'm just Milo."

"I suppose that would be all right," the receptionist said. The Count threw up his hand with impatience.

So they did it that way, and Milo became the thirteenth contestant in the Magical Scavenger Hunt.

2

Milo Finds His Place

The reporter rushed off to make her deadline, and the others went back to the park. Count Yeroen, who was clearly uninterested in socializing with the young people, returned to his camp, leaving Analisa, Milo, and Bori to themselves. They appropriated a picnic table, a place they were entitled to as fully registered contestants in the Hunt. Since neither Analisa nor Milo had any gear, they had no camp to set up, Analisa sat cross-legged in the middle of the table with Bori on her lap. She was giving him long, gentle strokes, and Milo could hear him purr and see his eyes closed in ecstasy and his paws making the opening/closing rhythm of a well-gruntled cat.

"So, is he your familiar?" Analisa asked Milo.

"That's the same question that the newspaper lady asked. I really don't know what a familiar is."

Analisa looked at Milo with puzzled curiosity. "A familiar is your magical companion. An animal helper who you can trust completely to assist you."

"Except for the magical part, maybe he *is* my familiar then. He certainly has helped me out all day long, but I haven't asked him if he would like to stay with me for the Hunt."

"Why don't you ask him then?" Analisa suggested. "You're going to need all the help you can get. You obviously don't have a clue, and you've already made a very powerful rival of the most renowned sorcerer in the Hunt."

"I take it you mean Count Yeroen."

Analisa rolled her eyes as though she was talking to an idiot. It made Milo feel very, very small.

"Yes, you silly. Count Yeroen."

Milo looked at Bori. Bori looked as if he were asleep, but the tip of his tail flicked slowly, so Milo knew that he had heard every word. Cats are like that.

"Bori? Would you care to stay with me and be my familiar?"

Bori stretched and yawned, his jaws opening so wide that it looked as though his head had split apart. Then he opened one green eye and fixed a gaze on Milo.

"I might consider it. I'm a free agent, and at the moment I have no other commitments. It's true that you're going to need help. And I was serious when I said that I believe you've got much better chances at winning than the Count High-and-Mighty thinks you do. We'll make a team, you and I."

That made Milo feel a lot better. He felt a frog in his throat, and not nearly so alone, even while he missed his own kitty, Gracie, very keenly. "Thanks, Bori," he said sort of gruffly.

"At your service," Bori replied. "You'll have to feed me, of course. That's part of the deal."

That reminded Milo that he was very hungry himself, that he still had only one kuzurian, and now he had an obligation to his familiar. It was bad enough to be hungry yourself with no prospect of eating, but to be responsible for feeding Bori as well really was daunting.

He still did have one kuzurian, though.

"I need to buy some cat food," he told Analisa. "Want to come along?"

She hopped down from the table and so did Bori who marched along just ahead of them, tail held in a high waving pose, proud of his new, important status. Maybe the prospect of regular meals helped out, too.

"How come you were so late registering?" Milo asked Analisa.

"I had to get away from my mistress, and I think she knew I was up to something. I finally escaped just in the nick of time."

"Your mistress?" Milo asked, puzzled.

"Yes. Technically, I'm still an apprentice. For another ten years, unless I can win this contest."

"Ten years?" Milo whistled. "That's a long time."

"Yeah, it is. She's a real...well, a real witch! She makes me do all her domestic work, like washing her clothes, making her meals, helping her dress, but never teaches me anything useful. About witchcraft, I mean. I just can't stand it any longer! So winning this contest is my only way to escape. Now that I've registered, she can't make me come back to her. For now, she and I are equals as contestants of the Hunt."

"Who is she?" Milo inquired.

"She's at the table on the other side of Tivik the wild man. Her name is Aulaires."

"You mean the one...," Milo broke off, blushing, because if Aulaires was who he thought she was, he'd spent half the afternoon trying not to look at her. "The one with the red tent?" he asked, rather lamely.

"Yes. The one with the red tent. Like you didn't notice," Analisa answered wryly.

"Uh...where were you?" he asked.

"What? Why, I was right there, all day long, working like a slave! I saw you. And your cat. In fact, I got out from under her eye only when you and Count Yeroen distracted her long enough for me to slip away. Milo, you *had* to see me!"

No, Milo had not. He had noticed only Aulaires. Her image seemed burned onto his retinas. And now, because of the way Analisa's eyes flashed, he realized he had made a major blunder.

"I...I was trying to figure out how to get the entry fee," he said, knowing that it was a weak excuse.

"You had your eyes glued on our camp all afternoon!" Analisa spat.

They walked on in an uncomfortable silence. Bori steered them to a shop where Milo could buy cat food.

"I'm sorry," Milo told Analisa. "I would like to buy us supper, but this is my last kuzurian." He paused. "And I'm sorry I didn't notice you this afternoon. Well, I did, but I didn't. You see, I've never seen anyone like Aulaires before. She's not your... ahh...typical witch."

"What would you know about witches?" Analisa snarled. "I don't believe you've ever even *seen* a witch."

"You're right," Milo admitted. "I haven't. Until today."

The shopkeeper who had sold Milo the cat food was still standing right there, having heard every word.

"Aren't you two the Hunt contestants who are in the paper this evening?" he asked.

"Yes, we're contestants, but I didn't know we were in the paper," Milo answered. "We did talk to a newspaper person, though."

"You must be the young man who didn't have his registration fee. The one whom Count Yeroen sponsored. And you must be the young witch who would have been the thirteenth contestant had it not been for this young man."

Analisa nodded, reluctant to acknowledge Milo's helpful gesture.

"And you just spent your last kuzurian to feed your cat," the shop-keeper stated. "But now how are you going to eat? Don't you have anyone backing you? How can you compete with no support?"

"I didn't exactly plan any of this. All I know is that I got here, so all I can do is the best I can. Like Analisa. She's got no better support than I do."

The shopkeeper looked at the girl and shook his head. "You'll both need sponsors, I think. But for now, I know you must be hungry. Come along back to the kitchen and let's see if my wife and I can't get you something to eat."

Supper was omelets with fresh-baked bread and butter, cheese, and fruit. Bori got a sardine and a saucer of milk. Then the shopkeeper and his wife served them hot tea with honey while they all sat around the kitchen table.

"How did you get to the Kingdom of Odalese?" the shopkeeper asked Analisa.

"It's been my dream—ohh, for as long as I can remember," she answered. "It was the reason I wanted to enter training in the first place. My mother is a witch, and of course I first learned from her. But I knew how tough the competition is for the Hunt, so I got into the best witch school I could."

"You're still so young, dear!" the wife spoke up. "The other competitors have been wizards, warlocks, witches, sorcerers, shamanesses, and mages for years before they put themselves into the Hunt. Don't you think you should wait for the next Hunt?"

"I...sort of didn't have a choice," Analisa said. "I came with my mentoress, and when I got here I decided that it was my big chance."

"Then," the woman began in a hesitant, shocked voice, "you didn't come to the Kingdom of Odalese on your own?"

Milo heard the unease behind the question. Analisa was quick to answer.

"Oh yes. I...found my own way."

There must have been more to the answer than that, but she didn't offer it.

The man turned to Milo. "What about you? How did you come to the Kingdom of Odalese? Was it an ambition like your friend's?"

"I really don't know," Milo answered.

"You don't know? Where did you hear about it? When did you decide to come?"

"I didn't. I was just sort of thinking, imagining what a magical scavenger hunt might be like, and then I was here."

The man and his wife traded glances. Analisa stared at Milo, a question held in check. Milo felt put on the spot without knowing why, or what they expected him to say. He glanced at Bori, hoping the cat might come to his rescue, but Bori was curled up into a neat ball in front of the kitchen fire, paws tucked in at the four corners and his tail wrapping up the package.

"Are you trained in sorcery?" the man asked Milo, as if posing a sensitive question.

"No. We don't have anything like that where I come from," said Milo. "Nobody believes in it."

They all looked at one another in amazement.

"How can you expect to win, then?" the woman asked.

"I guess I don't," Milo answered, thinking of this for the very first time. "I just expect to have an adventure."

Either his answer was that good, or it was so shocking, that it ended the conversation. The man and woman quickly changed the subject to other things and were careful to stay on safe subjects.

Finally Milo and Analisa decided that the time was right to thank their hosts and take their leave. When they were outside in the street again, Analisa sprang the question she'd held back.

"Was that the truth you told them in there, or were you just being coy?" she demanded.

Milo had Bori on his shoulder, and the cat was purring with the luxury of not having to walk under his own steam. "What do you mean?" Milo asked.

"About coming here without even knowing about the Hunt," she insisted.

"Sure it was the truth," he said, annoyed at her accusation. "Nobody at home has ever even dreamed of a thing like this, about a place like the Kingdom of Odalese or the Magical Scavenger Hunt. I still don't have a clue what it is."

That seemed to silence her. So now it was his turn. "What did you mean when you told them that you got here on your own? Did you come with Aulaires or didn't you?"

"You *have* to get here on your own to be considered a contestant. You know that much. I wanted to come here, and I secretly planned to come, without Aulaires. But she decided to join the Hunt, and I had no choice but to come along with her. So maybe *technically* she brought me, but since I'd *planned* to come anyway, I really came on my own."

"And so that makes it sort of problematic," he observed. "Since *technically* you're her apprentice."

"So I'm her apprentice," Analisa said defensively. "I shouldn't say this, but I think she knew I was planning on coming, and she tricked me into bringing her instead of the other way around."

"Then she shouldn't be here at all! She's the one who shouldn't be a contestant."

"Shhh! Don't say that. You have to understand the sort of magic Aulaires uses. She's a very powerful witch, and vengeful. She would turn you into a toad in an instant if she heard you say that. Forget what I told you and don't dare ever say a word to anyone about it."

"All right, I promise," Milo said.

"And another thing I should tell you about Aulaires and her magic. She gets other people to do things for her. It's her special skill."

"What sorts of things?"

"Anything she wants that you can provide. That depends on you and whether she wants something or not. She got her hooks into you already this afternoon when you stared at her like a fool."

Milo felt stupid again. He wished that he hadn't made all these blunders. He knew that Analisa thought he was an idiot, and he really wished that she would think he was cool.

When they reached the park, Analisa blurted, "Why did you help me out this afternoon?"

"Because they weren't going to let you enter, although I really don't understand why. That was unfair." Milo was proud about what he had done, and he hoped Analisa would think so, too. It hurt his feelings that she didn't.

"Milo, I can't lose this contest," she told him. It was not at all what he thought she would say. "So don't expect me to help you out. Besides, you said you really think you couldn't win anyway." She turned away to go.

Where she would go, he had no idea, and maybe she didn't either. She could hardly expect Aulaires to share her tent with her. But that was Analisa's business, Milo decided. He turned away so he wouldn't see where she went.

Camping out without equipment isn't much fun even in warm weather. Milo missed his bed. Even if the night wasn't very chilly, he wished a thousand times for his pillow and a blanket. The ground underneath the picnic table was cold and studded with rocks, or at least it felt that way. Bori slept in Milo's arms, which was uncomfortable in one way, but the cat was warm, and that helped in another way.

In the early morning, when Bori left to take care of his feline affairs, Milo got up, too. There just wasn't any point in trying to sleep.

He wandered up the streets of the town, incredulous that he had spent only twenty-four hours there. It seemed like weeks and weeks. His old life seemed more like a story that someone had told him rather than something he had lived day by day for fifteen years. Except for specific details, like a bed or a blanket and pillow or the smell of coffee that his mother would be making in the kitchen as he awoke, his "other life" was rapidly slipping into a never-never land of nostalgic memory.

The streets of the town faced him with the same doorlessness that had greeted him the morning before, along with the same uncertain prospect of breakfast. Wondering how he might get something to eat occupied most of his thoughts as he wandered higher up the streets. Suddenly he became aware of a sound. From faint, indistinct fragments of tones, the call strengthened into quavering music. He followed it into a ruined garden, a neglected labyrinth within broken walls.

As he came out onto the top of the hill, the notes became a long, lonely, drawn-out melody of a single flute. Sunrise had begun with color washing into the sky and melting downward, turning gray-toned leaves to green and illuminating lichen-patterned stone walls. The scent of lilac drifted into the air, as if released by the fresh light of the sun. It reminded him of his grandmother's garden.

He found himself inside an ancient and deserted citadel. Passing through a once-proud arch, he was led on by the call of the flute. Then he stopped, caught by a yearning so keen that it brought tears to his eyes.

The sound of the flute stopped, too. Milo looked around. The sky was now soft blue and rose. Sunlight gilded the ragged tops of the citadel's crumbling turrets and roofless cornices. He saw no one. The entire world could have been emptied of people, leaving him as the last. The yearning pooled in his heart in a formless sadness.

"You are the penniless boy who would win the Hunt," a deep male voice said, seemingly from nowhere.

Milo spun around. A lone figure, his tawny cloak pulled carelessly over hunter green clothes, sat cross-legged on the rampart wall. A wooden flute dangled in his fingers.

"Who? I—" Milo stammered.

The man laughed gently, a low and warming chuckle. It soothed Milo's homesickness.

"A boy who professes no magical training yet joins the ranks of the finest mages, drawn here by magic itself. Aren't you magical, Milo?"

"How do you know my name?" Milo asked.

"I read the paper," the man answered. "Everyone knows who you are. 'The Boy Mage,' 'the stealth contestant.' And, of course, the 'Thirteenth.' They don't know what to think of you, Milo."

Milo didn't know what to think of this, either, so he said nothing.

The man unfolded himself and sprang down, all in one flowing motion not unlike a cat. He landed on the grass so lightly that it appeared his feet didn't bend a single blade.

"What do you know about the Magical Scavenger Hunt, Milo?" he asked, looking into Milo's eyes. His features were tanned and weathered, his cheekbones lean and his nose aquiline. His eyes were deep and dark, sheltered under thick eyebrows but filled with warmth. His long hair, swirling in a dark mass around his head, was charged with a vitality of its own. Milo felt he should be suspicious of this man, but he wasn't.

"I called you here so that we could talk," he said. "You see, I participated in the Hunt myself once and have some knowledge of what you'll be facing. Since you know nothing—profess to know nothing, anyway—about the Hunt, I thought you might like an opportunity to talk to someone who knows something."

Milo considered this offer, but he was still doubtful.

"For a boy with no magical training..."

"That was in the paper, too, I guess," Milo commented.

"Actually, I got that from your host of last night. He's worried about you, you see. He likes you and he knows it's a hard trial, with many ordeals and sharp competitors. But you *can* win."

"How?"

"That's up to you, Milo. You might say that it's part of the test. But I believe that you have some advantages if you learn to use them. What others believe to be their best credentials can sometimes prove to be handicaps."

"Who are you?" Milo asked.

"A wise question. My name is Tinburkin. At your service."

" 'At your service.' That's what Bori said when he introduced himself," Milo observed. "Is that a polite way to give your name here in the Kingdom of Odalese?"

"Some might use it that way, but it's a statement of purpose. Boriboreau is a valuable ally. You were wise to take him on. He's a cat of substance."

"You know Bori?"

"We've met. But let's get back to you and your place in the Hunt as the thirteenth. Why did you pick that number?"

"I didn't. It just came out that way."

"The paper said you chose it."

"Don't believe everything you read in the papers," Milo advised. "Analisa was going to be the last one, and they said she couldn't because she's a witch. I don't get why that's important, but I'm not a witch, so I let her register before I did, which made her twelve and me thirteen. So what?"

"That's why I wanted to talk with you," Tinburkin said, his features stern.

All of a sudden, everything Milo didn't know and didn't understand settled on him like a huge pile of stones. He felt defeated. How could he hope to do anything in all of this? How could he even presume that he could do something as unlikely as this? Why was he here?

"I don't know why I'm here," he said, exhausted.

"Do you remember *how* you got here?" Tinburkin asked him with a surgical intent in his voice.

"I was just thinking about a fantasy scavenger hunt. What it would be like and everything."

"Keep doing that. You'll find yourself in various situations. Keep imagining what you could do with them. Today is the start of the Hunt. The mayor will announce the first challenge. Each contestant will devise his or her own strategy to solve it. You come up with your own strategy, and when you find the first clue, it will suggest what the next one might be. Just like getting here in the first place. You shouldn't follow or copy another contestant. Whatever you come up with is as likely as what another contestant might interpret. Sure, each one of them will believe that his or her decipherment is best, or even the *only* one. You can believe the same, if you like. Just believe in yourself. Remember how magic works in the Kingdom of Odalese. Use your imagination."

"But I don't have any idea how magic works!" Milo said emphatically.

"How did you get here?" Tinburkin reminded.

"I imagined."

Tinburkin grinned. "Exactly. Was it magic?"

"I guess so."

"Then you know. Stay with that. You'll do fine if you don't start relying on somebody else's ideas. Use your own."

Tinburkin laid his hand lightly on Milo's shoulder. "Have you had breakfast?"

"No."

They went down the hill together into town, to one of the cafés on the square. Boriboreau was waiting there as if by prearrangement. Tinburkin ordered for all of them. They ate, and then Tinburkin was off. "Business to attend to," he explained. "Don't worry about the bill. It's been worked out. After the article in the paper yesterday, I expect that every shopkeeper in town will back you, and you don't even have to wear their logos. Good luck!" He vanished around the corner in a few long strides.

"Who is he?" Milo asked Bori.

"Didn't he tell you? He's Tinburkin," Bori said, and went back to washing his paws. Milo knew better than to inquire further.

Bori urged Milo back down to the park. Since dawn, it had been transformed. Brightly colored banners fluttered everywhere, and a grand-stand, now crowded with people, was in place. Milo wondered how every-thing could have been put into place so quickly. But then he remembered the doors that weren't there until they were needed, so he guessed that the grandstand was a similar thing.

In the middle of the park, in front of the grandstands was a platform flanked by banners with all sorts of designs, crests, and symbols. Milo didn't recognize any of them or know what they signified. But judging by the official-looking people on the podium, he assumed that they stood for their organizations and whatever else was involved in the Hunt.

"See the person at the middle?" Bori pointed out a tall woman with long, raven-black hair. It was streaked with silver at the crown. She brushed this forelock from her face from time to time, as if it insisted on having the best place for whatever she was doing. Her dress was black velvet trimmed in silver. "That's the mayor."

Milo looked around at the rest of the assembly. He could see Ali-Sembek, resplendent in silks and brocade and a crimson and gold turban. His winged steed had been brushed until his coat glistened like darkened bronze. Count Yeroen, as grandly dressed as Ali, was talking cordially with Aulaires, who was more arrayed than clothed, causing Milo to shift his eyes away from, then to, then away again until he picked out Analisa some distance away. He felt a pang of something. He didn't know quite what it was, so he decided that it was sadness or just disappointment.

Analisa was alone, and Milo thought she looked a bit dejected. She was dressed just as she had been the last time he saw her, and he wondered if she'd had breakfast. He would have liked to go over and ask, but then he thought she wouldn't want him to talk to her. That definitely made him feel sad.

Closer to where he and Bori waited, Milo saw Tivik pacing like a wild animal, his eyes shifting about nervously. He appeared to be watching a statuesque black woman who was dressed in a swirl of colors, her mane a vigorous coil of dreadlocks.

"That's Obeah Reah," Bori told him, noticing the direction of his gaze. "She's skilled in the art of prognostication, and it's said that she can bring the dead back to life."

Bori continued his commentary, moving Milo's attention to the next contestant, whom Bori said was called Wei Jain. He was a rather rotund, smiling man with a wispy beard and eyebrows like wings. His head was bald and he carried a staff. He was in conversation with another contestant, Braenach, who just then was in the form of a bear. He was a shape-shifter. Milo was not sure that being able to take different forms would be an advantage, or just confusing.

Another woman, with pale, pale hair and a wiry figure, was listening to a man who was as gracile as she and had an elegance that was not from the clothing he wore but from his movements. He had a stringed instrument slung over one shoulder, and she was carrying what appeared to be a freshly cut branch of some sort of evergreen.

"The woman is Sarakka," Bori explained. "She uses that branch to fly. The man with her is Lute. He weaves spells with music."

Bori directed Milo's attention to the other side of the park where a woman dressed entirely in white stood. "That's Vianna. Her powers come from water."

Milo thought about the comic books he read at home, like X-Men, with each of the heroes, heroines, or super-villains having attributes that gave them special powers. Would the Magical Scavenger Hunt be like a comic book adventure?

"I count only twelve contestants, including us," Milo pointed out to Bori. "Where's the last one?"

Bori looked around. "I don't know. I can't count, but I'll take your word for it."

"You can't count?" Milo asked in surprise.

"No, I'm a cat. It's like pockets. Cats don't have pockets and they can't count. But I can see everyone who is here to compete, and I don't see the one who is missing."

Just then, trumpets blared as the mayor stepped forward on the podium.

"Contestants!" she called out, bringing silence over the park. "Citizens of the Kingdom of Odalese!"

Milo assumed that this covered everyone who was there because the mayor continued.

"This marks the beginning of the 77th Magical Scavenger Hunt. I wish to thank all the brave and distinguished contestants for coming to the Kingdom of Odalese to join the ranks of notables who have participated over the seven hundred and sixty years of the Hunt's history.

"Of course the Hunt has changed during that long time, but its purpose has remained true."

Milo pricked up his ears. (Bori didn't. A veteran of many speeches by the mayor, he was settling in for a nap beside Milo.) Milo hoped to hear some sort of definitive explanation for this odd undertaking that he found himself caught up in. Perhaps if he listened closely, he would get a clue.

"As you know, only the most accomplished of the wizardly are invited to come to participate." (Milo was baffled by this because he was not of the wizardly trade, and he could not recall an invitation of any sort.) "And only the greatest can hope to finish the contest. They compete purely for the prestige of the competition and the reward of joining such a prestigious group."

"Surely you win *some*thing," Milo commented quietly to himself.

He startled at a bright, girlish laugh right next to him. He turned to look, but no one was there.

"No need," a melodious voice that matched the laugh continued. "If you can win the Magical Scavenger Hunt, why would you need riches, fame, or any ordinary prize?"

Milo jerked around trying to find anyone close enough to be the voice. He thought he felt the tiniest, faintest brush of warm skin, but there was no one there. Not there, or anywhere else nearby. No one.

Almost before he decided that there was something wrong with his hearing, the voice gave a light, tinkling laugh.

"There's nothing wrong with you. I'm right here."

Right here? There was nothing there!

"What...where...who are you?" Milo asked, completely baffled.

"I'm Stigma, and I'm a contestant. The one you couldn't find just now, although I can't be named the thirteenth one because you're the thirteenth one."

"Who...where..." He wasn't expressing himself too well.

"I'm invisible. Nevertheless, I'm here, and I've been here all along. Perhaps we'll have a chance to talk more later, but for now we should listen to the mayor."

The mayor, of course, had been talking the whole time that Milo's attention had been hijacked by a person who wasn't there, but really was there but was invisible. So Milo had missed a lot of what the mayor had said. Sort of what happened to him when a teacher at school was talking and he was hearing the words but somehow they wouldn't stick in his mind.

He knew that the mayor was talking about the Hunt and how everyone should do their best, play fair, and so on, but that was about it. He wouldn't be able to pass a pop quiz on it. He kept thinking about who could be standing next to him.

He thought he could see a slight shimmer in the air where he'd heard her voice, but he couldn't be sure. He wondered if he might reach out to try to touch her, but that seemed impolite. The temptation was strong, though.

"And so the contest is run," the mayor was saying, "not by how swiftly or elegantly or knowledgably a contestant completes each portion of the Hunt, but by what the contestant has accomplished by the *end* of the Hunt."

Milo's ears did prick up at that. Bori's didn't. He was still napping.

"That means that being the first to return to the Kingdom of Odalese may not be the most significant thing. It can be, but as it has been on many occasions in past Hunts, the last one to return is named the leader. A panel of judges, most of them from past Hunts themselves, makes the final judgment. Magical skills and abilities do not ensure success. It is the *way* in which those skills and abilities have been employed that makes the Hunt a superlative expression of the magical art."

It still didn't tell Milo much about what he wanted to know. He needed practical information, like where the starting line was. But what the mayor was saying was something, and something is better than nothing.

Which drew his attention back to the empty spot next to him where he presumed the invisible contestant still to be.

"Do you understand what she's talking about?" he asked the empty air.

"No, not really," said the voice. "How could one know until one has been through the Hunt and discovered all the clues? They're never the same, you see, so you can't know ahead what to expect. They might not even be the same for you as they are for me. The only thing that counts is that you get from one clue to the next until you end up back here. Then the judges ask what you have found and you tell them, and they decide if you have completed the Hunt."

That made sense to Milo, though it sounded like a strange sort of game. But then, everything was pretty strange already.

"How do you know what to look for?" he asked his inapparent companion.

"Shhh!" she said. The mayor had reached the point of introducing each of the players.

"In the order of their registration, may I now give you the 77th Hunt's contestants!" she called out in a ringmaster's voice.

The crowd cheered. The mayor continued when she could be heard again.

"Ali-Sembek, of Qutan!"

Ali left his winged horse with the squire and mounted the podium to the applause of the crowd.

"Tivik, of Macassar!"

Looking dangerous and half-crazed, the wild man took his place on the stage.

"Lute, of Lyonesse!"

As each contestant mounted the podium, the ones yet to be called moved forward to be in position for their turns.

"Sarakka, of Pohjola!"

"Wei Jain, of Tuliang!"

Milo moved forward, too, drawn by the vacuum on the ground as the podium filled.

"Vianna, of Tarxien!"

"Obeah Reah, of Sofala!"

"Aulaires, of Acrotane!"

Milo studied his hands so he wouldn't stare as the resplendent Aulaires took the stage. He noticed that his fingers were trembling in anticipation of his turn to take the podium.

"Braenach, of Dowth!"

The shape-shifter mounted the podium, looking like himself, or what he presumably looked like when he was in the shape of a rather handsome man.

"Stigma, of Cumae!"

Milo thought he felt motion near him, but he saw nothing but the empty steps that led to the podium. Then a robe held by someone at the back of the stage swirled and then settled to reveal the shape of a woman, but one with no head.

Count Yeroen, who was still left on the ground with Analisa and Milo, noticed their looks of bewilderment.

"If either of you pups were better acquainted with the magical community, you would realize that Stigma has just wrapped herself in the cloak to make herself visible, but because her head is still bare, you can't see it. Only the parts of her that are clothed can be seen."

Milo suddenly thought of the soft, warm touch of skin when she first spoke to him, and blushed as he simultaneously re-evaluated Aulaires' at least partial style of dressing.

"Count Yeroen, of Avebury!"

Yeroen mounted the stage with grand style and inflated dignity, leaving the two youngest contestants as the last to be announced.

"Analisa, of Annwn!"

Milo was left on the ground alone. Bori got himself ready to stand beside Milo, tail high and ears turned up toward the podium.

"And lastly, our thirteenth contestant, Milo, of... of..."

Milo swept Bori into his arms and gave him a place on his left shoulder as he climbed up the steps, mind racing for where he should say he was from. An idea hit and he spoke it as he came into place alongside the mayor, recalling the slogan that his home state used to identify itself.

"The Land of Enchantment," he told her.

"...of the Land of Enchantment!" she announced triumphantly.

The crowd, who had applauded each contestant warmly as they were announced, exploded in cheers. Milo wasn't sure if he should take this as approval of him—why should they?—or approval for all the contestants, since he was the last.

"Now that all the contestants have been introduced," the mayor continued, to even greater applause, "let the Hunt begin!"

She turned to welcome an old man wearing white robes. He had long white hair and a white beard, and he carried a tall oaken staff.

"I give you Lord Barenton, the chairman of the judges of the Magical Scavenger Hunt, and winner of the 74th Hunt. He shall announce the first clue for the contestants."

"You will seek," his voice rang out, more like steel on steel than that of an enfeebled old man, "the first clue: the *Tor Vitrea*, the Tower of Glass!"

3

Milo Gets Off the Starting Line

As soon as Lord Barenton announced the clue, and well before the crowd stopped cheering, the contestants flew into action, some of them quite literally. Sarakka rose straight up into the air on her evergreen branch and in less than a minute was no more than a tiny speck up in the blue sky. Ali had to but spring onto the back of his winged steed and with a powerful beat of wings that sent dust and small children swirling, rose into the air, gone almost as quickly as Sarakka.

Obeah Reah came off the podium and marched to her camp where she took out some knuckle bones—Milo hoped they were from a pig and not human—from a silken bag, tossed them on the table, and studied them. Then she packed her things together and tied them up in a kerchief, sprinkled a powder around herself in a circle, and was gone.

Count Yeroen waved a wand that either created a mist or congealed the very air into a cloud that then rose away into the sky.

Analisa had her broom. "So long," she told Milo. "Good luck."

"Wait!" Milo called after her. "Where is this Glass Tower"—but she was gone, leaving him standing alone on the rapidly emptying field.

Braenach changed into an eagle, Stigma shed her cloak and vanished by means that gave no trace of technique, and Tivik loped away on all fours like a wolf. Aulaires—well, Milo had no idea how she got away because he didn't look. Even the crowd had dispersed by the time Milo and Bori got around to departing. Milo looked at Bori.

"What do we do now?" Milo asked the cat. "I don't have the slightest idea where—or what—this Glass Tower thing is. Do you?"

"Meow," Bori replied, with a dismissive inflection and a certain flip of his tail that added to his remark.

"I thought you were here to help me," Milo said peevishly.

"Yes, when I can," Bori answered, as airily as his meow had been. "You're the contestant."

"Do you at least have a suggestion?" Milo asked.

"Let's take a look at the situation. The first clue has something to do with a glass tower. Barenton called it Tor Vitrea. So it must be a definite place or thing. Everyone but us took off, presumably because they knew what it was. Right? So I suggest we find that out first."

"Like, duh!" Milo said, exasperated.

"Well, do you have a better plan?"

"No," Milo said, even more glumly.

"Then let's go to the library," Bori suggested, and set off, tail high, clearly full of himself. Milo had to tag along.

The library was one street back from the Square, on the opposite side of the building that contained the Mayor's office. As they came into the hushed interior with its smells of old books and waxed wooden bookshelves, Milo opened his mouth to ask Bori a question. A sharp look from the librarian made him close it again. Bori went straight up to her.

"We would like information on the Glass Tower," he told her after hopping up onto her desk.

The librarian smiled sweetly and nodded. "Do you have a specific glass tower in mind?" she asked in a near whisper.

"Are there many?" Milo responded. "I mean, other than the one the Mayor sent the Hunt contestants off to find?"

"Oh, then you must mean the Glass Tower. It's been written about extensively, although I don't believe anyone knows exactly where it is or if it actually exists outside of mythology. Selton recently published a book arguing that the Glass Tower, the Tor Vitrea, is actually a folk name for the Krystalien Geberge, of Upper Pharcia, and that the stories about it originate in Old Pharcian, but most scholars consider it to be pure folklore," she told him.

This sounded bad to Milo. "Then can we look at what you have on the topic? I'm supposed to go there, you see, and I don't know anything about it."

She gave him an odd look. "The tales of the Glass Tower appear in everything from fairy tales to scholarly literature. If I were to bring you everything in the library where it's mentioned, you would have more material than you could read during a ten-year sabbatical."

Milo stopped to think, wishing for a computer and access to Wikipedia. "Then could you pick out a book for me that you think would give a general overview?" he asked as politely as he could.

She smiled, and gestured them to find a place at one of the long tables in the reading room behind her desk.

While they waited, Milo whispered to Bori. "I never read anything about the Glass Tower, and I like reading about stuff like that."

The silence in the place was impressive. Milo could hear the rustle of a page being turned two tables away, and the crisp plop of a book being laid down on a table by another reader. Someone's subdued cough echoed through the galleries like a rumor. A man sitting on the opposite side of the table from Milo and Bori, and three chairs down, sat with head bowed into a thick volume opened before him. Apparently he was fast asleep.

The librarian returned, carrying two heavy books, one with a rather worn leather cover and the other with a dark green one. Her tweeds rustled softy, and her footsteps echoed in the hushed room.

"Thank you," Milo whispered as she piled them on the table before him.

She smiled at him again. "Let me know if you need anything else." She returned to her desk with quick, efficient steps.

Milo stared at the thick volumes, feeling his heart sink. He opened the worn leather one first. The print was tiny and antique, crowding each page in two dense columns. "It'll take ten years to read just this one," he said with a groan. "Everybody will finish the whole hunt before I can finish the first chapter."

"Not necessarily," said the man from the other side of the table, in a lowered voice. The librarian shot him a harsh look.

Milo saw a flute poking out of his coat pocket as he rose and moved directly across the table from Milo.

"They have to find it first," the man commented.

It was Tinburkin.

"Do you know where it is?" Milo asked.

"That's not important," he answered. "What is important is that each of the contestants must be able to identify the clue and use it to discover the next one."

"How can I go about doing that?" Milo complained. "I don't even know what it is."

"Every schoolchild has heard of the Glass Tower," Tinburkin answered.

"Maybe so, if they live in the Kingdom of Odalese," Milo retorted. "But not in...where I'm from."

"The Land of Enchantment?" Tinburkin grinned. "Then I'll tell you a story. It's a well-known tale, so I won't be breaking any rules if I repeat it for you. The Glass Tower is a place that can be found only by one who either knows how to look for it, which is very rare, or one who has the right attitude to find it. I'm sure there's a long chapter in that book there"—Tinburkin tapped the cover of the one Milo had opened—"that discusses those requirements at great length, even though it's quite simple in reality. The Glass Tower is located in a realm ruled by the Fisher King, who is the guardian of a great secret. You can get to the Glass Tower only by his invitation, but you must find his hidden kingdom first if you are to get his permission."

"I've read stories about the Fisher King," Milo said excitedly. "He's the guardian of the grail that King Arthur's knights were always looking for!"

He must have said this too loudly, because he caught the librarian's attention. Instead of putting her finger to her lips in a shush, she sprang from her desk with a deafening shriek, pouncing like an eagle on a rabbit. Her face was contorted into a glaring attack, all mouth and sharp teeth.

Needless to say, it startled Milo into speechlessness. He toppled over in terror as she launched at him. She no longer looked human. But then just as quickly she looked like a librarian again, standing in front of him with her hands on her hips.

"I won't tolerate this racket in my library!" she chided. "I'm afraid I'll have to ask you to leave!"

Heart pounding and weak-kneed in fright, Milo was all too happy to get out of there. Only when he was outdoors again did he remember Tinburkin. Thinking back, he couldn't recall seeing Tinburkin anywhere as he and Bori hurried out the door.

"What happened?" he asked Bori breathlessly, looking up and down the street to see if he could locate Tinburkin.

"The librarian is a banshee," Bori explained.

"A banshee? Jeez, she must have scared everyone in there half out of their wits, screaming like that."

"Actually, no one else heard a thing. It was meant for you."

Milo's ears were still ringing. He wasn't sure if he completely trusted Bori's explanation.

"Where's Tinburkin? Did you see where he went? I need to find him."

"You won't. You can find him only when he's looking for you, not when you're looking for him."

"That's too weird," Milo said in exasperation. "I'm getting awfully tired of all this...this magical stuff. Now how can I find out about what he was telling me?"

"If he left, then he's already told you all he intended to tell you," Bori suggested, rather distracted by a large dog on the other side of the street. "Let's go someplace else."

Judging by the way Bori's tail was swelling, Milo thought that leaving the area before the dog caught sight of the cat was a good plan. Another consideration for Milo was that he was feeling hungry again, and eating something before going off to search for the elusive Glass Tower was a reasonable idea. You never knew if there would be much opportunity for eats once they left the Kingdom of Odalese.

Over lunch, Milo brought up another concern. "Bori," he asked the cat, "how are we going to get to the tower? Everybody but me has a means of travel. I've got squat. We can't really walk there, can we?"

Bori, who was nibbling on a fish head, agreed that walking to all the places this scavenger hunt was likely to take them seemed impractical. "How do you usually travel?" he asked.

"My mom takes me in our car. But there aren't any cars here, and besides, I don't own one. I don't even have a driver's license yet."

"Then do you usually walk?"

"That or use my skateboard."

"What's a skateboard?"

Milo told him about skateboards. Bori confirmed that a skateboard didn't sound very useful for cross-country travel where there was so little pavement. "Anything else?" Bori asked.

Milo thought of his bike, but that didn't seem any better because he hadn't brought it with him either.

"You know, this Glass Tower sounds like it's an imaginary sort of place anyway," Bori observed. "So how would you get to an imaginary place?"

"When I was a kid, I used to build imaginary conveyances out of boxes and boards and strings and stuff."

"Did they work?"

"They worked fine for imagining," Milo answered, unconvinced about the practicality of those contraptions applied to the current necessity of getting from here to some other place.

"I think it's worth a try," Bori told him. "We're not getting anywhere now, so if it doesn't work, we'll still be here."

As odd as it sounded, it was sort of logical, so when Bori insisted, Milo went along with it. Bori took Milo into the alleys behind the shops where things got delivered and showed him discarded packing crates and garbage bins.

"This looks like a good place to build the sort of cart you described," Bori observed.

And rightly so. Milo started rummaging through stuff, halfheartedly at first, but with growing interest as the possibilities of the materials fired his imagination. He started having fun. He hadn't built a fantasy contraption for some time, and when the creative knack for it took hold, he could really see the potential.

"It has to be built without nails," he told Bori, who was mostly watching. "Iron nails impede the flow of magic."

"They do?" Bori asked.

"Sure," Milo said, not because he knew that they did or didn't but because it seemed right. Besides, he didn't have any nails. There were, however, lots of pieces of string left over from opened packages. Instead of cardboard, there were wooden slats that merchants used for making boxes.

Slowly the vehicle took shape. Someone looking at it without knowing what it was would have thought Milo was building a box with slatted sides, floor, and top, tied together in a fairly ramshackle way. But it was substantial enough to hold together when Milo pushed and pulled on a corner to test its structural integrity.

"What does it do?" Bori asked as Milo demonstrated how to crawl into it through an open space at the top.

"It flies," Milo answered as if that were obvious.

"Oh," Bori agreed, perhaps a little less than enthusiastically. "How do you steer it?"

Milo hadn't thought of that yet, and acknowledged that Bori had raised an important point. Clearly it would need a steering mechanism. His eye caught on some shipping labels, and the answer was obvious. He began sorting through the junk, pulling out the appropriate labels that had been attached to various crates.

He tore the label that read THIS SIDE UP so it read simply UP. He found directional arrows to use to point to the right and to the left, then found signs for DOWN, FORWARD, REVERSE, FASTER, SLOWER, and so on.

By making a paste with old pieces of bread ground into powder and wetted with the juice squeezed from overripe grapes, Milo stuck his signs to the inside slats of his crate.

"That's our control panel," he told Bori. "We need just one more thing," he continued. "We need a navigation system."

"How's that?" Bori asked.

"You know how Tinburkin said that you can get to the Glass Tower only through the invitation of the Fisher King? It just so happens that I know what the Fisher King looks like. I have a book at home with his picture in it."

Milo was thinking of one of his books with stories about King Arthur and the Knights of the Round Table. One of the stories was about the visit that Sir Gawain made to the Grail Castle. It included a picture of the Grail King, who was also known as the Fisher King. In the picture, he was on his boat, fishing in the lake that surrounded the Grail Castle, of which he was the guardian. Milo could see that picture as clearly in his mind's eye as if he held the book open in front of his face.

"How will that help?" Bori asked. "The book is there and we're here. Besides, how is a picture of this king going to help us get to the Glass Tower?"

Answering all those questions seemed like a lot of trouble to Milo, especially since he didn't have the answers, but he felt like he was on to something. If he could pull it all together, then having the answers wouldn't be important because he could show how it worked.

"I don't need the book," he told Bori. "What I need is some paper and colored pencils so I can draw the picture."

Although he didn't boast of it just then, Milo knew that he was a pretty fair artist. Drawing pictures was, in fact, a major factor in why his teachers got upset with him. Although they believed that drawing fantasies was an inefficient use of his time, he felt that this was an opportunity to demonstrate just how practical that particular talent could be.

"Where can I get the things I need?" he asked Bori.

Bori, though he seemed less than convinced that Milo's plan was one hundred percent reliable, took Milo to look for paper and colored pencils.

"Let's go, Boss," he said to Milo, and led off with his tail about half raised. "Let's see what we can do."

Bori took Milo to a stationary store stocked with cards, paper, pens, pencils, notebooks, calendars, planners, and so on. There were things for everyone from schoolkids to housekeepers, tradesmen, and merchants. Milo quickly found what he wanted: a notebook with blank pages and a box of crayons. He took them up to the counter.

"How much will this be?" he asked, wondering how he could buy them.

"That comes to one kuzurian fifty," the clerk said. She was a nice-looking woman who sort of reminded him of his favorite teacher from last year.

"Would you like me to put them on your credit?"

"My credit?" Milo asked in surprise.

"Yes, your credit's good with any merchant in the Kingdom of Odalese."

"Oh! Why...sure!" Milo said in relief.

As soon as he and Bori got outside the shop, Milo sat down on the curb and started to draw. A picture rapidly took form. Bori watched Milo with great interest, at least until he spotted a mouse fiddling along the wall beside the garden gate on the opposite side of the street.

When Milo finished coloring in everything, he called Bori.

"Got it! Bori, let's go!"

Off he dashed, the cat galloping behind as fast as he could to catch up. Back at the crate, Milo got in and Bori hopped up to be lifted inside. Milo opened the notebook to show him the picture of a misty lake with a skiff where a man sat with a fishing pole and line, waiting for a fish to take the bait. In the background, you could make out the top of a tower and some parts of a castle wall that were obscured in the mist.

"Hold on tight," Milo warned Bori. "We're off!"

Milo touched the sign that said START.

Bori didn't notice anything, but he kept quiet, not wishing to disturb Milo's fierce concentration. Milo's fingers moved from START to UP. To Bori's amazement, the crate shuddered and slowly lifted off the ground. Milo's other hand touched the FASTER sign, and the box began to lift more quickly. It cleared the eaves of the houses that surrounded them until they were looking down at the roofs. The Kingdom of Odalese opened up beneath them. Up and up they went, watching the town shrink and the world expand.

4

The Crane King and the Glass Tower

A raven surfing the air currents sailed near, giving them a curious look-over with his black winking eyes. Milo let out a whoop. Bori dug his claws into the floorboards, unused to the sensation of being cut loose from Mother Earth.

A few wisps of cloud cued Milo that they were high enough, and he moved his fingers to touch the FORWARD sign. The craft obeyed, moving now straight ahead. He and Bori could see the vast expanse of countryside down below, with the neat but irregular layout of the town directly underneath them, threaded by the silvery snake of the River Dulcy coming from the distant blue of mountains, through woods, and past checkerboards of farms, then going away in the other direction in reverse order. Milo saw roads, paths, farms, meadows, hedgerows, ponds, forests, lakes, and higher mountains behind the wooded hills, their stony joints angled out through holes in their cloaks of trees. Soon they left the valley of the River Dulcy.

Milo touched the picture he'd drawn of the Fisher King, breathless to know if this, too, would work. The crate—craft, that is—slowed and turned in a testing circle and then stopped, adjusted itself, and moved off once again in an altered direction.

Milo let out a sigh of relief. He gave Bori a pat of assurance, and the cat immediately responded by pushing his hindquarters high to receive it, tail awave.

"Well, we're finally on our way," Milo told him. "I bet you thought I couldn't do it."

"Why would I think that?" Bori said, nonplussed. "You're the Hunt contestant, not me. Why wouldn't you be able to do what you need to do?"

Milo couldn't answer that. He realized that he, not Bori, was the one who was surprised that this had actually worked. He considered for a moment as the craft zoomed ahead, thinking about how he had always just assumed that he wouldn't be able to do all sorts of things expected of him.

By afternoon and many miles later, they were both shivering with the altitude. Milo touched the SLOWER sign and then the DOWN sign to bring them closer to the ground where they could look for a place where they might find shelter for the night. Shadows stretched long across the land, converging to gather into pools of evening.

They were over an enormous, unbroken forest. Its borders, if there were any, were lost in the velvet robes of drawing night. Looking for a way to reach the ground, Bori spoke.

"There! There's a point of light."

"Where?"

"There. See?"

Milo saw a break in the treetops, albeit a small one, and a thread of white smoke. As they came over the spot, they could see a small campfire, and began to carefully descend. They could make out a lonely figure squatting near the fire, feeding twigs into it.

"Hello?" Milo called, not wishing to overly startle the fire maker. "Mind if we come down?"

The person looked up. With a start both of gladness and dread, Milo saw that it was Analisa.

"What? You! How did you find me?" she demanded, standing up with defiance.

"Why...I didn't *find* you; I...we just came down here," Milo answered. We need a place to put down for the night, and this is the only one we could find."

They sort of hovered in the crate a few feet off the ground, rocking back and forth from Milo's uncomfortable shifting, while Analisa glared at him.

The glare softened a little. "All right," she said at last. "Come down."

The crate landed with a bump. Milo found that he was quite stiff as he stood up and then lifted Bori out of the crate. Bori stretched and yawned, then hopped down and disappeared almost immediately from the small circle of light that the fire made. He blended into the darkness as if his gray fur had turned him as invisible as Stigma.

Milo climbed out next. "Where are we?" he asked.

"If you don't know, I'm not going to tell you," Analisa said. "Milo, tell me the truth. Are you following me?"

"No," Milo said, his feelings hurt. "I'm not following you. I may not know where we are, but I got here entirely by my own effort. I don't mean to intrude."

He began to move away, but Analisa stopped him. "Since you're here, you should share my fire. It's not much, but it's pretty lonely. I wouldn't mind having somebody to talk to.

"To tell the truth," Analisa continued, settling down near her fire again, "I don't really know where we are either. I've been flying over this forest for hours without a sign of anybody or anything."

Milo noticed her broom, an implement made of a stout, rather crooked wooden handle with a bundle of pliant willow switches bound tightly to its end. It was lying on its side near the fire.

"Have you seen any of the others?" she asked, meaning the other contestants.

"No, but I got a late start."

"I was beginning to think I'd taken a wrong turn," she said, chafing her arms against the cool night air. "Do you think we're on the right course?"

"I'm positive," he said with conviction while wondering what knowledge she had used to pick the route she was on.

His answer seemed to make her feel better. She put some more sticks on the fire, then settled a small, round pot onto the glowing bed of coals. "It isn't much, but you're welcome to share my porridge." She smiled at him for the first time. "To return the favor."

Milo took out his pocketknife (something that would have gotten him in big trouble if his teachers at school had known about it), picked up a branch from Analisa's pile of firewood, and began whittling it.

"What are you doing?" she asked, curious.

"Something my grandfather taught me how to do. I'm making a spoon."

She laughed. Milo thought he detected a tone of surprised admiration instead of derision, so he kept on whittling.

"Milo, you are an odd one."

They sat in silence for some time while he worked, Analisa staring into the dance of flames and Milo turning his work this way and that in the fire's light, looking for where to take the next curl of shavings. From time to time she stirred the contents of her pot with a stick. The pot was bubbling softly, emitting an inviting aroma that made Milo's mouth water.

"Analisa," he started, then faltered. "I know I'm sort of an idiot at times, and I don't know much about any of this." He gestured in a general way with his pocketknife. "But I intend to do my best to play fair and not take advantage of anybody else. I just want you to know that."

She looked at him for a minute.

"Milo, you're sweet. That's the problem, or at least part of it. The Hunt is serious business. Do you think for a minute that any of the others will play fair? The judges know they won't, nor do they expect them to. Do you think, for instance, that Count Yeroen paid your fee out of kindness? No. He did it as a ploy. He calculated that it would build his image, humiliate you, and possibly add an element of confusion that he could profit by. And you, instead of registering the insult that you are inferior to him, turned it on him by letting me in.

"I owe you for what you did," she continued, "but I still haven't decided what to think of you. Either you are very clever and deceitful—much more so even than Count Yeroen—or you really are a complete..." She stopped herself and groped for a different word than the one she had been about to use. "...innocent."

She turned to gesture toward Milo's crate. "Now you show up in that incredible contraption and sit here like..." She didn't complete the sentence, but after an awkward silence, she faced him. "Milo, if you're as big a fool as you say you are, how in the world were you able to build that out of...out of trash?"

Milo set the newly finished spoon on the stone next to Analisa's pot and retrieved the next stick he'd chosen to work on. Analisa picked up the spoon and looked it over. It was crude, but it was a spoon. She stirred her porridge to test it.

"Milo, do me a favor. Don't tell me anymore how clueless you are."

Milo wanted to protest, feeling his need to share how confused he felt. But she had taken that away from him. She had beaten him to it. He was stuck now with the responsibility of being a fully qualified Hunt contestant.

Bori saved the moment just then by strolling into camp, obviously pleased with his own prowess and appeased appetite. He sat down between them by the fire and began washing his face as he always did after a meal.

"Thank you for not sharing," Milo told Bori, imagining in spite of himself what the cat had had for dinner.

Analisa broke out in a laugh. "Oh, you two!" she said. "Milo, Bori—thanks for dropping in."

That made Milo's night. Not even the meal from Analisa's little pot made him feel as warm and welcomed as that.

Warm is a relative thing. Before dawn, they were all three huddled together and wishing for morning. It came, however tardily, and the new day sent them on their separate ways. Analisa left first, mounting her broom while Milo studiously looked down at something he was doing so she would see that he wasn't watching what direction she took.

After making sure that the fire was completely out, Milo and Bori got back into the crate and lifted off. "One of the floorboards is a little loose," he told Bori. "Remind me to tighten the lashings when we land again."

They flew on and on, the forest reaching out endlessly beneath them. Milo flew lower today, and perhaps a little slower—the better to see where they might be. He felt that he needed to be vigilant. Without being able to say why, he believed that they were getting close. By noon, the forest canopy had thinned, revealing stretches of open ground with tall grass.

"What's that up ahead?" Bori asked.

Milo knew that Bori's eyesight was much sharper than his. He squinted to see where Bori indicated.

"Looks like a bunch of animals," Milo said, "all milling around the base of that granite outcropping."

"It looks to me like a pack of dogs that has a cat cornered," Bori asserted.

Milo brought the craft lower and slowed it as it came in at treetop level over the commotion.

"What are those?" Milo asked in amazement when he was able to see the milling creatures on the ground. He and Bori could also hear their yelps, growls, and howls. At first Milo thought they were wolves, but then he saw that they didn't have fur, and they sometimes stood up on their hind legs. They had huge, hulking shoulders, suggesting massive strength. He thought they might be something like baboons, because they looked like misshapen humans except for their long ears and long muzzles, which had heavy, gaping jaws and long flashing white fangs that looked capable of ripping and crushing. The creatures were completely naked except for a bristly mane that continued down in a ridge between their shoulders and played out on their spine at the small of their back.

"Can you see who they're after?" Bori asked, looking into the focus of the frenzy.

Milo saw a man, and soon enough recognized Tivik. Just as savage as his attackers, he fought them off, his back to the boulders. He was glistening in sweat and streaked with blood. It was clear that he couldn't fight his way free.

"Tivik!" Milo shouted. "Grab hold of my crate! I'll lift you away!"

Tivik looked above him, unable to take more than a glance away from the lunging, snapping attackers. Without a thought to his crate's ability to lift the extra weight, Milo dipped in and dropped down as low as he dared. The sudden appearance of the craft surprised the weird beasts, and they shied back just long enough for Tivik to spring up and grab the open slats of the bottom of the crate. Anticipating the sudden jerk of Tivik's weight, Milo touched the UP sign just as Tivik gripped fast, and with a heavy shudder the crate lifted out of the reach of the snarling jaws that lunged to catch their eluding prey.

"Lopers!" Tivik said, panting. "Ambushed me this morning. I've been in a running fight all day. I wouldn't have lasted more than a few more minutes if you hadn't come along."

Milo flew the craft clear of the tops of the trees and rapidly away from the spot where the lopers, looking up and emitting a terrible howl, were already galloping to chase them from the ground. Tivik held on, struggling to maintain his grip from where he hung so precariously.

"I'll set 'er down," Milo told him, worried that Tivik might lose his exhausted hold.

"No! Put more distance between us and them first. They'll trail us by air scent, for days if they need to, and they can run faster than deer for hours and hours."

Just then the crate gave a lurch as the loose lashing broke. Tivik spun, jerking the crate in a yawl as he struggled frantically to get his free hand onto a different slat.

"I've got to set down!" Milo shouted, his hands flying over the signs to maintain the craft's equilibrium.

A yowl from Bori caught Milo's attention, and he saw that the cat was puffed up, back arched, tail bushed, and spitting. Bori was looking up, not down at the following lopers. Glancing up over his shoulder, Milo thought he saw large birds circling in fast.

"What's that!" he screamed at Tivik.

Tivik, still dangling precariously, saw what was closing in from above.

"Harpies!" Tivik shouted. "Dive, dive before they rip us out of the sky!"

Milo needed very little encouragement to send the craft plummeting as he searched for a place to get cover from above. He spotted a thicket of trees ahead and steered the wobbling, yawing crate into them, dodging under their crowns and between the boles, painfully aware of the heavy rush of powerful wing beats just above them.

Women's screams of rage and frustration rang out as Milo skimmed between trees, feet from the ground. The crate gave another lurch as Tivik dropped off and rolled onto the grass. The sudden change in weight sent the craft out of control and crashing into a tree trunk.

"Brilliant!" Tivik exclaimed with glee as Milo and Bori, bruised and disheveled, extracted themselves from the ruins of the crate. "Neither the lopers nor the harpies will follow us into the sanctuary of the willows," he asserted.

Milo looked up through the branches and leaves that separated them from the wheeling, screaming aerial pursuers. They looked a lot like eagles, only much bigger, and they had women's heads, hair, and breasts.

"I guess they don't know Victoria's Secret," Milo said to himself. "Willows or not, I don't think I like the idea of hanging out in this neighborhood. Do you, Bori?"

With a swish of his tail, the cat agreed.

"We can expect to find a stream farther in under the willows," Tivik said. "I'm thirsty, and I wouldn't mind washing off the blood and loper slobber."

Although Tivik didn't strike Milo as the sort of guy who would be overly concerned with personal hygiene, he agreed with the wild man. Sure enough, they found a delightful clear little stream. By now the screaming of the harpies and the howling of the lopers had converged, then faded into the distance. Tivik said that the mutual hatred between the two groups had moved their interest in the humans into a battle with each other. Tivik, Milo, and Bori were forgotten.

Bori and Milo drank the sweet, cool water upstream of Tivik, who waded in to wash off the gore. As the caked blood and dirt melted away, the various gashes and wounds appeared, but then they too closed and faded. "It's an enchanted stream," Tivik observed. He looked up, his senses cocked like a hunting hound's. "I wonder if there's anything to eat here. I haven't had a meal since I left the Kingdom." Tivik's appetite gave Milo a shiver.

"Look!" Tivik whispered.

Milo looked, and saw a white deer—a hind—standing some distance away, watching them. "Aha!" Tivik exclaimed, glancing craftily at Milo. "A sign—or a meal." Instantly, Tivik dashed away in pursuit as the hind took flight, vanishing into the thicket. Tivik crashed in after, the sound fading until Milo and Bori could no longer hear.

"I hope he doesn't catch it," Milo said with a shudder. "He doesn't strike me as being that much different from those loper things."

Milo and Bori decided to continue on, following the general course of the stream. The ground became boggier, and cypress trees, trailing long beards of moss, replaced the sorts of trees that like drier ground.

The sky opened up between the branches and exposed the surface of a misty lake. Balanced silently on one impossibly long leg, a crane, snaky neck cocked, stood motionless as a statue. Milo and Bori moved cautiously nearer. It was all white, with black on its folded wings and long red wisps of feathers like a crown above its eyes. Milo and Bori moved nearer and nearer without so much as a flicker from the bird until they were at the water's edge. The crane stood a little way out in the water.

Milo started to whisper to Bori, but the crane, without the slightest break in its concentration, silenced him.

"Shhh!" the bird admonished. "He's here! If you frighten him, I'll spear you instead."

Milo and Bori sank down. Milo decided there was no reason to be surprised that the bird spoke. After all, he had a cat that could. He thought it best just to wait.

Minutes passed. The crane didn't move. If he hadn't spoken, Milo would have begun to suspect that he was artificial, despite the way the faint breeze ruffled a feather here and there.

Feeling thirsty, Milo lay down very slowly and carefully on his belly, taking his queue from Bori, who was crouched down to lap water from the lake. Milo lowered his hands into the crystal coolness.

"Look!" Bori whispered, hardly louder than a faint hiss.

Milo saw his own reflection flicker on the water's surface. "What?" he whispered back.

"There! Almost between your hands!"

Milo looked through his own reflection down into the water itself. He could see his own arms and hands, pale beneath the surface. And sure enough, almost between them, he saw the dark, nearly invisible shape of a large fish hovering in its own element. All Milo had to do to catch it was to slowly, gradually close his hands together and...

Pop! Milo pulled up the huge, slippery fish and flung it onto the grass. As his balance shifted, Milo almost fell into the water. Bori jumped on the flipping fish before it could fling itself back into the lake, and Milo joined the fray, wrestling with the cool, solid body.

As the two of them managed to get the fish in their grips, the crane hopped above them.

"By Jove, you've gotten him! It's the salmon! I've fished for him for years, you see, and now you've caught him, just like that!"

Actually, Milo was more surprised by his catch than Bori or the crane was. Although he'd heard of catching fish that way, with your two hands held down in the water, he'd never actually done it, or even tried it.

"It just...happened, I guess," he told the crane. "Would you like to have it, since you've tried to catch it for so long?"

The crane looked quite taken aback. "You would...just *give* it to me?" the crane asked in astonishment. "You would freely give me the Great Salmon?"

"Well, I can't really do anything with it, and since you've been trying to catch it and all...Maybe you could share some with Bori here."

The crane stared at the cat as if the whole idea was beyond comprehension.

"Umm," Milo said. "What are you going to do with it?"

"Take it to my castle for proper cooking, of course," the crane proclaimed.

"Your...castle?" Milo asked incredulously.

"Why, yes. I'm the Crane King, and my castle is just over there, across the lake. You, and your companion here, of course, are invited to be my guests for the night if you will. And I hope, after this generous—oh, so much more than generous—gift, that you will allow me to host you, to honor you with every gratitude that my kingdom and I can offer."

That sounded pretty good to Milo. He wondered why this fish was such a big deal. But then, this *was* a king of cranes. How would Milo know what to expect from him?

"My cat and I would be delighted," Milo replied.

"If you would be so kind as to bring the salmon to my skiff over here—it's rather heavy, and I have trouble carrying heavy things due to my...infirmity."

The salmon *was* heavy, but Milo managed it okay, with Bori walking proudly along beside him, casting hungry glances at the fish.

"Bori," Milo told him under his breath, "you'd better leave that fish alone until the crane offers you some. He's making such a big deal out of it, I don't think you should try snitching a piece."

The bird hopped ahead on one leg. The other leg remained folded up under his body, clearly moving with effort and pain. Milo wanted to ask what was wrong, but he thought it might be impolite to mention the king's disability. He didn't want to seem nosey.

The skiff was nearby, although Milo had to wade into the lake to put the fish into the boat. Bori jumped from a log and onto the boat's bow, and from there onto one of the wooden seats. Milo's climbing in over the gunwale set the boat rocking, but it seemed stable enough not to tip over. He gave the cat another warning look.

The Crane King took a hop up onto the bow, and Milo pushed off. Standing on his one leg from his position on the bow, his balance stately, the Crane King asked Milo to row.

"It's impossible for me to row myself," said the crane, "so if you would be so kind, as you're the only one who can grip the oars," the Crane King said apologetically.

"No problem," Milo said, setting the oars and beginning to row. "I've rowed a boat before, with my grandfather, fishing. Milo wondered what the bird would have done if he hadn't come along to do the work. But he didn't ask that either.

Just the same, though, Milo was very curious. How did a crane become a king and have a castle? Why was he so keen on this particular fish, and what made this fish peculiarly special? How did the crane become injured? Milo thought he saw the fletching of an arrow—very old and bedraggled—lodged in the thigh joint of the leg that the bird kept drawn against his body. Milo remembered the wildlife rescue operations back home that might be able to remove the arrow and heal this magnificent bird. Only, to the best of his knowledge, that sort of organization didn't exist here.

The lake was really a swamp with very little open water and lots of tangles of rushes and islands of cypress. The Crane King indicated to him which way to take around the islands and what channels to follow. Milo soon had no idea where he was or how to get back to where they'd started. That bothered him, since he would have to find the crate again in order to fix it so they could get on with their search.

"What's that?" Bori whispered.

Milo turned. A tall gray castle soared above the layers of mist, its towers partly obscured by the trails of fog that hung above the surface of the lake. It had an air of forlorn magnificence, its color muted, perhaps by the fog.

"That is my castle, friends: Crane Castle," the bird said gravely.

Attendants—humans dressed in white liveries trimmed in black and red—met the skiff. In silence and with grave respect, they drew it up to the stone pier. They bowed to the bird and helped him onto a litter, where he lay to be carried by two of them.

"These are my new friends and guests for the night," the Crane King told the attendants as he gestured toward Milo and Bori. "This young man has captured the Great Salmon, which now lies in the bottom of the boat. He has gifted it to me. Please extend him and his cat every courtesy in honor of the guest oath."

The attendants picked up the crane's litter. "Cedric, my seneschal, will see to your needs and conduct you to your chambers. I will see you for supper by and by."

The crane was borne away, leaving Milo and Bori with Cedric.

"Come this way, if you will," the man said formally. Milo noticed that another servant was handling the still flopping fish with something like reverence, as if it were of immense value.

It wasn't as if there was anything unfriendly about any of this. It was just so solemn. It gave Milo a chill, and he wished he were anywhere else. He picked up Bori, glad to have him near. The cat rode on his shoulder, looking around with his big green eyes.

"I wonder if they have dogs in there," Bori noted as they crossed the drawbridge into the castle.

"I just hope they give us supper and a dry place to sleep, and show us how to find the crate again tomorrow," Milo said in his turn.

Cedric led them through a courtyard, up flights of stairs, into a hallway, and down corridors and more stairs. They turned corners and passed various rooms filled with tapestries, heavy wooden furniture, and all the sorts of armor and weapons that one would expect to find in a castle. The scene was every bit as confusing as the lake. Although the castle was ornate and stately looking, it also seemed ancient and stale, as if everything had been placed on hold for a long, long time.

Cedric brought them to their rooms: yes, rooms plural, a whole suite of them. A fire burned brightly in a fireplace as big as some people's living room, making the suite much more welcoming than the rest of the castle. In attendance were four beautiful maidens dressed in white with the black and red trimmings that seemed to be the fashion here. They curtsied and bustled in a rush of satin to take Milo and Bori in hand from Cedric, speaking only when he had left.

"Come this way if you please, my...Lord," the leader of the maidens said as the others hid their giggles. Milo was embarrassed by the whole thing.

But not as abashed as he was by what happened next. They insisted on helping him to undress, and then put him into a hot bath. Not that he had anything against a nice, hot bath, but, after all, nobody had actually given him a bath since he was maybe five years old. Especially not young women, hardly older than he was. But they insisted that he do exactly as they ordered. He was very glad to sink down into the water and take cover under the thick layer of bubbles and veils of steam.

This really is a strange trip I'm on, he thought to himself, feeling the heavy blush on his face.

Bori, on the other hand, was enjoying himself. While Milo soaked, the young ladies lavished attention on the cat, carrying on over him and brushing his coat to remove all the burrs, tangles, and mud.

Milo soaked for a long time, dreading the moment when he'd have to get out of the water, and trying to devise a way to do it without help or onlookers. But, alas, the time came. Two of the maidens stood by, holding towels to assist. As Milo rose half out of the water, he reached up and snatched away a towel to wrap himself in before he rose all the way out of the bubbles. The maidens tittered, but he didn't care.

"Listen, this may be what you're supposed to do," he said to the maidens, willing down his blush, "and I appreciate the help and all, but I prefer to do this myself."

As they tried to squelch their giggles, the leader said, "As you wish. We have fresh clothing here for you, and we can help you to dress or, if you prefer, leave the clothes here for you. You may call when you're ready. We'll be just outside the door."

"What about my own clothes?" Milo asked.

"They'll be laundered and ready for you on the morrow," she promised.

He chose to dress himself, and they left.

"Why are you making such a fuss?" Bori asked. "They're very gentle, kind ladies."

"It's...You wouldn't understand. It's a human thing. Like you not having pockets. I'm not used to having help this way."

Bori didn't look convinced. He sat looking at Milo with his wide, round eyes, tail wrapped primly around his feet, but he didn't say anything more.

Milo would have preferred his jeans to the tights they had left him, but the long white linen shirt was okay. The tunic that went over the shirt felt stiff and heavy because of its brocaded stitching. The boots felt a lot warmer than his marsh-soaked sneakers, and more trustworthy for the rough walking he'd been doing. His sneakers were wet enough to make a home for frogs.

"Okay," he called. "I'm ready."

The four maidens came at once. He was relieved that they didn't giggle this time. Instead, they complimented him at how handsome he looked. One of them had a comb and worked down his bath-tousled hair.

"We shall lead you to dinner now. The king and his court await you."

"They're waiting for me?" Milo asked, abashed. "I'm sorry! I had no idea they were waiting for me!"

"It's all right," the maiden told him. "They aren't waiting exactly. They're just ready to serve dinner when you arrive. There's a sort of ceremony that we do for our guests."

"Let's go then," Milo said, picking up Bori so he could see everything from the vantage of Milo's shoulder without anyone thinking he was just some stray cat.

The way down to the dining hall was just as confusing as the way in had been before. Milo could make no sense of the layout of the castle. They arrived in a cavernous gallery lighted like Christmas with banks of candles that somehow made the unlighted corners and the high ceilings appear even darker. People wearing satins, velvets, fur trimmings, and gold sat at long tables set with plates and flatware, cups of wine at hand. Milo looked for the Crane King. He wasn't there. On a raised dais at the head of the table sat a stately man who had white hair and a white beard, clipped short. He looked grim and worn despite his fine clothing. To his left sat a woman, the most regal person Milo had ever seen. He had no idea if she was young or old because she could have been either, or both at the same time. Mature was as close as he could get. Her hair was silver, but he couldn't say whether it was from age. It looked as though it might have always been that color. Most impressive was her beauty. A beauty of kindness. It just melted him to see her.

"Ahh! Our young friend has arrived!" the man said with pleasure but without standing up. "Please forgive me. Accept our welcome from where we sit. Come here. Your seat is the seat of honor, to my right."

Milo was blushing again. He came to the place indicated.

"I see you don't recognize me from our encounter earlier today," the man said. "I am Alerik, the Crane King, whom you met this afternoon.

I was in my fisher's form then. I find it…more suitable than my human shape for my pastime on the marsh. It's been that way ever since…" He broke off and hesitated as if he were unsure about what to say before finishing his sentence. "Since my infirmity." Milo noticed then that he was wrapped with blankets from the waist down.

Alerik continued with introductions. "This is my wife and the Crane Queen, Ayuthaya."

The queen smiled warmly and regally. Milo thought to stand and make a bow, hoping that this was the proper thing to do. His ears burned again.

"And you are…?" Queen Ayuthaya prompted gently.

Milo realized suddenly that he had not introduced himself. Not to the bird, not to the seneschal, not to the young ladies who had attended him, and not yet to his hosts. His ears burned even hotter.

"I…pardon me…I'm…it's all unaccustomed. I've never met a king and a queen before. I'm Milo, and this is Boriboreau," he said.

"Milo. And Boriboreau," Alerik said. "Welcome to Crane Castle. May I ask what brings you to such an out-of-the-way place as ours?"

"I came to look for the Fisher King," Milo answered. "You see, I'm a contestant in the Magical Scavenger Hunt, and we were told to find the *Tor Vitrea*—the Glass Tower—and someone suggested that the Fisher King could tell me where it was."

Alerik looked thoughtfully at Milo, and Ayuthaya looked down at her hands, as if something were slightly embarrassing. Milo's ears colored further.

"We shall speak of these things later," Alerik said. "But first, we shall proceed with our dinner."

A glance around the room told Milo that, although the places were set, the plates were empty. There was no food on the tables. Everyone was silent and waiting.

A door opened at the end of the dining hall and a page, dressed in the white, black, and red livery of the castle, came in. He was carrying a crossbow, held out in front of him as if to offer it to someone. If this were not odd enough, the response from the people at the tables was even odder. They began to weep and moan as if in terrible grief.

"What's going on here, Bori?" whispered Milo to the cat, hoping that Bori could give him some reasonable explanation, like doors that were there only when you needed them.

"I have no idea," Bori answered. "Some sort of silliness you humans call customs, I suppose. I hope the fish arrives soon."

The page stopped right in front of Milo and lifted the crossbow as if to offer it to him. Milo sat still, hoping that he wasn't expected to actually take the thing, and Alerik nodded to the page silently, releasing him. The page turned and left with the crossbow through a door on the opposite side from the one where he had entered.

Now three young women came in the same way that the page had. Their heads were bowed and they wore veils, all in white, without any of the red or black. It made them look like apparitions. A shiver ran down Milo's spine.

A fourth girl followed them. She was dressed the same way, except she held her head high and carried a large platter. On the platter was a large baked fish.

Milo recognized the girl. She was the same one who had been the leader of the maidens who had waited on him earlier. He blushed, in memory of the—at least for him—unusual bathing experience. The three maidens ahead of her stepped to either side as she stopped before the king, held up the heavy platter with the same formality that the page had displayed the crossbow, and bowed her head in respect.

The platter with the fish must have been very heavy, because Milo could see the strain in her arms as she lifted it. He hoped that someone would help her, but no one did. The king nodded, and she slid the platter onto the table before him, took a step back, and waited.

"May I introduce my daughter, the Crane Princess Erisa," Alerik said to Milo. "You may serve, now," he told her, with the formal introduction done.

She used a serving knife and fork to separate the tender, thick flesh of the fish from the bones. The three other girls came with plates to receive a serving before placing them in front of the diners. Milo received his plate first, then the king and queen. Even this large fish would not be enough for the whole table of at least two dozen. Yet the four girls set out serving after serving.

Milo wondered how this could be managed. Before he really considered what he was saying, he turned to his host. "Excuse me, Sir. Who is to be served?"

Dead silence took the hall. Erisa and the attendants froze. If it had been subdued before, the silence was now deafening. Milo's ears flamed and the heat spread. He had really done it now. Why oh why hadn't he kept his mouth shut?

Alerik cleared his throat. "What...did you say?"

"I just said"—Milo took a deep breath—"that even if that's a large fish, it can't be enough to feed so many."

Alerik sat breathless, as if someone had just whacked him senseless. Ayuthaya's face, which had instantly brightened as if in expectation, collapsed again. A muted groan rose from the onlookers.

What had just happened? Milo wondered. He guessed that he had committed some terrible blunder, but he hadn't the faintest inkling of what it could have been. Something about that blasted fish, but what?

"I mean, I . . ." he stammered. "If the fish . . ."

Ayuthaya recovered her composure first. "It's all right, Milo. You see, it's a very special fish and a very special platter." She touched the rim of the plate that held the final parcels of the meal. "The platter provides enough for all no matter how many there are to be fed. You couldn't be expected to know that."

Milo, though he appreciated how thoughtfully she had released him from blame, could not disregard the feeling that he had failed them in some way. Something very important had transpired, something that the king and queen, and all the others, had expected of him. He felt awful.

Meanwhile, Bori had retreated from the noise and confusion with Milo's portion of fish, slipping under the table to eat it in peace. Milo, when he noticed, decided that it was only fair. Bori had been so keen on that fish ever since they'd caught it, and besides, Milo didn't really have much appetite left.

"Milo, this must be amazing to you," Alerik told him. "You can't know what all this is about. I'll tell you the story. This was once a prosperous land. Its citizens had all they needed, no more and no less. We were not rich, but we were not poor either. We did not require wealth because we had a purpose, of which I, as the king, was the keeper. We kept the Grail. From the Grail flowed justice and nurture. We cared for the welfare of our land, for whatever guests Fate brought to us, and for one another. As long as any of us had enough, none of us would want.

"But envy and greed can sneak in to anyplace, no matter how blessed it is. There was one among us who wanted to be the keeper of the Grail and control its bounty for himself, dreaming of the power that it would bring. One day, as I flew out over the lake—as Crane King my lineage gives me that ability—bitter envy and ambitious greed drove this would-be usurper to shoot a bolt from a crossbow at me. He failed to kill me, but his dart lodged in my body, crippling me and limiting my ability to serve as keeper of the Grail. He was banished, but the spell he had laid on the dart made it impossible to extract. Since that day our people have become virtual prisoners of our wounded land, leaving us filled with sorrow and dull suffering. We could only wait until chance brought release from the curse.

"This was made even more unlikely, since our land was hidden from all but those travelers who sought the Crane King and the blessing of the Grail. We are not permitted to explain the nature of the curse or the meaning of the Grail.

"Today, when you caught the Great Salmon of Wisdom, which I have sought for so long, it fulfilled an old hope of mine—that by eating its flesh, we could earn release from our misfortune. As you observed, the flesh of even this large fish is not enough to serve all who are present, but the bounty that the platter provides gives us all a portion of the fish so we may gain its blessing. Partaking of the salmon's flesh is a sacrament all can share."

Everyone present sat reverently at their places and ate their portion of the Great Fish. It was only then that Queen Ayuthaya noticed that Milo's plate was empty.

"Oh, Milo!" she exclaimed. "What happened to your portion of the fish?"

Milo looked at his empty plate, then at Bori, who sat washing his face and licking his fur, satisfied with a full stomach and the last lingering taste of his fish feast.

"Ahh...the cat ate it."

Everyone sat shocked. King Alerik broke the tension. "Then Boriboreau shall be a paragon among cats."

Everyone laughed. What was done was done. But Queen Ayuthaya noted, "Milo, for all he has done for us, will receive none of the benefit of his catch."

Just then, Princess Erisa stepped up to Milo's place. "Then he shall have this," she said, and kissed Milo full on the mouth.

Milo sat back in surprise, licking his lips in reflex. The princess, her own lips shiny with the oil of the fatty salmon, smiled broadly in triumph. "There. That should bestow the wisdom of what an honor it is to receive a kiss from an admiring lady."

Milo licked his lips again. They felt like they were buzzing, but not, he thought, from the effects of magical fish.

More food was brought by attendants. This time there were normal dishes served through conventional means.

After a time, Milo was able to speak to Alerik privately. "Can you tell me," Milo asked, "whether other participants of the Magical Scavenger Hunt have come before me? I'm worried about a friend of mine who might have come this way shortly before I did. Her name is Analisa, and she's about my age. She rides a broom, and I'm worried that she might have gotten in trouble with the same harpies that chased me and Bori."

Milo decided to say nothing about Tivik, thinking about how the man had gone off chasing a white hind that was perhaps as magical as the fish had been.

"She would have had no trouble with the harpies," Alerik said. "They save their enmity for males. But no one else has come to the Crane Castle except you. Why would they be coming here?"

"The first clue of the Hunt was to find the Glass Tower. I was told that the Fisher King could give me directions."

"So you wish to find the Glass Tower?" the Crane King said. "And find the Fisher King?"

"Yes, Sir," Milo replied. "Can you help me?"

"I can, and I will," Alerik promised. "You see, I am also known as the Fisher King. The Glass Tower is near here. It belongs to Queen Ayuthaya's sister. I'm sure she would be glad to take you there and introduce you. After what you have done for us, I'm certain that Blai will help you however she can.

5

A Rainbow and a Clew

Sleeping in a real bed with real sheets and blankets was a welcome luxury, Milo learned, when at last Ayuthaya and Erisa delivered him to his rooms themselves. It had been a long day and a long evening. By the time they left Milo and Bori to burrow under the covers, both were ready to sleep for a week. That wasn't going to happen, of course. Ayuthaya had promised to take Milo to her sister's early the next morning.

Really early the next morning. "We should be there before sunrise," she insisted. "We must make the trip to the Glass Tower in the dark."

Milo promised to be ready, but when the knock came on his chamber door, he couldn't believe that he had been asleep for more than a few minutes. Part of him heard the knock, but the other part was so comfortable and snug under the covers that the sound had to go on for some time before the part of him that had promised to get up early got the upper hand. Bori, burrowed deep under the covers, was still fast asleep and didn't stir at all.

The visitor was persistent however, knocking until the noise dragged Milo out of sleepyland. One of his eyes struggled open just enough to see that it was still dark. "Okay, Mom," he said with a groan, forgetting entirely that he was not at home in his own bed, but on a grand adventure as a contestant in the Magical Scavenger Hunt. "But it's Saturday. Can't I sleep just a little more?"

It wasn't until Ayuthaya entered the room—admittedly in her mom mode—that the present situation came crashing back. Milo sprang from the bed, now fully awake. He *was* very sorry to make a queen wait like that, but also sad that it wasn't Saturday and this wasn't his mom.

"I brought you some clothing better suited for a hard walk," Ayuthaya said, piling the bundle on the chair where Milo had placed the clothes he'd worn for the dinner the night before. Bori tunneled himself out from under the covers with a yawn and an arched-backed cat stretch while Milo rushed around.

"We must hurry now," Ayuthaya said. "I'll wait just outside your door."

Milo splashed his face with water and rubbed his teeth clean (he was lacking a toothbrush), then pulled on the clothes Ayuthaya brought for him: a wool sweater and a pair of sturdy leather trousers. The cat dropped to the floor as Milo dashed out the door. Cedric appeared with a lantern and Ayuthaya handed Milo a felt cloak. "Here, put this on. You'll need it this morning."

When they stepped out of a side entrance to the castle it was still dark, and very wet. They started down a path with Cedric leading with his lamp, followed by Milo and Bori, and Ayuthaya at the rear. Milo apologized for oversleeping, but Ayuthaya excused it, saying only that they must hurry.

They plunged into the deeper darkness of the forest, the trees dripping with the rain. Milo had to watch closely to avoid tripping over rocks and tree roots in the path yet staying near enough to Cedric's light to see them. Ayuthaya either knew the way so well that she didn't need the light, or maybe she could see perfectly well in the darkness.

Milo was puffing from the pace after a quarter of an hour, and Bori, trotting along at his side, began a "meow, meow" protest until Milo carried him.

The trail climbed more abruptly from its initial gentle slope to steep switchbacks. It was like trails in the forests and mountains back home, only wet and cold instead of mostly dry and hot. Milo was panting hard as the tree cover thinned, the ground became rockier, and the slope grew more precipitous. The sky lightened; it was now pewter instead of deep black, with pink streaks washing across it here and there. Despite the chill, Milo was sweating under the felt cloak. At last they topped the ridge, and Milo could see a tall tower rising a short distance ahead.

It was a ghostly thing that gleamed on the side toward the rising light and turned a darkened transparent opposite. In between, the colors of the morning landscape were reflected almost as if there was nothing there at all.

"The Glass Tower. My sister's home. Hurry now," Ayuthaya urged as if they hadn't been hurrying the whole time. "We must arrive before the sun can clear the horizon."

They reached the base of the tower in the next few minutes. Close up, the translucent surface of the tower reflected their images and all that lay around them, without giving any indication of what was inside.

The thing was monolithic. Milo could see no seams, no indication of how it was put together. It soared into the sky out of the rock like a titanic crystal. Ayuthaya opened a door into the tower that Milo hadn't seen until she opened it. "Come this way," she said, and stepped inside.

Cedric remained behind as they began to climb the winding steps. Light came freely in through the walls, but because of their thickness they distorted the outside views. Milo could see through them but the outside was wavy and distorted. Even the steps were transparent. Milo could see into them, through them, and down into the turning stairway below until the very thickness of the glass obscured the view. It made Milo feel a little queasy and disoriented.

They climbed and climbed, following the dizzying twist of the stair-case. Milo was puffing like a porpoise. But Bori, who was on his own again, bounded up the stairs just ahead of Ayuthaya as if he knew where they were going and was eager to get there.

At last Ayuthaya came to a halt. They had reached the last landing. Above, through the glass at the top of the tower, Milo could see the dark blue sky and pink-tinged clouds of morning. Ayuthaya opened a door into a room inside the tower and Milo could see what he had glimpsed through the walls as distorted movement and wavy colors.

"Step inside," Ayuthaya told him. "I'll wait for you."

Bori trotted through the door and Milo followed. Inside was a graceful woman dressed in a shimmering silken gown. He noticed several things immediately. First, that she could be Ayuthaya's twin, which she was. Second, that her long-fingered hands held brightly colored yarn, which she wound into a ball so swiftly that he could hardly discern her movements. The room held no furniture except for a spinning wheel, and next to it was a pile of multicolored balls of yarn like the one in her hands.

"You must be Milo," she said without taking her eyes away from her work. "I was expecting you to arrive somewhat earlier. Take a seat over there. We'll talk later. The sun rises in just a moment."

Milo didn't understand what the point was, but he did as he was told. Blai pulled the last loop away, wrapped it into her ball, and tossed it onto the pile. It rolled down onto the floor, where Bori began to swat it back and forth. Blai moved immediately to the spinning wheel. No sooner had she taken her place than the sun broke the horizon with the first edge of its disk.

The tower filled with light. The rays of the sun shot through the walls and shattered into the banded colors of the rainbow. Blai reached up with her long, dexterous fingers and seemed to snatch up the banded colors and twist them as she began to spin. As she spun, the bands were drawn into the same colored yarn that made the balls in the pile.

Milo, mesmerized, watched her work as the sun lifted free of the horizon and climbed higher, shooting its rays into the tower. Blai spun at a furious rate, her concentration fierce. The light in the room was so bright that Milo had to shade his eyes against it. On and on she spun, creating a cascade of many-hued and intensely bright yarns. The sun lifted higher and higher until, all at once, the rainbow rays vanished, leaving ordinary light in the room. Blai stopped spinning.

"Wow!" Milo said in astonishment. "That was cool!"

"Cool?" Blai said, swabbing her forehead. "I'm rather warm."

"I meant..." Milo started to explain. "It's a manner of speaking. What I really meant was that it was awesome. Incredible. How do you do that? Spinning yarn out of light?"

"Well, first you have to have a glass tower to break the sunlight into colors."

"Like when light passes through a prism?" Milo asked.

"Or when you see a rainbow," Blai added.

"Yeah!" Milo went on, recalling what he remembered from physical science class. "Rainbows are created when sunlight strikes drops of rain at a certain angle. I don't remember what angle that is, but when it does, the light is refracted by the raindrops just the way it is in a prism, and the sunlight breaks into its component colors according to wavelength. The angles of refraction define which color shows at that angle. So, depending on where you are standing in relation to the way light strikes the rain-drops, you see a rainbow with bands of primary colors. I think that the most incredible thing about a rainbow is, although you can see it, there's really nothing there. The thing you think you see as a rainbow is an illusion, because there's nothing there except rain and light, which isn't what you think you're seeing. The only way you can see a rainbow is to be standing at the right place at the right time." (Milo was impressed that he remembered all this. Maybe he really heard more than his teachers believed he did.)

"Hmmm," Blai said. "An interesting thought. Seeing a rainbow, then, is like anything that happens to you in your life, isn't it? Being in just such a place at such a time, and seeing it from that angle. Miss it by just a little bit, and something very different happens to you."

Milo thought about that for a moment. "Yeah, I guess that's right. I hadn't thought of it that way before."

"Like arriving here just as the sun was rising, to seek your next clue."

"You already know why I came here?"

"You saw the rainbow. Would you have seen it if you weren't meant to see it? Milo, I think you came to the right place at the right time, not because someone put you here, but because something inside brought you. An ability to see what's in front of you, perhaps. That's how magic works. The question is, what will you do with it?"

Milo wasn't very clear about what she was talking about, so he went back to his first question as a way to change the subject.

"How do you turn light into yarn?"

Blai shrugged. "That's my form of magic. It's still light, only I've twisted it to hold a permanent shape in the form of yarn. I use it for a special purpose, which I'll show you later, if conditions are right. But I think you came here for a purpose of your own: you want to ask me a question. Correct?"

"Yes, you see—" he began, but she broke in.

"You're a contestant in the Magical Scavenger Hunt. You came to seek the Glass Tower. I know all that, but what can I do to help you?"

"I need to know the next clue."

"Well, I don't know what it is, either. I expect that discovering it requires using your own magic. While you work that out, you can help me."

She put him to work as she took the spun yarn off the wheel. She had him hold the looped yarn while she wrapped it into a ball, warning him not to drop the clew, which is what the spun thread is called. If he did, the loops would turn into a tangled mess. She showed him how to hold them tight between his outstretched hands as she drew the thread away.

It seemed like a good time for Milo to learn a little more about this idea of what magic was. "So, I guess you're a...a magician of some sort?" he asked. He had almost said "witch," but stopped himself for a more neutral word.

"No. I'm of another order completely. You humans have magicians, sorcerers, shamans, and so forth, but we don't. What you practice as magic is as much a part of us as...as breathing."

"You aren't human?" Milo asked in astonishment.

"I'm of what you call fairy blood, as is Ayuthaya. We belong to the Elder Race."

"What does that mean?"

"Those who came when the world was still young. We aren't

immortal, exactly, though our life spans reach beyond many of yours, and we have kennings of which your race has yet to imagine. Not even by your greatest sages, craftsmen, and scientists. This tower, for example. Your people call it magic, and magic it is, but magic is very different for us than what your race ordinarily considers."

"How so?"

"Tell me what you mean by magic," Blai requested.

"Well, magic is... ahh...making things happen that can't happen in the ordinary world."

"But they *do* happen. And they happen in the 'ordinary world,' as you put it, don't they?"

Milo shrugged his shoulders. He was careful not to slip a loop of yarn off his hands as she drew it away. She was winding her ball and pulling it from his left hand, then the right, then the left, and so on, more and more rapidly, as they developed a rhythm.

"Magic isn't something that's separate, or outside the real world," she said. "Rather, it's a part of the real, physical world, but at such a deep level of refinement that most people overlook it. Because they don't notice how things function at such a subtle, interconnected level, they believe that magic is *supernatural*.

"You explained to me how light is broken up to reveal the rainbow," she continued. "That's an application of magic. You also said that the most amazing thing to you is that you see a rainbow, but there's not an actual thing there to see. That's even closer to what magic is, because magic is not the thing itself. It's how and when we perceive a subtle interaction of the physical world and our perception of it. Do you understand?"

"I think I'm starting to see what you mean," Milo said, aglow with that eureka feeling. But it was still confusing to his factual mind.

"You, dear Milo, are a magician. You haven't been trained as others of your race who call themselves magicians, but you are, nonetheless. You just don't know it yet."

"Is King Alerik a magician? Or is he one of your people?"

"No. Alerik is like you. He has fairy blood, of the Crane lineage. His ancestors married into the Crane Clan of my people long ago when first they came to this land, but he's still mortal. His clan pledged to protect the Old Magic, taking as their charge protection of the Grail and this Glass Tower. Ayuthaya and I are the only surviving members of the original Crane lineage. Alerik is the last of his line, save for his daughter, my niece, Erisa. Although she is mortal herself, the Old Magic has a strong flow in her, for she is related to the Elder Race through her mother, who is of the Blood and through her father's clan, which carries it."

"So, a mortal can marry someone of your race?" Milo asked. He thought of Erisa, and of marrying her. It made him blush a little.

"Yes," Blai answered, smiling knowingly. "If you were to marry Erisa, your children would be tied very strongly to the Old Magic, and you would found a new clan of your own."

"I don't have a clan."

"Yes, Milo. You do. You just haven't remembered it yet."

She continued. "It's through the female lineage that the Blood is passed down from generation to generation. Although the subsequent generations aren't immortal, the special characteristics and gifts of the Blood cast a much longer shadow across their circles of influence than that of a non-Blood mortal."

Blai paused. "King Alerik will pass from this world, as will my niece. Ayuthaya and I will outlive them as we have many others. So you see, our long lives are also a curse, because we are doomed to lose the people we love, who come and go, leaving us to linger on. Ayuthaya will grieve Alerik and she will grieve for Erisa in turn. It's ultimately our demise. The grief wears us away. That's why I've chosen to live in this Glass Tower instead of out in the world with your people. I have already lost too many."

The depth of the sadness behind these words made Milo's heart ache. He thought that she faded a little bit as she said this, almost in the way he could see through the walls of the tower itself. Her face still looked nobly beautiful, though ancient.

Her sadness passed, and she smiled again.

"You are young and have much to learn, but you also have the heart to see into things. I'm sure that your cat, Boriboreau, who has tasted the flesh of the Great Salmon, understands that. It's good that he's your guide. He'll make a fine mentor. You, Milo, are fortunate. I'm honored to have made your acquaintance."

She finished winding her ball, freeing his arms from the last loop. This felt like the end of the conversation, but Milo wasn't ready yet.

"Wait!" he cried. "I still don't know the next clue!"

She tossed the ball she had just wound, and he caught it in his hands.

"You already hold the clue, Milo," she told him.

Milo looked at his hands holding the ball of sun-yarn. "This? This is the clue? I don't get it."

"That's my gift to you, to remember me by."

Just then the sun broke through a layer of cloud that had hidden it since Blai's spinning. Brilliance flooded the tower.

"Wow!" Milo said, forgetting his quandary.

"Ahh!" Blai said in satisfaction, and picked up another ball of her yarn. "It seems that the conditions are right. I can show you another part of my magic. The sun breaking through is the sign I was watching for. Let's go down now," she suggested.

Down they went. Ayuthaya was waiting inside the base of the tower, and the sisters embraced. Milo saw that they were crying, but he didn't know why. He felt embarrassed and out of place to be witnessing this mysterious scene between sisters of fairy blood.

"I think they have their own shared hopes. And disappointments," Bori whispered in Milo's ear. Milo was holding Bori on his shoulder. "Perhaps we should slip out the door and wait for them outside."

They did that. Outside, the earth was still soaked from the rain, but the sun sparkled in the jewel-like drops. The vibrancy and freshness of green on every leaf and blade of grass was in marked contrast to the somber colors they'd seen earlier in the morning. Cedric was still there, shaking the water out of his cloak. Blai and Ayuthaya came out of the tower, arms around each other's waists. It was like seeing a single woman hugging her own reflection. They both looked much younger, no older than Erisa.

"Time to go down to the castle," Ayuthaya told him. "Come along, Milo. I have something for you before you set off on your way."

"And I want to show you what I promised," Blai said to Milo, holding up the ball of color that she had brought along with her. "Here," she said, peeling away the end of the yarn from the ball and handing it to him. "Hold on to that. Hold tight."

She unrolled more yarn, then tossed the ball into the sky. Hard. High up into the air. It unrolled as it flew, higher and higher, like a kite going up. As it flew farther and farther away, it made a long arc, leaving a ribbon of color that spread as it went, instead of remaining in a single string. It reminded Milo of the vapor trails made by jets back at home, except this one shimmered in the colors of the rainbow. It arced away, across the tops of the mountains and off toward the far horizon.

A rainbow! Blai had just thrown a rainbow across the sky!

6

A Long Walk and New Friends

The five of them—that included Bori, of course—came off the ridge and through the woods by the same path they had taken before sunrise. Only this time they could see where they were going.

The castle looked much brighter in the fresh sunshine. Alerik, resting on a litter with Erisa at his side, waited for them high on the battlements where he could see across the lake and the forest, all the way to the gleaming Glass Tower.

Alerik greeted Milo as warmly as if he had been Milo's own father. "You are welcome to stay as an honored guest—nay, as a member of my family—as long as you wish," Alerik offered.

"Thank you very much, but I should see if I can find the next clue now that I've found the Glass Tower. I can't quit the Hunt just like that. I need to finish what I started."

"I understand, and I agree," Alerik replied. "I thought no less. But where will you go now?"

"I...I don't know."

"You are a seeker," Ayuthaya interjected. "Perhaps you must set out on the Seeker's Path. I think, Milo, it's time you became a pilgrim."

"A pilgrim?" he asked in dismay, thinking of people who wore tall, odd-shaped hats with a buckle on them, like the ones worn by the Pilgrims of the *Mayflower.*

"Continue your journey as a traveler, a pilgrim, to the End of the Earth," said Ayuthaya.

"What's the End of the Earth?" Milo asked uncomfortably, for it sounded like a very distant and dire place.

"It's a place where people with a purpose go to fulfill their goal or where people without a goal go to find one," Blai said with a knowing smile.

"You mean, like a clue?" Milo asked, suddenly getting Blai's suggestion. "Is it far?"

"Very far," Alerik said.

"But it's said that the journey itself is wonderful and important and provides whatever the pilgrim is seeking," Blai added.

"And they say that the End of the Earth is a remarkable place," Erisa added enthusiastically, and perhaps wistfully as well. "Think of the adventures you'll have just getting there!"

"Yeah. I am," Milo replied. He was having no shortage of adventures.

Milo was beginning to distinguish between the romantic notion of adventure—which was what Erisa seemed to be thinking, perhaps because she'd never had the chance to leave home—and the grim reality of hardship and danger. Adventures, he decided, are a lot more fun to hear about than they are to have. He was thinking about adventure more along the lines of exhaustion after long, hard days of walking, uncertainty about where his next meal would come from, and nasty things like lopers.

"How do I *get* to the End of the Earth?" Milo asked, resigned to a destination that looked like his only choice.

"You must go by foot, the requirement for every pilgrim who seeks that place," Ayuthaya said.

"You follow the Pilgrim's Path, also called the Rainbow Way," Blai added.

The rainbow? But the one she had thrown had already faded and was gone Milo had begun to think that Blai had made him a sign to follow, but if it was no longer visible, how could he follow it? When he turned to look at Blai for an explanation, she pointed. His eyes followed, and caught a brightly colored butterfly flitting on the breeze. It followed the general direction where Blai's rainbow had appeared. Then he saw another butterfly, and another.

"They're the pilgrim's guides," she said. "When the butterflies come, it's the sign for the pilgrimage seekers to follow them from every shire and hamlet. The path is clear enough, for over the ages, many, many feet have followed the Pilgrim's Way. But it intersects with other paths and may be hard to find in some places, for it's been a long time since the last pilgrimage opened the way to the End of the Earth. So you'll have to follow the butterflies. Whenever you're in doubt about which way to go, watch to see where the butterflies are going, because they all go to the same place."

"You'll need the right equipment," Alerik said, sitting up from his litter with some difficulty. He handed Milo his walking stick. "I've used this these many years," he said. "You should take it, to aid you with your walk. Take it with my blessing. It will support you when your limbs are weary, and hold any threatening dogs at at bay."

"And please take this," Erisa said next, stepping forward to give him a rucksack. It was made of tough canvas, with leather for the bottom, the reinforcements, and the shoulder straps. "Inside there's a blanket and special biscuits for when you find nothing else."

"Eat sparingly," Ayuthaya advised, "for the food is made with the Blessing of the Grail. You'll find that a little bit is filling and packed with nourishment. It will not run out until you reach your destination. The blanket is exceptionally warm and light, and will keep you warm and dry even through the wettest of nights."

"Here's a hat to keep your head from the ravages of weather," Blai said, handing him a broad-brimmed hat of oiled felt. "That and the walking stick mark you as a pilgrim and earn the respect of all who meet you. Because you're a pilgrim, people along your way will offer you their hospitality, so you can expect to receive a meal and a dry place to sleep, at least in the parts of the path where people live. It's an old custom that even bandits honor, although that could be because pilgrims rarely have much money or anything worth stealing."

"You must never spend two nights in the same place, no matter what," Ayuthaya instructed. "Follow that rule and you'll reach the End of the Earth for the Mid-Summer Games."

"Mid-Summer Games? What's that?" Milo asked.

"It's the celebration that marks the reason for the Pilgrimage," Alerik explained. "It's a tournament that goes back to the Elder Race and the founding of the first clans."

"How long is it until mid-summer?" Milo asked just as a group of butterflies swirled in spirals around his head.

"In twenty-nine days," replied Alerik. "Watch the moon. Tomorrow it will be full. You must be there when it's full again."

"But how far is it? How will I know that I can get there in time?"

"It's twenty-nine days from here," said Alerik. "Unless you stop and spend more than one night in the same place, or act rudely to a host, or stray from the path, you'll arrive in time."

"And when do I start?"

"Now. You have already spent one night here. You can't spend another."

Alerik shook Milo's hand. "Godspeed," he said.

Erisa stepped up and kissed Milo on the cheek. "Come back one day when the Hunt is done and tell me all your adventures."

Ayuthaya kissed him on the other cheek. "Milo, you are indeed a hero. Remember who you are, even when you doubt yourself or when other people underestimate you."

Blai took the ball of rainbow yarn that she had handed him back at the tower and dropped it into his backpack. "Who knows? Perhaps this is a clue," she said as she winked.

"Go now, with the blessing of the Grail," Alerik said.

Tears glittered in all their eyes as Milo, dressed in the clothes and boots that Ayuthaya had given him for their walk to the Glass Tower, put his hat on his head, slung the pack on his shoulders, and took the staff in his hand. Bori led the way, tail high with pride.

As he passed Cedric, the old man stopped him to shake his hand. He also handed him another gift. "A water bottle," Cedric offered. "It's just an ordinary bottle, but you'll need to have it if you're walking. And take this, too." It was a belt knife with a sturdy blade. "Utrea," Cedric then said.

Milo didn't understand the word, but he would learn it soon enough. Everyone at the castle was extending their hand to shake, wishing him a safe journey. And then he and Bori passed through the gates and out into the forest.

"Gee, that was weird!" Milo told Bori.

But Bori ignored his comment. He just trotted along by Milo's side, tail high with the end tipped over, like a hook. He was looking left and right. "I wonder if we might find a saucer of milk somewhere?" he said.

It was still morning, but Bori's comment reminded Milo that they hadn't had breakfast. The path they were following through the forest didn't look very promising in terms of available meals. After several hours of walking, the prospects hadn't improved. Milo had picked up Bori when the cat tired from the steady pace. He let Bori settle into the backpack so Milo could do the walking for them both. Unlike dogs, cats just aren't built for long, steady endurance. Their strength is of the supple sort, and their natures aren't suited for dogged duty. Besides, Milo discovered something special about this pack: Even after Bori—and he was by no means a small cat—had made himself comfortable on the blanket inside the pack, the burden felt no heavier.

Milo thought briefly about going back to search for his flying crate, but he quickly abandoned the idea. First, the crash into the tree had splintered the wood, and he wasn't sure he would be able to repair it. Second, Ayuthaya had told him that as a pilgrim he must walk, and he had to be a pilgrim if he wanted to get to the End of the Earth. And third, he would have to leave the path in order to go where the crate had crashed—another pilgrim prohibition—and he doubted he could find it anyway.

A bit farther ahead, they came to a fork in the trail. One way looked as well traveled as the path they had been following, and the other way seemed to be rarely used. Milo saw a sign lying on its side, perhaps blown down in a storm. When he turned it over in order to read it, he saw that the faded, weathered lettering read "End of the Earth." But because the sign had toppled, Milo couldn't tell which side of the fork the sign had indicated.

"So which way do we take?" Milo asked.

Bori had hopped down to make his own appraisal of the situation. "We wait," he advised.

"What for?" Milo asked.

Bori looked around. "For that," he said, fixing his green eyes on a spot back the way they had come.

Milo followed the direction where Bori was looking. A large, iridescent blue butterfly came floating along, sailing on easy wings. It passed just above their heads and, with a couple of deft flicks of its wings, turned along the path less traveled. Soon it disappeared up that trail.

"Okay," Milo said. "Let's go."

Bori sprang up to the pack and got his lower body inside so he could sit with his paws on Milo's shoulders and see the path ahead.

"How did you know to do that?" Milo asked him.

"I'm smarter than you are because I ate the Salmon of Wisdom. Besides, I was listening to Blai's instructions. Didn't she tell you to listen to me?"

Milo had to admit that she had, though he sort of resented Bori's superior attitude about it.

On they walked. Or, at least, Milo walked. When Bori wasn't giving directions, he napped. As the day wore on through the afternoon and toward evening, Milo was getting really, really tired, as well as seriously hungry. He said as much to Bori.

"Think of it as an adventure," Bori told him. "You'll get used to missing meals. I've missed plenty in my time, though I'd rather not have."

Milo thought that that was easier to say from Bori's position riding in the pack.

Despite such bravado on the cat's part, he seemed glad enough to accept a saucer of fresh milk when they came out of the woods at last and stopped at a farm. The farmer called them in to accept some pilgrim's hospitality, and Milo got a cup of milk, too, along with fresh bread with butter, some cheese, a bowl of stew, and a couple of apples to take along. Milo gave Bori some pieces of meat from his stew—after all, it was the wage they'd agreed upon for Bori coming along as Milo's guide. And Bori preferred the meat to the carrots and potatoes. By the time Milo pushed back from the table happy and full, the farmer and his wife had offered to let them spend the night in the hayloft of the barn.

Looking out from the hayloft and onto the path that had brought them—and in the morning would take them to the End of the Earth—Milo noticed a figure loping along. The man was headed the same way that he and Bori would take at sunrise. It was Tivik.

"Look!" Milo alerted Bori. "I wonder if he caught that deer."

"And also found the next clue," Bori suggested.

"But how? He wasn't at the Crane Castle."

"Maybe the rainbow and the butterflies were enough. That Tivik is a sneaky one."

"Do you think he has to be a pilgrim, too, to get to the End of the Earth?"

"Ayuthaya said it's the only way. But remember what Tinburkin told you: Contestants may find their own clues in their own way, and they might not even be the same clues, as long as the chain of clues gets them back to the Kingdom of Odalese."

"Maybe you're right," Milo agreed. "Can you imagine Count Yeroen or Aulaires walking the whole way as pilgrims?" He thought some more. "If Tivik could figure out the next clue without getting to the Crane Castle, I guess the others, with all their knowledge, might be able to figure out the same thing. And that whole business about an ancient tournament from the Elder Race sounds intriguing."

"They may know more because they're wizards and all, but we've gotten a lot of help," said Bori. "And I think we're doing just fine, wouldn't you say?"

Milo had to agree.

The next morning was a beautiful day to be walking. Milo was swinging Alerik's walking stick in tempo with his own strides as the sun rose into the sky. When Milo noticed a huge oak tree standing alone in the field ahead, he thought at first that it was in autumnal foliage, which was odd because it wasn't yet mid-summer. Then he saw that the tree was filled with butterflies. Yellow ones, purple ones, orange, green, violet, and blue ones. They were taking flight and streaming away in the same direction that Milo and Bori were headed. Very soon, the tree was green again with only its leaves for color.

"That must mean we're on the right path," Milo commented, feeling a marvelous sense of awe at the sight. "I wonder why all the butterflies are going to the same place as we are?"

"Maybe it's Ayuthaya's and Blai's magic," Bori suggested.

"Or maybe it's something else, something that their magic is based on," Milo proposed, remembering Blai's explanations.

They—or at least Milo—walked all that day. And the next, and the next. In the evenings when Milo stopped for the night, Bori went exploring and managed his own feline business. He did the same whenever Milo took a rest. Milo didn't ask him for details. As Blai had promised, people welcomed him everywhere along the road without asking him who he was, what he did, or why he was doing what he was doing. Just being a pilgrim was enough. They fed him whatever they had, whether simple or fine. Milo was thankful for whatever they offered, knowing how hungry he would be without it. They offered places to sleep, sometimes a hayloft and sometimes a feather bed with thick, warm blankets. Sometimes he washed his clothes in a river and bathed himself in the cold, flowing water while his things hung over bushes to dry. Sometimes he had the luxury of a real bath in a real tub, with hot water and soap—but that was rare.

For the first several days he was exhausted after walking for hours on end. He was sore-muscled and blister-footed. Then a deeper weariness set in. He feared he would not be able to go on. Dragging himself up each morning felt hopeless. Only determination—which each day he doubted would sustain him—and the fear of failure pushed him on. But gradually, this faded. The wonders that he met each day helped him forget how hard it was to keep going, and the kindnesses that people offered gave him the courage to continue being a pilgrim. That's what was expected of him, and what he wanted to be. By and by, the walk became an adventure in its better sense.

He met other pilgrims, recognizable by their hats and their staffs, their cloaks and their rucksacks, and by the direction they were headed, led by the butterflies. They met one another like old friends, telling their stories, what they had been given to eat, and what they had seen as they walked through the countryside, whether marvelous buildings, grand vistas, or the sweet water from a particular spring. Milo learned about the traditions of the Pilgrim's Way and the reasons that pilgrims had for finding the End of the Earth, a place that was sacred in the old histories. And he found that there were many mysteries and legends about the site—a likely place, Milo surmised, to find arcane clues that could show him where to look next in the Magical Scavenger Hunt.

Meanwhile, walking was all that mattered. Milo woke up early to walk. He ate and he rested so he could continue to walk. He washed his clothes, took care of the little gear he had, and took care of himself in order to keep on walking. Some days he walked with other pilgrims for company until the road sent them on ahead separately. Sometimes while they rested, they shared whatever food and drink they had. It was that simple. Despite the continual work of walking, it wasn't a bad life, Milo decided.

Over and over he was told by the other pilgrims, "When the butterflies migrate, the End of the Earth draws them and us like a magnet."

"But why?" Milo would ask. "Why do the butterflies want to go there?"

His question was often met with a shrug. "Maybe they're pilgrims, too. We go there for the same reasons as the butterflies. And for the slinger tournament." Although Milo didn't know what a slinger tournament was, he decided it was something he would learn when the time came.

One day Milo was waiting at a crossroads for a butterfly to show him the way when three pilgrims came up the road. Unlike most pilgrims, they where whooping, and dashing this way and that, using some sort of scoop-like things attached to their right arms to toss a ball back and forth. The pilgrims were noisy, high-spirited, and generally so congenial that Milo liked them immediately.

"Utrea!" he called to them as they came to the crossroads. He had learned that this word was the customary pilgrim greeting. As far as Milo could tell, it meant something like "Onward!"

"Utrea!" they called back and then walked toward him. Milo looked at the scoop-like objects they carried—elongated, curved woven baskets as long as a forearm, closed at the neck where the boys' hands reached through to grip a handle. The ball they tossed about was the size of a fist—just right to roll along the trough of the basket. The ball looked to be made of hard rubber. The three boys—a few years older than Milo, he guessed—tossed and caught the ball with the basket with amazing speed and dexterity.

"Look!" said one. "He's got a cat!"

"That's Bori," Milo said. "Boriboreau. He's my companion." Milo was used to the attention that Bori drew. No other pilgrim was traveling with a cat. "I'm Milo."

The new pilgrims stopped tossing the ball and, one after the other, pulled their hands free of the bats to shake Milo's hand.

"I'm Teryl," said the first.

"I'm Deryl," said the second.

"And I'm Beryl," added the third.

They all looked exactly alike to Milo. They could have been identical twins if there had been just two of them. They had red hair and freckles, and all three were very lean and agile. Real jock types, Milo decided.

"Are you pilgrims?" Milo asked.

"That we are," said one.

"We're headed for the End of the Earth," said the next.

"We're going to play in the End of the Earth slinger tournament," said the third. "We're a team. We're the best."

Whatever slinger was, Milo decided, the tournament must be a good reason to be a pilgrim.

"Yeah!" said the one who Milo thought was Beryl. "We're going to prove it at the End."

"Players come from all over to play at the End," explained Deryl.

"But since you have to be a pilgrim to get to the End of the Earth, we're pilgrims," added Teryl.

"What *is* slinger?" Milo asked. "I'm guessing that it's some kind of ritual game that's played at the End of the Earth, but what is it exactly?"

"What's slinger? What's slinger!" Teryl replied, as if Milo had committed heresy. "Slinger's the best, the fastest, the most amazing game there is!"

"Only the best teams come to the tournament at the End," chimed in Beryl, "because only the best ones need bother."

"Winning there is the absolute top honor there is!" enthused Deryl. "The winners are the heroes of the whole world."

Sort of like the Super Bowl, Milo thought, recalling his own world for a comparison.

"After we win there, nobody anywhere can tell us what we can or can't do, or where we can or can't go, or that we're nobodies," Deryl continued. "We'll prove that we're the best. Slinger is what we should be doing instead of something else."

Milo detected a story behind that outburst. He decided not to go into it just yet. Maybe he'd ask again when he knew them better. "So, how is slinger played? You see, I come from another place altogether. We play soccer, football, basketball, baseball, hockey, tennis, and stuff like that. I never heard of slinger."

"I don't know about those other games you mentioned," Teryl said, "but with slinger, we don't need 'em. Slinger is the *absolute* game! Here, we'll show you."

"I'm the goalie," said Beryl. "Nothing gets past me. I can catch anything."

"I'm the forward," Teryl said. "When Beryl catches the ball, he fires it out to me. I put it through the midline ring and into play for our side. I can outrun anybody, so the other team can't pluck the ball before I can pass it to Deryl—"

"Most of the time, you mean," Beryl corrected him.

"Yeah! Most of the time I get it!" Teryl said with fervor.

"—so I can attack the opponent's goal," Deryl went on, breaking into the other two's bickering. "Teryl and I work the ball back and forth until I get an opening on the opposing team's goalie, then—bam!—I shoot the goal."

"Deryl's our striker," Teryl explained. "Nobody can shoot with the same speed that he can. And if he misses—"

"Which doesn't happen very often," Deryl asserted.

"—then I'm there to pluck it off before the other team's forward, also called a runner, can recover it," Teryl continued.

"Let's show him!" Beryl said. "Go long, Teryl!"

Off went Teryl like a shot. In no time at all, he was way up the road. Beryl, with the ball resting in the basket of his scoop, whipped it out, sending the ball in a fast, hard arc. Teryl caught it in a lunge with his scoop and whipped it high into the air.

"That's what he would do to shoot it through the ring at the center of the court," Beryl explained. "Until he can get the ball through the ring, it still belongs to the other team. You can't score until you've ringed it for your side."

Then Teryl fired the ball to Deryl, who had run forward to meet him partway. Then they came running back, tossing the ball back and forth between them in all sorts of complex passes until they drew up short just in front of Beryl. Deryl suddenly fired the ball with terrific force at Beryl, who reached out easily to snag it out of the air.

"That's how he would score—by putting the ball past the defending goalie and the two pillars of the goal," Beryl said. "You see, the striker can't run with the ball, but the runner can. You have to imagine that the defensive players are doing everything they can to deflect Teryl's and Deryl's attack and intercept the ball. If they can do that, then they have to get it to the mid-court ring so it can go into play for their side." Beryl was rocking the ball gently in his scoop while he finished his explanation.

"So that's slinger," Teryl said. "Sort of."

"It's the best we can do without a real court to play in," Deryl added.

"And without another team to play against," concluded Beryl.

"We'll show you the real thing when we get to the End," promised Teryl.

"How long have you been playing?" Milo asked.

"It's a long story," Teryl said. "Walk with us if you like, and we'll tell it to you."

So Milo did. By and by, Teryl, Deryl, and Beryl told him how they had become slinger pilgrims on the Pilgrim's Way.

7

Of Pilgrims and Ballplayers

"We grew up on an island that didn't have a flat place on it," Teryl said. "The closest thing to a flat place was a tiny beach where fishermen pulled their boats up out of the water and dried their nets."

"We grew up as the sons of one of those fishermen," Deryl said, "only it was pretty fishy that we looked so different, with our red hair and green eyes. Our parents, and everyone else on the island, have black hair and dark eyes, and are short."

"That, and we hated fishing," Beryl asserted. "That made our fisherman father very unhappy. 'How're you gonna make a living?' he'd yell at us every time we tried to slip away from mending nets and cleaning the catch."

As their story unfolded, Milo learned that what they really liked to do was to run around on the island away from the other fisherfolk. It wasn't an easy thing to do, first because someone was always watching them, and second because the island consisted mostly of steep-sided mountains of bare rock and thorny scrub brush. Wild goats were the island's only other large inhabitants. But by following the trails that the goats made crisscrossing the island's flanks, the boys found a place that was nearly flat. It was on top of the highest mountain and dropped off steeply to every side. When they were up there, they could see the whole island below them surrounded by the sparkling blue sea. It was a magnificent sight and inspired the boys to imagine what might lie out of sight beyond the horizon.

T, D, and B went up there whenever they could slip away from their chores. It was their secret spot. They were the only ones who went there and the only ones who knew about the place because the other people on the island were interested only in the sea, their boats, and fishing.

It was on the flat place where they—especially Teryl—learned to run, *really* run, because it's not possible to run on steep ground interrupted by canyons, cliffs, and thick thorny brush. They learned that their long, hill-trained legs were good for something besides getting tangled up in the nets on the fishing boats.

They also learned that they were good at throwing and catching things. All three of them had been throwing and catching things for as far back as they could remember. Things like net-weaving awls, cork floats, water jars—even fish, as slippery as those creatures tend to be. Up on the mountain they would throw a cork float back and forth, and then forth and back while they ran around on the flat space.

Another odd thing about Beryl, Teryl, and Deryl was that they were the only ones on the island who didn't have birthdays. When they asked their parents about it, their father blustered and their mother tried to change the subject—another sign to the boys that something fishy was going on.

"When we were about fifteen years old," Teryl explained, "we met someone on top of the mountain."

"Yeah, a very extraordinary someone," Beryl added.

"A lady," Teryl continued. "A lady very unlike the women in the fishing village. She was tall and slender and had bright red-gold hair. She wore a shimmering white gown with green trim. It was clean, and there wasn't a patch on it."

Teryl, the spokesman for the three, had demanded that she tell them who she was. She said, "I'm your fairy godmother."

"Our what?" Deryl had blurted out in disbelief. "You've got to be kidding."

"Then she said that she'd come to show us our birthright," Teryl continued. "She told us that we were all born exactly fifteen years ago, on that exact day."

The upshot of it all was to show them a cave hidden behind an extra thorny bush just below the peak. Inside were three slinger scoops and a basket of rubber balls. "She told us that those were our birth gifts," Teryl explained, "and that she had hidden them there long ago when the three of us, as babies, first came to the island."

"How did you get there?" Milo asked.

"We washed up on the beach in a boat without oars or a sail," Teryl explained. "Our father—that is, the man we thought of as our father—found us. And he and our mother—or who we thought of as our mother—raised us as their own children. They gave us all they had to give even though they knew we didn't belong to their trade and place in life."

"Anyway," Beryl took up, "the lady would tell us only that we would have to find out for ourselves where we belonged, but that the bats and balls were ours and were given to us the day we were born. Then she disappeared."

Since the boys had never seen slinger played, or even heard of it, they hardly knew what to do with these new implements. So they experimented. Before long they were using the bats to catch and throw as they ran to and fro on top of the mountain.

It was around then that their foster father took them on their first trip to the mainland. They were old enough and strong enough to ply the oars for the long voyage across the open sea to deliver salted fish to the market.

The boys were so eager to get away and see something besides the island and the sea that they didn't mind the long, hard work of rowing. When they reached the port, they first helped to unload the boat and pull it up above the tide line. Then they were free to wander around the town.

Even though it was in reality a small and ordinary sort of harbor town, the boys, gawking at the sights, were amazed by it all. They had never seen anything but a dozen or so fishing shacks before.

On the edge of town they came upon a slinger match. They didn't know what it was, but they watched the game the way a cat watches a bird through a glass window. They recognized the bats and balls instantly, although the rules of the game remained a mystery to them. But after a while, they had the basics puzzled out.

"We asked them if we could play," Teryl explained. "They asked if we had our own bats."

"When we told them we didn't have them with us, they told us, 'Then you can't play,'" said Deryl. "It was a huge disappointment."

They continued to watch with avid interest, until their father located them just as the sun was setting. They left the match, walked to their boat, and set out for their home island with the tide.

Back on the island, they took advantage of the next time they could slip away to go up the mountain. It was with the specific objective of trying out what they had seen and to practice what they had learned. They practiced and practiced. When it came time to make the next delivery to market, they hid their bats, wrapped in oilcloth, under the fish. As soon as they had the fish unloaded and the boat drawn up safely on the beach, they fetched the bats and were off.

It was a festival day, and the slinger games were not just the usual pickup games they'd seen before. This was a real tournament. At first they were refused a chance to play. But by listening to the other teams announce themselves as representing this place or that place, the boys tried again, announcing themselves as representing their home island.

They didn't mention that they were the only slinger players on the island.

"We hadn't ever played against another team before, so that gave us trouble at first," Teryl said. "But the trio of slinger players that we drew wasn't very good. They couldn't get a ball past Beryl, and then Deryl drove one in during the last few minutes. That allowed us to advance to the second round."

"That posed the next problem," Beryl went on. "The next scheduled game was the next day, and our father had planned to leave before then. We hunkered down on the beach and watched the waves surf in. And while we watched, we noticed the seabirds coming in to shore."

"We pointed it out to our father," Teryl said, "because that's a sign that a storm was on the way. Of course he had noticed because he's a fisherman, and fishermen always watch the weather and the sea. Somewhere out to sea a storm was brewing and sending in waves that rose gradually higher and higher. Waves like that can topple a boat and smash it to bits. Our father decided that we would have to wait out the storm."

Deryl took up the thread. "We'd never been so happy to see a storm. As we watched the breakers pound the beach, a white bird landed nearby and trotted up, eyeing us with its sharp black eyes. Then something happened unlike anything that had ever happened to us before. The bird said, 'I've sent the storm. You have three days. You must win this tournament if you are to ever leave your home island and win a chance to reclaim your birthright.'"

"We figured out pretty fast that the bird was really our fairy godmother helping us out again," Teryl said. "We thanked her and promised to win the slinger tournament no matter what."

The boys played every game with utter abandon. What they lacked in finesse they made up for in energy. What they lacked in skill they made up for in valor. By the second day, word had gotten around that there was a phenomenal new team playing in the festival tournament. Someone asked the boys' father if he knew them seeing as he was from the island that they represented. He went to see what was going on.

Even he, who knew nothing of slinger—man of the sea that he was—was impressed to see that his three boys, whom he had considered lazy and frivolous, could run and throw rings around the players of the other teams. "When he saw us," Beryl exclaimed, "he said, 'Those are *my* boys!' to anyone who would listen."

The boys advanced to the finals on the third day. Exhausted and battered, they knew that this last match would be their hardest. They were facing a team that had played for years, traveling as professional players from tournament to tournament. When they weren't playing or traveling, they were practicing. They even had a full-time trainer. These were no local boys who fancied they could be champions; they were the real thing. They had trounced every team they had played at the tournament, sending players home not only with lost games but with bruises and a few broken bones. They had coldcocked at least one other player with a hard rubber ball to the back of his head.

Since this was a local boy, and since it was rumored that he was in a coma, the team responsible for the injury was less than popular with the local crowd. Because T, D, and B were the last team left to play the despised one, and they were more or less local boys to boot, the whole crowd was rooting for them against their opponents. Other teams even lent them pieces of equipment that the boys didn't have.

"Still, things didn't look good for us," Deryl remarked.

"These guys really played mean," Beryl told Milo. "They were planning to slaughter us."

"I felt almost like giving up," Teryl said. "Deryl had a sore ankle that he'd had to wrap up. I was limping even worse than Deryl, and Beryl's arm was so sore that he could barely lift it above his shoulder. Then a man walked up and, without us saying anything, he told us we needed a trainer."

"I asked him who he was," said Teryl, "and what did he think he could do for us."

"'First,' he told us, 'a certain lady thinks you might need some professional help just about now. She sent me,' the man said. He said his name was Savoy and that he knew just about all there is to know about slinger, and how to keep young whippersnappers like us playing instead of falling apart. He pointed out that there wasn't much time left since we were supposed to go on the court in just a little while. Then he told us that he'd seen one of the players on the other team wrapping flat rocks into his hip belt. He said that was an old trick to cause nasty bruises when the player used a hip-check against his opponent. The man also said that the opposing team's goalie was slipping a special ball into his belt that weighs more than the standard one. 'You sling that sucker out with enough force,' Savoy said, 'and it'll wreck a bat or break an arm.' He told us that we'd have to be extra careful not to be hit directly by their balls. He pointed out that those are old tricks that could work because we were so green. He said he could help us counter them, but first we'd have to be in better condition before we could go on the court. He broke out liniments for our bruises and sprains, and gave us something to drink—some sort of fortifying tea to help with our exhaustion."

"I wanted to know how he got there," Beryl said. "I asked him about the lady who sent him, and he said, 'She's the one who looks after you. You know who she is even if nobody else does.'"

"How do you—"

"Know her? Let's just say we're old friends. You aren't the only slinger players I've stepped in to help at her request. But there's no more time for chitchat. Get out there and play. Play clean, even if the other team doesn't. Play hard, and don't let those guys bully you or trap you into changing your own play. And don't try to take revenge for their tricks."

"As he talked, he helped us put on our gear," Deryl told Milo. "The easy way he adjusted it proved more than his claims that he knew what he was doing."

Off they went. Deryl described how the local mayor's wife threw out the ball to start the game and how they finessed the ball around every attempt the opposing team made to take it back. When the moment came as Deryl caught the ball off a high bounce, he was open to toss it leisurely between the posts to score.

The crowd erupted. No other team had scored so neatly and quickly on this feared juggernaut. The roar echoed off the stone paving of the court and walls. The opposing players shouted instructions to one another, but these were lost in the tumult.

In desperation, the opposing runner brought his dirty tactics into use. He tried to slam into Teryl with his hip belt load of stones, but Teryl, well warned of the threat, slipped him. The goalie and runner managed several passes, trying to throw Teryl off, but still the runner could get no clear shot. Meanwhile, the frustrated striker had to wait on the other side of the court until his runner could get the ball into play for their side. They were yelling at each other, trying to coordinate plays, but the crowd, sensing that their cheers had become an effective deterrent to the despised team's plans, kept up a steady roar.

T, D, and B needed no spoken instruction among them. They maneuvered as if they were a single player. "That's when I saw how the other team's runner slipped a second ball out of his belt," Deryl said. "He exchanged it for the game ball when he received the next pass. I gave Beryl and Teryl a nod, enough to warn them what was coming. The goalie shot his pass out with all the force he could put into his vault. He threw straight at Teryl instead of to his own man, not caring if Teryl caught the weighted ball or if it hit him directly. Either way, the unexpected weight of the ball thrown with such force would be plenty to break Teryl's bat or wrench his arm."

"But I knew better than to try to take the ball," Teryl said. "I feinted instead. The goalie's own runner saw the move for an opportunity, and threw himself at me to smash me with his stone-loaded hip belt. Only that put him right in line with the ball."

Deryl continued the commentary, relating how the runner caught it with his shoulder. The cannon shot took him down in a writhing explosion of pain. Meanwhile Teryl scooped up the ball as it rolled away from its victim, lifted it adroitly now that its venom was spent and put it into play. He tossed it lightly to Deryl, who caught the pitch, turned with the pull of its weight, and spun it once, twice, adding speed to each turn before firing it down the court with all the leverage he could coax from his bat. It was a goal shot that depended on sheer brute force. The waiting goalie knew better than anyone what was coming at him—and that what was coming would be impossible to stop. He saved himself instead. He dodged as the ball blasted between the goalposts for a score.

"If the crowd had been wild before," Teryl commented, "it now went ballistic. People were jumping up and down, hands in the air, howling with something beyond exhilaration Vindication, perhaps, and rage, as well as celebration."

"It was sort of frightening," Deryl told Milo.

"Yeah," added Beryl. "There was this poor guy rolling around on the court with a broken shoulder, and maybe a broken hip from falling on the rocks he'd stuck in his hip belt. And it made people glad!"

"We were really sort of happy to get away from there," finished Deryl. "Right after we were declared the tournament winners, the sea smoothed out and we left with our dad for the island."

"You went back home?" Milo asked. "What about Savoy?"

"He told us where we should go next, and said he'd meet us along the way," Teryl explained.

"We couldn't just leave our parents without going back to the island first," Deryl said. "We wanted to say good-bye to our mother and the other people we'd known all our lives. It was like, all of a sudden everything had changed. We weren't part of the island anymore. We weren't fishermen. Everything we had ever known up to that point was rubbed out. We were strangers there."

"Leaving was scary, even if leaving was what we wanted," said Teryl.

So they went back to the only home they had ever known, said their good-byes, and returned to the mainland. Savoy met them as he had promised, and started training them as they traveled from tournament to tournament. They lost some games, but never a tournament. Their reputation grew, but they were always poor, without a sponsor, and looked on by the established teams as upstarts who had no business playing in the major leagues. That cut them out of the tournaments that would have brought larger purses and full acknowledgment.

"But then when we saw the butterflies, Savoy told us we had to play in the End of the Earth tournament," Teryl explained. "And that's why we're here."

8

At the End of the Earth

The five of them—Teryl, Deryl, Beryl, Milo, and Bori—sat in the shade of an apple tree on the side of a hill munching some honey rolls that a kindly person had given them. Except for Bori, of course, who didn't like honey rolls. He was eating a piece of cheese that Milo had saved for him from their last meal. They were overlooking the road and noticing how many butterflies—and pilgrims—there were now.

"There's more every day," Deryl observed.

"The closer we get to the End, the more there are," Beryl added.

"I guess we must be getting close, then," Milo said. "It should be a full moon in just a few more nights."

"So?" Deryl asked.

"My...uhh, the person who suggested I go on the pilgrimage said that I should be there by the full moon."

Just then, Milo saw a pilgrim he recognized: Count Yeroen. Even from a distance he looked put upon. He had a companion—a lackey apparently—who tugged along a mule loaded with baggage. Since Milo and the boys were a ways off the road, Yeroen didn't see them, or at least seemed to take no interest in them. Milo, for his part, was okay to let Yeroen go on his way without trying to hail him. It wasn't something Milo felt particularly obliged to do.

"Do you know that man?" Milo asked his companions as Yeroen passed on up the road.

"Looks like a wizard or something," Deryl commented.

"We've seen several," Beryl added.

"And some witches and stuff," Deryl noted.

"There must be some sort of Walpurgis Night or something at the End of the Earth this year," Teryl speculated.

"So I've heard," Milo said.

Bori, who hadn't said a word since they had met the boys, gave Milo a significant look and expressive wave of his tail.

"How do you know a wizard or a witch when you see one?" Milo asked.

"Oh, I dunno," Teryl answered. "They just have a certain look about them."

"They're serious," said Beryl.

"Self-absorbed," Deryl added.

"Do I look like a wizard?" Milo asked.

"Are you kidding?" Deryl laughed. "Of course not."

"Well, what do I look like?" Milo pushed on.

"A pilgrim! What else?" Beryl answered.

"If you were a wizard or something," Teryl explained, "your cat here could talk, I expect."

Bori gave Milo a sly, self-satisfied look that seemed to say, "There you go."

Milo let the topic drop.

The day before the full moon, Milo, Bori, and his three ballplayer friends arrived at their destination. After all the long, hard days of walking, the End of the Earth was a bit of an anticlimax. Milo was even sort of sorry because as long as he had been a pilgrim, with walking his only concern, he didn't have to worry about the Hunt and how he'd figure out what to do next.

Not that The End wasn't a beautiful place with a wild and windswept coast overlooking an ocean where waves smashed into the cliffs and sent white spray high into the air. But there was no town, no houses, no signs of any habitation. Milo hadn't known what to expect, but this wasn't it. If you looked underneath the wiry branches of the heather, you could find ruins of old stonework, as though something had been built here long ago but had fallen down and been forgotten.

"No, nobody lives here," Teryl said when Milo asked. "It's been generations and generations since anyone has."

"Why's that?" Milo asked, looking at the heather-covered roll of the land with flower-filled little valleys. Clusters of butterflies flitted everywhere, often swirling together in spiraling columns. They looked happy to see one another, and ready to play.

"Just because," Teryl said as an explanation. Then, "Come on, let's go see the ball court."

The ball court was in much better condition than the rest of the place. It had been built in a deep notch in the hillside, allowing the onlookers to look down into the court from the slopes around it. The court itself was built of gigantic slabs of stone. Weeds grew out of the cracks between them, probably because there hadn't been a game played there since the last pilgrimage. But pilgrim/slinger players were already cleaning out the debris and de-weeding it.

"This is the oldest court there is," Teryl told Milo. "They say it's the birthplace of slinger."

Milo believed it. The monumental walls were so old that they looked geologic, and the granite surfaces were mottled with lichen. The slabs of the floor were set so closely that the cracks between them almost disappeared. The goalposts were granite uprights and were so weathered that the carved designs that had once adorned them could no longer be deciphered.

While B, T, and D joined in cleaning the slinger court, Milo and Bori climbed the slope above it. Milo wanted to get a better view of the whole place from the knoll above, the highest point in the immediate area. After wading through the scratchy brush, they reached the top and looked around in all directions. The peak—well, the highest point on the ridge—was mostly free of brush, with a flat shelf of weathered granite that served as a fine viewing point. Milo could see plenty of other pilgrims camped out in the dips and swales. They apparently chose to take a low profile: white threads of smoke from their modest campfires were all that gave away their location.

At first, Milo assumed that the stone underfoot was bedrock, until he noticed that the cracks in it were too geometric and regular to be the result of natural forces. In fact, when he studied them, he thought that they looked like paving, not unlike the floor of the court below. If so, they were very large stones cut and fitted with remarkable precision.

As Milo walked to and fro, tracing the lines of the joints in an effort to decide whether they were really man-made, he noticed that a smaller stone, seemingly fit into a large one, rocked a little underfoot. Curious, he pried at the edge and found that he could lift it, if only slightly. Gravel in the joints prevented the stone from being lifted out, but after digging with the tip of his knife, he freed it. It was heavy—almost too heavy—but after some prying and tugging, he heaved it out.

To his surprise, he found that it was set very precisely into a socket cut into the larger stone. Inside the socket a pocket had been cut, and inside the pocket someone, apparently a very long time ago, had placed another stone of an entirely different sort. He could see that even though this stone was caked with moss and old mud that had probably washed in over the ages, the stone had a polished surface and a carved shape. Prying it out of the cement of mud and moss, he saw that it was roughly disk shaped, less than half an inch thick. He rubbed at it with his thumb to clean it, and old gunk broke away to reveal four evenly spaced notches around the edges. The disk looked like a skewed "X" or a warped cross, depending on how you held it, with four short arms of even length. It was made of very hard, well-polished stone, maybe a dark green jade, and it fit very neatly into his palm. It was shaped like this:

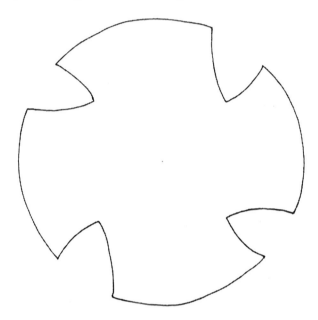

Milo liked it immediately. Someone had gone to a lot of trouble to put it there. On the other hand, that had been done a very long time ago, and it was unlikely that whoever had taken the trouble to hide it so well would be coming back for it. He rubbed it until its polish came up. Old dirt still stuck in what looked like scratches on one side and pits on the other, but after studying the scratches, he decided that they really were an inscription of some sort.

Why not keep it then? he thought. Although it could be considered an artifact in an archaeological sense, and as such should be left in place to be excavated properly, as far as he knew there were no archaeologists here to do that. He slipped the disk into his pocket and wrestled the stone cover back into place. Then he scattered loose dirt and gravel over it, brushing the debris back into the cracks so that he left the spot looking the same as he had found it.

He wanted to see if he could find any of the other contestants, especially Analisa. As he and Bori went down the slope away from the ball court, he rubbed the disk inside his pocket, liking the smoothness of it. It felt, well, very special.

Walking through the webs of trails in the heather, he saw several of the pilgrims he had chanced to meet on the road, but none of the other contestants. Who he did find, however, was a surprise.

Milo heard a flute. He looked at Bori and Bori looked at him.

"Do you think that's who I think it is?" he asked the cat.

"If who you think it's the same person I think it is, I think you're right," the cat replied.

They followed the notes of the flute, and sure enough, the floating tones led to Tinburkin.

"So!" Tinburkin said, putting down his instrument. "You've made it this far."

"Did you think I wouldn't?" Milo asked.

"I thought you would," Tinburkin said lightly. "And you have. How are you faring?"

"Okay, I guess. I've seen a few things I never dreamed I'd see, and I've become something I would have never thought of being: a pilgrim."

"I'd heard about the Crane King, and something to do with his Grail," Tinburkin said. "Do you know anything about it?"

"No, not really."

"You'll have to figure that out for yourself, but you've got time, I think. How do you like being a pilgrim?"

"It's okay. Did I do the right thing by guessing the pilgrimage could be the next clue?"

"I hear you came with some friends," Tinburkin said, not answering Milo's question. Or did it? You never knew with Tinburkin what an answer was. Milo wondered what Tinburkin *didn't* know about his affairs. "Yeah, some slinger players."

"That's good. Have you seen any of the other Hunt contestants yet?"

"No."

"They're around. Everybody seems to have arrived for the slinger tournament in time. Do you know yet what you need to do next?"

"No. I guess I need to puzzle that out, but I haven't a clue how."

"Don't worry. The others haven't figured it out either."

"What are you doing here?" Milo asked him.

"Pilgrim. There hasn't been an End of the Earth pilgrimage in my lifetime, and I wouldn't miss it for the world."

"Can you tell me what this whole pilgrimage thing is about?"

"Didn't Ayuthaya explain that to you? It's about coming to the End of the Earth at precisely the right time."

"I still don't get how that's supposed to help me."

"Someone from your own homeland said something like this: eighty percent of success is showing up. You showed up. You need only the last twenty percent."

"You've been to where I'm from?" Milo asked in surprise.

"I've been to a great many places. I'm a Ranger, after all. It's what I do."

"A Ranger?"

"Sort of like a monitor or a scout for magical affairs."

"But you don't exactly answer questions, right?"

"Oh, I answer questions. You just aren't ready to understand answers."

"Then tell me what this pilgrimage is about. I've walked for weeks without knowing why, and not meeting anybody who did—at least, not really. All I know is that Ayuthaya and Blai said I should."

"And you trusted them?"

"Yes. Shouldn't I?"

"Don't ask me who you should trust. How do you know you can trust me?" Milo didn't answer that. Two could play that game, he decided. "I'll ask you another question," said Tinburkin. "Are you stronger today than you were when you started your walk?"

"Yeah, I guess so."

"Then you've already gained something tangible from it, not so? What else have you learned?"

"That I still haven't got a clue. Those other Hunt contestants...they all got here okay. I don't think they had to ask Ayuthaya and Blai where to go and how, like I did."

"They had to walk every day to get here just like you did. You knew nothing about the pilgrimage at all, but it was something they've known about all their lives. Yet you got here just as quickly as they did. I'd say you've learned a lot."

"If you say so," Milo answered in resignation.

"I can tell you something about the history of the End of the Earth pilgrimage, if you like," Tinburkin offered.

Without waiting for Milo's consent, Tinburkin launched into his story. "Long, long ago, the Elder Race built a special place here. They probably came the same way you did, following the migration of butterflies, just as pilgrims have ever since. They may have known why the butterflies come here and why it was here that they built their ritual ball court to commemorate their legends. *I* don't know why, but they knew a great many things, especially about the primeval world. As newer races came into the land, the Elder Race taught much of their lore to those who wished to learn. Some, but not all. They taught the newer people skills, trades, and ways of thinking. They helped the newcomers to develop the arts that we often call civilization. But not all the contacts were peaceful. Some of the newcomers were quarrelsome and unwilling to live in peace side by side with the Elder Ones.

"The people of the Elder Race were very long lived but always few in number, while the newcomers multiplied quickly. As time went on, the numbers of Elder Race dwindled even more. Some, worn down by struggle with the newcomers, left these shores and vanished over the seas. They sailed away to the West in ships from this very place. That's why it's called the End of the Earth. Legends have it that they went to a refuge hidden from us. We're known as the race who displaced them.

"As they left, they took most of their secrets with them, leaving behind fragments and structures that they had built, and also what they had taught those of the newer peoples who had been willing to learn from them."

He stopped, cocking his head to one side to fix Milo with a teasing look.

"In your homeland, you have very similar stories about an older race. And over time, you've reduced them in stature, but not in awe. You call them fairies. Or gods. In either case, they aren't around to be encountered anymore, though some say there are a few of them to be found in special places.

"But of course, you're one of the few people who would know about this better than anyone else, right?" Tinburkin pointed out.

"What do you mean?" Milo asked, with an answer already dawning on him. "Do you mean Ayuthaya and Blai?"

Tinburkin nodded. "Do you think that just anyone can walk up to the door of the Glass Tower—or of Crane Castle, for that matter—and knock to ask for dinner and directions?"

"I...don't really know," Milo said. "But I think Tivik may have."

"Tivik, if you recall, is a highly accomplished warlock and seer, as all the other Hunt contestants are. How he, or any of the others, might have guessed the clue relies on his or her skill in deciphering evidence and lore. In Tivik's case, I believe he was led by the chance sighting of the White Hind, a huge stroke of luck that was enough in itself to tell him what he needed to know to discover the next clue. But the renewed migration of the butterflies worked the way a neon sign does in your land to tell the Hunt contestants where to look."

"It wasn't obvious to me," Milo protested.

"Were you there? Did you find the Glass Tower? Did the butterflies lead you here?"

"Yes...but I didn't know what I was doing."

"Milo, did you get here? Yes. How you did it isn't significant. Doing it is what counts. Don't discount your accomplishments because you achieved them in a way different from how you assume it *should* be done."

He stopped chiding Milo so he could get back to his story.

"The End of the Earth was the last stronghold of the Elder Race," he told Milo. "When the last of them left, it fell into ruin, but our traditions reminded us that it was a special place and that it retains connection to ancient wisdom. It became a place for pilgrimage and the reenactment of the ritual tournament."

"I guess that means that this slinger game is more than a sport."

Tinburkin gave him another mysterious look. "Some still think so. Maybe it is. People tend to find what they seek and overlook what they didn't think to look for."

"So the whole point of the pilgrimage is...?"

"...to submit to what you find."

Milo didn't think this conversation was likely to get any more enlightening. "So now that I'm here, what am I supposed to do? What do the pilgrims do once they get here?" he asked.

"It might be a good idea to watch your friends play in the slinger tournament."

The three ballplayers were back at camp, simmering a pot of stew for supper.

"We've seen some of the other teams," Beryl told Milo as he and the cat came up to the fire.

"We've already beaten some of them," said Deryl confidently.

"The Black Hawks are here," Teryl said, with notably less confidence.

"Who are the Black Hawks?" Milo asked.

"They're awesome," said Beryl, his tone expressing dread.

"We've heard of them everywhere we go," Deryl added.

"If half of what we've been told about them is true," Teryl continued, "then they aren't even human."

"What are they then?" Milo asked.

"How should we know?" Beryl replied. "But they can do things that just can't be done by humans."

"Unless you use some sort of magic," Teryl added.

"Is that allowed?" Milo asked.

"It's not fair, but if you get away with it, who can stop you from doing it?" Deryl exclaimed.

"The question is, how do we play against it?" Teryl asked.

"Where's Savoy? Would he know what to do?" Milo asked.

Before any of the boys could answer, Savoy stomped up to the fire and sat down, reminding Milo of a tree falling or an avalanche. "I'm here," he stated. "Are you boys ready?" he asked, dishing himself a steaming bowl of stew. "Has the drawing been held yet?"

The drawing was the first thing to be done to start the tournament. Each team that wanted to play tossed its marker into a pot, then each team drew in turn to determine who would play whom. The first team to draw a marker played the team that owned the marker it drew. That would be the first game to be played. The next team to draw would play the team whose marker they had drawn in the second game, and so forth. By the time all the teams had played once, and the losers were eliminated, the winners would toss their markers back into the pot and a new drawing would determine the order of games for the second round. The final round would be between the two teams that had won each of their games.

"We play the Raging Rabbits first," Teryl told Savoy. "We beat them when we played them at the...wasn't that the Tomaine tournament?" he asked his brothers.

"That was last year," Savoy pointed out. "They're better now, so don't get cocky. There's nothing to say they won't eliminate you in the first round."

"We're better than that!" Beryl insisted.

"Those guys are good, I tell you," Savoy said, shoveling in a spoonful of stew. "And they've got a grudge against you. They'll want to kick your—"

"Okay," Teryl broke in. "Point taken. We have to win the first game before we think about the second. One game at a time."

"And when do the Black Hawks play?" Savoy wanted to know.

"In the sixth game."

"You're really worried about the Black Hawks," Savoy said, sort of gurgling his words through mouthfuls of hot stew. "They use magic, you know."

"We know," the three said in unison.

"What if you could counter their magic?" Milo asked. "Could you beat them if their magic wasn't working?"

Savoy quit chewing and looked at Milo, as if he had seen him for the first time. "Who's this?" he asked.

Teryl explained how they had met Milo on the road and gotten to be friends. When Savoy started chewing again, the topic returned to the Black Hawks.

"At least we would have a fair shot at beating them," Teryl said in reply to Milo's question.

"Save the Hawks for later," Savoy said, wiping his mouth on his sleeve.

Actually, Milo had a purpose in mind. After eating, he went off with Bori. "Let's see if we can find Analisa," he told the cat. "Maybe she can think of a way to counter the Black Hawk's magic."

"And maybe we'll come across a vole or two while we're at it," Bori commented. "They're especially spicy here in this heather habitat."

The moon was full and it was easy to find the paths through the tangle of heather. You could see little fires here and there marking the campsites of pilgrims. Milo thought there were so many of them that it was almost like a mirror of the stars above down here on the ground.

Instead of Analisa, they found Tivik. Milo didn't really feel like asking him for help, even if he owed Milo for saving him from the lopers, but he didn't mind asking him if he'd seen any of the other contestants. Sure enough, he knew where Analisa was camping, and gave Milo directions.

First, they had to find a standing stone. After they did that, locating Analisa's camp was easy. From the darkness looking into the ring of light from Analisa's fire, Milo recognized her and felt a twang inside his chest.

"Ahh...knock, knock?" he called, not wanting to barge in without some sort of invitation.

"Hello, Milo," she said without taking her eyes off the pot she was tending.

"How are you?" he asked, coming up and squatting down, uncertain that she had actually invited him. Bori marched right over and rubbed against her leg. He got a pat.

"I'm fine. And you?" Her tone was formal.

"I was worried when I didn't see you at the Glass Tower. With the harpies and all."

"A little late for concern, isn't it?" she replied coolly. "Besides, I can take care of myself. When I saw the Pilgrimage Rainbow and then the butterflies, it was pretty obvious. What took *you* so long?"

"I had to walk," he answered.

"We *all* had to walk, Milo," she said in exasperation. "It's the only way to get here."

Milo winced. Did she have to make him feel like a fool? On the other hand, he told himself, he was making it pretty easy for her.

"I came," he began, deciding to get it over with, "to ask a favor. Not that you owe me anything, and not for me. It's for my friends."

"You mean those three ball heads you're hanging out with?"

"How did you know—," he began, then dropped it. "Right. Teryl, Beryl, and Deryl."

"The Fish Sticks." She rolled her eyes. "How clever."

"They're good guys. But they have to play a team that uses magic, and I was wondering—"

"If I could do a little spell to help out," she completed his thought. "Why don't *you* help them?"

"I'm no wizard or anything," he insisted. "You know I can't do magic. But I was hoping you could. I mean, I know you can, but I wondered if you would be willing to use your ability to just cancel out the Black Hawks magic so it can be a fair match."

"Listen, Milo. The Black Hawks, or so I've heard, always use magic. So taking away their magic would be like making your guys play on one leg."

Milo had to think about that. He could sort of see how her logic was running about taking away magic from someone who always used it, but it still didn't seem right to use an uneven advantage like that in an event that was supposed to be about athletics, not magic. He tried to explain his point.

It didn't work. Analisa stuck to her argument.

"Listen," Bori broke in. "Analisa, Milo's your friend. It won't hurt to do him a favor. If those other guys are using their own magic, that's one thing, but what if it's somebody else's magic they're using? By using something that isn't their own talent, they're not playing fair. If that's the case, you *should* strip it away and let the match be played on even terms."

Milo had to think that one through, seeing a new idea in it about how the Black Hawks were cheating. Apparently, it made sense to Analisa, because she agreed.

"Come and get me just before the Black Hawks play. I need to see what they're doing, and whether Bori is right and someone else is doing the magic."

The next morning, the first game began as soon as there was enough light to play. Savoy and the boys were watching to study the teams in case the Fish Sticks met the winner in a future game. Milo told Savoy about the arrangement he'd made with Analisa while he watched the start of the game, but Savoy just grunted. Milo wasn't quite sure that Savoy had heard him.

Savoy sent B, D, and T back to camp at the end of the third game. "I'll stay to watch the matches," he told them. "You rest and get ready to play. I'll tell you what you need to know when the time comes."

Milo hung around until after the boys had gone. He wanted to ask Savoy a question. "Why is slinger such an important event at the End of the Earth pilgrimage?"

"Because it always has been," Savoy answered.

"But why?"

"How should I know?" Savoy answered gruffly. "It's tradition. How do you explain tradition? People always do whatever tradition dictates."

It wasn't much of an answer. Milo decided he would try to find Tinburkin and ask him. Even if Tinburkin's answers were indecipherable, Milo was sure he would have one.

He waited until the fourth game began before he went to fetch Analisa for the start of B, D, and Ts' game, which was to come up next. He thought that if she saw the Fish Sticks play, she might be more sympathetic to their cause.

She agreed to come, but she took her time doing it. By the time they arrived, T, B, and D were already on the court.

"I don't see the point of the whole thing, anyway," she protested.

"Well, it's a major element of the whole End of the Earth Pilgrimage, isn't it?" Milo insisted. "So it must be important."

"How so?"

Milo didn't want to be caught stumped yet again. "It's tradition," he said. He was relieved that she didn't question him further on his answer.

He explained to her what was going on down in the court, the object of the game, and what the rules were. That is, until she commented, "Nice pass off the rear wall. Beryl—Beryl's the goalie, right?—used the rear wall cleverly to make the pass without giving away his shot."

"You...you know the game?" Milo asked in surprise.

"Sure. I played it until I went to witches' school. Didn't have the time after that."

"Why did you act like you didn't care for the game?"

"Because I have something more important to do than play a sport that, frankly, I'll never be really, really good at. But your guys are excellent. I like watching them. They deserve to win."

The Fish Sticks won the match. Milo introduced Analisa while the next game was being set up. She commented about several of the key plays of the match, things that Milo hadn't even noticed, clearly making an impression on the guys. They were still talking to her when the next game started, and Savoy sent them away. Milo guessed he didn't want them watching the Black Hawks, who would come up in the next game.

Analisa stayed until the Black Hawks stormed into the court. Not only did they glower like television wrestlers, but they burned with malicious energy. The snaggle-toothed goalie snarled at everything through the gap in his grimace, and the runner whipped a long black topknot from his otherwise shaven head. The striker whooped and did salmon jumps down the court, shaking his bat like it was a club.

It was obvious from the first instant when the play began that the Black Hawks were not content merely to score on their opponents. They wanted to destroy them. They ran the score up rapidly. It was already five to zero when Analisa whispered to Milo, "I see what they're doing. Bori was right. Somebody else is creating opportunities for them with time management."

"What's that?" Milo had to ask.

"Have you noticed that when they're running a play, there's a sort of shimmer in the air? That's from slowing down time. It allows them to do things that nobody else can see. That's how they pull off their incredible shots. They know how to use the advantages of magic, but the things they seem to be doing are not possible, if you go by what you can actually see happening."

"Who's helping them?"

"I don't know. Whoever it is has to be here somewhere, but he or she is doing a good job of cloaking him or herself."

"Can you counter the magic?"

"I don't know. First I have to figure out who's doing the magic. Then

I have to see if I can override it. If it's someone really good, I may not be able to."

When the match ended, Analisa returned to her camp, and Milo sought out Savoy to tell him what Analisa had discovered.

This time, Savoy was listening. "Dealing with a magician is no simple thing," he told Milo. "They're dangerous. You can't just scare them off or drag them away. But I know some people here. If you can point out the Black Hawks' ally, I'll see if I can't get the boys a fair chance when they play them."

Milo felt pretty good about the negotiation. He told Bori about how Analisa had warmed to helping the guys, and what she had discovered. Bori, however, was not quite as overwhelmed with this success.

"This whole thing isn't over yet," Bori pointed out. "Analisa has to find the magician who is helping the Hawks, and then someone has to be able to deal with him—or her. And don't think you can stay clear of that muddle, because you've put yourself into it. Now you'll have to deal with whatever happens. Something tells me that there's more to all this than a simple matter of what's fair or not in a slinger match. And you still have to figure out what the next clue is."

That took the wind out of Milo's sails. Why did Bori have to devour the Salmon of Wisdom, Milo lamented privately as his feeling of satisfaction dissolved into dread.

The first round of play extended throughout the day before the winners drew markers for the second round. The Fish Sticks played early, and Analisa showed up for that game as well as later in the day when the Black Hawks played.

At the end of the second round, both the Fish Sticks and the Black Hawks had advanced to play in the third round. Analisa had still been unable to identify the magician who was giving the Hawks their advantages, however.

"I'm fairly positive it's a man," she told Milo, "but I think he's on to me. I almost had him, then I felt something slip, and then a void. He may have caught me as I was zeroing in. If he did, then that's it. I won't get another chance."

"Isn't there anything else you know?" Milo pleaded. "Something more than just that he's a man? There are lots of men watching the games."

"No. Nope," she asserted. "Old. I get old. Old and very mean. In fact, when I got the feeling of his meanness, it was so strong that I shuddered.

That's when he slipped me. I wish I could do better."

With the second round done, the order of play for the third round had to be decided. There were four teams left, drawing for the semi-finals. Teryl pulled for the Fish Sticks. It was the Black Hawks' marker.

That was a blow. After the drawing, the mood at the Fish Sticks' camp was grim.

"So we don't know who's helping the Hawks and we have to play them next?" Teryl asked Milo after he heard Milo's report.

"We have to play them with a handicap," Beryl moaned.

"Look at it this way," Deryl suggested. "We play them in the first game of the day. That round will be over by noon. If we win, we play in the final. If we lose, then we'll be free to enjoy the last game by watching."

It was a weak attempt to put on a good face. His comment just contributed to the atmosphere of gloom.

"Whatever happens," Savoy ordered, "you three must play your best. Let Fate take care of what you can't. Win or lose, you'll be remembered by how you play."

Milo gave Bori a pat. "Come on," he told the cat. "Let's go see somebody."

As they left the somber camp, Milo was thinking about talking to Analisa again. Maybe she would be able to learn something more during the game that could help T, B, and D in time to save them. But as soon as he left the light of the fire, he had changed his mind.

"Let's see if we can find Tinburkin," he told Bori.

The cat took the lead. Not only could he see in the dark, he could smell and had a superior sense of direction.

"How's Tinburkin to help?" he asked Milo.

"I don't know. It's just a hope, I guess. Tinburkin told me to trust myself, and right now I feel like I need to talk to him."

Bori found Tinburkin's camp, even though it was not at the same spot as before.

"Good evening, Boriboreau, Milo," Tinburkin greeted as they entered his circle of light. "I've been expecting you. How are you?"

"Not so good," Milo said, then explained the situation with the Fish Sticks, and about Analisa's failure to identify the magician to interrupt his unfair help for the Black Hawks.

"Have you figured out the next clue?" Tinburkin asked without commenting on anything Milo had said.

"No. You advised me to watch the tournament. That's what I've been doing." On an impulse, Milo reached into his pocket. "And I found this."

He pulled out the jade cross and held it out on his palm to show Tinburkin. Tinburkin startled, then looked away.

"Put that away," he ordered, looking elsewhere. "Where did you get that?"

"I found it."

"Have you shown it to anyone?"

"Only to you."

"Then don't show it to anyone else. Not to anybody. Don't mention it, and don't take it out where someone could see it even fleetingly. You never know who might be watching."

"What is it?" Milo wanted to know as he stuck it back into his pocket.

"I can't tell you. You'll have to figure it out for yourself. I can warn you though. It's more profound than meeting the Grail King. And more dangerous, as well. Guard it with your life. That goes for you, too, Bori."

That was bad news—and nothing like what Milo had been expecting by coming to Tinburkin. Bori's prediction of going from the frying pan and into the fire seemed to be coming around.

"Is there anything I can do to help out Beryl, Teryl, and Deryl?" Milo asked listlessly.

"I have no idea," Tinburkin said. "Be very careful, Milo."

Although the next morning was bright and sunny, it might just as well have been an overcast day with the threat of rain. Milo tried to act cheery, but it fell pretty flat. Savoy was all business, and B, T, and D said almost nothing at all. Analisa showed up hoping she would be able to locate, and perhaps to distract, the sorcerer who was helping the Hawks, but it was clear that she was less than optimistic about her chances.

"Stop thinking about losing and concentrate on playing!" Savoy barked. "If you don't play as well as you can, you really don't have a chance to win, and if you don't give it your best, you don't even deserve to win!" he told them harshly.

Milo couldn't see that Savoy's advice helped improve the morale of the brothers. Their game was the first one to be played that day, and they were just waiting to go on court. Waiting made the tension worse. Milo had such a bad case of butterflies, he couldn't imagine how Teryl, Deryl, and Beryl were feeling. Sure enough, Teryl threw up just before they were leaving.

"I'm better now," he said grimly, wiping his mouth on his sleeve. "That, and mad! Hey, I don't care how the Hawks cheat! Remember all we've done to get here? Maybe they'll beat us. So what? I want to make sure they know that they have to be cheaters if they want to win! Come on, guys! Let's kick their butts!"

His fury was infectious. Deryl and Beryl lifted out of their funk and turned vicious. Even Milo felt like he wanted to start a fight.

As the Hawks came onto the court with their usual taunting braggadocio, the Sticks came out in grim silence, taking positions without a word. Their silence was heavy enough to still the crowd, so the Hawk's catcalls reverberated emptily around the court.

The first ball was thrown out by the judge. The opposing team's runner attacked instantly. As the Hawks' player faked to intimidate Teryl away from the ball, Teryl ignored him and scooped the ball for a pass through the center ring, done so rapidly that the Hawks had no time to react. The ball went through the ring with such force that it sailed all the way in a straight line down the court to ricochet off the rear wall behind the Hawks' goal. As the ball bounced into the air, Deryl and the goalie jostled each other for position as the two runners came dashing down the court, nearer the goal.

Analisa, standing at Milo's side, gripped his arm and called his attention to a faint shimmer in the air. Although Milo couldn't see how it had been done, the Hawks' runner had the ball and was dodging Teryl's defense to take the ball up for a shot through the center court ring. When he took his shot, Teryl made a prodigious leap to catch the ball before it could reach the ring, crashing into the wall, but still in control. The attack on the Hawks' goal resumed.

Milo felt like he might puke, too. The game went on like this, with the Sticks unable to score, but with the Hawks unable to escape their courageous defense. Analisa squeezed Milo's arm hard enough to make him wince, drawing his rapt attention from the play.

"He knows I'm on to him," Analisa breathed. "I don't know if he's figured out where I am yet, but it won't be long. What he intends already hurts. He'll attack as soon as he finds me. I don't think I can fend him off!"

"What'll we do?" Milo's hackles rose.

"I don't know. It's going to be bad."

Milo's hands went deep in his pockets. For the first time, he realized he was rubbing the stone like mad. Teryl had the ball back in play for the Sticks and made a pass down the court to Deryl. Deryl scooped up the ball and fired it into the rear wall on a trajectory to take it between the goalposts from the rear. It would be a score if the goalie, who had placed himself into position in anticipation of a more direct attempt, couldn't reach the ball in time. The shimmer began just as Milo expected it to, masking the time delay that would give the goalie the instant he needed, but then faltered. The ball shot through the goal as the goalie threw himself hopelessly behind it.

The crowd went nuts. The players on both teams, expecting the magical help for a save, stopped stock still, their jaws gaping. The Sticks recovered first, leaping around and high-fiving one another.

"What happened?" Milo shouted to Analisa over the tumult.

"I don't know," she replied. "Something broke up the spell. Just as it was taking hold, it melted. Whatever it was, it wasn't anything I did."

Both were mystified. "Whatever it was," Analisa went on, "he thinks I did it. He's searching for me like mad. And boy, is he mad!"

Too mad, apparently, to pay attention to the game. The score they had made galvanized the Sticks and unraveled the Hawks. It almost seemed that the magic that had failed the Hawks had transferred to the Sticks, not by giving them extra time to make plays, but by putting wings on their feet. They flew around the competition, and before very long they scored again.

Meanwhile, Analisa was going into a panic. "He's narrowing in on me!" she told Milo. "I can feel him scanning for me, and building up a spell to blast me with!"

Milo was so concerned that he forgot the game, too. "We've got to get you out of here!" he told her.

"No! He'll see us trying to leave and then he'll know us for sure. I've got to sit it out, mask my own magic, and hope he doesn't identify me before the game is over. Maybe then we can get away in the crowd."

Trying to watch the game like all the other people was harrowing. Down in the court, it was clear that the Hawks were on their own and the game was being played on equal terms—only the Sticks were playing with such lightness and the Hawks weren't even all that good now that they were stripped of their advantage. The game ended with a score of 4-0, Fish Sticks.

The crowd went wild, and Analisa grabbed Milo's arm. "It's not me!" she shouted at him. "It's you!"

At that instant, Milo felt the smooth stone in his pocket. He was rubbing it between his fingers compulsively out of anxiety.

"Run, Milo!" Analisa shouted. "Get out now while everybody's milling around!"

He did. He thought he could feel a target on his back, as if he were dodging through people with the crosshairs on him as he attempted to escape. As he came clear of the crowd by passing out of the gallery and over the ridge into the open heather-clad slope beyond, a hand reached out and grabbed him, jerking him aside.

"Tinburkin!" he exclaimed, expecting much worse.

"Come on!" the Ranger growled. "Let's get you out of here! You're in terrible danger."

"What? Why?"

"You've been using the stone."

"The—" and he felt its smoothness inside his pocket. "Why? What's the problem?"

"It's something that you must keep secret, although it seems the secret is already out. It's power is something sought after, at least by a knowledgeable few. Those few, however, happen to be very clever, very determined, and very, very dangerous. And you just blew the cover of one who has spent a long time developing it. His name in Kayn Smith, and I think he'll do anything to get his hands on that stone. Then he'll take revenge on you."

"I'll give it to him!" Milo exclaimed.

"You'll do nothing of the sort! Besides, it would do you no good. He wouldn't return the favor. You'll be safer with the stone than without it."

"Then I'll put it back where I found it."

"That would be the same as giving it to him. Smith apparently knew it must be hidden here, and came for it. He holds his grudges dear. He won't forget you. You're already on his short list of people he dislikes."

"Why? What did I do?"

"You, with your visit to the Glass Tower, opened the Pilgrimage."

"Oh geez," Milo said, thinking about the evil sorcerers in the stories.

"Yes. Kayn Smith's not likely to become a reformed citizen now," Tinburkin pointed out. "He must be very frustrated to find out that you beat him to the thing he has spent so long trying to track down. It's ironic, actually. He's been unable to find the stone because the Pilgrim's Way has been closed for so long. You show up and open the Rainbow Path, giving him the opportunity to get here, then you beat him by picking up the very thing he came to claim."

This was a lot for Milo to absorb. What Tinburkin had just told him brought up so many questions that he could hardly sort them out. But one issue outweighed them all.

"What's he going to do to me?"

"Good question. Whatever it is, you won't like it. So you have to keep him from catching you."

"How?"

"Use the Hunt. Find your own way. It's your shield as well as your challenge. The stone is the cipher and you are the wild card, so he might have a hard time anticipating what you're likely to do. That, and don't let *anyone* know about that stone, and don't lose it."

9

Fish Sticks and Red Herrings

"I know who it is!"

Analisa gripped Milo's arm and whispered sharply into his ear as soon as she came into camp the next morning. Milo and Bori had spent the night moving from place to place to avoid the risk of being found. B, T, and D had left to play in the final game. "He's called Smith. He's a dark-side sorcerer."

"I know," Milo said miserably.

"You know?" Analisa replied, surprised and looking crestfallen. "How?"

"Another friend warned me. What else did you find out about him?"

"Not much. I went to the other contestants and asked if they knew him. The only one who did was Count Yeroen, and he acted like if I didn't know who this Smith guy was, he wasn't going to tell me. But then Aulaires—would you believe she would offer me information?—told me that she had heard about him. She said he's very secretive, hardly unusual for a dark sorcerer, and that he has an exceedingly vicious reputation."

"But you're all right?" said Milo. "He hasn't tried to do anything to you, has he?"

"No. This Smith guy dropped me when he switched to you. I think he knows who I am because he gave me this...this look when I was trying to leave the gallery. It sent a chill clear through me."

"What does he look like?" Milo asked, hoping to be able to pick out his enemy in the crowd.

"Old. Very intense, shifting eyes that go everywhere. Smallish, but otherwise nothing in particular about him stands out." She stopped, then asked another question. "What did you do to him, Milo? Why did he turn on you?"

"I don't know," Milo answered. He couldn't tell Analisa about the stone in his pocket and how he had been rubbing it, like a worry stone. Or a wishing stone. "But I wish he hadn't." Milo was careful not to touch the stone as he said that. He decided that he had to do something with it, put it someplace where he couldn't touch it as easily as when it was just sitting in his pocket. Someplace safe, where it wouldn't get lost. "I'm glad he left *you* alone, though."

"He gives me the willies," Analisa said, hugging herself as if she were chilled. "I've heard about sorcerers of his kind, but he's the nastiest person I've ever actually encountered. You'll have to be very careful, Milo."

"What about the boys?" he asked, changing the subject.

"They played the final, and won. Even the team they beat was happy. Nobody likes the Hawks. Savoy said that the way the Hawks played was a stain on the integrity of the game. He said that playing just to win destroys the true significance of slinger that reaches back to the earliest of times. And if they'd won using magic, it would have been an insult to the pilgrimage and the tournament."

"Why's that?"

"Because this place is about people's hopes and ideals. It's sacred. The slinger tournament as it's played here is about respect, honor, and heroism. When the boys won, the very first thing they did was congratulate the other team on a game well played. Each of them grabbed the hand of one of the guys on the other team. Then they all linked up holding their hands high in victory. It was the best part! The audience cried and cheered at the same time. I wish you'd been there. It was the perfect expression of what slinger's really supposed to be."

Milo thought about that for a minute, wishing he *had* been there to see it. He wondered if this guy named Smith had been there when the guys won. Probably not. After all, he had been quite willing to slander the tournament. Then Milo asked Analisa something else. "Have any of the Hunt contestants figured out the next clue?"

"If they have, nobody's left yet. So I doubt they have. It has to be something that's unique to the End of the Earth or that arises because of the pilgrimage here. Like the way the Glass Tower initiated the pilgrimage in the first place."

"I don't suppose you know what it is," he suggested.

"No. Not yet. If I did, Milo—no offense—I wouldn't tell you. Each of us has to figure out what makes sense and how that suggests the next clue. That doesn't mean that the clue is necessarily the same for each of us. Besides, we're still competitors, and like I told you, I have to win."

"I know," he said in resignation. "You're right. It's just that..." He was about to say that he had to get away from here fast, but he changed his mind about how much to tell her. "I don't have any idea how any of this works."

"You promised me not to play stupid, Milo. Remember?"

He nodded, remembering the promise he had made back at the forest camp.

Then he and Analisa went to find B, T, and D to congratulate them. When they did, they found lots of other people crowding around the victors. There was no way to reach the three boys through the mob, at least for the time being.

They found Savoy, though. He was off to the side, sitting on a rock to watch the whole thing from a safe distance. Bori sat with him, with as philosophical an air as Savoy's.

"Congratulations, sir," Milo greeted.

Savoy ignored the greeting. "So you managed to lift the magical advantage," he stated, looking at Milo, then at Analisa. "Whichever one of you accomplished that, my thanks. I owe you one."

"That's—" Milo started, but stopped himself. If he took credit, wouldn't it be giving away part of what Tinburkin had warned him must be kept secret? "Analisa worked very hard."

She gave him a curious sidewise glance as she added her comment. "I'm very happy that the boys won."

"They'll want to thank you themselves," Savoy said. "Might take a while, though, before you get a chance." He glanced over at the throng of well-wishers around the three young heroes. "Everybody recognizes how they won, fair and square."

"Not everyone," a new voice spoke from behind. "I think that somebody else might have left here in a hurry. He wouldn't have been so warmly celebrated for his part in this."

Milo and Analisa jerked around in surprise. It was Aulaires. Milo blushed as he always did when he saw her, and Analisa glanced around uncomfortably, clearly avoiding eye contact. Aulaires studied her carefully.

"Hello, Milo," she said in her silky voice. "Hello, Analisa."

They both muttered a return greeting as Aulaires stepped forward to extend a hand to Savoy. "And to you, Savoy. Seems you've done it again. Congratulations. Your boys did very well. I expect you'll be leaving soon?"

Savoy looked her over with his appraising eye. They clearly weren't strangers to each other. "Yep. Taking them home. This one has been a long project."

"Ahh. I suppose you've been working with...?"

Savoy nodded. "An old colleague. She is these boys' special

protectoress and has been looking after them since their birth. She asked me to fetch them back home to their parents. Their parents will be very happy—and very surprised—to see them."

"I expect so. The Aken Clan—or Oak Clan—once ruled the End of the Earth before it was destroyed, didn't they? I recall the incident when the clan's heirs—triplets—went missing at their christening."

Savoy nodded. "And the Oak Clan has always been deeply associated with the game of slinger. Looks like the tradition continues."

"The clan has produced many slinger champions," Aulaires mused vaguely. "Very interesting. Well, I'm sure you'll be going soon, and so will I." Milo noticed a smug smile on her face as she said this. "Good luck to you, and good travels." She turned back to the two young people standing there. "And to you two, also. I expect we'll meet again somewhere along the Hunt's clue-lined road, no? Take care, Analisa."

As Aulaires made her charming exit, Milo watched Analisa instead. Analisa turned a tight face to Milo. "Time for me to go, too. Good-bye, Milo. Good-bye, Bori. It was nice to meet you, Savoy. Give the boys my best wishes."

Just like that, she was gone. Milo realized that whatever Aulaires had picked up from Savoy had also worked for Analisa, but it hadn't given him anything he could understand. He felt the lump of the stone cross in his pocket, and recalled the extraordinary way that Tinburkin had reacted to it. He felt sure that it held more significance than whatever Aulaires and Analisa had picked up from that little conversation about slinger and the Oak clan. But what?

He thought about the inscription on its face. Would that be the clue he needed? How could he read it? Could someone who knew old languages read it for him? Tinburkin had warned him not to show the stone cross to anyone, but maybe he could take a rubbing of the marks and show it to some expert.

"Savoy?" he asked the old trainer. "You get around a lot and know a lot of people. Like Aulaires." Savoy just grunted, watching the crowd around the three boys. "Do you know anybody who might be good at translating old inscriptions?"

Savoy looked at him with his appraising eye. "You Hunt contestants. Always with your secrets. I owe you one. I have a friend, a librarian at the university in Inverdissen. If anybody can read an old text, it's Samuel. Inverdissen's a long walk from here, and a different direction from the one

I'm taking those boys, or I'd take you myself. But you find Samuel and tell him I sent you. He owes me, so tell him to pay me back by helping you." He pointed to the distant blue line of mountains opposite the coast where they were sitting. "Take the road that goes to those mountains. When you get to the top, take the middle road from there. Inverdissen is on the middle of three peninsulas. If you take that path, you can't get lost."

10

Travels with Senster and Dexter

The trail did nothing but climb for the next three days—except for when it dropped into a deep ravine, then climbed out again on the other side. Milo felt quite pleased with how little the strain of such difficult hiking caused him. Days on trails such as these would have left him breathless and moaning before, but now the weeks of travel on the pilgrimage had hardened him to a relentless walking pace. Now he could even think of it as fun!

Milo and Bori—Bori riding in his usual place in Milo's pack—climbed the long ascent to the pass that Savoy had pointed out back at the End of the Earth. As Milo walked, he wondered about the other contestants. "Looks like we're the only ones who came this way," he said to Bori.

"We haven't seen anyone on this path at all," Bori observed. "In fact, we haven't seen anyone off it, either." Both of them had noted this fact, especially when they were getting hungry and hoping to see a farmhouse where they could ask for a meal. Milo was munching one of the biscuits that Ayuthaya had provided him that he really hadn't needed during the days on the pilgrimage trail. Bori continued his observation: "By the time we'd said our good-byes to Deryl, Teryl, and Beryl, not even one of the Hunt contestants was still at the End of the Earth. They all left as fast as Aulaires and Analisa."

"That's right," Milo confirmed the cat's observation. "But remember what Tinburkin and Blai both told me about trusting my own instincts."

"Or something like that," Bori muttered. "Self-preservation—in this case getting a meal occasionally—is an instinct, too."

"Don't complain. You've done pretty well on the rodents living in these mountains. I'm the one living on dry biscuits. Besides, I feel certain that the stone cross is my big clue." He laid his palm on the lump where it rode on a leather thong Savoy had given him off some slinger equipment back at the End of the Earth. He wore it under his shirt where he couldn't touch it directly, but he could feel it and make certain that it was safe.

They ceased talking to make the last steep pull up the ridge they'd been climbing all morning. At the top they took a break. As Milo sat down and slipped off his pack, Bori hopped out to do a little reconnaissance.

He refused Milo's offer of a piece of the hard cake, insisting that if it had never had blood coursing through it, it couldn't be cat food.

"Remember what Savoy told us to do when we got to Inverdissen?" Milo reminded. "We should find the university and ask for...for..." Milo momentarily forgot the name that Savoy had given them.

"Samuel. The librarian," Bori filled in. "I hope he isn't a banshee."

"Savoy said he was an old friend, so I doubt he's a banshee. Savoy said that this Samuel owes him a favor and I should tell him to transfer the debt to helping us. The problem is showing him the inscription without showing him the stone cross. If I had some paper and a pencil, I could make a rubbing, but since I don't, I've been trying to copy the marks onto this piece of slate I picked up." He showed Bori the flat rock, about the same size as the stone cross, where he had been making a copy by scratching marks with the point of his knife. "I'm pretty sure I've done it just like the inscription on the cross, but what if it isn't? The marks are fairly complicated, and maybe they won't make any sense at all."

Bori, who was poking around through the weeds, gave a dismissive flip of his tail. "What you humans call books and writing and make such a fuss about seems to us cats like nothing more than a nice place to sit. Besides, those marks you're making look like what happens to a good scratching post." Bori had found nothing but a couple of lizards, which weren't his idea of lunch, either. But now he called Milo's attention to an old sign chiseled into a marker where the trail started back down the slope.

"I think it says Inverdissen," Milo read. "So if this really is the right pass, we're on the right road, and it's all downhill from here. Maybe we'll start seeing habitation again."

"That would be fine by me," Bori grumbled. "I could use a nice saucer of milk to wash the lizard scales off my tongue."

It was still a long walk through the mountainous wilderness. There was no sign that anyone lived in these mountains, meaning no chance for hospitality. Bori had to continue to rely on his hunting skills while Milo still made do with the dry cakes.

It took another couple of days before they had descended far enough for the trail to enter foothills that showed signs of inhabitants. Shepherds with their flocks—herded by dogs, which made Bori nervous—wandered the rolling pastures, and small farms with tiny garden plots and orchards were tucked away along the creek beds.

"I hope there's someplace to get something to eat soon," Milo said as they dipped into a valley, the largest so far. There was a farmstead near the road at the place where the trail crossed the stream. It was a low building built of fieldstone with a red tile roof that looked close to caving in at one end. A part of the roof that had already collapsed had been repaired with thatch. There was a breezeway with a similar structure on the other side, but it hadn't been as fortunate—based on the condition of its sagged-in roof. A few chickens ran across the courtyard between the house and the shed.

During the pilgrimage, Milo had become confident of approaching strangers whenever he needed a meal or a place to spend the night. The cardinal rule of this dependency was to receive whatever you got with good grace. "Some hard cheese and a chunk of bread would taste pretty good right now," Milo told Bori, shaping his appetite's expectations to match his economic impression of the area.

"Would a saucer of milk be too much to expect?" Bori added to Milo's wish list.

When a woman came out of the shed, following the flutter of chickens, Milo called out to her. Her head was covered with a scarf, and she carried a pail, giving him encouragement that Bori's wish for milk might come true.

"Good day!" he called. "Does this road lead to Inverdissen?"

The woman stopped and stared at him without setting down her pail. Milo waited a moment, expecting an answer to his question, and then an invitation to sit down out of the sun and an offer of cool spring water or even fresh milk, if that was what she had in the pail. Instead all he got was a suspicious look.

Seeking to break the impasse, he followed up his first question with a second. "Is Inverdissen a long ways yet?"

The only answer she gave was to scamper the rest of the way across the courtyard and into the dark door of the farmhouse. She slammed the door behind her.

"I guess we'll have to wait for that saucer of milk," Bori commented.

"Maybe being an ordinary traveler doesn't entitle us to the same sort of hospitality that being a pilgrim does," Milo observed. "Bori, if everybody here is this unfriendly, then we're in trouble."

In his pocket, Milo knew, was not a single kuzurian, if that was the currency here. Without the ability to be generous, he was no better off than the homeless people he saw in the streets back in his town. He and Bori had no choice but to move on. Milo smarted a little from his humiliation. Being rejected like that made him feel like a beggar, a feeling he'd never had as a pilgrim.

It was well after noon when, hot and parched, they passed an orchard. The trees were small and gnarled, but the fruit on their limbs looked tempting after a diet of crackers. He stopped, looked one way and then the other, and, seeing no one, slipped off the pack and hopped up onto the dry-stacked rock wall in order to go over it.

"Hey!" came a shout. "What do you think yer doin'!"

A man brandishing a hoe appeared from among the trees. Milo jumped down just before the first stone whacked into the rock wall he was on. He grabbed his pack and started to run. Bori, who had hopped out of the pack when Milo put it down, bounded along beside him as a puff of dust in the road just ahead of them announced the arrival of the second stone.

By the third stone, they were almost out of range, but they kept on running anyway. When Milo felt safe, he stopped to catch his breath and get Bori back into the pack before slinging it onto his back. "Guess we can't expect much hospitality out here in the countryside," he said, heart and hopes sinking. "Maybe it'll be different in town."

On they trudged. As they turned a bend in the road, they saw some sort of cart rolling slowly along up ahead. Simultaneously they heard it: a tinkle, clatter, rattle-clunk. Despite the heat and Milo's weariness, he picked up his pace out of curiosity to see what this odd conveyance might be. Coming nearer he saw a high, two-wheeled green wagon that looked like a cottage on wheels. It clunked and creaked as the wheels turned on their single axle, and the pots and pans hanging underneath provided the musical accompaniment. The little house had a door in the back with steps that hung suspended partway to the ground.

An RV with no engine, Milo thought. Instead of a motor, two large bovines pulled it, and driving them, sitting high up on the box at the front, was a man. Milo couldn't see him very well from behind, but he could hear him singing. A deep and happy-sounding voice, singing as if the rattle/clank/clunk of his cart were all the accompaniment he needed.

Milo pressed on to pass around the cart until he could see the face of the driver perched up on the seat. He wore a battered felt hat, and his full beard was grizzled. He wore a tan coat, ragged at the collar and the sleeves, over a red shirt, baggy black pants, and deeply scuffed boots. He held a whip in one hand as if it were a badge of his status as the driver.

Two enormous oxen plodded along in their traces, pulling the cart as if its weight meant nothing to them. Flies swarmed their muzzles and their rumps, and the animals seemed completely absorbed in their pleasant bovine boredom and the singing of the man who sat behind them.

The man didn't seem to notice Milo until he pulled slightly ahead of the wagon. "Hello!" Milo called. The man stopped singing and looked down. "Good day!" Milo added.

"And a good day to you, too!" the man called back as if this were the first greeting he'd ever heard.

"Does this road lead to Inverdissen?" Milo inquired.

"Indeed it do! Where would yuh be hopin' it would lead?"

"Inverdissen is good," Milo replied. "Is it far? Inverdissen, I mean."

"Oh, far 'nuf, I spose, but not too far if yuh like a nice walk. Or might yuh be carin' for a lift?"

That was just the sort of invitation Milo was hoping for. He unslung his pack as the man reached down for it, and up it went, Bori and all. Milo grabbed the rungs of the ladder to the box, and climbed up without the cart ever changing its ponderous progress. The man scooted over on the seat to accommodate Milo and the pack as Bori hopped out of the pack and jumped onto the roof of the house just behind the man's shoulder.

"That's Bori," Milo said in introduction. "Boriboreau. And I'm Milo."

"Milo, then. Glad to make yer acquaintance." He offered his hand and he continued his introduction as they shook. "I'm Einter. And this one here"—he flicked the whip out toward the rear end of the ox on the left without touching him—"is Senster. That one's"—and he flicked toward the one on the right—"Dexter. They're brothers, but yuh wouldn't know it by lookin' at 'em."

Milo thought they looked identical except that the one named Senster was white and Dexter was black.

"An' what would be bringin' a young traveler such as yerself to Inverdissen, if yuh don't mind my pokin' inta yer business?"

Actually, Milo wasn't eager to reveal those details. "Oh, just on the suggestion of a friend of mine," he said, wishing to keep a long story short. "Do you"—he continued quickly, trying to head off more questions of this sort—"travel this way often?"

"Often, dependin' on how yuh look at it," Einter replied good-naturedly. "As yuh can see, I'm a tinker, an' my travels take me on the roads. I travel over a regular circuit, so I comes down this way, oh, 'bout twice a year."

"A tinker?" Milo asked, having never met one before. "Like...you fix pots and pans?"

"That an' other things made of metal. An' I trade in 'em, too. It's a livin' and lets me breathe the good country air. What trade would you be a'followin'?"

"Ahh..." Milo stalled. "I went on the pilgrimage, and now that it's over, I thought I'd see some of the world before I settle down."

Einter nodded sagaciously. Apparently Milo had offered a plausible answer. "You're still a young feller, so it's a good time to be a'wanderin'. I was like that when I was a striplin'. Never felt right sittin' still fer long. Reckon as how I still feel that way, happy on my wagon with them two fellers fer company"—he gestured toward the oxen—"an' always curious 'bout what's around the next bend in the road."

He glanced at Milo before continuing. "But I wouldn't of pegged yuh fer no vagabond. More of a student type. Reminds me of somebody with a purpose, even if yuh haven't got it nailed down yet. I would've guessed you was on yer way down to the university in Inverdissen. It's sposed to be a crackerjack one, yuh know."

"No, I didn't know that," Milo answered. "I don't know much of anything about Inverdissen, except my friend said that it lay down this road."

"Well, I'm told that if a person wants t' know a thing or two, 'specially 'bout the Old Times, Inverdissen's the place to go. Got the biggest, oldest library what is."

Milo was getting a little uncomfortable with the way this conversation was moving. This man either knew a lot about him already—how could he?—or he was far shrewder than his simple looks and mannerisms revealed.

"I knowed a fellar onct," Einter said, gazing off toward the place where the road met the horizon, "what spent some time down in Inverdissen. Trainin' slinger players down there—you wouldn't be a slinger player, would yuh? No? I thought not. Anyway, we got to be good friends. We was much younger then—older than you are now but younger than I am now—and we liked to do that carousin' around together. Not that I'm suggestin' yuh ought to try that out. That's bad business, an' now I'm wiser than I was back then. My words to young fellers like yerself would be to stay away from that sort of life. Anyway, we was good friends. Wonder where ol' Savoy is off to these days. He suffers from feet as itchy as mine."

This really rocked Milo. He didn't know what to say.

Apparently, he didn't need to say a thing, because Einter read it off his face.

"Got word from ol' Savoy just the other day. Said he was sendin' a young feller Inverdissen way, an' wondered if I might be on the lookout for him. Said he had a big gray cat." Einter was patting Bori, who sat on the bench between them. Milo glanced at the cat. Bori appeared to be oblivious to the conversation while enjoying Einter's pats. But he had one ear cocked toward Milo, as if giving him a signal. Milo didn't know how to read Bori's message, if it was a message, so he kept quiet. Einter continued.

"Ol' Savoy said I should look after that young feller an' see that he stayed out of trouble. Said there was good reason to watch after him, though he didn't say what the trouble might be, an' I'm not a feller to be sticken' my nose into other folk's business. Savoy did say I was to see that the young pup got matched up with another ol' friend of ours, ol' Samuel. He's down at the library in Inverdissen."

Milo's composure was now in tatters. How could this man know all that? How could Savoy have gotten the information to Einter, and if it wasn't from Savoy, how could Einter know all these details that Savoy had given him with no one else within earshot?

The cart was drawing near to a farmstead, announcing its arrival with its clink/rattle/groan. People came out to meet it: several kids of different ages, a younger and an older man, and three women wearing aprons and headscarves. They all welcomed Einter warmly.

For his part, Einter hailed them all by name, even the kids. The younger man took Senster's halter and guided the oxen to a halt. Einter rose stiffly from his seat and climbed down from the bench at the bidding of the older woman. He introduced Milo and Bori, and they were welcomed with cool lemonade for Milo and Einter, and a saucer of fresh milk for Bori.

"Friendlier than folks from earlier," Milo commented to Bori.

"They's friendly enough in these parts when they knows who yuh are, or who yer with," Einter put in, having overheard Milo's comment. "Tend to be just a mite suspicious of strangers, though."

The man who had unhitched the team of oxen led them away to a watering trough while the rest of the people gathered in the shade of an arbor. Soon a table was set with clay mugs and a pitcher, the pitcher damp with condensation. There were olives and bread, goat cheese, and a plate of plums. Einter sipped his drink between answering questions or commenting on bits of news. The women brought out pots that needed fixing and the men arranged buckets with holes to plug and tools to be sharpened.

After finishing his lemonade and gossip, Einter got up from the table and rubbed his large, hard hands together.

"Wup! Time to get some work done. Want to come along an' help me with my setup, Milo?"

For the next hour, Einter worked with easy dispatch. Milo marveled at how efficiently he handled the repairs, talking the whole time as if his attention were in the conversation, but with dexterity in his hands that seemed to defy their size. He completed repairs so smoothly that his skill seemed magical. When he finished, coins changed hands and the oxen, still chewing fodder, were re-hitched. Milo helped Einter stow his tools in the cart. Bori, who had made friends with a lady cat, dashed up to the driver's box and onto the roof of the cabin in three quick bounds, showing off for his new acquaintance. The women brought out a basket with fruit, bread, and meat. Einter thanked them and passed what would be their supper up to Milo, who was already on the box. Einter wished the family a farewell as he climbed up himself. Snapping his whip over the backs of the two oxen without touching them, he called out "Whoop!" to urge the oxen to move into a slow, amiable stroll.

"Good business, nice folks," Einter commented as the cart swung onto the road.

Maybe it was the heat, his full stomach, the rocking of the cart, or the lumbering cadence of the oxen that made Milo sleepy. He fought the stupor, but his eyes glazed over and his lids took on a will of their own. He flopped this way and then that, struggling not to fall off the box. He didn't know how long this battle with the sandman went on, or if he actually lost the struggle and his consciousness, but a cessation of motion woke him up. The cart was standing still, and the oxen were swaying and slinging their tails at the flies. They were under some huge willow trees beside a bright, friendly river.

"Good place for a camp," Einter announced as he uncramped himself before he tried to climb down.

Bori was well ahead, jumping onto the sandy bank, tail in a playful arch to bat at a fuzzy seedpod before dashing off. Senster and Dexter stood in patient, swaying repose, waiting for Einter to unhitch them and lead them into the clear water for a deep, long drink.

After the oxen had been watered and staked out to chew grass in the adjacent meadow, Einter and Milo unloaded the gear for their camp and set it up, and then enjoyed the simple supper that Einter prepared from the provisions the farmers had given them. Then Einter and Milo rested in the deepening twilight. They watched the dancing embers of the dying fire that had heated their supper, and eased into relaxed conversation, Einter picking his teeth with a twig.

After idle talk about the farm they'd visited that afternoon, and other farms that Einter knew from his circuit, Einter asked Milo, "How did yuh come to be in the Magical Scavenger Hunt?"

Since he hadn't said a word about the Hunt to Einter, Milo was taken aback by the tinker's inquiries about his affairs.

"For a person who likes to keep out of other people's business," Milo blurted, "you seem to know an awful lot about mine."

Einter shrugged as if it were a matter of common knowledge, and picked his teeth again before answering. "Savoy thought I ought to know what I needed to know if I was to look after you proper."

"How did he tell you all that?"

Einter shrugged again. "Ol' Savoy must think pretty good of yuh to have clued me about yuh. We has our own way of keepin' in touch. He wanted yuh to get all the help yuh need for whatever it is yuh need to get done."

"And what would that be?" Milo wanted to find out just how much this traveling stranger knew about him, and was just a little piqued about what he knew already.

Einter picked at an especially difficult tooth. "Reckon you got to know that yerself. I'm to help yuh find it out. Somethin' to do with ol' Samuel down there at the library in Inverdissen, I reckon. That, an' to make sure yuh don't go hungry tryin' to get there."

Milo, glad to have his stomach filled, decided to leave it there, at least for the time being. "What can you tell me about Inverdissen and the library?" he asked, deciding a less personal subject was in order. Besides, it was a topic he needed information about.

"Well, Inverdissen's all about the university what's there. It's the place where the bards an' the scholars want to go to learn the deep stuff. All the priests an' lawyers, them what holds high office in the government, the teachers an' the scribes, an' just about anybody that needs the sort of education to do what they do. Even yer wizards and yer mages is goin' to visit the university in Inverdissen. An' there's reason for it, 'cause that's where the library is. That library's been there just about as long as dirt, so that's where everything is. The story I got from my pap, what he got from his pap, what came to him by way of his pap—which would be my great granpappy, what he got from his great granpappy...well, see, back then my family wasn't tinkers like I am now. They was masons, an' it was my great, great (Einter counted it out on his fingers) great, great granpappy who built the tower of what's nowadays the main library. There was a library back then, too, but the librarian of Inverdissen at that time wanted a new building for all the books they was gettin'. An' he wanted a scriptorium for the scholars. My pap told me that his pap told him"— Milo sort of zoned out while Einter went through his genealogical line for the second time, until Einter got to the next portion of his story—"that the library's got books in there so old that there' nobody left what can read 'em. That's where our friend Samuel comes in. See, Samuel's special on old languages. Why, back in our carousin' days, me an' Savoy an' ol' Samuel would hang on a real snorter, and there'd be Samuel a'cussin' out some poor hitch 'n' snitch in some tongue what hadn't been heard in a regular pub since the time of Abracadabracus's granpappy. Me an' ol' Savoy knowed that when Samuel started in like that, it was time to haul him off, 'cause sure as dirt the hitch 'n' snitch he was cussin' was gonna take offense, even if he didn't have no more than blue sky what it was Samuel was callin' him. There'd be trouble, an' the constable would come, an'...well, it'd get complicated."

"So, Samuel can speak the old languages that nobody else knows?" Milo asked, wanting to keep the conversation on track.

"Yep."

By now, Milo was feeling decidedly less anxious about Einter knowing his business, or at least some of it, and about his participation in the Magical Scavenger Hunt. In fact, it was a relief to know somebody that he might be able to think of as a friend in this place where he knew not another soul. He dug around in his rucksack until he found the flat piece of slate with the markings he'd copied from the cross.

"I came across these markings," he told Einter, showing him the slip of stone. "I think it may help me figure out the next clue in the Hunt."

Einter looked at the piece of slate in the firelight, then passed it back to Milo."We'll jest have to ask Samuel. Still, there's another side to all this. See, some of that old stuff's been forgotten so's there's nobody left what understands it even if it *can* be read. I never seen letterin' like this, what suggests it just might be that sort of stuff. Samuel will know. If Savoy recommends yuh to Samuel, I'll back yuh, too. That should convince him to help yuh out, even if it's some of that secret stuff."

The two of them rolled themselves into their blankets soon after that. Bori was off tomcatting at the next farmstead as the stars wove their patterns across the firmament above, wheeling their way to bring on the next dawn.

11

What Was in the Cards

They reached Inverdissen shortly before noon, the first place Milo had seen that could really be called a city. It stood behind a wall, like the kind that a castle would have, with towers over its gates. The houses, like the ones in Kingdom of Odalese, were built right up together with common walls, but they seemed bigger and there were more streets crowded with shops and shoppers. The street was wide enough to accommodate Einter's oxen and his cart, although it might have required some tricky driving had they met a similar cart coming the other way. Senster and Dexter plodded forward into the crowds with no more perturbation than they showed for the usual swarms of flies that surrounded their muzzles.

It was clear that the oxen knew the way, because they turned off the main road into a cross street without direction from Einter, and then again. They stopped on their own before a tall double-hung gate and Einter got down to open it and lead the brothers through a tunnel-like passage into a courtyard lined with three-stories of windows. Once inside, Einter took the two out of their yokes.

"This'll be where we're stayin'," Einter told Milo. "Belongs to a lady friend of mine. Help me see to the boys, an' then we'll clean up a bit ourselves. After a spell, when it's cooler, we'll go on down to the inner city t' find Samuel." Just then, the lady of the house came out and Einter swept her up in his bear-like arms to twirl her around.

Einter was big and stocky, and this woman was small and compact, of an age to place her in Einter's generation. Her costume was a swirl of red, yellow, and brown, her bare arms and face were the hue of coffee-with-cream, and the yellow-and-red headscarf was tied on so snuggly that it seemed part of her head. Gold bracelets and bangles adorned her arms, rings her fingers, and bright glass beads hung in strands around her neck. Big gold hoops peeking out from under the headscarf gave her a gypsy look. When he put her down again, she turned on Milo.

"An' who may be this young pup?" she demanded.

"Milo," Einter told her, then turned Milo's way. "Milo, this would be the Dame Reyna Renee."

She reached a hand out. Milo couldn't say if it was to be kissed or to be shaken. Feeling more familiar with the hand-shaking form of greeting, he reached out his, but just as he touched hers, she drew a card, apparently from his palm, and held it up to study it quickly.

"Ah!" she said, as if the card was more an introduction than Einter's had been. "An' 'ow did you come by him?" she asked Einter.

"Savoy sent him," Einter replied.

"Ahh! That explains this," she continued, waving the card in her hand. " 'The Wanderer.' It iz also known by some by another name: 'The Fool'."

Milo wasn't sure what she meant by this, but it made him uncomfortable to guess, by the way she locked her eye on him.

"Dame Renee would be what yuh would be callin' a soothsayer," Einter explained. "She's the Mistress of the Cards, that's for sure. She can finagle the future out of that deck of hers like nobody I ever seen, nor my Pappy nor his pap before him. I bet she could tell yuh what yer up to better than you could say yerself. Why, I bet she could tell yuh about that odd writin' of yurn as good as ol' Samuel, or better."

He stopped, clearly struck with the brilliance of this realization. "Yuh know, that itn't a bad idea; no sir! not a'tall!"

Milo didn't feel as overwhelmed with the idea as Einter.

Dame Renee, a keen observer, read him as well as one of her cards. "Perhaps. But that can come in another time. Just now I think a wash and something to eat, followed by the afternoon sleep would be more agreeable."

Milo thought that was it.

"But wait!" she cried, pulling them up. "It's not done! There's another card to be read and a reading to be recognized. Who iz this?" she demanded, pointing to Bori, who was sitting patiently at Milo's foot.

"Oh, that's Bori," Milo answered. "Boriboreau."

"Ahh! 'The Messenger!'" she announced, flicking a card out from somewhere, using her first and middle finger, like an accomplished Vegas dealer. It had the ornate picture in full color of a wing-footed man releasing a dove with one hand and holding out four cards with the other.

"It...doesn't much look like him," Milo ventured.

"Oh, the cards, they do not work that way," she said.

"What she means," Einter explained, "is that the card what she just showed stands for the way Renee saw the future this morning, which is now."

"Every morning," she told Milo, "I lay out the cards to see what they may tell me about the day. And then I discover what they told me as the day unfolds."

"Is that helpful?" Milo asked in innocence.

"It depends," Dame Renee answered. "But now, you two wash the grime of the road away; then we'll have lunch. From the smell, I can't tell you two from Senster and Dexter."

"I hope there's a saucer of milk for me," Bori commented as he sat beside the basin where Milo washed his face and hands in his best effort to get cleaned up. Einter had gone somewhere else to do his hygiene.

"What do you think of that 'Messenger' card?" Milo asked Bori as he lathered his hands. "Have you checked your paws for wings lately?"

"Don't laugh," Bori advised. "Maybe I will. Maybe it just hasn't happened yet. After all, she foretells the future, doesn't she? I could become something like Ali's horse."

"You aren't big enough for me to ride," Milo pointed out.

"No, but think of the birds I could catch..."

Milo preferred not to.

They had lunch with Dame Renee and Einter. Not only did Bori get his milk, but he had some smoked fish as well, and then they all retired for the midday nap.

Milo was awake when he heard Einter out in the courtyard, whistling as he fiddled with his cart and curried his oxen. Bori was curled in deep sleep. Milo went out to see Einter.

Dexter was standing calmly, tied to one wheel of the cart, chewing his cud and stringing drool like the complacent bovine that he was. Einter brushed the muck and tangles from his huge sides and flanks.

"Dame Renee don't know all that much about where yuh been," Einter told Milo as he came up, 'but she probably knows more about where yer goin' than you do. Yuh might think yuh know and yuh might not, but she's got one uncanny ability to see what's t' come."

"Sorry," Milo apologized. He didn't want for his earlier comment about doubt in the cards to be an insult.

"It's all right. I have to see proven what I'm to believe, too. An' she just don't see the future the same way you or I look at it. Well, when we looks about us at this courtyard, we sees the courtyard. What she sees is the shape of things an' how they be changin'."

"How can she do that from those cards?"

"Hard to say. Part natural talent, I guess, and part havin' an affinity for the cards. She got it from her Ma, and her Ma got it from her ma before her, an' her ma before her...an' so on. Them cards was made way back. Back, long ago when the folks what thunk 'em up had the ability to make things like that. Which, for the most part, we don't. Only some people what still has the talent an' the skill to use 'em."

"When do we look for Samuel?" Milo asked, changing the subject.

"Oh, I reckon we'd best wait till after the afternoon pause. He's a grouchy so-n-so if yuh wakes 'em up."

Milo took over doing Dexter's legs while Einter led Senster out to hitch him to the other wheel of the cart.

He started in on Senster's broad back. "I took the liberty of askin' Renee to find yuh a proper clean outfit. No offense, but yuh look like yuh been livin' in them clothes for a spell."

"I have," Milo replied, looking at what he was wearing. He thought it interesting how used he had become to wearing the same clothes all the time, with very little chance to wash them or even himself. Another way his life now was unimaginable to the one he'd always had before. "I don't think I want new clothes," he told Einter. "I like these."

"Be that as it may, an' all," Einter said, "they needs cleanin'. In the meantime, yuh can't go through the streets of Inverdissen the way yuh was borned into the world. So Renee's goin' to give yuh somethin' proper like."

That settled, and as soon as the oxen had been taken care of, Einter took Milo to a big stone trough in a side building. The water wasn't warm and the soap wasn't scented, but it did the job. Milo had to think with nostalgia to the luxury of his bath at Crane Castle, and he blushed a little just thinking about Erisa. The way her lips had felt when she passed on the taste of wisdom....

He was still thinking about that wisdom as he walked with Einter and Bori through Inverdissen's streets, dressed in the clean clothes that Dame Renee had provided. They were okay. Trousers, sandals, loose shirt, and a tunic over that. Especially the tunic: a bright blue, sleeveless, with silver clasps instead of buttons. Nothing for the roads like the gear that Ayuthaya had given him, but okay for the streets of the city. Renee and Einter had both assured him he looked handsome in it, and he agreed, secretly of course.

The inner city of Inverdissen was magnificent. Nothing in ancient Rome could have been more imposing. The broad avenues were tree-lined and the buildings were monumental, as if they had been built for a race twice as tall as mortals were now. Grand was the thing. Milo was impressed even before they reached the university, and, at its center, the library.

The library's tower soared above everything else and the blue enameled dome glistened the same blue as the sky above the main body of the building, itself so high that the pigeons wheeling around it looked like gnats.

"They keep a light burnin' way up there in the tower for the ships out at sea. It signals 'em where the city is exactly as they come up over the curve of the horizon."

Something in that statement caught Milo's attention. "You mean... the world's round?"

"Why, of course the world's round!" Einter answered in indignation. "What would it be otherwise, square? Everyone knows that!"

Milo had assumed that the people in this world would picture the earth as flat. It was an assumption that went with not having electricity or gasoline engines. "Sure, you're right," he answered in embarrassment for misjudging Einter's and this world's sophistication. "I know the earth's a globe, but it's so big that you could think of it as flat."

"Well, just you think for a minute. If it was flat, then it'd have to have edges somewhere, wouldn't it? If you was to go in one direction yuh'd have to reach the edge. Either that or the world would just go on forever. But it don't! Go in a straight line an' eventually, yeh'll come back to the place yuh started. Therefore"—he said with a triumphant flourish, "the world has to be round."

He continued, telling Milo how maps were made and how problematic it is to represent them on a flat page of paper that couldn't take into perspective the curvature of the earth's sphere. He explained how it wasn't noticeable for a smaller area, but how it distorted the perspective when trying to represent the entire sphere. Milo was surprised at how knowledgeable Einter was on the topic. Maybe he wasn't as simple and uneducated as he let on.

By now they were mounting the flight of steps to the library's huge bronze doors, decorated with scenes in relief from events that meant nothing to Milo. Passing through into the marbled vastness of the foyer, Milo stopped. Gilded statuary mounted the walls, story after story, like gods. Galleries lined with books radiated away from each of these levels, sort of like at the Library of Congress, which Milo had visited with his fifth grade class, only bigger.

Instead of entering any of these wings, however, Einter steered him through a side door, down a narrow stairway, and into a much tighter, musty-smelling environment. This region was also stuffed full of books, but more like a delapidated used bookstore than the Library of Congress. They turned one way, then another, down narrow, low-ceilinged passages, until Milo had no idea where he was.

"Samuel's study is down here someplace," Einter explained, and mumbled under his breath, "I'll be getting' to it directly." After one more turn, he stopped outside an open door. Inside was a study crammed with books, piles of them, with only narrow little trails between the stacks. The room was dim, lit by a single lamp behind mounds of books atop what supposedly was a desk or worktable.

"Samuel? Yer in there?" Einter called into the room.

"Uhm...?" came a reply, but with such effort that it sounded like whoever had made it might be in the process of being crushed by a topple of heavy, leather-bound books.

Bori went in first, carefully, looking for possible mice as he penetrated the room. Einter went next, easing his way along to avoid tipping over any of the piles. Milo followed, recalling the banshee librarian in The Kingdom of Odalese.

What they found was different. Samuel, as Einter soon confirmed, was unlike anyone Milo had ever met. The first thing he noticed was Samuel's huge eyes which appeared to be glaring, oversized disks until Milo saw that he was wearing thick glasses. But the horns really were his: two of them, thick and mounted where they should be, on his forehead. His features were also wrong, out of kilter as if they had been assembled out of wood scraps, knot holes, twisted roots, and oak galls. His thin, lank hair reminded Milo of Spanish moss more than ordinary hair or even hair that has been neither washed or combed in a long time. Then, there was the smell. Barnyard with an extra punch of something reminiscent of mushrooms.

"Samuel! Yuh ol' bas...uh, feller!" Einter enthused. "How yer be?"

The figure at the table stood, his face cracking open into a gap-toothed grin, and Einter threw his arm around his old friend to pound him on the back.

Samuel was no taller than Milo. Shorter, actually, but substantial, like a tree stump. He was dressed in a coat and trousers that reminded Milo of bark.

The friends tossed familiarities back and forth in a very uncouth fashion for a couple of minutes until Einter turned to introduce Milo and Bori. Samuel's hand was as hard and as rough as a piece of wood, although it moved perfectly well to accommodate Milo's. Bori hopped up onto the table to stand on the open book that Samuel had been studying, waving his tail in an offering of friendship. Samuel complied, stroking Bori's head and chucking him around the ears.

"There's a fine cat," Samuel exclaimed. "Might have an opening for a good mouser if he wants to stay on."

"Sorry," Milo said. "I can't do without him. He's my Guide."

After some round-about conversation in which Einter explained who Milo was, and how Savoy had sent him, he got around to what it was Milo needed from Samuel. Milo took out the piece of slate with the symbols scratched on it. "Is this writing?" Milo asked.

Samuel took it and turned it this way and that. "Hmm..." he said. "Where'd you get this?"

Milo didn't really want to tell, so he tried a route more circular than direct. "I...came across it. Do you know about the Magical Scavenger Hunt? You do? Well, you see, I'm a contestant, and I'm looking for my next clue, and"—

Samuel broke in. "You're a wizard?" he asked in obvious disbelief.

"No, but I *am* a contestant. So when I came across this, I thought it might tell me about finding my next clue, but I have no idea what it says."

"That's not odd. This script—if it is a script—hasn't been used or read by anyone since..." Samuel broke off. "Is this a copy? Because it can't be original."

Milo didn't want to tell that, either, and he sure couldn't show Samuel, or anyone else, the source of the writing, but he was having a hard time coming up with a plausible tale on the spur of the moment. "I'd rather not say, if you'll pardon me. There are circumstances...it may be dangerous for you or anybody else to know where I got it. I know it's dangerous to me. That's part of the reason I really need to know what it means. The fewer people who know about it, the better. Savoy said I could trust you, and that you should help me as a favor to him. He said to tell you that. He said—"

"I see," Samuel said, breaking him off. "As much as I'd like to know where you got this, I won't insist. I will tell you why I'd like to know, though. I think this is a very ancient script. So ancient, in fact, that it's the grandfather of the oldest known writing. The language it represents is the ancestor of the oldest language that any scholar today can decipher. Luckily, I am that scholar. I can't read it, but if you'll give me some time,

I may be able to tease out the meaning. It's written, you see, in symbolic ideograms. That means that this script isn't made up of letters that correspond to the sounds of a language, so they aren't alphabetical. The figures represent abstract pictures suggesting ideas and concepts instead of linguistic words, so in theory, it *could* be read without knowing the language it was created in. The hard part is to identify the meanings that the author used these symbols to refer to, since even if I can recognize the patterns of the ideograms, I may not be able to interpret the correct concepts the author intended. The huge void between his time and our own makes his cultural understanding alien to the way we think about things. I'm an antiquarian, but this makes even the earliest culture I know seem almost recent."

That sounded bad. Milo didn't have much choice, though, but to let Samuel have a go at it and hope for something meaningful to come out. When they were back in the street, Milo just had to ask this question: "What sort of...person is Samuel, anyway?"

"Oh, he's like me brother, but of course he idn't, 'cause he's an Ogma. My Pap found him under a cabbage leaf when he was but a wee little thing. Pap knowed right off he was an Ogma, an' left him there a spell, hopin' his mum would come back for him, but when she didn't, he had no choice but to bring him back to the house. So Samuel grew up like me brother, only Samuel always had an intellectual bent where's I was dull when it came to sittin' still through lessons an' all. Samuel got into the university an' I got an apprenticeship with a tinker. I don' know how he can sit down there in the bowels of the earth, surrounded by all them dusty, smelly books all the time, but then he's an Ogma."

"Why? What *is* an Ogma?"

"They's woodfolk. Very shy. Keeps t' theyselves, mostly. Us humans rarely, if ever, even sees 'em, even when they's our neighbors."

"How do they live?"

"Like I said, they's woodfolk. They takes care of the natural countryside an' live so close with it, they's like a part of it. They's so much a part, that yeh kin look straight at 'em an' never see 'em. Samuel, of course, since he growed up like part of our family is more like us. But he's still Ogma and looks like 'em. He went off for a spell with 'em once, but then he came back. Guess he preferred the academic life over the sun, the rain, an' huddlin' under some big ol' oak instead of in a house."

Milo changed the subject. "Do you think he can translate the writing I gave him?"

Einter shrugged. "If anybody can, he can. He speaks—oh, I don't know—dozens of languages, I guess, an' half of 'em nobody speaks at all no more."

So Milo waited. While he waited, he spent time with the only people he knew: Einter and Dame Renee. Gradually, he realized that Dame Renee had picked out one hint after the other during their conversations, and soon had a fair idea of what Milo was doing.

They were drinking tea and nibbling cakes as they talked one afternoon. "So you started out as a contestant in the Magical Scavenger Hunt, but there seems to be more to it than that. Some sort of danger."

Milo was perturbed that she had come so close to his private business.

She continued. "And the thing you have Samuel working on has to do with the danger as well as the Hunt."

"I don't want to talk about it," Milo told her. But he liked her. She had been very good to him and to Bori and he didn't want to seem ungrateful. So he added, "It's...well, the less you know, the safer for you."

Einter put in. He told Renee, "That's what he said when Samuel asked into it. From the message from Savoy askin' to help the boy out, I got the idea that Savoy thought so, too."

"Oh, the cards told me the same," Dame Renee said, flipping one into view. It had a picture of a stealthy man dressed in black slipping around the corner of a house in a street at night. "Thief in the Night," she said, naming the card. "The card of secrecy, doubt, and the unknown." She put the card down on the table. "But then there's this—" snapping down a second card.

Milo couldn't see where she had her deck, although he knew she always had it with her. The card she'd shown had a picture of a king with armor, a drawn sword set point down before him, a shield behind him and banners whipping in the breeze to the right and left.

"Noble Purpose," she said. "The card of service and honorable intentions. It indicates a high level of idealism, but it can lead to disaster if not balanced with practicality."

She nudged it into a position alongside the first card and produced a third one to lay across the first two. One by one, she put down twelve cards on the table, telling the face meaning of each one as she did so. "And now, the thirteenth."

It was one Milo had seen before, the first one she'd ever shown him, 'The Wanderer.'

"That's the card that identifies you, at least within this spread," she explained. Milo couldn't tell if the cards had come up randomly, or if she had sorted them to come out that way. "These other cards," she said, pointing out the ones that already lay in the pattern she had created, "describe the actions and relationships between the major cards, like your Wanderer, or The Thief. They operate the way verbs connect nouns in a sentence to produce a statement."

She pointed out the card with three cups in its picture, explaining that cups have the energy of water. Stars showed fire, stones were earth energy, and spirals gave air.

"Now I can tell you about your quest," she said. "Maybe not the details, but I can outline the path you'll encounter. You must follow a way that takes you into a place of shadows, and the shadows will tell you the way to a place suspended between the underworld and the heavens. The heavens will teach you what you must know to enter the underworld, and still return. You *do* want to return, don't you?"

A cold shudder accompanied that idea. Milo indicated that he did.

"Stay true to your teachers and you shall." She tapped him on the chest. "Your heart. That's the card of Noble Purpose. Don't forget it."

"Thank you," Milo told her, unsure still about what practical advice he'd just received. "I'm really not sure I understand it all."

"Of course you don't! If you did, it wouldn't be a quest! Stay with this"—she tapped the card with the king—"and you'll find your way. The Way will show you your purpose. After Samuel translates your inscription, you must seek the place of shadows. It won't be long."

Indeed it wasn't. That very evening, Samuel came to Dame Renee's.

"I believe I have it," he announced with a smug look on his gnarled face. "It's an ingenuous cryptograph, but when translated into modern parlance, it could go something like this:

The dragon's cross must hold the door
Of that which can't be opened;
The stone womb is the sacred tor
That heals the bond that's broken.
A crossroad is an open door
That's closed until you take it;
An opened tomb lies just before
The choice before you make it.

It's an incantation, I think."

"What does it mean?" Milo asked, perplexed.

"I have no idea," Samuel said. "Maybe I didn't get it right. It could be:

A crossroad is an open door
That's closed until you take it;
An opened tomb lies just before

...and then something about repairing. It's not all that clear. Very intriguing. Are you sure you can't tell me where you came across it? That might help make its meaning more precise."

Milo assured him that he couldn't offer more information, and thanked him for what he had done. After that, Dame Renee invited Samuel to stay for dinner, and they talked about things that old friends talk about until late at night. The food was delicious, though Samuel's odd scent put Milo somewhat off his appetite, and the yarns the three adults entertained themselves with were engaging, making Milo rather envious of the many adventures their lives had had.

That night, Milo discussed the situation with Bori. Bori said, "I think it's time we moved on. You have what you came here for."

"But where? I don't know which way to go."

"You never have. Why does that bother you now?" Bori pointed out.

"Do you know where this shadow place is that Dame Renee read from the cards?"

"No, but it's your quest. I'm just along to help out. Do what everybody's telling you to do. Follow your heart."

$$12$$

Into the Dark

"So...where're yuh headin'?" Einter asked when Milo announced that he would be going soon—the same day, in fact. He made his announcement when he came down for breakfast, dressed in his pilgrimage gear. Dame Renee pressed a small purse of coins into his hand after assuring him that she'd known he would be leaving this morning. It had been in the cards.

Milo answered Einter's question honestly. "I don't know. Down the road, I guess, wherever that takes me."

"Well, if yuh don't have more of an idea than that, why not go along with me for a spell? I hitched up ol' Senster an' Dexter an' mean to be hittin' the road myself. I'm sure the brothers wouldn't mind addin' yer weight to the load an' havin' yer company. Me neither."

With Bori stretched out on top of the box and Einter with the whip slack in his hands, Milo found himself once more up on the bench, watching Inverdissen fade away into open farm land, and then into wilder country beyond that.

"Where are you headed?" he'd asked Einter as Einter urged the oxen into motion that morning to pull out of Renee's courtyard.

"I take up the circuit down the coast ever year 'bout this time. Couple of days travelin' up an' down the rocks along the water, then I skirts Korrigan Forest an' head on inland into the wheat lands. Flat, wide open country with plenty of farmers watchin' for me to come along. Easy goin' on the boys"—he flicked out his whip over the rumps of his oxen without touching their hides to indicate who he meant—"onct we leave the coast. A couple of days of real work won't hurt 'em after their vacation at Renee's."

It was true. The road worked the rocky coastline up steep hillsides and across the rocky spines of the ridges. Arched stone bridges crossed smaller gullies and noisy, bouncing creeks, or rollercoastered longer spans of linked arches crossing swift-flowing rivers that gushed into the sea. Gulls swirled and yelled as if Einter's cart reminded them of the crabbers' boats that were visible out on the water, bobbing on the long rollers that relentlessly smashed against the rocky coast in high sprays of foam. The clean salt air tousled Milo's hair and stiffened it with the aerosol of salt from the thundering surf.

For the several days this passage took they made a few stops at remote fish camps before leaving the coast and climbing away from the fading sound of the surf. The cries of gulls were replaced by the lonely, hollow croaking calls of ravens and the chirruping of crickets. Low ridges stood along the horizon in shades of blue baffles, turning to dark green as they drew nearer. "Korrigan Forest," Einter announced. "So deep an' thick that nobody much dares to go in. They says it reaches back to the beginnin' of time, from before the Age of Man. A road from the earliest days goes into it. Right up ahead, in fact; see that notch between the hills up there?"

"Why don't people go there?" Milo asked.

"Because the place 's haunted."

"How do you mean, 'haunted'?" Milo asked.

"Shades. Shades of the Old Folk. The folk what live here say that the Ogma use it, but common decent folk stay away. They won't go in there at all, 'cept in broad daylight."

"Shades?" Milo asked. "Like...ghosts?"

Einter shrugged. "Don't know exactly. Ghosts be like the spirits of dead folk, an' I always got the feelin' that Shades was somethin' different. Anyways, they be hostile to human folk. It's said they play tricks on 'em to get 'em lost, an' makes 'em go mad, they does. But not to worry; we go around it, here on the road. The wheat lands start up beyond them distant ridges there, and that's where we're headin'."

Shades. Shadows. Milo wasn't so sure about going into the wheat lands, but he didn't think much of the alternative, either.

They camped at the place where the ancient road broke off from the one Einter was following and plunged into Korrigan Forest. Long ago it had been paved with cobblestones, but now they were uneven and weathered, matted with untrampled grass. Still, the old road showed a clear passage into and under the trees that made an arched tunnel, their tall and ancient limbs sheltering the passage into the gloomy forest. Bori, prowling for voles, called Milo's attention to something at the side of the road, hidden in a tangle of brambles.

When Milo picked his way to the place where Bori called him, he saw the cat sitting on a toppled marker stone. It was etched with lichens, telling its great age, but its shape was unmistakable.

"It's the same shape as the cross on my..." Milo said, touching his shirt where the little sack with the cross hung.

"Thought you might think that was interesting," Bori stated.

"What do you think?" Milo asked him. "Shades—shadows, and now this? Do we go in?"

"Einter doesn't like the place much," Bori observed.

"But if we've got to learn a secret, wouldn't an unknown place be a good place to look?"

"Would going into a dangerous place be sensible?" Bori retorted.

"Yes, if 'dangerous' is already part of everything we've got to do. Besides, I have a feeling about this place. I felt it right away. I think I've got to go here."

"Then I guess we go."

Milo told Einter about his intention while they chewed their dinner.

"If yer plannin' to go there, I suppose I ought to do what I can to give yuh some sort of protection from the shades what haunts the Korrigan." Einter said.

The next morning, Einter took Milo and Bori out into the edges of the forest. "Look," he told Milo as he pointed out a very large, obviously ancient tree. Its trunk was of incredible girth, and its limbs towered over them, spreading out over a huge space. "See the leaves an' the bark? That's an oak. This one's the guardian of the forest, so to speak. Climb up into its limbs an' then introduce yerself to it. Ask it for protection. When yer feels its acceptance, pluck the acorn it offers yuh an' then come on down."

Milo did as he was told. He climbed the trunk, using the rough bark like the stone of a cliff face. The trunk was so thick that he couldn't begin to reach around more than just a little part of its girth. He climbed until he felt the movement of the tree responding to the wind. Looking down he could hardly see the ground below the many thick limbs he had climbed up and around.

What an incredible tree, he thought, wondering how many centuries it had taken to get to such a size. "I'm Milo," he told the tree, admiring the solid feel of it under him, holding him up. "I'd like to go into your forest, if I may."

Leaves rustled on every side, and he felt the ponderous sway of the living wood around him. Not knowing what to expect, he looked around, noticing how the sunlight filtered through the canopy. An ant ran out along the branch he was sitting on. As he watched, he saw it move farther and farther out, and then his glance fastened on an acorn lodged in a crease in the bark. "Is that it?" he asked the tree. "Is that the acorn I can take?"

The tree swayed slightly, and Milo took it for a nod. He had to work himself out on the limb, straddling it like the back of a horse. Carefully he lifted and runched himself forward. It wasn't particularly difficult, but it was an awfully long way above the ground. When he got out to the place where the acorn was he picked it up. "Thank you," he said before working his way back to the main trunk to climb down.

With his feet on firm ground again, he patted the trunk. "Long life to you," he told the tree and then turned to where Bori sat waiting.

"Where's Einter?" he asked the cat.

"He went that way," Bori said, rotating his ears to hear the sounds that were too faint for Milo to catch.

Milo followed as the cat marched through the grasses and weeds that covered the ground beneath the trees. They found Einter beneath another tree, wrapping a red string around two twigs that he had taken from the tree to make a cross.

"This tree's called a rowan," Einter said, handing Milo the little charm he had made. "This little cross will introduce yuh to whatever yuh meet in there. Did yuh get yer acorn?"

Milo showed it to him.

"Put that into yer pocket. It'll keep yuh from getting' lost. Let's see about findin' some other trees to help yuh out."

"How do you know this stuff?" Milo asked.

Einter tapped the side of his nose as if that explained something. "My Pap," he said. "He got it from his pap and his pap before him got from his pap an' so on. We in my family haven't forgot the Old Ways like some. An' these Shades—they'll see that you know somethin' about the Old Way, an' that'll make 'em curious. Then maybe they'll show theyselves to yuh."

"Here!" he said, stopping beside another tree. "This one's an alder." He patted the gnarled trunk and said some quiet words to the tree, then cut a small branch with his knife and began peeling the bark. He used another twig to poke out the soft pith in the center of the finger-sized section of branch, then cut a slot into one end.

"Here," he said. "Blow into it."

Milo did, and to his surprise it made a whistle.

"That's a fairy flute," Einter told him. "Yuh blow that ever so often as yuh walk along. It'll announce yuh to whatever Shades are around."

They moved on to another tree.

"This one's an elm. Take this..." He handed Milo a small flask. "Ask it for its help in findin' the folk yuh want to meet up with. Then pour out a little of the mead in the flask for an offerin'."

Milo did as he was instructed, then thanked the tree and moved along with Einter and Bori.

"Yuh see this tree here?" Einter asked, directing Milo to make note of its details to insure he could recognize its type on his own. "It's a haw-thorn. After yuh been travelin' a while until yer deep into the woods, an' yuh been blowin' on that whistle from time t' time, an' yuh find a whole grove of hawthorn in a bunch, go into 'em an' sit down. Blow the flute to call out the Shades an' wait." He patted the tree like an old friend before they moved on.

"One more," he told Milo. "This one's an elder. Not an *alder*, like the one we made the flute from: an *elder*. Ask it if yuh can take a few twigs, an' cut 'em like so."

Einter indicated how Milo should cut them and weave them into a circlet. "When yuh sit down in that hawthorn thicket, put that on yer head like a crown. It'll let yuh see the Shades when they come. Without it, yuh won't see nothin'. All yuh'd see is motion out of the corner of yer eye, an' they'd be tryin' to trick yuh and get yuh lost an' crazy. When yuh see one of 'em, look 'im straight in the eye an' ask his name. When he tells yuh, then yuh'll have a conversation to ask 'em what yuh want. If he knows, he's bound to tell yuh. But only if yeh've got his name first. He'll lie to yuh if he can. But not if yeh've got his name first. Be sure to ask exactly what it is yuh wants to know. Think about that as yuh travel through t' woods before yuh meet 'im. Rehearse what yer needin' to ask over an' over in yer mind, because he'll answer the question yuh asks, but not necessarily the one yuh mean. Don't worry about keepin' yer secret. He won't be tellin' yer secret to nobody else."

"These...Shades. They're dangerous, aren't they?" Milo asked apprehensively.

"Yep, but not the same way a bear or somthin' like that is danger-ous. Dangerous tricky. Malicious. They hates humans, because people have forgot to respect 'em and the forests they live in. Folks have come to hate anything they can't own, and they can't own the deep forest. They want to cut roads through it, clear land for farms, cut trees for timber or just to burn 'em up to clear 'em away. That destroys the forests an' the homes of the deep forest folk what ye'll be lookin' for."

They returned to Einter's wagon and Milo helped him hitch up Senster and Dexter.

"Well, I best be on my way an' yuh'll be on yers," Einter said, offering Milo his hand to shake. "Been good travelin' with yuh." He gave Bori a couple of pats as the cat lifted his tail high in farewell. "Remember all what Renee told yuh, and what I taught yuh about the trees, an' yeh'll be all right. Take care," and Einter mounted his cart.

Milo wanted to say something to thank Einter for all his help and companionship, but the lump in his throat kept him from saying a thing. Einter flicked his whip and the brothers started off, setting the cart into creaking motion, clanking away to some place beyond Milo's part. Milo just stood there, watching the cart recede as the hole inside him filled with an awful sense of loneliness.

Einter, the cart, and the oxen had vanished—even the sound had faded—before Milo could gather himself again.

"We better be going," he told Bori in a diminished voice.

"I wonder if these Shades we're looking for have saucers of milk?" Bori mused.

13

The Seen and Unseen

The forest ran on and on. There were no breaks in the canopy once Milo and Bori penetrated its depths, and the forest floor lay in gloom. The road, its bed filled in with leaf litter, was only discernable from any other part of the forest floor by a relative absence of trees, leaving an open path to walk along.

Milo's spirits had not improved from the low point of watching Einter's cart fade out of sight. Homesick, lonely, and frightened, he dreaded the arrival of night and tried not to think about what unknowns might be afoot with full darkness.

"I like night time," Bori offered when they stopped and Milo buried himself into his cloak and a nest of leaves. "I'll stand watch." Bori hadn't followed his usual habit of slipping away for a hunt as he usually did come nightfall. "I can see just fine, and hear and smell. I'll let you know if there's anything out there you need to know about."

Somehow, this assurance hardly helped Milo's mood. If there was something out there, what could one cat—even a fairly large one like Bori—do about it? Knowing something was out there would be no better than being afraid that there *might* be.

"Why did I come here," Milo whined, fighting back tears and having second thoughts about facing the forest alone. The choice he'd made by daylight, out in the open under the bright sun and blue sky, seemed to be foolish bravado now that he was alone in the dark.

"You came to look for help," Bori reminded him. "And you're just worried now because it's dark. There's no difference between day and night except you can't see in the dark. A human limitation. Try thinking of yourself as a cat. I can see just fine. Night? Day? Same threat. Think how you felt while it was daytime. You were confident enough then."

"No. I wasn't."

"Okay, so you weren't. But that wasn't because of your surroundings. It was because of how you felt inside. Either way, I'm here and you aren't by yourself."

Milo patted him. It made him feel better, and Bori's purr was worth more than Milo could say. "Come on," he told the cat. "Crawl under the cloak and let's get some sleep."

Milo didn't remember when he went to sleep, but he knew when he woke up, so he knew that he had slept, finally, after listening to what had seemed like hours and hours of sounds out in the darkness. He knew that it was morning, or nearly so, even though it was still as dark as it had been, because the sounds he heard now were of birds twittering and making dawn talk up in the treetops. Bori was snoring. He did that. Milo lay still, trying to sort out the dream he'd been having just before he woke up. He remembered the feeling of swaying. He had been in the oak tree. He also remembered parts of a long conversation. He remembered asking the oak, "I don't know what to ask."

"What do you want to know?" the oak asked back.

Dreaming Milo hadn't noticed that it was strange that the oak talked, because he remembered that was why he was up in the tree: to talk with it. "I need to know what to do with the cross." In the dream he had known it was okay to mention the cross, because the oak already knew all about it.

"Why do you think that the forest folk will know that?" the tree asked.

Milo shrugged. "Because Dame Renee said I was to go to the place of shadows. And because I'm supposed to follow my instincts. This seemed like the right thing to do. What do you think?"

The tree swayed gently. "I think you're right. The forest folk know things like that, because they are very old, at least for legged folk. They've crossed over entirely into the magic realm and since the cross has everything to do with Magic, it's logical that they would know."

"Yeah. I guessed that." Milo realized right then that he *did* know that. "If I can return it to the place where it belongs, it'll heal a rift in the magic realm. So I have to know where to take it."

"Perhaps it isn't quite that simple. Perhaps you should let the cross lead you to the place it needs to go. So if you asked the forest spirit straight out, he could tell you where to take it, but that would be his trick because it isn't as important to take it to that place as it is to find out what the cross needs in order to return to the place it must go."

"What do I ask, then?"

"How about: 'Who knows the source of the cross?' Then you'll know who *can* tell you what you need to know about the cross."

"But how will I know how to find out where that person is?"

"You get three questions," the oak told him. "Did you know that?"

Milo shook his head no, without even wondering how the tree could see that.

"So that's your first question. The next question is: 'Where do I find him?'"

The oak was silent, except for the shush of breeze through its leaves and branches until Milo had absorbed the first two questions. "The last question is more a request, but because you have learned his name, and he has answered your first and second questions, he'll be obliged to comply with the third. This is it: 'Lead me to the place where I can find the one who knows the source of the cross.' Remember—the forest folk are full of tricks, but whatever his answer is, it must be truthful. They know that the truth can be as tricky, depending on how it is given, as a lie. So do what he says. It may be something that makes no sense at all, but if you discard it as complete nonsense, you'll be falling for his trick."

That's all Milo could remember from his dream conversation. There was more, but he couldn't draw it back together.

Bori woke up and stretched. "Time to go?" he asked.

"Yeah. I think so," Milo told him.

They walked all day through the woods, with Milo blowing the flute from time to time. Milo believed it must be a bright and sunny day. Yesterday could have been overcast. The forest didn't seem as dark as it had the day before, although he still couldn't see the sky through the canopy of leaves.

He also noticed motion that hadn't seemed to be there the day before. Each time he turned to look in the direction of the movement, there was nothing to see. By late afternoon, with twilight already settling in beneath the trees, he and Bori came onto a grove of trees like the ones Einter had pointed out to him. "Those are hawthorns, I think," he told Bori.

"Like the ones you're supposed to sit under?" Bori asked.

"Yeah. That's them." He blew the flute and adjusted the little crossed-twig talisman Einter had given him, then put the elder wreath on his head.

They chose a place and Milo sat down with his back against the bole of one of the bigger trees and between the buttresses of two thick, gnarled roots. Having the tree wrapped halfway around him felt comforting without restricting his ability to see. Bori sat at his knee, using his night vision to peer out into the gathering darkness.

As night fell, the motions Milo saw fleetingly from the corners of his eyes increased. "Do you see what's moving around out there?" he whispered to Bori.

"No. Nor do I smell anything that smells any different from the forest," Bori answered. "Every time I look to where something flits, there's nothing there but shadows."

Milo blew the flute. It had one tone only, so he tried making up songs that had only one note. He readjusted the elder-twig crown and then he saw something.

A face. Scowling at him. He also heard whisperings that seemed to call to him, urging him to follow them. Instead of moving away from the shelter of the tree bole, he focused on the peering face.

It was barely discernable in the darkness and could be nothing more than the configuration in the bark of a tree, but then it blinked.

"What's your name?" Milo asked aloud. The whispering suddenly stopped. His own voice sounded over-loud. The scowl on the peering face deepened to a grimace of unspeakable hate and spite.

"What is your name?" Milo repeated.

"Musail!" spat out the reply, like an insult. "Who are you to invade our forest?"

"I came to talk to you. Talk to me and I'll go away again." Milo felt Bori's tail bushed up and his body crouched, wound up like a spring ready to explode.

The face edged in closer, and a body became discernable, bearing it.

"I would like to ask you some questions," Milo said, meaning the ones from his dream that he had rehearsed over and over during the day.

"How do you know the craft of the woods?" Musail accused.

"I had a teacher who knows something of the Old Wisdom. He sent me here to find you."

"You may ask, then," Musail said, somewhat assuaged.

"Okay; first, then: Who knows the source of the cross I carry?"

"Let's see it."

Milo held Musail with his eye as he opened the little sack he kept the cross in. He worked it free and held it up, feeling a disturbing tingle as he did so.

Musail's scowl softened. "Where did you get that?" he asked Milo.

"That's unimportant. Where I take it is my concern. Answer my question."

"Ask Heronsuge. He knows it well."

Milo noticed the look of cunning that passed across Musail's features.

"Where do I find him?"

"Beneath the Great Barrow," Musail answered with a sneer. "It's not a place for mortals unless they wish for immortality." The sneer became a spiteful grin.

"Direct me to the one who can take me to the source of the cross."

No sooner did Milo say this than he knew he had said it wrong. The look of glee on Musail's face confirmed it. "Seek a guide you cannot see!" he cackled, then vanished.

All motion around them stopped. Milo kicked himself for losing his concentration. He should have asked, "Lead me to the place where I can find the one who knows the source of the cross." He wasn't sure what the implications were between what he had intended to ask and what he had actually said, but he had been warned, and Musail's reaction verified his mistake.

Bori was still growling deep down in his throat and his fur was ridged. Milo took off the crown.

"I messed up," he told the cat. "I needed to have Musail actually help me find whoever I need to find and the way I said it let him off the hook. Now it's up to us to find whoever it is we need to talk to by ourselves," he told Bori. "I hate the idea of staying here all night, but unless you've got a better idea, I don't think we've got a choice."

Bori agreed. It was a sleepless night. Nothing else happened, but expecting something was just as bad. The something that might be out there kept Bori's green eyes and Milo's brown ones wide open all night.

As soon as there was enough light to avoid stumbling into a tree trunk, they were moving. With Bori's help, they found their way back to the track of the old road. "I hope we get to the other side of the forest soon," Milo said as they shuffled along, with the light improving moment to moment. "I don't know how we're supposed to put Musail's advice to work, or what it means, but right now, I don't care. I just want to see the sky again!"

"Then follow me," said a voice from just a couple of steps away.

Bori went straight up, hissing and with every hair on his body rigid. Milo jumped sideways so suddenly that he slipped and went down in the loose leaves.

A bright laugh erupted from the empty space where the voice had come from. Milo thought it sounded familiar.

"Stigma?" Milo inquired, recalling the invisible contestant from the park at the starting line of the Hunt. "Is that you?"

She laughed again. "Yes, Milo. It's me."

"You almost scared us to death!" he shouted, his heart racing so hard that it felt about to burst through his shirt.

"I'm sorry." The giggle that accompanied the apology made it sound less sincere.

"What are you doing here?" he asked, brushing off the dried leaves and debris.

"Looking for you. You took a different way from the rest of us back at the End of the Earth. As it turned out, the way the rest of us went was a false lead, or at least a disastrous one. Interesting, but wrong. When I realized you weren't there, I decided that you might be on to something that the rest of us missed."

"I doubt that," he grouched.

"Why did you come here, then?" she asked.

"How I got here's a long story, and one I don't feel like telling just now. If you think I can show you anything, then I'm afraid you've taken another wrong turn. I don't really understand it myself."

"That's all right by me. I like you," the empty air said. "Maybe I can help you, then. I heard you say that all you want is to see the sky again. If you really do, I can help you find it. Just follow me."

"How can I do that if I can't see you?"

He felt a hand slide into his. "I'll lead you," she said. "Come along this way."

Bori took up his place in Milo's rucksack, his bushed-up tail back to normal and his cool demeanor as smooth as if nothing had happened. The invisible hand drew Milo into motion.

"How long have you been following me?" Milo asked.

"Several days, I guess. I followed your signature emanations until I caught up to you."

"When was that," Milo asked suspiciously, wondering what 'signature emanations' were. Instead of asking that, however, he was thinking about how long she'd been near and if she had been spying on them.

"Oh, just now. I felt you were close by, then I saw you coming up out of that hawthorn grove. Is that where you spent the night?"

"Yes," he said simply.

"Wasn't very restful, I bet."

"No, it wasn't."

"Where are you going now?"

"Out. Just out," Milo answered, still uncomfortable about how much she knew and wondering if he could trust her.

They walked for some time. There was a division in the old road, with a lesser track—so much lesser, in fact, that Milo could barely discern it. The invisible hand that drew him along drew him onto it.

"Not long now," Stigma said.

"How do you know? Have you come this way before?"

"I haven't, but others have. Most of them long ago. I'm following their emanations. Just like I followed yours."

"What is that?" Milo demanded. "Emanations?"

"The trace of intent people leave behind. Like a track of their wills. It's part of my magic, like my invisibility."

"Must be nice to have powers like that."

"Or not. It's a heavy price sometimes, Milo."

"So..." Milo continued, edging into his question without committing more than he had to. "You weren't with us last night?"

"No, I hadn't caught up with you then. Why?"

"It wasn't a good night. There's some sort of...people, I guess, or spirits or something—here that don't let you rest. And you can't really see them."

"Oh. Forest Folk. They don't like us. But they don't bother me because they can't see me, either, so they leave me alone."

"I wish I had that ability," Milo said, thinking how much easier the night would have been without Musail's relatives.

"No Milo. You don't. My invisibility is a curse. If I could, I'd be visible with more joy than you can imagine."

A thought came to Milo just then: what Musail had said about a guide he couldn't see. "I told you that I really can't help you find the next clue. That's because I need to find something—or someone else first. See, I got involved with a...a difficult situation that I have to take care of before I can learn the next clue. I think. Maybe you could help me if you know something that I don't understand at all. If you'd be willing to help? I mean, if you can?"

"Of course, Milo. Like I said, I like you."

"Okay. Do you know who Heronsuge is?"

A thoughtful silence came from the place were Stigma was. "No, I don't think that means anything to me."

"Well, then do you know anything about the Great Barrow?"

"Ahh! That I know. It's from very ancient lore. A place that dates back into the Age of Heroes. That was when the Avatars were wresting the world away from the Elementals. It was a time when Magic was released into the Realms."

"I don't have any idea what you're talking about. I mean, is the Great Barrow a place I could actually get to?"

"Yes, and no. It isn't a place like the Kingdom of Odalese. It lies in the realm of enchantment, sort of like the Tower of Glass, only even more so. It's a place that only those who follow the right path can get to."

"Could I get there?"

"Look!" Stigma said. "Up there! A break in the trees!"

Milo looked, knowing that the diversion had ended the answer to his question, if the answer had been there in the first place.

Sure enough, blue sky showed through the canopy ahead. They scrambled up a slope slick with leaf litter and peered out into bright sunlight. They had reached the forest's boundaries.

"There!" Stigma said smugly. "You wanted out of the forest, and there's out!"

Milo gazed over the rolling landscape beyond, laced with woods, and open to the sky. Bori jumped down from the rucksack, as relieved as Milo to see out. They saw the horizon where a pale blue chain of mountains met the sky. That was the only feature he could pick out as a destination.

"It looks like a long ways to anywhere," Stigma remarked. "If you like, we can travel together. I'll do what I can to help you find the Great Barrow. I think you've helped me with the next clue, whether you planned to or not, so it's the least I can do."

Milo couldn't think how he might have given her a clue he didn't know himself, but if she would help him, it didn't make any difference. "By the way," he asked, "how are the other contestants doing?"

"I don't know. Like I said, I decided to follow you when I realized we'd made a wrong turn. Everyone made it to the End of the Earth—how could they miss a clue like that? A clue, I understand, which you had a hand at opening—and after the slinger tournament the obvious clue had to have something to do with the three brothers and their homecoming in Akenwald. Everybody took off to get there first. Except you. If I had been paying attention, I would have noticed that. Instead, I went where the others were going. Just too arrogant, I suppose. I didn't even notice that you were the only one who wasn't in Aken Forest, and while we were all casting around looking for the next clue and acting like we knew what we were doing, we were watching each other to see if someone really *did* know something. Since I have the advantage of spying on others without them knowing I'm there, I knew when Count Yeroen took off, Aulaire hot on his heels. I followed like an idiot, afraid that I'd loose out if I didn't. I think the others did the same, because we all started arriving behind Yeroen, one after the other, at the Valley of the Stone Knights.

"That was an even bigger mistake, as it turned out," she continued. "The Pass of the Stone Knights is the site of one of those legendary places from the Age of Heroes. There was a huge battle there when the Elementals trapped the army of the First King who happened to be the founder of the Oak Clan. They would have been completely annihilated if the knights of the King's Table hadn't sacrificed themselves to serve as a rear guard. The rest of the army got away while the knights held the pass. They placed themselves under the Stone Spell in a desperate effort to hold the pass."

"What's that: 'the Stone Spell?'"

"It's a terrible oath. They turned themselves into invincible stone. They could still fight, but they had to surrender their living bodies for bodies made of stone. It meant that they could remain animate, and remember their purpose of fighting, but they lost their living flesh.

"So that's the curse on the Pass of the Stone Knights: nobody can go across the pass, because anyone who tries will be attacked by the Stone Knights. But the Knights hold one other characteristic, which I think Yeroen thought he could exploit. They retain their knowledge about the Ancient Days. If a person can defeat a Knight—or trick him into thinking that he *has* been defeated—he must tell you what he knows. So it seemed like a perfect place to learn the next clue. Anyone who could get information from a Stone Knight would have to be a very clever and knowledgeable mage. Of course, we all believed that we were up to that challenge. One of us after the other entered the pass to try. It was awful. I entered the pass, and since the Stone Knights couldn't see me, none challenged me. But I saw what was happening to others. You see, if you fail, you get petrified. That's when I noticed you weren't there. I decided I would be better off trying to find you, so I backtracked until I found your trail and followed the way you'd gone, all the way through Inverdissen and along the coast until I found you in this forest."

"Who?" Milo asked in horror. "Who got turned to stone?"

"I don't know. I know only who I saw with my own eyes. Ali and Tivik."

"Analisa?" Milo asked. "Or Yeroen and Aulaire?" he added, mostly to hide his particular interest in Analisa.

"I don't know. I think they may have made it, but there's no way to know what they might have learned. Maybe they *did* learn the next clue. You know, there are many clues to the paths of the Hunt."

With a shudder, Milo thought about what would have happened to him if he had gone into the Pass. Then he hoped Stigma was right about Analisa getting away safely.

He could see Bori bouncing through the tall grass beyond the trees, a grey-bodied porpoise in green waves. Gesturing toward the cat and assuming that his invisible companion was watching the same thing that he was, he said, "I guess Bori has plans for his own lunch. I've got a little food that my friend gave me when Bori and I went into the forest...want to share it with me? You.... You do eat, don't you?"

"Yes, Milo, I eat. I'm pretty much like you, except you can't see me."

He took the food out of his rucksack and began separating it into two portions. The one he'd laid out for Stigma began to disappear, a bite at a time. "How does it work?" he asked. "Being invisible, I mean?"

"Do you mean: how did I come to be invisible, or how is it that you can't see me?" she asked back.

"Both, I guess, but mostly, how can you be here but not be seen?"

"Well, for one thing, I'm not invisible to myself. I can see myself as well as you can see yourself. Invisibility is, like, a talent I have, but someone laid a curse on me that made it permanent. It's almost like the curse works not so much on me as it does on everyone else. If they can see, then they can't see me. Once, I could be invisible or visible when I wanted to, but the curse took that control away. I've made it part of my magic, but if I could learn to reverse it, I would be thrilled. I would be forever grateful to whoever could do that for me."

"When we were being introduced back in the park at Kingdom of Odalese, you put on a robe and I could see you."

"Yes, when I want to be seen, I can put on clothes. You can see the clothes, but you can't see me."

Milo hesitated. "You mean, you're..."

"That's right, Milo. If I don't want to be seen, I don't wear clothes. I'm not made up of air, or invisible flesh or something. I'm just as solid as you are."

He felt a grip of a hand on his arm.

"The curse just makes it impossible for you to see me. I'm here, it's just that…that you can't see me. If we were in a totally dark room…in other words, if you couldn't see anything at all, then I would be there just as much as you would be. If we touched, it wouldn't be any different than touching anyone else in the dark.

"Here; let me borrow your knife for a moment," she continued.

Milo gave her his knife. The handle disappeared, and the blade sawed away in the air. Suddenly a hank of hair, along with the knife, appeared on a rock beside him. The hair was pale; so pale that it matched the color of the moon when full He touched it. It was fine, straight, and soft.

"You're blond?" he asked.

"Yes. All the sorceresses of my line have moon-struck hair.

"Are they invisible, too?"

"Some of them. Only, they can control when to be invisible and when they want to be seen."

"Why did the person who cursed you do that?"

"That's a long story. One I don't feel like telling. Like you don't want to tell me why you want to find this Heronsuge."

Milo could respect that. "It looks like a long way to anywhere from here," he commented, looking out across the wilderness ahead.

"Yes, at least, by foot, the way you travel."

"How do you travel?"

"My magic is Air Magic. I travel on the wind if I'm not walking, as I have been to follow you. It also has something to do with why the curse works on me the way it does. But don't worry. I can walk as well as you, and I'll be sure we don't get separated. Since you can't see me, you can't really follow me, so I'll tell you where we're headed. Like now; do you see that hill? The one with the single pine tree growing out of its peak?"

"Yes. I see the one you mean."

"Well, that's where we're going next. If we get separated, or walk at different speeds or choose different routes, that's where we can meet up next. From there I'll pick out another rendezvous point, and so on. Okay?"

Milo agreed. As he packed, he came across the acorn he'd taken from the oak at the beginning of the Korrigan. He dug a small hole, dropped the acorn into it, and covered it over with loose earth.

"There," he said, patting the earth into place. "Live long and prosper."

He called Bori, who showed up on cue to take his place inside the pack. They set out, following the arrangement that Stigma had suggested. He never knew if she was nearby or not, but once as they were crossing a muddy stream bank, he saw fresh footprints made by a small bare foot and new ones appearing up the bank on the other side.

They traveled this way for several days without incident or signs of other people. That was the problem. The land was vacant. They were out of food. Bori offered to share the mice he caught, but neither of the humans were hungry enough to take that offer. They ate berries and nuts that they found along the way, but it was hardly enough to term a meal.

"I think I'd better travel ahead," Stigma told Milo. "I could move much faster and locate the nearest place to get real food."

"How'll we find each other again?" Milo asked.

"I'll take care of finding you," she assured.

"How will I know where to go?"

"See the mountain range that we've been walking towards?" Milo nodded. "See the highest peak? And then a low spot before the next set of peaks? Aim for that pass. I'll meet you there, or along the line you'll be walking for the next couple of days."

It meant he would have a long way to go on an empty stomach until Stigma returned. Milo didn't care for the idea much, but what else could he do?

They walked. Stigma was gone and Milo walked. And got hungrier. And worried. That meant that he was getting tireder. How long would he be able to keep on without food? All he could do was to hope that Stigma got back sooner, rather than later.

14

Burrowing Into the Barrow

M ilo walked. And walked. One day turned into two. He reached the pass that Stigma had pointed out and waited there. She didn't appear. Or didn't show up, since she couldn't appear and Milo was too hungry to wait for long.

"She said she would find us," Milo told Bori. He recalled something he had read somewhere. An adventure is nothing more than a long walk on an empty stomach. "Let's keep moving. I'm afraid if I wait, I'll starve. Let her find me while I look for a place to get something to eat."

Bori did okay, since the countryside was well provisioned with field mice. With nothing left in his rucksack and no place to get a meal, Milo began to wonder how long he could go before taking up Bori's offer to share the meals the cat procured out in the grass and rocks. He still wasn't *that* hungry, and besides, he considered this a breach in his contract with Bori; he was supposed to furnish the meals, not the other way around.

For two more days Milo ate nothing more than the wild foods Stigma had shown him—far, far longer than he had ever gone between meals in his whole life. Then, from a high place on the morning of the fourth day, he saw a thread of white smoke on the horizon. Smoke meant fire and fire suggested a chimney where food could be cooking. Admittedly, it was still a long way off, but it offered a real destination to aim for.

That day turned out to be the longest day of all as he walked and walked, exhaustion dragging at every step. Finally, by afternoon, he could see the chimney that the smoke came from, and the building it belonged to. His stride picked up a little in anticipation. Would he find hospitality, or would the people there prove to be unfriendly? No matter, he decided. One way or another, he *had* to get something to eat.

As he and Bori walked up to the well-heeled complex of stone buildings, dozens of curious young people surrounded them, surprised to see anyone walk out of the wilderness beyond the school, for that was what it was. They clamored around, asking each other questions—they didn't ask him anything directly—and exchanging theories about his arrival among themselves until a couple of teachers arrived and immediately took charge. He was only too glad to explain his plight and ask for help.

They took him at his word (and famished looks) and steered him straight to a place that emitted such delicious aromas that his empty stomach nearly jumped out of his throat in anticipation. The presiding staff member there, the head cook, quickly took over, since feeding hungry young people was her vocation.

She fed him a wonderful, thick broth, with crusty bread still hot from the oven. She had to intervene when she saw how he wolfed down the food, cautioning him to slow down before too much food on an empty stomach made him sick. After he had spooned out the last drop of soup and munched the last crumb of bread he was still hungry. Actually, he felt even hungrier, because what he had eaten had alerted his appetite that it was back in business. He thanked the cook while the young people gawked at him from several tables away, chattering on about this unusual wayfarer. Bori, of course, had gone among them after finishing his saucer of milk, and was making friends, making a hit, as usual, with the young ladies.

A new person now appeared, one who wore the air of authority so pompously that Milo had no problem believing, on being introduced, that he was the school principal.

"I am Headmaster Treverthorne," the inquisitor announced. "What brings you to our Academy, young man? What possessed you to go off into the wilderness?"

"I'm Milo, and this is Boriboreau," Milo replied to the headmaster's demand for his identity. "We travel together, and I haven't eaten in some days. Thank you"—and he turned to include the cook, who was still standing nearby, bare arms folded over her ample bosom—"for the meal. I don't think I could have made it much further." With the soup soaking into his body, he felt the exhaustion drain away the last of his resolve.

"I...got separated from my friends. That is, I knew where I was but I didn't know where I was going." Milo was quickly losing any interest in conversation. He was feeling an increasing disorientation, rubber-legged and even sick. The headmaster must have noticed, because he ended the interview. "Let's get you into bed. You'll feel more like talking once you have a long rest and another meal."

Milo woke up with Bori on his chest, staring into his face. "It's about time," Bori told him. "You've been asleep since yesterday, and now it's today."

"That long, huh?" he replied groggily, rubbing the gravel from his eyes. He hadn't decided if he was ready yet to wake up, but he did feel better. He recalled that the headmaster had sent him and Bori with a staff member to a cottage out behind the building where the kitchen was, and that he had collapsed onto the bed without bothering to undress, or even to turn down the covers. He now had the covers pulled up to his chin, and from the feel of his body underneath, he didn't have on any clothes, either. "So, what's this place like? Where are my clothes?"

"They took your clothes to be washed, because they stank. They said they'd see you got a bath when you woke up."

Milo felt for the string with the little bag at his throat. It was gone. "Where's...where's my—" he asked, instantly in panic. Bori jumped down and started batting something around on the floor from under the bed. "Bori! This is no time for play! My...my..."

"Is right here," Bori finished the sentence, nonchalantly, and swatted the little bag into clear view. "Don't get fumblefluxed. I thought you wouldn't want anyone messing with this, so when they took it off you, I just knocked it down and batted it under the bed for safe keeping."

Milo sighed and leaned back in relief. "Thanks, Bori. You really are a paragon of cats." He picked up the bag and slung it back around his neck. "Any sign of Stigma?"

"Now, there's a dumb question. There wouldn't be any sign of Stigma if she were sitting right next to you."

Even if what Bori had said was true, Milo rather resented it. "You know what I mean. Do you think she came here? I feel pretty disappointed that she might have just left us like that and not come back like she said she would."

Actually, he felt more than disappointed. He felt angry, and betrayed. He'd trusted her as a friend, and she'd left him lost and hungry.

"There's a basin over there for you to wash in," Bori told him. "I'll take you to see the headmaster when you're ready."

"Ready? Like this?" Milo gestured to his nakedness.

"Oh, you humans!" the cat exclaimed in exasperation.

A knock at the door interrupted their discussion about human customs. Without waiting for an answer, the visitor opened and came in. Milo dived deeper beneath the covers on the bed.

Tinburkin stood there. "Well! Awake at last!" he exclaimed.

"Wha...how—" Milo stammered, forgetting for the instant in his surprise that he was not prepared for a social visit.

"Hup! Hup!" Tinburkin urged. "Get up! It's impolite to keep the headmaster waiting!" He turned to Bori. "Didn't you tell him that he was to see Master Treverthorne immediately upon awakening?"

"Yeah, he told me that," Milo said. "But I'm naked. I can't go traipsing around like this, in my birthday suit now, can I?"

"Birthday suit!" Tinburkin laughed. "That's good! That's funny!"

"It's what my grandmother called being naked when I was little," Milo mumbled. "Where are my clothes? Somebody took them!"

"And left you these," Tinburkin said, pointing to a pile of folded, clean ones lying on a chair that Milo had not yet noticed. Bori was sitting on them. "Your's are on the line to dry after being laundered. But more important, do you still have the..." Tinburkin left the question open to make his meaning, and Milo touched the bag at his throat in answer. Since it was all that he was wearing, the significance of the gesture wasn't hard to figure out.

Milo huffed over to the chair and Bori jumped down as Milo reached to snatch up the stack of clothes. "Oh," the cat said. "That's what this is. I thought it was a cushion. Certainly more useful than the silly things you humans think you have to wear all the time."

"Why are you here?" Milo accused Tinburkin as he began putting on the pants. "If you're keeping tabs on me, you could have come when I was lost and starving."

"I'm here on business. My business is to check up on the progress of the Hunt contestants."

"Checking up on the...? Why? How?"

"I'm...what you would think of as a referee. I keep up with the Hunt players and validate their progress."

"How's my progress, then?" Milo demanded.

"How do you think it is?" Tinburkin riposted. "My job doesn't include judging how you may be doing."

"I'm doing just fine," Milo grouched. "I'm lost, someone I trusted let me down, or even worse, she might be in trouble herself. I couldn't find her if I tried, I'm sick of being hungry, walking endlessly to I don't know where. And I'm tired of not knowing just how bad it can still get. How's that for a report?"

"So...you're doing fine, you'd say?"

Milo decided not even to answer that.

Tinburkin continued. "I can tell you this. You don't need to worry about Stigma. She's quite capable of taking care of herself. Also, based on what you know right now, you don't have enough information to judge her. Keep focused on what you need to do."

Milo leaked all the sarcasm he could into his voice. "Great. I feel much better, with your valuable advice. What about Analisa? I heard about the encounter with the Stone Knights and that it went badly for some of the contestants. Was she one of them?"

Tinburkin gazed away toward the ceiling as if the answer to Milo's question had been posted there. It wasn't. Milo looked.

"Oh, I really can't tell a contestant anything about the progress of others," Tinburkin replied.

"I don't care about that!" Milo snapped. "I just want to know if my friend's okay."

Tinburkin ignored him. "So. What are you planning to do next?"

Milo gave him a scathing look. "Talk to the headmaster, I guess. And have some breakfast, or whatever I can get. I'm hungry. That's all I have any plans for right now."

"That's a good start. Then, perhaps it would be a good idea to find out where you are?"

"Yeah. Sure. I guess so. I expect the headmaster—I think you called him Master Treverdoor?—will fill me in on that, since I'm sure you won't."

"Trevorthorne. Master Trevorthorne. Yes, he can tell you about Rykirk Academy. That's where you are. A place with a distinguished history. Interesting that you should show up right here, seeing as how you were lost and all."

"It was accidental, I assure you. As far as I could see, and I mean that very literally, it was the only place I *could* see. Yeah, it was an accident, just like every other thing that's happened to me."

"I suppose so. But I shouldn't keep you any longer. Run along. Don't keep the headmaster waiting. He's not at all used to that, you see."

Milo and Bori did just that. Milo commented to Bori on how Tinburkin showed up the way he did and that he thought it was curious how he popped up over and over. He also asked Bori what he thought about it.

"Tinburkin's a Ranger. He travels a good deal. He told you that he's a referee for the Hunt, so I guess keeping up with you and the others must be what he does."

"All I am is lost. But he found me anyway." The thought hit him that if Stigma had found him and Tinburkin, too, what about that other one, that Smith guy? Milo's small feeling of safety by eluding his enemy vanished.

"Whatever," the cat said. He changed the subject. "I've heard that Tinburkin was a contestant in the Hunt once. That was before my time, so I don't remember it myself. So was Barenton; remember him? The chairman of the Hunt committee? I believe the Mayor of the Kingdom of Odalese was, too."

"Why? Why are all those people so interested in playing this hunt game?"

"I don't know, but then I'm a cat. That sort of thing is none of my business."

They arrived at the office of the headmaster, which Bori knew from his reconnaissance while Milo was sleeping.

"Ah! Master Milo!" the headmaster greeted. "Please, come in and have a seat. I hope you're feeling much refreshed since I saw you the last time."

Milo shook the headmaster's proffered hand, expecting it to feel oily. It wasn't. It was very soft and a little damp. "Yes, thank you. I...ahh..." he stammered, not able to decide just what he should say.

"The Ranger told me about your long trek across the wilderness. All the way from Korrigan Forest? My, my. You must be a ranger yourself to complete such a journey. Did you actually enter the forest?"

"Yes, I did. I...I wanted to learn something about the lore of the place."

"That would certainly give you first-hand experience, though I would say most of us would choose a less *risky* way of getting it. A very reckless choice indeed."

"I had some coaching about how to go about it. I think that it was worth the trouble. That is, if I can take what I learned to where it leads. Perhaps you can help me with that part. Can you tell me how to get to the Great Barrow? Or who Hersonsuge is?"

Headmaster Trevorthorne sat as if poleaxed. His mouth actually gaped.

"I...ahh...I..." he stuttered at first, then turned stern, as if admonishing a wayward pupil for some infraction. "How did you come by these... these questions?"

Milo answered calmly. "Musail suggested that I go to the Great Barrow to speak with this Heronsuge. Musail is the Shade I met in Korrigan Forest."

The headmaster rubbed his forehead as if it suddenly ached. "These are...uncommon questions. And things that should not be so...casually spoken. Musail, you say? How did you know him? How did you make his acquaintance?"

Milo was pleased that his question had rattled the headmaster's control, taking him off his high horse. He also guessed that the headmaster's answer would not likely be a simple one, either. "As I said, I met Musail in Korrigan Forest. I had been counseled to find him because I needed information which he could give. Because of the nature of my quest, I really can't or shouldn't say more, but the information is important. I was hoping you could help me. Tinburkin—the Ranger—urged me to speak with you."

"Yes. Of course. But you must understand, Master Milo, that you ask about things that are not to be discussed lightly, or by the uninitiated."

"I'm a contestant in the Magical Scavenger Hunt and figuring out puzzles is a key feature of that. What I'm asking for, if you have the information, is essential. I'm not asking about it lightly at all."

"My, my, but you are a determined young man. The Ranger advised me as such, and now I understand what he was telling me. Still, these things cannot be approached in a casual way, nor are the answers simple, like filling in the blanks on an exam. Generations...well, I must stress to you that the things you seek answers for are weighty matters that have absorbed the earnest studies of many committed scholars, and have inspired incredible advances in scholarship."

"I won't try to tell you that I understand, because I know that I don't know what you're talking about," Milo confessed. "If I had the choice, I'd just walk away from the whole thing and forget it, but apparently it doesn't work that way. However it works, I'm caught up in it and if you can't help me, I have no choice but to look for someone who can. The sooner I can get to the Great Barrow, the better. So, can you give me the information, or can't you?"

Milo's direct method was clearly unsettling to the academic. The headmaster bristled and he wrapped his scholar's robe tightly around himself. "I'm afraid that the Great Barrow and what it conceals are too complex and powerful to pass on so lightly. If you are willing to invest the time and hard work to accomplish the disciplines required to approach such a profound endeavor, perhaps I might help you, but without such a serious commitment, I'm afraid there is little I can do. I offer you what I can by extending the hospitality of the Academy for as long as necessary for you to recover from your rash ordeal, but I cannot offer you the information you seek as if it were passage on a tramp trader's ship."

That done, Milo and Bori took their leave. "Either he knows about the Great Barrow, or he doesn't know but is trying to let on that he does," Milo told Bori when they left the office.

"He knows, but only as an idea," Bori observed. "The sort of knowing that's wrapped around maintaining what he knows to differentiate himself from the uneducated. I think we should snoop around here to see if we can't find something that he doesn't want us to find."

They agreed to split up. Instead of returning to the cottage where Milo had slept off his exhaustion, he decided to look for the school's library. Bori said he would explore the place for its less obvious nooks and crannies. "Besides," he added, "places like that are likely to hide a mouse or two."

Since Bori seemed to be putting his appetite ahead of the business at hand, Milo decided that he should detour his errand to the kitchen.

His nose led him there. The head cook greeted him right away, and swept him into the aroma-filled refuge. In moments he was seated in front of a plate piled with eggs, bacon, and a basket of fresh, crunchy bread with butter and marmalade. A chilled pitcher of milk topped off the bounty, and Milo forgot the urgency of his mission. While he ate, the cook talked.

"This is such a highly touted school," she told him, "you'd think they could pay us better than they do. The students all come from the best—and richest—families."

"Is it—the Academy—any different from other schools?" Milo asked. "I mean, I really don't know much about schools here or anything. Back at home—where I come from—I go to school, but it's…well, in a very different place and we study lots of things unlike what I've seen since I joined the Hunt."

"What hunt would that be?" she asked. "You don't look like a hunter to me. I'd guessed you would be more a thistle-downer."

"Oh, no! I'm not a hunter, like in hunting animals. You know what the Magical Scavenger Hunt is? You do? Well, I came to be a contestant in the Magical Scavenger Hunt. It's…more confusing the longer I'm doing it. What's that other thing you mentioned? A thistle-downer?"

She looked him over with an appraising eye. "I can see how you might be with the Magical Scavenger Hunt. It explains how I took you for a thistle-downer. A thistle-downer is a person who looks for traces of the Old Ways on his own instead of going to a school, such as this one, to learn the history of the Ancients. He or she wanders wherever the winds take him or her, like thistle down. 'Course, thistle-downers are frowned on by the likes of Headmaster High-and-Mighty. Hates to get his hands dirty, grubbing around in the old places and sleeping on the hard ground instead of reading about it in books and sleeping in a soft, warm bed."

She moved in conspiratorially to whisper to Milo. "Personally, I have more sympathy for people like you who are willing to take the risks and the hardships of thistle-downer's life to learn about things on their own. I figure you get what you pay your dues for, and these pampered scholars? They get what their families pay for, and that's about it. When they go home from here all they really have is a piece of paper that says they're better than the rest of us, and they spend the rest of their lives thinking it. Does anything come of it? 'Course not! It's just to be able to say they know about the Old Ways without gaining anything of the Old Wisdom. You go on," she encouraged. "You learn all you can your own way. Maybe you'll learn a few things that'll help out the rest of us someday." She gave him a smart wink and another serving of scrambled eggs.

"Maybe that's why Master Trevorthorne refused to help me out," Milo mused.

"That old stuffed shirt!" she spat. "He doesn't know what he knows, but he's jealous about that! He had you pegged for a thistle-downer even when that Ranger showed up looking for you. 'Course, he wouldn't think much of a Ranger, either, even if a Ranger carries a lot more weight than a schoolmaster. Even the schoolmaster of Rykirk Academy. That makes him dislike you even more."

She continued. "So, what wouldn't he tell you?"

"I asked about the Great Barrow," Milo offered.

"The Great Barrow, now!" the cook exclaimed. "And he didn't know? The thing that Rykirk Academy claims to hold the key to? Hah!"

"The key? To the Great Barrow?" Milo asked in astonishment.

"Oh, yes. I may be no more than a servant at this school, but I've been here all my life and come from a family that's worked here for as many generations as the school's been here. I've picked up a thing or two. Yes, Rykirk was put here to be the gate to the Great Barrow."

"Where is it, then?" Milo asked.

"The Great Barrow? Well, I don't rightly know; that's what these scholars are here for. But I know about the Gate."

"Where's that?"

"Up there, on the hill." She indicated the hill behind the school with a kip of her head, obviously proud of her knowledge. Milo looked out through the open door in the direction. The low hill there was encircled by a massive stone wall. On the hill top was an odd-looking pile of enormous stones. "There! That's the Gate," she asserted, verifying that he had seen what she meant.

"That's the Gate?"

"Yes, of sorts. But you can't just go up there. You have to get through the gate in the wall first."

"The Gate has a gate?"

"And a key. To prevent unauthorized access to the Gate. They don't let just any riff-raff, like thistle-downers, go poking around up there. You have to have the permission of the headmaster to go up there, and he has the key."

"I think that's a problem," Milo ventured.

"That's right. Trevorthorne's not going to let you in. It's the last place he would let you go."

"Can I climb over the wall or something?"

"Not easily, so I would advise against that. There's still another way."

"What's that?" Milo asked, puzzled.

"My husband," she said, smugly. "He's the grounds keeper. He has a key so he can go inside to cut the weeds. I just might be able to influence him to leave the lock open. If he does that, you have to promise not to give away how you got in. I don't want him to get into any trouble."

"Sure! I understand. I'd be glad to promise that. Can you do it?"

"Let's just say that I don't have anything against poking a hole or two into Master High-and-Mighty's self importance. Come back after dinner tonight before the procession and I'll let you know if my husband can help. This would be a good night since it's the dark of the moon. The procession is over by midnight and the students and faculty leave the hill. The headmaster will probably expect my husband to lock up then. You could slip in when everyone else is in bed."

"Procession? What sort of procession?"

"Oh, it's Samhain. The night when the boundaries between the worlds are at their thinnest. The whole school goes to the hill for a procession of lights around the Gate. It's a tradition."

Milo left the kitchen with a full stomach and an eager heart. Bori was waiting for him outside the cottage door. "I found something I think you should see for yourself," Bori said.

"What is it?" Milo asked.

"I said, you need to see it for yourself," the cat repeated. "Come on."

Bori bounded away, forcing Milo to scramble to keep up with him. He led Milo to the wall surrounding the hill where the cook had told him the Gate was located. Bori showed him a grated iron door.

"I thought this might be a perfect habitat for voles," Bori told him. "So I came up to look around, and when I did, I saw this."

Milo was nervous that someone might see them. "The cook told me about this place just now," he told the cat. "We're going in tonight, but I don't want to be seen here or show any sign that we're interested in the place."

"This you have to see. Look."

Milo looked through the rusty wrought iron bars to see the jumble of huge stones on the crest of the hill. Although they seemed partially tumbled, they were clearly some sort of an ancient monument. Bori drew his attention closer, to the place where the iron gate sat in its jamb. Milo saw a hank of moon-pale hair lodged in the heavy lock.

"Stigma's," Milo whispered.

"That's what I thought," Bori confirmed.

Milo plucked it out of the lock. "She was here!"

"Yes, and I think she left this as a sign for you. She knew you would come here, and she knew the only thing she could leave you that you might recognize was her hair."

"I think you're right," Milo said, a wash of relief coming over him. This sign confirmed that Stigma hadn't simply abandoned him. It also suggested that she had been true to her promise to guide him to the Great Barrow, even if it wasn't in person. "Come on, Bori. Let's get away before anybody notices us."

They wandered away, as if they had been on a random ramble. "Everything we've learned confirms that we have to get inside," Milo told Bori. "The hank of hair Stigma left us backs up what the cook told me."

"Either that or she got her tail caught in the door when she slipped though," Bori observed. "It happened to me once. I was dashing through a door that someone had opened, and it slammed—bang!—on the very tip of my tail. Caught the last tuft of hair. If I had been just a shade slower, I'd have a door-jamb shaped kink at the end of my tail."

"I guess that shows how risky it is to dash through closing doors," Milo said, thinking about the possible dangers of slipping through this one.

"I have something else to tell you as well," Bori told him. "Before I came to the gate, I was hunting over by the groundskeeper's shed. Master Trevorthorne came by, talking to the cook's husband. He told him to lock the door to our cottage as soon as we went in tonight. He said he didn't want you to take part in the procession, whatever that is, and he didn't want you wandering around unsupervised."

"That could be a problem," Milo admitted.

"I thought so, too. Then I had an idea. He can lock the door, but what if we weren't inside? Then we wouldn't be inconvenienced. We just have to be sure that everyone *thinks* we're inside. I've found a suitable hide-out where we can stay until it's safe to try the gate."

Milo got his bath before dinner, then went back to the dining hall. The students were clearly in a festive mood, but Milo and Bori were placed at a table separate from everyone else, the 'visitor's table.' Only, since they were the only visitors, it kept them in isolation. When the students began clearing out, the cook came with Milo's own clothes: patched, clean, and folded.

"It's all set," she whispered. "My husband will leave the gate unlocked and ajar. You only have to promise to lock it so no one notices that he 'forgot' to close it properly."

Milo agreed. Nothing was said about the instructions from the headmaster about locking them in for the night.

They went back into the cottage, but only long enough for Milo to change into his own clothes, and to fix the bed to look like he was in it, wrapped up in the bedclothes. Bori kept watch while Milo got ready.

"Hurry!" the cat said. "Someone's coming."

At the last instant, Milo decided to take his rucksack as well, and slipped out into the heavy shadow and around the corner before the footsteps Bori had heard arrived at the door. They heard a key stealthily turning in the lock. "Sorry, young fella," a man muttered, "but I have to do as I'm told."

Milo was glad that it was a moonless night, and the deep shadow hid them as they made their way to the hiding place Bori had picked out, a dip in the rock beneath the wall some ways from the gate.

As they crouched down in the hole-like depression, Milo looked up at the stars blazing in incredible profusion in the black satin of the night sky.

"See those stars there?" Milo said, pointing to a group of three bright stars in a diagonal in the eastern sky. "Those are the stars of Orion's Belt.

I don't know much about stars, but my grandfather taught me those. That star up above is his shoulder, and the ones down the side are his sword or club."

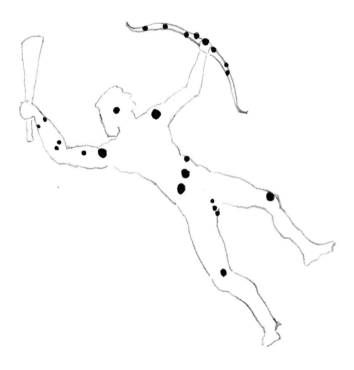

"They just look like stars to me," Bori responded.

"Yes, but it's a human thing, seeing patterns in the stars and making stories from them. We see them as constellations, even though they don't really have any relationships except the way they look from our point of view. Orion, for instance, we call the Hunter."

Milo stopped for a minute, a strange idea dawning on him. "If I recognize the same pattern of stars here as I do at home, then, this must be the same place! I've always thought that being here meant that I was in a completely different world, but those stars tell me that I'm not! It's the same place in relation to the stars. This is *weird.*"

"So, what does it mean, you think?"

"I don't know. That's the mystery. How can it be so different if it's the same place?"

"Let me know when you figure it out," Bori said, and yawned. "Look! There's more stars!"

Milo looked down to where the cat was staring. "No, those are candles. The procession must be starting and everyone coming out of the courtyard is carrying a candle."

A flow of bobbing, flickering points of light emerged from the school and flowed up the hill, clogging up briefly against the wall by the gate. Milo realized that if the cook's husband thought that he had locked Milo and Bori into the cottage, he probably wouldn't be leaving the gate unlocked for them.

"We've got to get in with the students," Milo told Bori. "We can't wait until everyone is gone to get in."

"Then we'll have to do it without anyone noticing us," Bori pointed out. "I can slip in unseen as long as I can avoid getting stepped on, but what about you?"

Milo shrugged. "We'll just have to risk it. You go through first so you can see the inside. I'll try to come through with the last ones."

Bori disappeared into the darkness almost instantly. Milo slipped along using the cover of deeper shadows along the wall for cover, thinking how Stigma would have no trouble doing this. He reached the place by the gate just as the last couple of students were passing inside, and joined on, candleless, to pass through. Once inside, he pressed himself against the wall in the deepest shadow and sidled away from the candlelight. Bori was there already, guiding him to a low place in the uneven ground where they could take cover.

They couldn't see much of the ceremony from there, but they could hear the indistinct drone of chanting and fragments of a single voice, probably the headmaster's, leading the chorus. Actually, it was pretty boring. Milo dozed a little as time passed. Orion climbed higher and higher into the sky before Bori woke him.

"They're coming down," the cat whispered. In silence the crowd moved back to the gate and filtered through. As the last one went out, they could hear a key scrape in the lock. They were locked in, alone.

Milo got himself up stiffly, glancing at Orion, which stood a little past zenith. He could dimly make out the silhouette of the jumbled shapes of the boulders that were on the top. Bori, however, could see it clearly.

"Come this way," he told Milo, and Milo followed him, more by motion than by actually seeing him. They picked their way up the rocky slope until they arrived at the pile of huge, smooth-sided stones.

In the starlight, Milo could make out their general shape, and distinguish a certain order to how they were situated. Bori lead him to a place where lozenge-shaped stones set on end to the right and the left made an opening. Between them was a floor of packed earth. He ran his hands over their surfaces. Except where weather had peeled away the surface, the stones were dressed and smooth. At the mouth of the opening a massive lintel of granite lay across the uprights. In the dim light, he thought he could discern a pattern of some sort pecked into the surface of the lintel, and traced it with his fingers until he recognized the shape.

"Bori! There's a sort of carving above the door! It's a cross figure, like mine!"

"Or like the one we found in the weeds at the side of the road when we went into Korrigan Forest?" Bori added. "Ready to go in? The opening's a tunnel from here on. It's okay, I can see and smell enough to know there's nothing inside that we should avoid."

They went in, Milo ducking under the first lintel and feeling his way into a darkness that was now total, except for an occasional space between stones that allowed a star or two to peek through. Bori had the advantage of his nose and whiskers to tell him all he really needed to know to explore the space. Milo counted the pairs of stones that held up the roof, noting that each set was taller than the one before.

"...ten, eleven, twelve..." Milo counted as he touched the flanking uprights. "Ouch!" He rubbed his forehead where he had bumped it against a lowered thirteenth lintel stone, invisible in the darkness.

"Come this way," Bori said. "It opens up on the inside."

Milo had to stoop to pass through this doorway, and as soon as he did he felt, rather than saw, that the passage opened into a chamber. The ceiling lifted away to at least three times his height. The gargantuan uprights held up a cap stone of immense size.

"I think I know what this is," he said. "I've seen pictures. It's an ancient tomb called a passage grave." The idea of having entered an ancient grave in the middle of the night made the hairs stand up on his neck. The feeling made him want to turn around and make his way out again, but his purpose in coming held him fast. He reached out to touch the upright stones of the wall, exploring them as he made his slow way around the circular chamber. The surfaces of the stones were tooled by the ancient masons to polished surfaces, revealing no features or carving that he could discern. Thirteen—there it was again—huge stones had been fit closely side by side, their lower ends buried in the ground and so huge that Milo couldn't conceive of how such enormous weights could have been moved. Even in his own world, these stones would have strained the ingenuity of modern engineers. "Well," he said with a sigh, "I guess we'll have to find a way to come back here by daylight. Maybe I could see something useful then. Let's get out of here."

Bori led the way and Milo followed, thoroughly unable to see the cat and waving his hands in front of him to find the passage. It was a relief to step out into the starlight under an open sky. After the total blackness, starlight seemed bright. Orion soared away to the west, headed toward its setting.

"Wait a minute," Milo said, puzzled. "Something's wrong."

Instead of the outline of the wall that ran around the hill, Milo was seeing the tall, soft shapes of tree tops. "Bori, I don't think we're in Kansas anymore!"

15

Out the Other Side

"I don't know anything about Kansas," Bori told Milo, referring to the literary reference Milo had made from *The Wizard of Oz,* "but the moist air and scents of forest smell like we aren't in Rykirk anymore either. I think we've gotten to some new place on our journey."

It was also a good deal chillier. Milo drew his jacket in tighter. "So, do you think we've gotten to the Great Barrow?" Milo asked.

"Yes. You have," came a female voice from somewhere close by. "I've been waiting for you. You found my marker?"

"Stigma!" Milo called. "You're here? We just came through!"

"As I was sure you would. Welcome to Inys Raun. I was only a day ahead of you. I found the Gate by following the groundskeeper. When he opened the gate in the wall, I slipped in. Then he locked it when he left, and I was inside. That's when I came through to arrive here. But I'd started to worry when you hadn't arrived. The Barrow opens at dawn."

"How do you..." Milo started asking before her last statement registered. "What? What do you mean, it opens at dawn? The Great Barrow?"

"Hold on. Let's go through this a step at a time. First, I'm glad to see you."

"And I'm glad to see you! I mean, I'm glad you're here, even if I can't see you. Uh...where are you?"

"I'm over here on this rock."

Milo saw a perfectly empty block of stone that looked like a perfect place for Stigma to be.

She explained. "When I reached Rykirk I had to steal food, and of course, nobody saw me, but I had to be careful to take only a little bit at a time so it wouldn't be noticed. Then you showed up. While you were sleeping—I didn't want to disturb you—Tinburkin arrived, so I thought it was best not to give myself away. I followed him when he went to speak in private with the headmaster. That's how I learned that Rykirk is the Gate to the Great Barrow, and since that's what Tinburkin was interested in, I realized that you had been on the right track all along. Tinburkin was expecting you to show up there, by the way."

"How...what do you mean?"

"He told the headmaster he's monitoring the progress of the contestants of the Magical Scavenger Hunt. He asked if anyone had come to Rykirk seeking the Gate. The headmaster got very upset, but he told Tinburkin no. No one had been there and if they had, he wouldn't let them use the Gate for some frivolous purpose. Tinburkin assured him that the purpose was anything but frivolous, and pointed out that you had gotten there that very afternoon. Then he went to wait for you to wake up. I stayed to see what the headmaster would do, and he called his groundskeeper and told him to make sure the gate to the Gate was locked. So I followed the groundskeeper and when he opened the iron grill to look around inside the compound, I took the opportunity to slip through. When he left again, I put the hank of my hair into the lock for you to find, knowing that you would understand the message. Then I went to explore the dolmen."

"The what?"

"The dolmen. That's what it's called. They were built in the Ancient Days and they're passages between worlds. Sometimes they're passages between the world of the living and the dead, and sometimes between the regular world and the legendary one. This one's of that sort. I waited until twilight—that's usually when a thing like this opens up—and I came through. That's how I got here. So I waited for you. All that's left for us to do now is to go over to the Great Barrow and see what we can find."

Milo looked around. Despite the darkness, he could make out a huge hump in the countryside some little ways away, a soft, rounded shape devoid of the trees that surrounded it. "Is that what you mean?" he asked, pointing.

"Yes. Shall we?"

He felt her hand slip into his and they started down the hill. They would have to cross through the forest below before they reached the Great Barrow, but it wasn't very far and should be fairly easy.

Bori was acting oddly. His ears were laid back and the hair along his spine was rising up into a ridge. He arched up his back, tail lifted and bushed. A whining growl came out of his throat, and Milo stopped.

"Bori? What is it?" he asked the swollen cat.

"Milo! Down!" Stigma screamed and jerked him sidewise. A blast of blue fire exploded just where he had been standing and he tripped and tumbled down the slope. He lost Stigma's hand and Bori went bounding down-slope.

"It's Kayn! Kayn's here!" she screamed. "Trying to kill me!"

"Kayn?" Milo yelled, scrambling in the direction he'd seen Bori go. Her hand grabbed his again. "Trying to kill you? Why?"

He felt the press of her body against his. "He's the one who placed this curse on me," she hissed. "But I don't know why he's trying to kill me now!"

She pulled him behind an outcrop of rock and made him crouch down. A bright light like a flare arched up to light the hillside. "It's not you," Milo told her. "It's me! He's after me. He doesn't care about you. Run! It's me, and he'll follow me. Stay with me and you'll just be collateral damage!"

"Wha…" Stigma began, confused. "Why"—

But Milo broke and ran. He crashed and rolled and ran again, trying to run the same direction, more or less, that Bori had gone. Another flare burst in the sky with a hard white light as he tumbled hard across a log he hadn't seen in the dark. It hurt. It hurt so bad he couldn't breathe.

Bori was on his chest. "Get up! Get up, Milo! Run!"

He did. Bori bounded away, and they were into the deep shadow beneath the trees. More flares burst above the canopy, but Milo and Bori were hidden. It was slower going under the trees where Milo had to feel his way to avoid banging into tree trunks. Bori hissed directions to him to turn this way or that to avoid obstacles. Suddenly, a man stood in front of them.

He had a small lantern. "There!" he said. "Come along this way. I'll take you to safety."

"Who…?" Milo started, but the man was already moving away. Milo followed, not knowing what else to do. He picked up Bori, who was still wired with excitement.

They walked for maybe ten minutes before the man stopped. "There. That should do it," he said. "You should be safe enough, now."

"Who…?" Milo said again.

"I'm Culebrant. I live here. When I saw the commotion, I thought someone might need my assistance. Nasty bugger, the one after you. Haven't seen his likes in these parts for a while. You'd best keep your head down until he moves along."

"I…I have to get to the Great Barrow. It's why I'm here. Can you get me there?"

"Yes, I can. But with that one trying to stop you, you might consider altering your plan somewhat. He'll have you fried to a crisp before you even reach the barrow."

"The...barrow?"

"The hill. The Barrow is a barrow. It was built, so it's not a natural feature like a real hill. But I expect you know that."

"No. I didn't and I don't know much of anything, really. I know who is after me, but I don't know why—or, I don't know exactly."

"Either he really doesn't like you and doesn't want you to get to the place you want to go, or you have something he wants that won't be damaged if he reduces you to a pile of ashes. Is that about right?"

"Yes," Milo answered solemnly.

"More's the reason I should help you. Who is this sorcerer who's after you?"

"He calls himself Smith. Or Kayn. I think his whole name is Kayn Smith. Anyway, he and I aren't on good terms."

"Hmmm...Yes, I know of him. He's been by here before. A very bad sort. If he's your enemy, then you can consider me your friend. If it's any consolation to you, he would treat me the same way he's treating you. If we were to meet."

"You know him?"

"After a fashion. He may, or may not, know of me. But his interests, or what he has in mind, would put us on opposite sides of the issue."

Culebrant looked around at the dark forest. "You and he aren't the only ones to come seeking the barrow just lately. There's been an unusual amount of traffic here this evening."

"There has?" Milo asked hopefully.

"Yes. Mages, witches, and enchanters of various sorts. Five so far, outside of you and Kayn. Is there some sort of convention taking place?"

"We're...contestants all looking for the next clue in the Magical Scavenger Hunt. Except for Kayn."

"Can't say as that...ahh...event rings a bell for me. But then, I don't get around as much as I did in the old days. Mostly, I live quietly here next to the barrow, in the woods. I'm a Woodcutter."

"A woodcutter?" Milo asked. He had been thinking—hoping—for something more along the lines of a wizard. A powerful one.

"That's right. And you? I don't think I caught your name."

"Oh, I'm Milo. And this is Bori."

Bori had settled down by this time and hopped out of Milo's arms. He walked over to Culebrant with his tail high in greeting, waving in friendliest fashion. "Boriboreau, at your service," he announced.

This startled Milo. Bori didn't talk to just anybody. Culebrant showed not the faintest sign of amazement at meeting a talking cat. "Happy to make your acquaintance," he said, stroking Bori's head in greeting.

"I believe we should be on our way," he advised. "You'll be much safer under my roof than you are out here in the open forest."

"Thank you, but I really do need to get to the Great Barrow."

"Because of this scavenger hunt?"

"Yes…or actually, it's gotten to be more than that since I got into cross purposes with Kayn. Kayn isn't part of the Hunt. He wants something, the same something I came here for. I can't let him get it, and I have to find out why he wants it so badly," Milo added, surprising himself by how much he had already told this stranger. "I don't really understand, except that I'm wrapped up in it, and that I don't have any choice but to succeed," he added, trying to cover for having said too much.

"Then I must help you. But walking straight into the place where this Kayn is waiting to finish you off seems decidedly self-defeating, wouldn't you say?" He didn't wait for Milo to answer such an obvious question. "I can help you in several ways: I can give you a safe place to hide from Kayn until you're ready. I can prepare you to deal with him when the time comes, and I can teach you how to learn what you seek from the Great Barrow. You see, of the two—Kayn and the Barrow—it's the Barrow itself that's much more formidable. I've seen many self-serving mages such as Kayn come here seeking what the Barrow holds, and it defeated them. They were rash. This Kayn appears to be so filled with himself that he is unwilling to put in the time and hard work necessary to solve the mystery of the Barrow. Without the proper preparation, the power they thought to steal is too great and therefore, it eludes them. Take your time, young Milo. Allow this Kayn to confront the enigma of the Barrow on his own. Wait for him either to move on or reap the harvest of his own sowing—without you or the thing he hopes to take from you. Meanwhile, apprentice yourself to me and I will guide you into the ways of a Woodcutter."

A woodcutter? Why, Milo wondered, would he choose to become a woodcutter with all the serious things he was facing?

"You're young," Culebrant said. "But by now you've surely noticed that those who announce themselves with impressive titles and claim high-sounding abilities may be no more likely to actually possess mastery than those who offer their services in humbler ways. Think, for a moment, of those you've met along the way. Which ones stood out offering extravagant claims, and which ones offered gifts with a modest hand?" He waited, watching Milo think. "See my point? It's time for you to practice the discipline of the Woodcutter."

Culebrant ended with a chuckle. "Besides, I have a nice porridge simmering on the fire and no one to share it with."

16

Woodcutting Lessons

The sky was graying when they arrived at a low cottage in a small clearing in the wood. Built of closely fitted field stones, it had a somewhat irregular oval shape with a tall, conical thatched roof that steamed softly in the chilly morning air. Milo had to duck slightly to pass under the door frame and noticed for the first time how short Culebrant was, who didn't have to duck. Inside it was humid and warm, with pleasant smells of herbs and wood smoke. It was illuminated by no more than the soft, reddish glow of a fire in an open hearth in the middle of the single, circular room. Its smoke rose straight up to gather in the high cone of the ceiling, where it seeped through the mat of thatch. A blackened cauldron hung above the fire from a hook made of an elbow of wood suspended from the crooked beams of the roof framing. The contents of the cauldron simmered enticingly, giving off an inviting aroma.

"First thing, let's see your injuries," Culebrant said, motioning Milo to take off his jacket and shirt. Even by the subdued light of the fire, the fresh bruise from smashing against the tree trunk on the flight down the hill was becoming visible. Culebrant looked at it, probed it gently with his fingers as Milo flinched, then began pulling down swatches from the herb bundles that hung in the rafters. While his back was turned, Milo quickly slipped the cord that held the pouch with the stone cross from around his neck and buried it in his pocket. Meanwhile, Culebrant mashed the herbs he'd chosen between his palms, added some paste from a small clay pot, and smeared it onto the skin where the bruise was and wrapped soft, fibrous strips around Milo's chest.

"Leave that on for a day or two and you'll be just fine," he said as Milo put his shirt back on. "Now that we've done your outsides, let's see what we can do for your insides."

Culebrant ladled portions of porridge from the cauldron into two bowls with a wooden ladle and handed Milo one of them. "Sorry, Old Fella," he told Bori. "There'll be fresh milk after I milk Bernice, my goat, in just a little bit. But don't worry. I won't forget. Neither Bernice nor Molly—she's my cat—would let that happen." As he spoke to Bori, he handed Milo a hand-carved wooden spoon. "Perhaps a bit of salt pork would tide you over until then?" he asked the cat.

Bori indicated that that would be acceptable. Culebrant carved a few slivers of meat from a smoked ham that hung in the rafters and gave them to Bori.

Milo sipped the porridge in appreciation. Peering up into the dim, smoky rafters, he saw all manner of objects hanging along with the ham and the herbs. He recognized items like smoked meats and sausages, but there were also bundles of sticks, tools, and implements whose purposes Milo could only wonder about. It was like the stuffed, messy closets that some people have. Despite the haze of smoke above, the air below where they were was clear, much to Milo's amazement. The whole arrangement was decidedly rustic, but it seemed to work in a comfortable, practical way.

"It's simple," Culebrant said, as if reading Milo's thoughts, "but it suits an old man's needs. I live here alone, except, that is, for Bernice and Molly." He turned to address Bori. "You'll be making Molly's acquaintance soon. She'll soon be in from dawn mouse patrol. Perhaps you'll be able to give her a hand. Keeping the mice in check around here's a full-time job."

"Perhaps I could lend my services for a bit," Bori replied. Milo knew that the mention of Molly had something to do with his disposition to help out.

Culebrant took Milo's empty bowl as Milo finished the last of his porridge. "I expect you could use a rest after your journey. I'll make you a pallet over there by the far wall where you can sleep undisturbed. As to the urgency of your mission"—he continued, cutting off Milo's haste as he put away the bowls after washing them in a wooden pail—"there's no need to hurry until you're ready to confront the challenges of the Barrow. It's been there these many, many years, and it can wait for you a bit longer. Rest for now and when you wake, we can start your apprenticeship."

"But...I got here with a friend..." Milo began to explain, worried about Stigma and how she might have fared with Kayn, but he felt suddenly so sleepy—had Culebrant put something into his porridge? He could barely hold his eyes open long enough for Culebrant to show him to a low bed of rushes covered with plaid wool blankets. He slept as soon as his head landed on the pillow.

Milo awoke hours later, much refreshed and in relaxed spirits. His bruised side didn't hurt and as he opened his eyes, two sets of peering cat eyes met his. One set (Bori's) was green and another set—unknown—golden. The face that held the golden ones was black and almost invisible in the dim light of the cottage.

"May I introduce Molly," Bori said, indicating the stranger. "I've told her all about you, and she's eager to make your acquaintance."

Milo sat up and stretched out his hand, allowing her to sniff the back of his curled fingers. That done, she allowed him to stroke her under the chin and ears. She purred.

"Where's Culebrant?" Milo asked.

"Outside. He told me to tell you there's soup on the fire if you're hungry, and then join him out-of-doors."

Milo wasn't hungry, so he went out.

"Ready to work?" Culebrant asked as Milo entered the yard, blinking like a mole in the hazy sunlight. Gradually unsquinting his eyes, he saw what he had not been able to see the night before. The trees were not summer green, but had turned into autumn reds, golds, tans, and russetts. The autumn air was crisp with a chill that resisted the efforts of the sun to warm it.

Culebrant was cutting tree limbs into firewood. He showed Milo where to carry the pieces to stack up alongside the cottage. It felt good to move and breathe clean air, and Milo worked happily for some time, matching Culebrant's wordless activity.

After a time Culebrant took a break and Milo sat alongside him on a log. Milo's question came out without thinking. "Does the name Heronsuge mean anything to you?"

"Yes, it does," he said without evidencing surprise. "Does it to you?"

"No, not really. He's the reason I came to the Great Barrow. I was told by a...a reliable source that he could tell me what I need to know."

"I expect that's right," Culebrant said and went back to work.

"Can you tell me about him?"

"Yes, I can and I will. Like you said, it's what you came for. It's why I took you as an apprentice."

"What do you mean?"

"You didn't think that helping me cut up wood was the reason I took you on, did you? There's more to it than that."

"What do you mean?" Milo asked again, more perplexed than before.

"Well, for one thing: shields."

"Shields?"

"You're wide open. If you meet Kayn like that, or Heronsuge, for that matter, he would instantly see how unprotected you are. Kayn would smash you for no better reason than you are unable to protect yourself. So you need to be able to create and deploy your own shields. And then there's the lore of trees."

"Trees? Why trees?"

"For their wisdom. You must learn how to understand what they can teach. The Art of the Woodcutter."

Milo saw that now they were getting somewhere—only he didn't have any idea where.

"I'm a Woodcutter," Culebrant said. "Not a woodsman. You see, trees are sentient, although they have a form and existence so different from humans who live such short, quick lives walking around in the trap of their five senses. Trees have an entirely different sort of wisdom and experience. A Woodcutter must learn how to listen to them."

Milo thought of the oak in Korrigan Forest. "So that's what you meant about me being your apprentice?"

Culebrant nodded. "You must learn from the heavens, too. In fact, it's the heavens that are the books you must study to learn what you must know. Then you'll be able to ask the right questions at the right times and understand the answers. Without knowing the stars, the planets, the sun and moon, you can't read the Wheel or understand the answer—much less ask the proper question—which Heronsuge could answer for you. If you got that far, which you wouldn't."

"How am I to learn all that stuff?"

"By listening and by asking measured questions. By doing what I tell you whether you can see the sense in it or not, because understanding often comes after the fact. Be patient and take however long you need to learn what I have to tell you. There's no need to hurry. That's the first rule."

"But"—

Culebrant stopped him. "What's the first rule?"

"Be patient. Don't hurry," Milo said, feeling his heart slide with the realization that he was trapped into a new situation. He decided to try another tack. "You said I could ask questions?"

"Yes, if they are considered."

"I'm pressed for time. I have to get to the Great Barrow as soon as possible, and I'm worried about my friends who may be there already. I believe that Kayn is as dangerous to them as he is to me. How can I take the time you tell me I must take if I don't have the time to take it?"

"That's more than one question. There was one word among all those others that was meaningful. It was 'possible.' You must get to the Great Barrow as soon as *possible*. Now, you could rush off, climb it, and stand there like a fool until Kayn blasted you off it. That's an option, but, I think, a completely useless one. What if I were to tell you that the time you think you don't have is irrelevant to what is possible? Submit to this apprenticeship and I will not only keep you safe from your enemy, but I'll also assure you that the time you think you don't have will be profitably offset. It is the only way you can do what is possible—and to help yourself and your friends."

Milo didn't answer. Not protesting was all the answer he had the heart for.

So began Milo's apprenticeship as a Woodcutter. Each day before breakfast, they began with exercises—breathing, stretching, and strengthening—that Culebrant insisted were shaped by the structure of the universe, something he indicated was related to circles of movement. He called these movements 'The Gyre of the Rule' or simply 'The Rule.'

"Train your body with interlocking spirals of motion and your spirit learns to move in a circular way, too. In that way you condition yourself to avoid running headlong into barriers of resistance," Culebrant insisted. "Supple body, supple mind."

After the exercises, they ate breakfast and did chores. There were long rambles through the woods, with talks about the things they saw around them. Collecting plants and discussing the types and qualities of trees played a major part of these walks, reminding Milo of the sorts of information Einter had given him before Milo's adventure in Korrigan Forest—only what Culebrant had to say about them went well beyond what Einter had shown him.

At night they watched the sky. Often Culebrant got Milo out of bed in order to see the sky at a particular—and inconvenient for his slumbers—time. Wrapped in blankets against the increasing chill as autumn faded into winter, Culebrant showed Milo stars and constellations, and how they progressed through the hours of the night. Gradually, as the seasons turned, he explained the constellations of the elliptic. He demonstrated how these were the star patterns that lay along the same path that the sun takes across the sky. He called this chain of constellations by several terms: the Wheel of the Seasons or the Wheel of Time, but mostly, he referred to them simply as the Rule.

One night as they were watching the sky, Culebrant pointed out the stars that made up the constellation Milo recognized as Orion. Recalling his revelation from that night in Rykirk, Milo told Culebrant about it. "Those are the same stars I see at home—the world I come from," he said. "And if those are the same stars I see at home, how can this be a different world?"

"Because you've shifted. This place is not the same place as Rykirk, and Rykirk isn't the same place you came from. But that doesn't mean that they're different worlds. They're just different phases of the same world. You call those stars Orion, and they no doubt have their own stories. Here they're known as Candaon. I would hazard to guess that the stories about Candaon have similarities to the stories about Orion but they also are different in a way that fits the place where you come from. What do you know about Orion?"

"Well, Orion was a hunter."

"So was Candaon. In the earliest versions of his myth he was called the Protector of Beasts, but in a later version he became a great hunter. Myths may shift and take on new details but the core of the story—it's deep structure and purpose—remains true to its original inspiration. If it doesn't, it usually vanishes and the story is lost forever. You see, myths are the oldest things that people have. They're always told about a distant past and are relayed by storytellers, one person to the next, and each generation retells the story in a way that makes sense in that generation. The retelling must suit a purpose and make sense to those who are hearing it, without forsaking its antiquity."

"Sooo..." Milo puzzled, "a myth sort of wanders around. It's a fiction with a meaning that's true?"

"You could say that. A fiction because it's told for a dramatic purpose instead of being told to preserve factual detail. It must possess an insight that goes much deeper than simple facts can, which in the end are unimportant and pass away. Myths can be nearly forgotten, but then if the need arises, they can be revived and rebuilt. But for now," Culebrant said, turning Milo's attention back to the stars, "let's look for other star patterns that have their own stories, but are still linked into the same web of tales as Candaon's." He pointed out a rather faint star off to the north of the blazing group that made up Candaon. "Do you know what star that is?"

"Ahh...is that the North Star?" Milo ventured.

"Very good! Yes. It's called a fixed star because the whole sky appears to wheel around it. It's at the hub of the Wheel."

Culebrant showed Milo the constellation he called the Great Bear next, which Milo recognized as the Big Dipper. That led to the Little Bear, which was fainter, with the North Star at the tip of its long, un-bearlike tail. Then Culebrant pointed out an even more difficult set of stars that snaked between the two bears. They twisted along an arc of sky around the North Star.

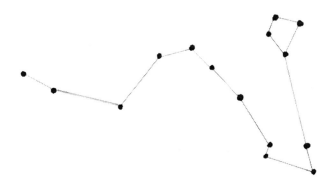

"That one's called The Dragon. I want you to memorize it and look for it every chance you get," Culebrant instructed.

Culebrant led Milo into the woods where they couldn't see the sky at all. "It's cold," he commented, wrapping himself tightly into his blanket. Milo, who was shivering and hoped that they might return to his nice, warm bed, followed along with some disappointment. "Let's walk and wait for the dawn."

Milo realized that they were moving close to the Great Barrow. Often on their walks they came near it, but they had always skirted around it. This time Culebrant took him right up its treeless, heather-choked slope.

"Tonight is Yule," Culebrant told Milo. "The longest night of the year. Tomorrow the sun will rise a little bit to the north of where it rises today, and begin its journey back into the summer sky. The day will be just a tad bit longer. This morning we'll watch the place where it rises."

They sat on top of the barrow, which Milo could see was shaped like a wandering ridge instead of a single hill. Its meandering shape undulated away toward the west. They were standing on the easternmost part. "Look there," Culebrant directed, pointing to the east. "Dawn is almost here and we need to watch the exact spot where the sun will rise." The darker mass of the earth was backlit by the waxing of sunrise, brightest at the point where the sun would clear the horizon. "Pay careful attention for the first flash of the sun's disk. Mark the exact spot. You can't watch for long, but I want you to be able to recognize that spot once the sun has lifted away from the horizon."

The whole rim of the eastern horizon was glowing now, and pink streamers of light trickled across the sky as it turned from black to a deep, luminous blue. The spot where the light was centered became dazzling just before the leading edge of the sun spilled across. Milo marked the spot, several finger widths from a wedge of rock jutting from the horizon line before he had to look away, blinking at the bright spots in his vision.

"Did you get it?" Culebrant queried.

"Yes. Just to the side of that bump."

"That was once a temple," Culebrant commented. "It was placed there to mark the winter solstice as viewed from this place on the Barrow. A dolmen was set to split the solar disk in half as it rose."

"Why? What happened? Did they put it in the wrong place?"

"No, they built it precisely, but that was a very long time ago. The hub of the sky has shifted. The earth has a wobble, making a slow circle that takes many thousands of years to complete. The sun rises in a different place now than it did back then. Besides, the dolmen has toppled since then and the temple is only rubble. You came through it when you arrived, though all you saw was a jumble of weathered stones. Woodcutters watch the slow cycle of the turning sky, marking it by the rising of the sun, the moon, and certain stars, and they pass these observations on to the next generation of Woodcutters so that they'll understand and track the cycle until the sun once more rises at the original spot at the old temple, though it will be completely gone by then."

"How long will that take?"

"A full cycle of the Wheel. Thousands of solar years."

"Why? That must be almost impossible. Is it that important?"

"It's the measure of Time. It's the calendar of each year and marks the seasons. It calculates the ages and it's the Book of Wisdom, because if you know what you must know in order to keep up with the precession of the Wheel, you know the cause and effect that the metaphysical world has on the manifest world. And for you, Milo, it will tell you what you've come here to learn."

"Are the stories about Candaon and the other constellations part of that?"

"Of course. They are the archive of the metaphysical world. For instance, did you know that Candaon played slinger? I believe you've mentioned your slinger-playing friends and the tournament at the End of the Earth." Culebrant stood up from where they had been sitting and started off down the slope. Milo had to hurry to catch up.

"You see, Candaon had been on a long journey far to the east. On the way back he met a giant who was terrorizing the land and blocked Candaon's way. This giant forced anyone who came by to play him in a slinger match. Candaon learned that the giant had a magic bat that killed at one end and resurrected at the other end. Candaon managed to steal the bat, replacing it with a normal one. Then he used the magic bat to overwhelm the giant. That bat became so much a part of Candaon that you can see it to this day in the stars of his constellation."

"So...that's why slinger is important to the End of the Earth pilgrimage?"

"Exactly. You see, Candaon was traveling back to be reunited with his wife. But when he got there, he discovered that her uncle, whose name was Severanus, wanted her to leave Candaon and marry an important ally, by telling her that Candaon was actually her nephew. The uncle's plot backfired, however, when her shame was so great that she threw herself into the pit of fire where she served as an oracle. When Candaon learned what had happened, he flew into an insane rage, howling with fury and grief, swearing to kill Severanus. Severanus fled, seeking the protection of Tholis, the Lady of Underground Places. Candaon raged on, killing anyone who came in his way until he came to the sacred isle of Elx, known for its labyrinth of caves. Tholis pledged to punish Candaon for these murders and called up from the labyrinth an Elemental. This was the great monster Heronsuge."

The name hit Milo like an electric shock. Not that he hadn't been listening to Culebrant's rambling story, but this name, heard so suddenly, made it very personal.

"What! What did you say?" Milo cried.

Culebrant chuckled. "So. You *have* been listening. I told you that these are things you must know. Now keep listening. The story's not done yet.

"You want to know who this Heronsuge is. It's time to make his acquaintance. You see, Heronsuge is often thought of as a huge dragon or serpent. Actually, he is an Elemental, one of the First Children of Anzu, the Creatrix, who divided herself into the heavens and the earth to create order—the Rule—from Chaos. Before that there was nothing but the unordered singularity that was Anzu. By dividing herself, things and beings came into existence, and as soon as there were individual things and beings, they had names. Thus, in the beginning there was Anzu. Elementals, only one step apart from the power of Chaos, were her first children. Her second were the Avatars. Later came the Elder Race of skilled magicians. Some of them wished to claim Creation for themselves, and they conspired with some of the Elementals and Avatars, who, after the rebellion was lost, came to be known as the Fallen. Not all of the Elder Race rebelled and they pledged to maintain the Rule of Anzu in opposition to their brethren and their bretheren's allies. This discord resulted in the War of the Elementals. Humans, for the most part, were pawns in this power struggle, battered this way and that.

"But let's return to Heronsuge," Culebrant said, noticing Milo's impatience. "The Great Dragon Heronsuge, tricked by Tholis into believing that Candaon was attacking the Gate that Heronsuge was set to guard, pursued Candaon as he stepped out of the sea onto the Isle of Elx. Candaon quickly learned that his arrows and even his slinger bat had no effect on the powerful Elemental, who was immortal. The abilities of the club—one end for killing and the other to resurrect, that is, an instrument of destruction and of healing—had no power over an Elemental who had come into existence before Death. All Candaon could do was to flee the monster by diving back into the sea and swimming away.

"He sought out Dawn, with whom he had consorted during an earlier adventure. She gave him a talisman shaped into the four corners of the Wheel, that the Dragon would recognize and respect. Its power was its ability to lock Heronsuge back into his underground lair."

Milo, hearing about the shape of the talisman, thought of the stone cross he wore in its sack beneath his shirt. He felt a hot blush rise into his cheeks and unconsciously covered it with his hand as if to hide it from his old teacher. If Culebrant noticed the gesture, he ignored it.

"Now, Elx was a sacred island. Tholis held reign over its labyrinth, but Therona, her sister, who was the Lady of the Moon and Patroness of the Hunt and of beasts, held sway of the island's surface. Therona was a great archer, and Candaon had learned archery from her long before. Tholis, who had gotten word that Candaon was returning to Elx, armed with the talisman to render the Great Dragon harmless, devised a new plot to stop him. She paid her sister a visit, and as they gossiped Tholis spotted Candaon swimming to the island. Only his head was visible, bobbing on the waves. Tholis pointed out the tiny target and taunted Therona that, great archer that she may be, she surely couldn't hit such a difficult target with one of her arrows. Therona, not realizing that the tiny dot was actually Candaon, accepted the challenge. She chose her best arrow and fitted it to the string of her crescent-shaped bow. She drew and let fly, the arrow arching up into the heavens. It reached its zenith and turned downward, falling with terrible force. It's said that it looked like a meteor as it fell, piercing Candaon through the forehead.

"When Therona learned what she had done, that she had killed Candaon with her own hand, she was devastated. She called on her father, Strellanus, the Star Herder, to set stars into the sky for Candaon as a memorial to him. Then she pledged that the moon—remember, she was the Moon Lady—would wane for half her cycle as a penance before waxing again to bring light back into the blackness of night. Candaon's stars would ride on the winter Star River—I believe you've called it the Milky Way."

Milo was puzzled. "How does all this relate to me and my need to speak to Heronsuge?"

"I agree. You have a problem," Culebrant confirmed, his expression so guileless that Milo knew he was up to something.

"Okay," Milo surrendered. "What is it I have to do?"

"Unravel the puzzle."

Milo groaned. "This is going to be a long winter."

17

The Widdershins Shuffle

The kittens were born just before the day Culebrant called Ostara, at the spring equinox. There were two black sisters and a little grey male. Molly purred as they nursed and Bori swelled with pride. The only time he would leave the side of his new family was to hunt for them.

"Fatherhood gives you a different perspective on things," he told Milo when Milo invited him to go on a ramble. "You'll see, one day," Bori assured him.

Milo missed the cat's company, but respected—admired even—the cat's devotion to his family. Besides, he looked forward to playing with the kittens as soon as their eyes opened and they began to explore their new world. After all, he was their godfather.

Culebrant kept Milo plenty busy. "First of all, you must learn to make a shield, following the proper procedures. Then you have to internalize it. The physical shield then becomes redundant, for it's the spiritual shield that thwarts the malignant energy that will be directed at you."

So they went about making a shield. First, they collected the materials Culebrant said Milo would need.

"Everything's right here in the forest," Culebrant told him. "This is how you become a Woodcutter. Not a woodsman, mind you, or a person who cuts wood with metal tools. Have you ever heard the term that hunters and trackers use? 'Cutting for sign?' That has the meaning I use. It means to look for the evidence animals leave behind, like tracks, droppings, hair, and grass and twigs bent by their passage. A skilled hunter can examine those things to learn a great deal about animals that he hasn't actually seen. A Woodcutter does the same thing, except instead of animals, he's tracking the wisdom of trees."

He handed Milo a knife made of beautifully flaked flint, with an antler handle. "A metal knife, saw, or axe destroys the energy in the wood when you cut it. This is much less intrusive and leaves the essence of the plant's energy in the parts you'll be collecting. They'll be much more powerful to you that way."

The idea of trees having some sort of inherent energy and wisdom was a hard idea for Milo to accept, but he wasn't going to say that to Culebrant. Culebrant said it for him.

"Remember, young Milo, these are beings much more like us than we realize. They have an experience of life that's alien to the sort of mobile existence we have, but that doesn't preclude their sentient nature. For now, accept that they can help you. I won't insist you believe it as long as you respect the possibility. Wisdom comes through believing nothing while remaining open to everything."

Culebrant showed him a succession of trees, explaining the properties and characteristics of each. He described how Milo should collect the parts he would use from each of them, avoiding contact with them himself. "To be your shield, it must resonate to your energy. My touch could alter that enough to cause a weak spot, and your enemies, especially the skilled ones you'll meet, would instantly recognize those points and exploit them.

"There are three things a good shield can do," he continued. "First, it can deflect malevolent intent. Second, it serves to camouflage your own intent from others, and third, it blocks the vampiric drain of energy that other beings can take from you, whether through malicious design or sheer neediness."

Loaded with materials, they trooped back to Culebrant's cottage. Bori left the sleeping kittens to come out into the yard to watch. Culebrant coached Milo in careful detail as Milo followed his instructions.

First, he had Milo shape a ring by bending willow branches and binding them together. "We'll hang that in the rafters where it can dry and adapt to its new shape," Culebrant told him. "When this part is done, we'll prepare the other materials to use as we need them during the construction of the shield. That should take a while—oh, say until Belthane, at summer equinox. After that, we'll start the process you'll need to go through to internalize the finished shield."

He directed Milo how to put together the unused materials to store them. "There will be an additional quality your shield must have," he added when they were done. "It must be able to conceal the talisman you wear underneath your shirt as well as shield you."

This shocked Milo. He had been very careful to keep the cross hidden from notice. "You...you...?" he stammered.

"Oh yes. I've known about that from the first instant I set eyes on you. It shines brighter than the brightest star to anyone with an eye for things from the Otherworld. You'll need to hide it better than your shirt can if you want to keep it secret from the sort who can see it, because it gives you away. You can't afford that."

Milo felt anxious and embarrassed at the same time. All this time Culebrant had known that he carried a secret that he hadn't shared. What if Culebrant had tried to take it? What if he had gone straight into a face-off with Kayn? It made him feel like a fool, ashamed and dependent on nothing more than just dumb luck.

The kittens were growing day by day as Milo worked on his shield. Culebrant encouraged him to spend time with them even as he held Milo to a schedule that would insure that he finish the shield before the beginning of summer. "Those kittens need to have the company of their human friends," he pointed out. "Otherwise they'll be too wild to be handled."

The kittens were soon tottering about, their bright little eyes eager to see everything. They held their little spike tails high as they practiced scampering and pouncing on imaginary prey, three fierce teddy bears.

"What are you naming them?" Milo asked Bori as Milo played with the little grey male, letting him chase the tip of a whippy switch.

"Oh, that's up to you humans. Cats don't need names among ourselves. We know each other by scent. Names are between us and our human friends."

Milo thought about that as he watched the little male, already full of himself and strutting like the world was there for his sole benefit. "I think 'Raster' suits him," Milo decided.

"Raster? Okay, how about the girls?"

The two female kittens were playing hide-and-seek under the apparent inattention of their mother, who, Milo knew, was aware of their every move and everything else in the yard. One of them stopped in mid-pounce to smell a recently bloomed crocus.

"Iris and Daisy," Milo said, deciding names right then. "I don't know which one is Iris and which one is Daisy, because they look exactly alike," Milo added.

"You would know if you were a cat with a cat's sense of smell," Bori answered. "I've always wondered how you humans get along without being able to smell what's happening around you, being blind at night, and lacking a good set of whiskers to feel where you are."

"We do the best we can, I guess. Besides, I've got you to help me out."

Raster left the switch to pounce on his father, who rolled him with a lazy paw and held him down until he struggled free and dashed away to chase his nearest sister.

"Family life suits me," Bori told Milo. "When this is done, I'm going to settle down right here with my family."

Culebrant insisted that the shield be finished by Belthane. "That gives it the strength of the waxing sun," he said, referring to the sun's return into summer skies.

Culebrant instructed Milo to choose his own materials to incorporate into the shield, though he was careful to make suggestions and explain what properties each choice might give as Milo went along. Milo wove strips of various woods together and layered them using glue that Culebrant taught him to make. In the days just after Yule, Culebrant had taken him into the forest to climb high into oak trees to harvest and mash the white mistletoe berries for their juice to use in the glue. He had given Milo a white smock to wear, insisting that he have it on whenever he did anything with the mistletoe. It had gotten stained with juice, moss smears, and glue, but Culebrant would not let him wash it. "That would dilute the strength of the mistletoe," he claimed.

Two days early, Milo had it completed, except for choosing a symbol to paint on the face. "What will it be?" Culebrant asked him.

"I was thinking of the stars that make up The Dragon," Milo answered. "But just the little points are sort of weak. I think it needs something to make it stronger than that."

"I think The Dragon is an excellent choice. Let's see if we can't figure out how to make the design more striking. How does the constellation make the most sense to you?"

"I've been watching how it turns around the axis of the sky every night, and I like the wheel-like path it takes."

"Then draw a picture of it on this piece of bark," Culebrant suggested.

Milo did that, easily placing each star where it appeared in the configuration, so familiar were they to him by now.

"Now, try this: draw the way they go in the opposite position," Culebrant directed, and Milo did that. They formed a shaft-like shape with hooks at the outer ends. "Draw another one at right angles, and then opposite to that."

When Milo finished, the design had the form of a cross with bent tips. "It looks like it's dancing," Milo said. "It also reminds me of a figure we call a swastika, though swastikas have a bad name where I'm from.

That's because they were used by some very bad people before I was born. Only, I think the one they used had the arms bent the opposite way. They made their swastikas look like they turned clockwise."

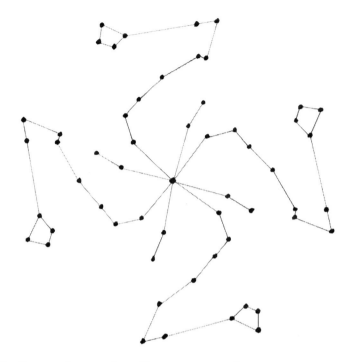

"That's very interesting. The way your picture turns is the way The Dragon turns in a gyre around the sky, marking the cycle of the Rule. We call that direction 'widdershins.' The other way would be anti-widdershins, and that gives it an evil spin."

"Wow! I wonder if they knew that?" Milo said, thinking about the Nazi symbol.

"Perhaps their intentions guided them whether they knew what they were doing or not," Culebrant said. "This picture you drew is a very old symbol, and very powerful. I think it's perfect for your shield."

Milo painted the whole face of the shield white by grinding white clay into the paste he made using mistletoe juice. He edged it with a black border around the rim, and then filled the middle with the wheeling widdershins stars. Instead of painting in each star as an individual point, he turned the four-armed shape into a solid figure in a rich crimson. He held the shield up when he was done, very pleased with the effect and how substantial it felt despite its light weight.

"That shield can stop a spear," Culebrant told him. "But it can't stop a spell yet. You have to internalize it first."

"What do you mean?"

"Between now and midsummer, at Litha, you must carry your shield with you everywhere you go. Use it for a pillow at night. Look for it in your dreams. By keeping it with you all the time, it'll become a part of you."

Milo made loops of twine so he could sling it on his back to free his hands while he worked, but the part about looking for it in his dreams seemed very unlikely. How do you control your dreams? But he promised to try. Meanwhile, Culebrant taught him more stories about the stars.

"When you painted the stars of The Dragon on your shield, you made the hub on the third star of the dragon's tail," Culebrant pointed out.

"I did that because it seemed to be the best one for the constellation to spin on. That way the four directions seem the most balanced" Milo offered.

"That's very interesting," Culebrant commented. "What if I were to tell you that that star was once the Pole Star, the North Star thousands of years ago? Back when the temple for the winter solstice was built?"

That caused a shiver to run up Milo's spine. It felt like he was hanging on the edge of a major revelation.

"Precession has caused the Pole Star to shift, like I explained to you before. Today the Pole Star is the last star in the Little Bear's tail, but back then it was the third star in the dragon's tail. That means that the Hub was in Heronsuge."

"In Heronsuge? The Dragon? Then...back when the hub was The Dragon, it would have been the most important constellation in the sky!" Milo exclaimed.

"Exactly. Heronsuge was set to guard the Hub and be the protector of the Wheel. Candaon, carrying his bat of destruction and of healing, had the talisman he received from Dawn to counteract Heronsuge. That means Candaon held the key to lock Heronsuge into place and thereby control access into the Gate of Eternity; he held the key to The Rule. So, you see, Candaon and Heronsuge are joined in a deep partnership. Together they preside over the Gate into the Otherworld. They administer the path of Wisdom, or Knowledge of the Rule, and guard the path that the soul must take to pass into the Higher Realm on the other side of the Wheel.

"Here's the explanation about how that came about. Remember

when I told you the story about the War of the Elementals? How some of the Elementals joined with The Fallen while other remained faithful to Anzu and her Rule? Heronsuge remained true, but Tholis was one of the rebels. Severanus was another. When Tholis called on Heronsuge to pursue Candaon, she convinced him that Candaon was trying to get into the Garden of the Higher Realm on the other side of the Wheel in order to steal the apples of immortality that grew there. In fact, she and Severanus were the ones who were plotting to steal them. If they had gotten the apples, they would have had the key to escape death and that would have been a huge advantage in the war."

Milo's mind spun with possibilities at this. "So...there were apples that make you live forever. We have a story about apples, too. They were in a garden when the world was created. The first two people, Adam and Eve, lived in the garden where the apple tree, the Tree of Knowledge, was until a serpent tempted Eve to eat one of the apples. She shared it with Adam and because the apples were forbidden, they were banished from the garden and condemned to live in pain and to die, them and all their descendants afterward."

Culebrant considered Milo's story, shaking his head in recognition. "Fascinating! It's the same story, only altered to fit a different culture. The apples, a tree of knowledge that's forbidden to mortals, and a serpent— that would be Heronsuge, the dragon who guards it."

Culebrant anticipated the tumult of questions Milo was about to ask and preempted them by continuing his story. "When Therona's arrow struck Candaon as he was returning to Elx, bearing the talisman from Dawn, he was carrying his slinger bat with him. As he sank into the waters of the sea, the end that gives back life struck him, preventing his death. Of course neither Tholis nor Therona realized this and presumed him dead. Weakened, but still alive, he made it to Inys Raun and dragged himself up onto the beach."

"Wait a minute!" Milo broke in. "I thought he was going to Elx. Where did this Inys Raun come from?"

Culebrant gave a mischievous grin. "Elx and Inys Raun are the same, the sacred isle presided over by Therona, Lady of the Moon and the High Priestess of the Western Maidens who live in the Garden at the Gate to the Otherworld. Tholis had made her labyrinth beneath the island to gain access to Elx. By hiding her realm beneath the island, she could keep it from the notice of those who were loyal to The Rule and at the same time give herself an unseen but convenient approach to the Gate.

"With Candaon taken care of and Therona distracted by her guilt and grieving, Tholis and Severanus made a dash for the Gate. She stood guard against Heronsuge's return while Severanus slipped through to steal the apples. Meanwhile, Therona found Candaon on the beach. With the talisman he carried, she used it to heal him and restore his strength. Overjoyed that he still lived, she took him to her temple, but on the way they met Tholis who had received the apples from Severanus. Tholis tried to slip past Therona and Candaon, but Therona stopped her to ask her what she was carrying. Tholis told her that she just had some apples that she had been eating, but Therona suspected what they really were. Therona asked Tholis if she would share them with her and Candaon since they hadn't eaten.

"Tholis couldn't refuse. If her ruse were revealed, she knew she couldn't take both of them on at the same time, so she had to give each one of them an apple, leaving her with only one. But one, she considered, was better than nothing and she slipped away with the remaining apple.

"With the two apples in hand, Therona was certain where they'd come from and turned in pursuit of Tholis, handing the two apples to Candaon to guard. Instead of waiting, however, Candaon used his slinger bat to volley the apples back into the Garden, a tremendous feat of skill and strength. Then he chased after Therona and the fleeing pair, Tholis and Severanus. They caught up with them, but not before Severanus called up reinforcements. A furious battle broke out with Therona shooting her deadly arrows and Candaon using the killing end of his bat. He engaged with Tholis, using his bat to scoop away the apple she carried. With Therona covering his retreat, he dashed back toward the Gate. Now the chase was reversed, with Tholis and The Fallen chasing Therona and Candaon. But as they approached the precincts of the Gate, Heronsuge, returned from searching for Candaon, had taken up his place as Guard of the Gate and confronted Candaon. As Heronsuge opened his jaws wide to snap the interloper in half. Candaon made another incredible leap that carried him straight down the monster's throat and out his tail, right at the entrance to the Gate. Saturated with Heronsuge's venom, Candaon used the last of his strength to toss the third apple back into the Garden where it belonged.

"Heronsuge's venom dissolved the hero in moments. Nothing was left but the talisman he carried and the nobility of his deed.

"Stellanus, the Star Herder, carried out the promise he'd made to Therona to place a memorial for Candaon in the sky. He took the brilliance from Heronsuge's stars and transferred it to Candaon's stars to blaze in the winter sky. There they arbitrate the destinies of all mortals through the influence of the constellations of the Wheel. Heronsuge, in remorse for his mistake in trying to prevent Candaon from completing his task, relinquished his position at the Hub, but he remains as the Watcher of the Wisdom Path."

"That's quite a strory," Milo commented.

"Yes, it is," Culebrant agreed.

18

Milo Dreams of an Otherworld

"How will I know when I've internalized my shield?" Milo asked Culebrant. He carried it with him all the time now but couldn't imagine how that was to lead to an end of the process.

"Oh, you'll know," Culebrant assured him.

"You said I should have it by summer solstice, right?" Milo pushed.

"Yes, I said that. But it's not about the amount of time. By the way, how's your dreaming?"

"Oh, okay." He knew Culebrant was going to ask him about the shield appearing in his dreams, which it hadn't. "Like, last night I dreamed that I was on top of the barrow. Bori was there, and we were looking for Raster. He'd gone off somewhere."

"Did you find him?"

"I don't remember. I think the dream slipped off onto something else at that point."

"Did you have your shield?"

"I don't think so. I don't remember it."

"I told you you should keep it with you everywhere you go. That includes when you dream."

That seemed impossible to Milo, but since Culebrant said it in his usual mild way, Milo didn't feel criticized by Culebrant's admonishment.

Bori and Molly were teaching the kittens to hunt. They were young cats now, not just little spike-tailed balls of mischief. The two girls were doing quite well with their lessons, catching grasshoppers, moths, and the occasional lizard, but Raster was set on greater prey, choosing to ignore the smaller stuff. He would skip over a perfectly good grasshopper, his eyes fixed on a blue jay that knew exactly what he was up to. It would hop around on the ground while Raster worked himself through the grass on his belly, ears flat and tail flicking with intent until he was almost within range. As he pulled himself into a knot for the final rush, the bird would casually hop up into the lower branches of a bush, just beyond the cat's reach.

"I don't know about that boy," Bori told Milo. "He just won't listen.

It's got to be all or nothing. I've shown him over and over the art of the stalk and how to control his excitement. I've advised him that it's best to practice on little things first, but no, he wants his first kill to be a bear."

"He'll get it," Milo assured the dad. Actually, he wasn't that sure. Raster had more energy than patience.

And then one day Raster came into the yard, dragging a woodrat that was almost his size. He growled at his sisters when they ran out to see what he had, and glared a warning at everyone else. He was much too proud of his kill to try eating it, and wouldn't put it down until Bori came home. Raster laid it at his father's feet and sat, his back turned toward his dad and the rat to show that it wasn't such a big deal, and went to work straightening out his roughed-up fur. Apparently the woodrat had put up a pretty good tussle. Milo couldn't tell which of the two—father or son—was the prouder.

Later, Bori made a comment to Milo. "You two are a lot alike: you and Raster. Not satisfied with practicing on the little stuff first. You both have to go for the big kill."

"What do you mean?" Milo asked, surprised and a little put-off.

"That shield. You're obsessing about it. If you wouldn't try so hard, I bet it would just be there, in your dreams like Culebrant said it should be. Are you sure it isn't?"

Milo shrugged. "Maybe I should just tell him that it's there, and let it go at that."

"Somehow, I don't think that would work. Not with Culebrant."

On the morning of the summer solstice, Milo awoke, bursting out of sleep in a state of excitement. He ran straight off to find Culebrant.

"I did it! It happened!" he announced the instant he found the old man, trimming kindling for the morning's fire.

"You did?" Culebrant asked mildly, not looking up from the axe chop.

"Yes! My shield!"

"It was there in your dreams, I take it," Culebrant said as if it were the most ordinary thing Milo could say. "Tell me about it—after we do our morning exercises, just like we do every day. Your dream can wait. Focus your thoughts so you can give me all the details later."

They did that. Milo unraveled the excitement and confusion of remembered dream images, remarking with increasing amazement at the richness of detail. By the time they had finished their morning sequence, they sat down and Milo began.

"At first, I didn't have my shield. It just wasn't there. I didn't miss it or think about it, or anything. But then, I saw someone."

"Who was it?"

"It was Kayn."

"How do you know? I thought you've told me that you never actually saw him."

"I...just knew. And I knew then that I had my shield and it was right there. I was holding it up in front of me. He looked right at me, but then—and I was terrified he'd seen me—he sort of gazed away like he hadn't noticed me. I realized that the shield had hidden me from him."

"Where's your shield now?"

Shock hit Milo. He didn't have it. Having it was second nature after carrying it around all the time, and he didn't have it. He hadn't even noticed.

"I...I guess I must have left it on the bed when I woke up. I was so excited. I'll go get it."

He rushed off toward the cottage, chagrined at his slip-up. Forgetting his shield just when he'd finally succeeded in dreaming about it was embarrassing.

It wasn't where he'd left it, right beside his bed where he put it last thing before he went to sleep so it would be there when he got up. It wasn't near the bed, or anywhere else in the cottage. With all sorts of wild thoughts about where it could be or what could have happened to it, he started out the door of the cottage and ran into Culebrant, coming in.

"Did you find it?" he asked Milo.

"No. I...I must have left it..."

Culebrant interrupted. "You won't find it. You don't need to. You've internalized it. When you needed it in your dream, it was there. That's where it is now. You've succeeded, my young friend." And he smiled warmly.

Milo was at first dumbfounded, but then what Culebrant was telling him began to sink in. And he understood what Bori had told him, and how cat and son had felt when Raster caught the woodrat.

Culebrant said no more about the shield for some time, until one day, with no lead in at all, he said, "You have your shield. Now you must learn to stalk. Kayn is searching for you, and you must find him first. That's your best protection. The hunter, believing he is controlling the hunt, will not realize that he is the hunted. Stalk *him*. Keep up with what he's doing and learn all you can about him. You must know your foe before the showdown."

"How? How can I do that?"

"By Dreaming." Culebrant paused, letting Milo comprehend that he didn't have any idea about what Culebrant was talking about before he continued. "Not sleeping, but by using the state of dreaming in a conscious way. That's Dreaming."

Culebrant had Milo sit in concentration, the same way they did every morning as the final part of the exercises they did, with his eyes closed and his body in relaxed focus. After Milo settled, Culebrant spoke. "Find his face," he told Milo, so gently that it seemed not to be actual words, but inside Milo's head.

Milo pictured Kayn's face, seeing it just as he had dreamed it. He studied it, slowly noticing that the rest of him filled in to make a whole image inside a setting. Milo felt his shield held in place, although he didn't feel like he was there himself at all. It was a little like watching television, except he could feel the air and smell heather and wood smoke. There was a crowd, with Kayn standing at its borders. Milo recognized it as the assembly at the End of the Earth ball court. Kayn was working his way carefully around the crowd, looking at the many faces and observing what had drawn the crowd's interest. The crowd was watching Beryl, Teryl, and Deryl.

Kayn, however, avoided them and continued to look for something else. Milo watched as he caught sight of Analisa and stopped to study her with an intense expression of spite on his face. Milo felt apprehensive for fear he would do something to her, but Kayn moved on. He found and watched Aulaires who was speaking with Count Yeroen. The crowd began breaking up, Kayn trailed along behind Aulaires and Yeroen until they separated. He then turned to follow the Count.

"Where do you go now, Lord?" Kayn, using the wheedling guise of Smith, asked as he caught up with Yeroen. The two clearly knew each other.

"To follow the next clue in my quest," Yeroen said confidently.

"And that is...?" Kayn—now as Smith—asked, leaving his question open.

"It will have something to do with how those three silly pups return to claim their heritage in the Oak Clan." Yeroen paused. "I don't have the details worked out yet."

Smith nodded in sympathy. "Of course, I'm no lore master as you are, but as you know, I have some knowledge. The obvious place to look, of course, would be Akenwald, where those three oak-heads will be traveling, but that seems too obvious, don't you think? No, there's another possibility. Very risky, but the sort of challenge suited to the competition in the Magical Scavenger Hunt. Certainly a risk within the abilities of an accomplished mage like yourself."

Milo wanted to scream at the Count. Surely such blatant flattery should trigger his suspicion of this charlatan, but Yeroen smiled smugly. "What? Out with it, man!"

"Well, you surely know of the Valley of the Stone Knights? Of course you do. During the War of the Elementals, the rebel army sacked the End of the World, ending its existence as a city. They moved on, expecting to gain aid with a secret weapon, but they ran into an army of the Loyalists first. There was a terrible battle. When the rebel army was forced to retreat, they made their way into a valley which is now known as the Valley of the Stone Knights. In order to hold off their enemies while the main van of the army could slip out across the pass at the head of the valley, the Knights of the Guard took a terrible oath. They swore to hold the valley against the insurmountable odds of the Elemental Army, fighting without quarter and asking for none."

"Yes, yes, I know the legend. They took the Lithic Oath in order to be able to stand against the onslaught of their foes. They succeeded, but the price they paid was dear indeed. They became the Stone Knights. Invulnerable and retaining their fighting skills, but turned into animated stone, soulless and capable of nothing but duty and combat. They have no alternative than warfare. To this day, anyone who ventures into the valley can expect to be attacked as soon as a Knight senses the intruder."

"Your acumen is impressive," Smith gushed, "but remember, they still hold their secrets—secrets from the time when they sacked the End of the World. Vanquish one of them, and he must reveal the secret that the End of the World holds. That, I would guess, would reveal knowledge that sheds light on the clue you're seeking."

"Hmm," Yeroen intoned, thinking. "You could be right. And what an extraordinary accomplishment that would be! *That* would impress the Hunt judges! But is it possible? No one of flesh and blood can defeat a Stone Knight!"

"Oh, there is another way, and it has been done, from time to time. I read about it in the great library of Inverdissen, in a book long buried in the catacombs of its vast collection. Clever subterfuge can trick a Knight into believing he has been defeated and then he will tell his secret to the person who defeated him. It's his price for failure and the loss of all he has left: his honor."

"How would you"—Yeroen began, but broke off as Smith grabbed his arm, warning him to silence. Milo had edged very close in order to hear what was being said, and jerked his shield into place as Smith/Kayn—sensed something. Smith drew the Count away, and Milo dared not follow too closely.

He trailed along at a distance, watching as they walked, heads together in guarded conversation, until they came to Yeroen's camp. Smith veered off and Yeroen began packing for departure.

Milo followed Smith. He seemed to be wandering aimlessly, but he soon came on Aulaires. He spoke with her, glancing around as if to avoid notice, and then continued on his way. Now Aulaires went into a whirlwind of action to hurry off toward Yeroen's camp.

Smith sought out three more of the Hunt contestants as Milo watched. After he had spoken with each one, that contestant went into a frenzy to be off. Milo, feeling the strain of his concentration, let the scene slide away. He sagged into Culebrant's presence.

"He sent them away," he said. "Kayn! Kayn Smith sent them into the Valley of the Stone Knights! Why would he do that? Why did he want to get them killed!?" The cold blooded horror of what had happened hit him harder than when Stigma had told him about it.

"They're not dead, not exactly," Culebrant said. "Just frozen in the stone spell which the Knights use to hold their prisoners. As to why Kayn would do that? He's cunning and ruthless. I'm sure he had his reasons, and my guess is that it had something to do with flushing you out. Perhaps he hoped to lure you there, either to ambush you himself or let the Stone Knights do it for him. How did you avoid his trap?"

"I didn't!" Milo said, distressed at the thought that he had caused what had happened to the other contestants. He thought of Analisa, and wondered if she had gotten a visit from Smith, and if she were now ensorcelled in stone. It made him wince, helpless to undo whatever he had contributed to. "He tricked them. I didn't have any idea where they went, because...I had a different idea about what I needed to do and the next clue. So I went a different way."

Another thought hit him, deflecting his remorse in confusion about another issue. "I was there," he stated. "Right there, right then, at the End of the Earth. And then there I was, as the me I am now, watching Kayn. Were there two of me there at the same time?"

"You weren't actually there at all," Culebrant explained. "You looked in on Kayn from Dreaming. In Dreaming, you sidestep the Rule. Even if you see yourself, you are seeing yourself as you were then, not as you are now. You're looking at the manifest world from outside it."

Milo's head ached. "I don't understand. I don't get it."

"Action within the manifest world belongs to the conditions imposed by the Rule," Culebrant explained. "You can watch Kayn in any time you choose, but you can't do anything to him, or act upon anything in the scene you're viewing."

"But...I got too close and he knew I was there. I used my shield, and I don't think he really knew it was me, but he knew *something* was watching him, because he moved away and made sure I couldn't hear what he was saying after that."

"Watching the manifest world from Dreaming is sort of like standing outside a room and looking in through the window. What you say about Kayn sensing you is very interesting, because it reveals that he knows about Dreaming. I don't expect he can use Dreaming himself—it's a very rare skill, and I would know if he were able to Dream—but apparently he's able to sense when a window is open. You made a mistake that Dreamers often make at first. You believed that you were actually there. It's like standing at a window when the light is on; it makes you visible to someone outside the window. Luckily you obscured yourself with your shield, so Kayn was unsure that he had sensed you and you didn't give yourself away. Let that be a lesson, and don't make that mistake again. You won't escape his notice a second time. If he figures out that you're watching him, he's clever and skilled enough to turn the table on you and he'll be stalking you as you are stalking him."

It all made Milo's head spin.

Culebrant kept Milo watching and learning everything he could about Kayn from Dreaming. Most of the time, there was very little of importance; he watched Kayn travel, apparently following the Hunt contestants as they converged on the pass of the Stone Knights. Kayn traveled in the humble persona of Smith in order to avoid drawing suspicion to himself. Milo saw how often he would pause, fixing his attention on someone, lip curled in a sneer. Especially Count Yeroen, who seemed to be oblivious to Kayn's presence. Milo learned to recognize Smith by his sidling walk and his studied, nondescript bearing. But he saw very little that revealed what Kayn's plans might be. Even this, Culebrant insisted, was important, because it allowed Milo to become acquainted with how Kayn looked, how he moved, and how he behaved within his disguise as Smith.

"Keep watching him," Culebrant insisted, "and you'll find the moments when he reveals his purpose. Then he'll be unable to fool you with some ruse when you meet him face to face. It's the whole reason to stalk him."

Bit by bit, Milo followed Kayn until he crossed the pass into the Valley of the Stone Knights. Kayn gauged his arrival well behind the Hunt contestants. Milo saw how he moved into the valley with extreme caution, seeking to avoid the notice of the once again dormant Stone Knights. He was methodical, seeking out the Hunt's casualties one by one. Milo saw how he took pleasure in the fate of each one, each one a person who had done nothing to deserve being petrified.

The first was Ali-Sembek, now a heroic statue astride his winged horse as it reared with Ali waving his granite sword like a warrior in battle. Apparently that had been a poorly thought-out strategy. Kayn showed little interest in the man except to note and sneer at his failure, and moved on quickly. He located each unfortunate for a similar look-over. Braenach, Tivik, Wei Jain, Obeah Reah and Vianna. Count Yeroen was not among them, nor were Aulaires (presumably her charms could melt even the stoniest males) Lute, Sarakka, or—to Milo's relief—Analisa. Because he had met her later, he wasn't surprised that Stigma was not among the ensorcelled, although he wondered if he would have been able to see her if she had been captured in stone.

After further searching without finding any others—and he seemed particularly frustrated by these results—Kayn made his way back to cross out of the valley by way of the pass. Just before the top, Kayn suddenly ducked into cover and Milo instinctively did the same. Each of them peeked out after a few moments to see what—or who—was coming in. Milo expected a Stone Knight. It wasn't. A figure dressed in patched, well-worn green made his way stealthily into the tangle of shrubbery. Tinburkin.

Kayn buried himself into the foliage. Milo moved in as close as he dared to watch as Kayn studied the ranger, the lip-curl more pronounced than ever and making wringing motions with his hands as if restraining a desire to do damage.

Milo could see that Kayn was poised to blast Tinburkin if he showed signs of detecting him, and Milo's tension mounted into a terrible urge to do something to keep Kayn from doing harm to the ranger.

The need didn't arise. Tinburkin passed out of sight into the valley and Kayn moved quickly over the pass and was gone. Milo relaxed and remembered that he had seen Tinburkin at Rykirk at a time that would have been after he visited the valley. Back in the present, Milo asked

Culebrant the question about warning the Ranger from his place inside Dreaming.

"It's good you didn't try," Culebrant reminded him. "You would have been unable to do it and Kayn would have detected you. Unless this ranger is as skilled as Kayn in sensing activity from the Otherworld, he would not have noticed anything and Kayn would have blasted him anyway. No, your purpose is as the observer, learning what to expect from your quarry. You've chosen a strategic action that you are now committed to follow. If this man, whom I suspect you know well, had fallen victim to Kayn it would not be your fault—as I expect you would be tempted to believe. Remember, each of us has his own destiny. We each must choose how to explore that destiny and what strategy to use in following it, but another person's destiny remains his own. It's not our responsibility nor do we have the ability to interfere. Sometimes our various strategies overlap, and when that happens we may aid each other, but as strategists we can't afford to waste energy. Remorse drains us when we think we should, or could, take an action to affect another's situation."

This seemed cold to Milo, and also shocking, coming from the otherwise gentle Culebrant. It revealed a hitherto unexpressed ruthlessness.

Summer was beginning to fade when Milo had a final—and definitive—episode trailing Kayn. Milo found him standing on the ridge that overlooked the forest he recognized as the same one that sheltered Culebrant's cottage. Behind the forest rose the shape of the Great Barrow. Kayn stood on the same ridge where Milo had tumbled in flight when he had arrived from Rykirk. Count Yeroen stood with him.

"This is where it all started," Yeroen was telling the man he knew as Smith. "You were right, my friend. The Great Barrow is the key to the final clue."

"No," Smith insisted. "Not the final clue. You have to learn what it is the Barrow holds if you are to learn that. You must enter it. What about the others?"

"Aulaires came with me. She knew that this island—Inys Raun—was known as Elx in the legendary past. With that connection, the importance of the Great Barrow to the Hunt became clear to me. As to the others, Lute made it here as did Sarakka and—to our amazement—that silly young witch Analisa. She must have tagged along on my coattails, as she's done all along. That won't serve her very well when it's her turn to face the Hunt judges when they assess our exploits."

"Was that boy with Analisa?" Smith wheedled.

"I haven't seen him or any of the others. I expect they failed in their encounters with the Stone Knights. Winnowing out the weak and the inept. When I left the End of the Earth, it was a regular exodus. They were all watching me, of course, knowing that I'm the most skilled of the Hunt contestants. They all chased me blindly in fear of being left behind. The ones who got here must have been clever enough to deal with the Stone Knights, but it's not been an easy trail to follow, even with the evidence wrung from those archaic stone heads. And of course, with the Barrow's special relationship to Samhain, the timing of our arrival guarantees that we would all arrive here at the same time. As to that stupid young whelp you asked about: if he's not standing in the Valley of the Stone Knights as a monument to foolishness, I expect he's off blundering around in Akenwald with his oaken-headed slinger friends."

"I think not, my Lord," Smith replied, rubbing his hands together in his most obsequious manner. "He has more...luck...than you give him credit for. I would guess that he possesses certain...resources. He is clever at concealing them. He is...unique."

"Oh, I doubt that," Yeroen said, and snapped his fingers. "That's how much credit I give him. He's no more than an opportunist, and not a very skilled one at that. No, after the contest with the Stone Knights, I believe the field of the Hunt contestants was thoroughly weeded and the true capacities of the candidates revealed. We're now down to the final test."

He turned to Smith and looked directly at him for the first time during this conversation. "By the way, you never told me what your interest in all this is, yet you arrive at the same places along the way."

"Oh, I have my own purposes. It's quite coincidental that your pursuit of the clues of the Magical Scavenger Hunt and mine converge. A true stroke of luck I find very convenient to the success of my purpose, for it has provided me the advantage of meeting someone of your stature as a lore master and mage. I've certainly profited from your knowledge and leadership, and I hope that I've been able to return the favor in some small way as well."

"Oh, indeed," the Count assured him, patting him on the shoulder. "Indeed."

Milo saw how Kayn Smith recoiled from Yeroen's touch, although Yeroen, already starting off down the hill, didn't notice or see the arrogant curl of his lip. Milo broke off the connection.

19

Reflections and Revelations

Of all his questions, one still stood way out in first place: "I don't have any choice but to deal with Kayn, do I?" he asked Culebrant.

"No, you don't. He's followed you all the way here. He'll follow you wherever you go, plotting and setting his traps until he has what he wants from you."

"And that is...?" Milo asked, knowing the answer but asking anyway.

"You must know that yourself, for without knowing what it is, he holds the advantage. You barely escaped a trap when you came here, and now you know what he'll do."

"But surely he's moved on by now. I mean, it was almost a year ago that I came, and he came, and I escaped, and we haven't seen him since."

Culebrant studied Milo carefully, considering telling him something that he should have already figured out for himself. "What?" Milo asked, dreading the answer.

"I provided you with refuge. Kayn was about to slay you and take what he came to get. I intruded in order to make it a fair fight. You weren't able to meet him then, but now you have the tools you'll need to deal with him, if you use them wisely. It's time."

"Time?" Milo's voice cracked. Terror swept through him. "I thought that time doesn't count in Dreaming."

"And in Dreaming you can't meet Kayn and act. It's time to take action."

"You mean, he's still around?"

"You've spent a year—a sun cycle—with me in order to learn how to deal with Kayn and carry out your purpose. You came here with a purpose, remember? But you weren't ready when you came. I have my purpose for having helped you escape. Our strategies converged. Did you think I saved you because I'm just a silly, kind-hearted old man?"

Culebrant was scaring him now.

"Milo, my young friend, I'm quite fond of you—that I won't deny—and I want—I need—you to succeed. But you must do that for yourself. I've given you the tools. Tonight you must return to your task. This is Samhain, the night when the doors between the world of the Rule and the

Otherworld are at their thinnest. You must step back into your own cycle and finish your mission."

What Culebrant was telling him was beginning to sink in. "I've been in the Otherworld for a whole year, haven't I?"

"Not precisely. I took you out of your own cycle and into mine. When you leave my cycle, you'll step back into your own at the time you left it, as if no time had elapsed at all." He gestured around him, at the woods, the cottage, and the family of nearly grown cats playing in the yard. "All this will belong to a long-forgotten past, as if it never was. Your destiny awaits you in your own cycle, where you still belong to the Rule."

Bori had come up during the conversation and sat at Milo's side. "I'll go with you," he told Milo. "I started this with you, and I'll finish. I think you'll need me. But when it's done, and my own destiny willing, I'll return here, to be with my family."

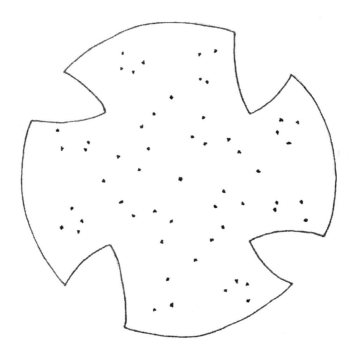

It was settled. The longest day Milo had ever known dragged out the afternoon. Milo thought a thousand thoughts, all of them pointless. Toward sunset, he took out the cross and looked at it, a thing he had avoided doing for the whole time he had been with Culebrant. He studied the inscription that he still couldn't read and then he turned it over to look at the back. It had a number of small pits in it which he'd never really paid much attention to, thinking them nothing but chips or imperfections. Now he saw something he'd missed. They were arranged in a repeating pattern, into each of the four arms of the off-kilter cross. Now they made sense. They were the same as the figure he'd painted on his shield. They were the pattern of stars, repeated to the four directions, that he knew as the Dragon. Heronsuge. He felt dizzy-headed, and his thoughts spun.

Culebrant came up to sit next to him. "You should put your things together—all you brought with you when you came. I think you should wear the old mistletoe smock when you go. The protection from spells that it's accumulated may come in handy."

Milo only half-heard him. "Culebrant? Can I show you something?" He remembered when Culebrant had referred to the cross without naming it, saying that it was visible to someone who could see such things.

Culebrant looked him in the eye, gently warning him, but of what?

"Yes, it's safe to show me. I know about it already. You have questions about it that you'd like answers for. Many of those questions can only have answers that come from you, but go ahead."

Milo held out his palm. The cross lay there, a charming artifact that held all its mysteries in perfect stillness.

"That's the Dragon's Cross," Culebrant said. "It has a remarkable purpose, for it's the key that opens a road that has not opened for a very long time."

"A road? A path...to the Hub of the Rule, right?"

Culebrant nodded.

"And I've been carrying it around with me all this time..."

"It's how I knew to help you. It's the thing that Kayn wants above all other things. It was taken away long, long ago, and hidden to keep it from such as Kayn. He learned of it and even figured out how to find it, but you intervened. It's a thing that can't be possessed, for its purpose is to serve."

"To serve? Who does it serve?"

Culebrant's face broke into a broad grin and he patted Milo's shoulder. "That's something you must still discover—on your own and at the proper place and time. For now, you'll find it will be the key you'll need to enter the final leg of your quest. It will be your guide as well as the key to the gate into the Beyond. Keep it safe. Use it to go, and use it again if you decide to return. Others may travel with you as your companions, but it's you who are the Wanderer."

Milo remembered hearing that before. The picture of the card that

Dame Renee had shown him flashed into his mind's eye. "The Wanderer... that was what Candaon was, wasn't it?"

"You've learned your lessons well. You're ready, with knowledge at least, to engage Kayn and to meet Heronsuge. Without the knowledge, you would have no hope of success, but unless your heart is strong and your actions true, knowledge won't be enough. Knowledge is never enough by itself."

"It's going to be dangerous, isn't it?" Milo asked, feeling how dread made his legs squishy.

"Of course. Kayn won't hesitate to do anything he can to take the Cross. Your best plan is to lead him to believe that you have the knowledge—which you do—that he needs in order to possess and use the Cross. Others will be there, too. Keep them near."

"You mean the Hunt contestants, don't you?"

"Yes. With them around you, Kayn will be more careful of his actions. Secrecy and stealth are a habit with him. Most likely, he'll use his disguise as Smith around others. Use Smith to hold off Kayn."

"I hope you're right about my knowing what I need to know. I don't feel like I do."

"You're scared. That means you understand the gravity of the challenge. Be very careful with what you know. Parcel out only enough to *suggest* you know rather than trying to impress by acting as if you have more knowledge than you do. Kayn understands how to manipulate braggarts. He's used that skill many, many times. He's built a career of it by flattering his marks into doing his work for him. You are ready, young Milo."

Many things came into Milo's mind as evening came on. Culebrant made him his favorite stew and encouraged him to eat, but he could hardly swallow. There were too many butterflies swirling inside his stomach to find room for food. He packed his rucksack and put on his old clothes, the ones he'd worn when he came, and then put on his mistletoe-cutting smock, as Culebrant had advised. The cats all sat around, ignoring him in catty sociability, except for Raster, who was off adventuring somewhere. Bori sat steadfastly at his side.

"Bori," Milo began, "I think you should stay here, with your family." He was worried what might happen—how this might turn out. "You've helped me this far, and I can't ask you to do more."

"No, I signed on. I'm a cat of my word. And I expect I might still be very useful to you. You never know what skills might be important, and the more you have on your side..."

Milo stroked his fur, glad for him to stay. Bori purred. Milo decided that just that—a bit of mutual comfort—was help aplenty.

Culebrant was being just about as sociable as the cats, nearby, but ignoring Milo's tense waiting. Minutes seemed like hours and hours like days, but at last Culebrant told Milo it was time to go. "I'll take you as far as the edge of the clearing at the barrow," he promised.

Milo felt like his legs had turned to lead as they walked through the dark woods. As movement brought his legs back to life, they began to tremble. The butterflies in his stomach wanted to escape, and he thought he might vomit before they reached the barrow. At the edge of the woods they stopped. Bori rubbed against Milo's legs and Culebrant patted the cat.

"Pay attention to your cat," he advised Milo further. "What you don't know, he does. You two are a team."

Milo couldn't speak. Tears smeared his eyes and dribbled down his face. He reached out a hand to shake Culebrant's and the old man gripped it in his strong, work-hardened palm, then pulled Milo into a hug. "Fare well," he said.

Milo choked on a sob as Culebrant released him and turned away back into the forest. Bori started away into the grassy clearing, tail high like a battle-banner. Milo followed, half blind, choking, and weak with fear. As he climbed the slope of the barrow, he concentrated on breathing the way Culebrant had taught him in order to collect his thoughts. The tremors that were flowing through his body in surges melted away and by the time he reached the top, the queasiness had drained away.

There were others already there, dark shapes in the dark night. As he came up on them, he heard a male voice asking, "That little battle must be over. I wonder if it was our contestants fighting?"

"Is everyone here?" Milo asked, surprised to hear his own voice.

"Milo?"—that was Analisa.

"Oh, my god!"—that was an irate Count Yeroen.

Sarakka was there, and Lute, whose voice Milo had heard. Aulaires was there, all aflutter in a robe of fur and feathers. He felt a soft squeeze to his elbow. "I'm glad to see you escaped Kayn's trap, Milo." That was Stigma. One, two, three, four, five, six. The seventh was Smith. Milo felt the hair on the back of his neck bristle. "Are we waiting for someone else?" he asked the group.

"Of course not!" Yeroen exclaimed. "If they haven't made it by now, that's not my concern. We're waiting for..." Yeroen fumbled.

"...for the gate to open," Smith filled in. He sat off to the side, watching Milo with wolf-intense eyes.

"And what gate is that?" Milo asked.

"The way into the Barrow," Analisa said as Yeroen made growling sounds of disgust.

"Why's that?" Milo persisted.

"You don't have a clue, do you, you silly pup!" Yeroen exclaimed. "How'd you get here in the first place?"

"We need to get into the Barrow," Analisa answered, "only, none of us knows how to do it. That's why we're all up here, waiting."

"That, and to keep an eye on each other," Lute said with a cynical laugh.

Milo glanced at Bori. The cat gave him a glance, got to his feet and took a good stretch. Then he started down the other side of the mound.

"Let's get started," Milo said, and followed the cat. He resisted the urge to look back to see if the others were moving. Sounds told him after a short delay that they were, each of them, as Lute had pointed out, afraid to be separated from the others whether they believed Milo knew something or not.

"I've spent time hunting voles up here," Bori told Milo softly. "I know where the gate is, or at least, where it should be. When we get there, the rest is up to you," he told Milo.

"He's a remarkable cat," Stigma's voice said from Milo's side. Milo reasoned that in her invisible state, she knew of Bori's abilities, which he generally preferred to be careful about showing off.

"Yes, he is," Milo whispered to the place were Stigma must be.

Bori stopped in front of several tumbled, weed-grown stones. One by one the others arrived, Yeroen and Smith last. "Now what?' Yeroen demanded. "If this was a gate, it's been ruined and caved in for ages."

Each of the others was examining the stones. Lute chopped back some of the weeds, revealing the largest of the stones. Smith hung back on the periphery, watching over the shoulders of the others as if his interest were only intellectual. Milo could feel Smith's eyes, however, as if his breath were right on Milo's neck.

A feeling of assurance came over Milo, and without saying what, he knew that Bori was right. This was the gate, the ancient entrance into this monument. He felt the Dragon Cross in his pocket, the 'key' as Culebrant had called it.

"What do you think?" Milo heard Yeroen in consultation with Smith.

"You must be inside before dawn, or the window will close," Smith told him.

"I know that," Yeroen assured him condescendingly. "But how can that be accomplished? Should we dig?"

Bori was walking over the stones, sniffing at them and apparently checking them out for recent vole activity. When he jerked his tail, Milo noticed the silent signal and went to him. He ran his hand over the surface of the stone, exploring the weathered hole Bori was showing him.

It was shallow, but Milo knew the shape. He took the Cross out of his pocket and pressed in into the depression. It fit. Bori hopped down and the stones began to shift.

"What? What's this?" Yeroen called excitedly.

"Looks like a hole," Lute said.

"There! There, see?" Yeroen said proudly.

"Looks like you've done it," Smith said ingratiatingly, but looked at Milo.

A flow of cold, musty air breathed out of the void. All five contestants peered into the total darkness inside. Milo felt Stigma's fingers wrap around his arms as she joined in. Smith was still behind the others, just behind Yeroen, and he continued to study Milo with a secret knowing smirk. Milo looked back at him, holding the contact of eyes for the moment.

"Well, shall we go in?" Yeroen commanded to the band, but without stepping forward. There was an awkward pause as each of them waited for one of the others to take the lead, until Lute broke the standoff.

"If you would be willing, ladies"—and he stressed the word to the group to allow the gender reference to be clear to the males present—"I'll go first to scout the way."

He lowered himself into the hole, the darkness swallowing him from sight. "There's some rubble at the beginning," he called out, his voice echoing out of the hole, "but the passage seems to be intact. Be careful as you come in."

Analisa went next, and then Sarrakka. Yeroen took the next turn and helped Aulairess descend into the darkness, leaving Smith, Milo, Bori, and the invisible Stigma, who still held on to Milo's arm, to go last.

Smith waited. Milo locked eyes with him and waited as well. At last Smith shrugged, smiled, and slipped in. Bori hopped down next and Milo and Stigma followed.

The silence inside was as total as the darkness. Each rustle that one of the party made was amplified by comparison and intensified the Barrow's feeling of long abandonment.

"Come this way," Bori whispered to Milo. "Even if I can't see anymore than you do with no light at all, I have other faculties."

Milo slipped his hand into his pocket and wrapped the Cross into his palm. He eased it out just far enough to let him glance at where his palm should be, turning it in his fingers. When the reverse side was up, he saw points of light. Each pit glowed, like the number on the face of a watch. The quadrupled star positions of The Dragon appeared, with the front two at the head glowing brighter than the others. He slipped it back into his pocket and began to shuffle forward deeper into the passage, following the brush of Bori's tail.

"I can't get a light spell to work," Lute called out from somewhere ahead. "Anyone with better luck?"

One by one, the others confirmed the inability. "What in blazes is going on?" Yeroen demanded.

"Our magic doesn't work," Aulaires responded in melodious tones. "Why not?"

"The Barrow," Smith said. "It absorbs your spells. Magic is useless here. The harder you try and the greater the spell, the more energy the Barrow will drain. I suggest you stop trying. It will only waste you. The Barrow was built to strip those who enter here from using the powers they have on the outside. Probably to humble them and make them receptive."

"But...but," Yeroen blustered. "What's the purpose of that? Where does it lead?"

"To the Hub," Milo said. "The place where time has no value."

"What? What!" Yeroen exclaimed. "What could you know about it, you insolent pup!"

"More than you do, you old fool!" Smith snapped, his voice revealing his transition from the obsequious Smith to the arrogant Kayn. "Tell us, Boy, what we should do?"

"Keep going, if you want to learn why you came here in the first place," Milo answered. "If not, I suggest you go back right away, before the door closes."

"You mean, we're trapped in here?" Aulaires asked in a diminished voice.

"Milo? Do you know the way?" Analisa asked.

Milo took the Cross out of his pocket and glanced at the glowing points. "More or less, I guess. Right now, we follow the passage."

"Then you should be our leader," Sarakka said.

"I agree," Lute added.

"That way we'll be warned when you tumble into a pit in the floor," Yeroen said viciously.

Stigma squeezed Milo's hand. "I'll come with you," she whispered, and Bori led the way with Milo and Stigma in the tow of his tail. They carefully passed each of the others, feeling their presence in the tunnel without actually touching, sensing the warmth of their bodies and the sounds of their breathing in the cold darkness.

"What are we seeking, do you think," Milo heard Yeroen say back somewhere behind him.

"The Well of Reflection," Kayn said. "The place where your deepest questions will be answered."

"I'd be happy to be able to see what I'm asking for," Aulaires said with a shiver in her voice.

Milo and his two companions moved forward carefully, taking the lead. "Join hands," he called back. "We should make a chain so no one gets lost." Bori's tail brushed his leg and he held fast to Stigma's hand with his right. With his left he reached back, groping the darkness until it contacted Lute's, and closed on his callused musician's fingers. He visualized the chain forming up behind him, each connection telling him of the next in the chain joined with the one ahead. A faint sensation of nausea hit him: Kayn linking in.

They traveled very slowly. From time to time, Milo let go of Stigma's hand so he could reach into his pocket to take out the Cross, peering through the dark toward the place where his hand should be. The glowing dots appeared there, suspended in nothingness. As they traveled, the earlier ones faded and the one ahead grew brighter. The progression of the bright dot was the only indication that they were making progress through the labyrinth.

Milo noticed that Stigma's hand was getting colder and colder. Half way through, he could feel her shiver and hear her teeth chatter.

"Are you alright?" he asked, whispering to the place where he thought her ear might be.

"I'm...I'm...freezing. My magic can't ward off the cold here."

"Stop," Milo called out and sounds of shuffling stilled. He let go of the hands he held and slipped out of the mistletoe smock he was wearing. If spells didn't work inside the Barrow anyway, it wasn't doing him any good to ward off enchantments, so it might as well serve as clothing for

Stigma. He pressed it into her hands and helped her as she got her arms through the sleeves and over her shoulders. He was very aware of her bare shoulders even in the dark, as his hands brushed against smooth, chilled skin.

"What's going on up there?" Yeroen called. "Why have we stopped?"

The rustlings Stigma made settling the smock onto her body stopped, and she took Milo's hand again. He groped until he found Lute's. "Join up," he called and the chain linked up. Bori's tail brushed Milo's leg and they began to move forward again.

It seemed like hours since they had begun to thread their way down the black labyrinth. Perhaps it had. Milo had no way of knowing the passage of time. His eyes burned from staring so hard into the impenetrable darkness, and his ears had become hypersensitive. He no longer felt afraid of what might lie around him or just ahead. The sensory deprivation became monotonous. He glanced at the Cross and saw—at last—the next point now the third from last: the hub of The Dragon. It was increasing in brightness, indicating its significance. That point represented the star that had once been the pole star when the Great Barrow was constructed, and Milo recognized that the Great Barrow's shape—although he had never recognized it when he looked at the serpentine layout on the ground—was a model of The Dragon.

Approaching the third dot, the blackness began to whiten. At first, Milo thought it was something wrong with his eyes, but then he began to actually see, like looking through milky glass.

"The passageway is changing," Stigma whispered.

"It's opening up," Bori said. "Getting wider, and higher."

Milo had noticed from the beginning that the tunnel sloped slightly downward. By this time, they were probably deep beneath ground level. "Stop," he called. "The passage is getting wider. You at the rear, move toward the left. I'll go to the right. Let's find out how wide it is."

The chain pulled out into a front. He could actually see his companions' shapes, washed in a white light, like moonlight. Every sound they made now echoed in a new way, and as they moved forward, the two ends of the chain lost contact with the walls. They were in a cavern.

The light seemed to glow. Tall, smoothly rounded presences stood in silence before them: stalactites and stalagmites of pearl-colored stone. Some joined together from above and below to create floor-to-ceiling columns, giving the cavern a cathedral-like look. Milo glanced to the left, seeing the other members of the party, and then right toward Stigma.

Stigma! He could see her! She was visible within the mistle-toe-stained smock. The stains glowed with opalescence, but it was the woman inside the smock that amazed him. Her moonstruck hair cascaded over her shoulders and clear down her back. Her profile was graced by a high forehead, delicate nose—thinnish—with well-formed lips, and lifted chin. Her long throat struck him as swanlike and her figure—what could be seen from inside the formless smock—was lithe and graceful. Her skin had porcelain evenness, in keeping with her moon-pale hair. As she turned to smile at him, he saw that her eyes were electric blue, large, the whites sparkling.

"Who's that?" Yeroen demanded.

"Stigma, of course," Milo replied, feeling a little light-headed as he looked at her.

"How did she get here?" Aulaires asked.

"She's been here all along, only...only now you can see her." Milo puzzled if this were an effect of the cavern, its eerie light, or its spell-absorbing qualities. He glanced past Yeroen to Kayn, at the far end of the chain. His face was twisted with a look of bitter hatred.

"I've dreamed of this place," Stigma said, her voice connected to her image for the first time and calling Milo's attention back to her, and then the cavern that she gazed out into.

"I've played it," Lute said, and he unslung his instrument from his back.

"This is the source," Sarakka said. "The place where life flows out into the world."

"It looks sterile to me," Yeroen grumbled.

"Be quiet, my Lord," Aulaires said, her voice afloat with awe. "This is Anzu's Womb."

Lute loosened an arpeggio into the still air. The sound fluttered out like doves into the space, dodging in and out of the pillars to return in echoes of complex, interwoven chords as if the delicate structures of cave-stone had joined their voices with the notes of Lute's instrument. Lute waited, his fingers poised above the strings, as the tones gradually receded. There was no magic except the magical purity of music. As the chamber returned to silence, he sent another chord out as if in reconnaissance.

The party stood frozen in rapture as the melodiless music returned, like wind chimes or distant bells. They stood enthralled as if each of them were witnessing true magic for the very first time.

All, that is, but one. "Let's get on with it," Kayn broke in, destroying the spell and fracturing the harmonics. "Somewhere out there is what we've all come for. Out there in that maze must be the Well of Reflection."

"Fan out," Yeroen instructed, asserting leadership. "Whoever finds it first can call the others."

Milo watched Kayn, who was watching him. Analisa watched Milo and Stigma, who had stayed at Milo's side with Bori.

"I'm visible again," Stigma said, her voice lilting in wonder. Milo decided to leave her joy intact instead of advising her that this effect was probably only temporary, due to the qualities of the Barrow. To escape Kayn's eye, he drew her away along the wall and behind the nearest column.

Bori spoke. "Kayn may make his move soon," he told Milo, ignoring that Stigma heard him speak. After all, she must have heard him many times in her invisible presence. "He knows well what you've got and that you have it with you."

"The thing Milo used in the dark, right?" Stigma put in.

"Yes," Milo told her. "It can do things Kayn wants, and I can't let him have it. I don't know what he wants to do with it, but just knowing he wants it means that he wants it for no good. I can't let him do whatever it is. I know some things about it, but I don't know what all its properties may be. For instance, I didn't know that it would glow in the dark and serve as a map to the labyrinth."

"What do you think we should do?" Milo asked Bori.

"You and Stigma look for whatever you need to look for. I'll guard you."

Milo imagined Bori accomplishing this as a lookout, like he had so many times before, even if the way he said it sounded...well, more comprehensive than that. He turned to Stigma.

"Do you know what Kayn is talking about? This 'Well of Reflection' thing?"

"No, I don't know what it is exactly," she said. "But in my dreams—I've dreamed this place my whole life!—there's a pool. Perfectly still, except when water drips into it and sends ripples out across the surface. They wipe out the reflection you're looking at, only, I've never seen what those images are in my dreams. But they tell you things. When the image gets wiped out, that's the end of what you see."

"Then let's find it," Milo said. "Let's be the first to find it."

"But...where? This chamber is a labyrinth."

"Your dreams...do you know where it might be."

"No, only that it's here. I'm in this space"—she gestured to include the entire surroundings—"and it's very sacred. And then I come on the pool."

"You said something about dripping water?"

"Yes. It's the drips that change the images in the pool."

"Listen...hear that? The drip? We follow that and we find the pool."

It wasn't nearly as easy as it sounded. The sound echoed back and forth, seeming to come from there, or was it there? Or that way? Maybe over there...

...until they found it. The three of them stood at the edge of a still pool that had more white stalagmites rising up out of it, like the trunks of cypress trees standing in a lake. It made Milo think of the cypress trees where he had met the Crane King so long ago. The water in this underground pool was so still, so crystalline-clear, that it looked like the same place repeated just beneath the surface, only upside down. Bori crouched down to lap water from the edge of the lake, his pink tongue doubled where it sent out ripples across the surface. The upside down world fractured into dancing fragments.

Analisa arrived. Milo saw how the two girls glanced at each other, and for the first time he saw how young Stigma really was—no older than he or Analisa. He also saw how completely different they were in their opposite types of beauty: Analisa with her dark hair and earthy immediacy, and Stigma with an ethereal look that suggested that she might rise as easily as a feather. She reminded him of the elegance of the two sisters of fairy blood, Blai and Ayuthaya. He also noted the look of pain—or maybe it was temper, mixed with disappointment or something—that crossed Analisa's face. It made him want to tell her all the things he had thought about saying to her these many past months, and how he had worried about her.

But this was not the time, and he said nothing.

He looked into the mirror of the water's surface. It had regained it's stillness following the ripples Bori had made. The two young women stared into the pool, too, totally absorbed in what they saw.

Milo wondered if each of them was appraising her own appearance, Stigma after not seeing herself for so long and Analisa, probably comparing herself to Stigma. He saw his own reflection and as he stared at it, he seemed to be looking through the reflection into inestimable depths. He had a moment of vertigo as the reflected image reversed as if it were above and he was below, looking up. And in that world, there were new settings, backgrounds of places quite unlike the cathedral cavern.

Staring beyond his own face, he saw something take form: the Dragon Cross. He was holding it. Then he wasn't. His vertigo switched and he was looking down again, into the water, but the Dragon Cross lay at the bottom of the pool. He stooped to reach in to recover it, but stopped as the scene underneath it began to revolve, evolve, and resolve. It was as if the substance of the water were generating images in which the Cross became the central point. His vertigo returned, and this time it carried away his sense of time and place, and he looked into the open universe, launching him into this place or that, sort of like Dreaming. He knew he was looking into Otherworld, and he let himself relax into the state of the witness. Milo knew, as if from some deep well within himself, what it was he was seeing. The Cross—the Dragon Cross—was the constellation of the Dragon, and it was Heronsuge, the Guardian of The Way. Heronsuge was thus both guard of the gate and the guide to The Way. A vast constellation of Time spun around this center, and Heronsuge stood fast at its center, watching the actions of the manifest world that were, unlike him, subjects to the Rule.

A single sound, as isolated as the toll of a bell, announced itself: a drop falling into water. The sound expanded out much faster than the ripples in the lake, but as the ripples arrived, they fragmented the reflection that he was seeing. The scene vanished and Milo was released into the measure of Time. His gaze pulled away from the pool and he looked at his companions, and the moon-bright columns of the cavern. The two women stood blinking and disoriented as if they'd awakened from a deep, deep trance.

Except for Bori, who sat waiting with paws tucked in and tail wrapped around, eyes closed for a nap. Milo thought he looked like a cat Buddha, sealed into deep meditation.

His eyes opened and then he came all the way into awareness. "Get ready," he said. "Time to go. Kayn is coming."

On cue, Kayn stepped into view from behind a stalagmite, and stopped, recognizing the three young people.

"You found it?" he asked. "The Well of Revelation?"

"Yeah," Milo answered, noting the shift in terms from the Well of Reflection, which he had used before. "It was right here."

Count Yeroen was right behind Kayn. "You were supposed to tell the rest of us if you found it!" he chided.

"Well...yeah. It's pretty big. Besides, you're here now."

"Did you...learn its secrets?" Yeroen asked, too eager for what it might reveal than he was dismissive of 'this pup.'

"I got a few things," Milo answered. "I suspect it has a few secrets left if you want to try it out. It's all yours."

He turned to his companions. "Are you ready? Let's go."

Trying to act very normal and uninterested—bored even—he moved away, leading Bori and the two women. His heart was racing, pounding inside his chest so hard that it sounded to him like a drum. He expected Kayn to do something the next instant. Bori, too, was half-swelled, his ears flat against his head and eyes slitted.

"I don't think he can do anything," Stigma whispered when they were a safer distance away from the two men. "His magic is useless down here. He has to wait until we're outside again."

"What?" Analisa asked. "What's going on? The tension back there was as thick as butter."

"Remember back at the End of the Earth? The wizard you were trying to identify at the slinger tournament?" Milo answered. "Well, that's him."

"What? You mean Smith? He's been so...helpful," Analisa said, then blanched.

"Yes, well, it was because he wanted to use you—and all the other Hunt contestants—to find Milo," Stigma said filling her in quickly, if not particularly gently.

"I've got something he wants," Milo told Analisa. "And by the way, this is where things get really dicey. I just want to get this all over with. And now I know what I have to do."

"The Well?" Stigma asked.

Milo nodded. "Did you see it, too?" He asked her.

"I saw something, but I don't think it was the same thing you saw. And something about my invisibility. I have you to thank. You have my unreserved gratitude."

That surprised Milo. "What do you mean?"

"For breaking the enchantment placed on me by a certain malicious wizard." She jerked her head to indicate who was behind them. Milo knew she meant Kayn.

Milo winced. "Stigma, it might not be permanent. It could just be the conditions of the cave that brought your visibility back."

"No, Milo. The Well showed me. You broke Kayn's spell when you gave me your jacket, saturated as it is with mistletoe power. And good will. It's the antidote." She paused and turned her head in an inquisitive slant. "Funny how that worked out. He took my own talent and turned it against me, but eventually it let me watch him without his knowing I was there. I followed him into the Valley of the Stone Knights and saw how he had tricked us all into going into a place of terrible danger. That's when I understood what he had done. The spell he laid on me saved me from the fate of the others who had been turned to stone."

"What?" Analisa said. "How...you mean, Smith planned to get us turned to stone?"

"Yes. So he could get Milo and take what it is Milo's carrying while Milo was helpless—forever, like the others who are his collateral victims."

"How did *you* escape?" Milo asked Analisa.

"Escape?" Analisa said, obviously very uncomfortable.

"Keep moving," Bori ordered. "If Kayn finds the way out ahead of us, he'll turn us all into cinders the minute we step out of here. You *do* know the way out, don't you?" he finished with a question to Milo.

"I...yes, I think I do. If we keep going in the same direction from where we came in, it should take us to the apples. That's in the garden, at the end of the labyrinth, so I bet there's a way out from there."

"The what?" Analisa said. "The apples?"

"Yeah. It's from an old story that seems to be the basis of this whole thing," Milo answered.

"How do we know which direction to go? I'm totally turned around," Stigma put in.

Milo took the cross out of his pocket and held it out where they could see it. He studied it carefully, just barely able to see the yellow glow of the points in the white light of the cavern. He turned this way and that until he believed he had the alignment of the points.

"There. See that?" he asked, holding it out to show. "It works like a compass. The one that's glowing the brightest is in the front, the way we're facing. We'll go that way."

As they went, they collected the others: Aulaires, Sarakka, and Lute. Each one of them had found the lake at a different point. All were subdued, affected by what they had seen in the waters of the lake, and searching for the way out of the cavern.

When they located the end of the gallery, the light faded. They linked hands as they passed into the dark tunnel, with Bori in the lead. As they left the last of the light, a broken call came from behind, fragmented by echoes.

"Someone? Is anyone there? Please! Someone?"

"It's Yeroen!" Aulaires said. "Wait!"

"We're here," Milo called back. "Come this way."

20

Milo Finds a Way

It didn't take very long to get to the last point on the Dragon Cross compass. Milo felt his heart leap when a shaft of light appeared up ahead, and he could see the difference in the dark between the tunnel and his own hand. Despite the anxiety that Kayn might somehow have gotten to the exit first, and was just waiting for Milo to emerge, he couldn't wait to be out into light again.

"I'll go first." Bori whispered to Milo. The statement wasn't an offer. It was a decision.

As the group waited, hoping for Bori to return with the report that it was safe, Count Yeroen moved to Milo's side. "I owe you an apology," he began. His voice was subdued and shaken. "I didn't realize...I didn't know what Smith is. And I...I have a great deal to atone for."

His voice broke. Milo didn't know what he had seen when he looked into the lake, but it must have been a doozy.

"I had no idea..." he tried to continue. "I just thought you were..."

"It's okay," Milo told him. "I really didn't fit into the Magical Scavenger Hunt."

"Oh, no!" the Count countered. "On the contrary! You're the only true contestant! What you've done, what you must succeed in doing, is the most notable feat to have ever been performed by a Hunt contestant in its entire history. I understand that, and the part I've played up until now. My duty is to help you complete the task."

"If it hadn't been for you, I'd never have been in the Hunt in the first place," Milo reminded him. What Yeroen was saying, astonished him. The Count's change of heart made him burn with curiosity to know what had caused it. What had Yeroen seen?

Bori returned, interrupting the exchange, drawing Milo aside to whisper to him. "The opening's going to be a tight fit for you humans. You'll have to go one at a time, on your bellies, crawling through a small space under the collapsed opening. I hope no one gets stuck, because I can't help you if you do. The weather's miserable and the passage is muddy." He looked soaked, his fur spiked from the wet and smeared with mud.

After Milo explained to the others, Lute volunteered. "I'll go first. I'm thin and wiry, and can help any of you if you get wedged in the crawl space." He handed his instrument to Sarakka. "After I go through, push this ahead of you until I can reach it, would you please?"

Milo suddenly remembered his rucksack. He hadn't had it since... He recalled he had left it on the stump at Culebrant's cottage. Lute had wriggled out of sight into the hole, cutting off the light that filtered through. They could hear his grunts and rustlings as he push/pulled his way through the passage, and then the light came back.

"It's not too bad, he called through. "A little tight—and very wet right at the end."

"Let me go next," Yeroen offered. "If Smith is out there, I'll take him on while the rest of you get through. Here," he said to Sarakka. "I'll pass Lute his instrument as I make my way through."

The light disappeared as Yeroen filled the hole. There was more rustling, grunting, and groaning as he strained to force his somewhat larger size through the hole.

"Do you trust him?" Analisa asked Milo as they waited, again in total darkness.

"Yes. I think so," Milo answered. "Something happened to him in there."

"To all of us, I think," Aulaires said.

Sudden light marked Yeroen's completed transit. Aulaires went next, then Sarakka. Bori, Analisa, Stigma, and Milo were left. "Milo," Analisa said, taking his hand. "We're with you."

"Absolutely," Stigma said, touching his arm. She glanced shyly at Analisa. "All of us." She cocked her head to indicate the ones who had already passed out of the tunnel. "We all have a role to play and we'll do whatever we can to hold Kayn off. When we get through, your job is to get away. Don't hesitate because of any of us. We know what we've got to do, and what you have to do only you can accomplish."

"Well, hurry up and do it," Bori admonished. "I can hear Kayn back there in the tunnel, stumbling along in the dark. He'll be here soon."

Milo went next. His slender body fit through the crawlway easily, and Stigma and Analisa were right behind him. They emerged into what at first seemed a blindingly bright day, but as Milo's eyes adjusted to full light, he saw that the sky was heavily overcast, the clouds no more than a few feet above the top of the barrow, pouring rain.

Bori shot out right behind Analisa and the perfectly visible Stigma.

"Come on!" Yeroen shouted. "We'll cave in the opening and leave Smith trapped inside. Without his magic, he can't blast out the passage! He'll be trapped."

"No," Milo said in horror of leaving someone—even Kayn—buried alive.

"Milo's right," Sarakka said. "The sorcerers of old had themselves purposely buried that way. It made them much, much more powerful, transcending the boundaries of death. But it turned them into banshees."

"Then we run for it," Stigma said. "Each of us in a different direction to confuse Kayn when he comes out. We'll regroup in the forest so we can shield Milo."

"Go! Go! Go!" Bori spat. "He's in the crawlway!"

Like a flock of startled birds, everybody took off in a different direction. Milo, his heart pounding, looked back just as Kayn emerged from the hole. Bori stood on the spot, back arched, ears flat, tail bristled and as rigid as a spike, hissing straight into Kayn's face. A slash of his paw laid four bloody stripes across Kayn's cheek.

"Bori!" Milo cried. "No!" Milo turned back in anguish, terrified for the cat's safety. "Run! Run! Run!"

Instead of running, Bori held his ground. Kayn jerked away with one hand to his wounded face and the other flashing out, open-palmed, to emit a ball of blue flame. It hit Bori and sent him rolling, fur smoking in the downpour. He was back on his feet even before his roll stopped, squaring off to face the sorcerer again.

As Kayn scrambled the rest of the way out of the hole and took up a stance for his next attack, Bori burst in a transformation. In one decisive move, he became huge, as huge and as formidable as a full-sized lion—nay, bigger. Something Milo had seen before—a live version of the bronze lions that guarded the steps of the courthouse at Kingdom of Odalese. Roaring, he leapt onto Kayn and they went down in a slashing, shredding ball of fury.

Another transformation happened as fast as Milo could blink. Kayn became a screaming dragon, spouting flame.

"Run!" Bori shouted. "Run! I'll hold him as long as I can. Get away!"

The others were well away now, leaving Milo as the obvious and identifiable target. As he stumbled in hesitation, the Kayn dragon reared and shot a ball of fire out to take him. Reflexively, Milo threw up his arm to shield himself...

...and his shield—the one he had built months ago—turned the ball away, leaving him singed but uninjured.

Bori launched himself against the dragon again, digging in all his claws and locking his jaws into the dragon's scaly flesh. They both went rolling down the slope, locked in a fierce battle, emitting growls, roars, and shrieks. Torn fur, smoke, and spurts of flame roiled the air.

Milo ran. Ran blindly, his face wet. He ran without direction until he found himself beneath trees, and someone grabbed his arm to bring him back to control. Stigma pulled him to face her.

"Bori..." he sobbed, unable to say more.

"I saw," she said.

"He was...he was the best..."

"Yes."

There wasn't really anything more to say. The others came up to regroup, singly or in re-joined pairs. Shock had them all by the throat.

"We've got to move," Yeroen said, his voice brittle. "Smith..."

"His name is Kayn," Milo said, his voice suddenly calm and cold. "Kayn Smith. He's done terrible, terrible things. He'll do worse if he gets his hands on this..." and he held up the Dragon Cross.

They all looked uncomfortable and confused by the sight of what was by now known to each of them. "We're here to help," Lute stated. "Each in our own ways according to our talents. None of us are a match for Kayn, but we can slow him down so you can escape, at least for now. Stigma? Analisa? Can you go with Milo to help him off Inys Raun?"

"And me," Yeroen said. "At least as far as the Gate. I can hold Kayn long enough for these three to get through."

Aulaires stepped to Analisa's side. "Be careful, child," she said, giving Analisa a kiss on the cheek. Tears leaked down Analisa's face as she joined Milo and Stigma to find their way to the door they had used from Rykirk.

The four of them moved away, leaving the others behind. "I need to visit one place before I leave here," Milo told them. He led them easily through the forest, familiar with its ways from the time spent with Culebrant. A fierce storm raged in the sky behind them. They all knew, without saying anything, that it was no ordinary storm. It was a wizards' battle.

Milo took them to the place where Culebrant's cottage stood. Or had once stood. Now there was nothing there but some scattered stones beneath the weeds, and in the place where Culebrant's hearth had been towered a huge and gnarled oak, centuries old. He stood speechless. First Bori, now this. He was beyond shock or even despair.

"Where are we?" Analisa began to ask. "What...?" Stigma stopped her.

"Meow? Meow?" came a call of a cat from somewhere out in the weeds.

"...Bori?" Milo called, his voice shaky with hope.

A grey cat came bounding into the clearing beneath the oak, obviously relieved to see Milo.

But it wasn't Bori.

"Raster?" Milo said, surprised.

"Yes! You came back!"

"Raster? You can talk?"

"Sure. Culebrant told me to wait here for you. He said you'd come. He said you'd be back for this, and for me."

Raster took Milo to the location where he and Culebrant had so often sat. The stump was gone, rotted away long, long ago. His rucksack sat in the place where it had been—the place where Milo had forgotten it.

"How..." Milo began, and Raster interrupted.

"When I got back from my hunt this morning, there was nothing left except what you see now. Everybody was gone. But then Dad...he was all burnt and bloody. Culebrant was carrying him. They told me to wait for you here. Dad said that I was to go with you. He said that you would take me to the place where I'm to be a Guardian, like he was. He looked... awful, but Culebrant said he'll be all right."

Milo scooped Raster up, hugging the young, squirming cat and choking his sobs into his fur. It was a long time before he could set Raster down again, wiping at his eyes and taking up his rucksack.

"How...when did you learn how to talk?" Milo asked.

"Oh, I've always known how to talk. Only, my Dad did the talking, so I didn't need to. But I guess I do now..." He seemed much less sure of himself than his usual, brash self.

"It's okay," Milo said, scooping him up again. "We'll do it together. Here, take your dad's old place in my rucksack. We need to be going." The sounds of the storm had moved from the west into the northeast.

"We should go quickly," Yeroen said. "The three of you—four, with the cat—should get through the gate and back to...wherever this leads. It's the quickest way to leave Inys Raun, and the quicker, the better. It sounds like the battle's headed this way, so I expect Kayn knows where you'll try to go, and is trying to cut you off."

Milo took one last look at the place where the cottage had been. "Thank you, Culebrant. Farewell, Boriboreau, wherever you are."

He had a hard time at first, following the others as they made their way through the woods, headed east, his eyes blurring with tears, but when they cleared, he took up the lead. They moved quickly over the terrain Milo knew.

They came to the ridge where he and Bori had arrived—was it really just night before last, by current reckoning? Time had gotten completely muddled for him. How long had they been inside the barrow? Had it been just hours? Or maybe months? Not to mention the year Milo had spent with Culebrant.

"They're moving this way!" Analisa said anxiously as they climbed the ridge. Lightning flashed, making the low clouds glow red, orange, yellow, green, and blue. The rain had slackened from the downpour it had been on the Barrow. It was now a steady drizzle, but rumbling sounds like thunder, punctuated by howling and sharp cracks rolled toward them like a violent storm.

At the top of the ridge, the lichen-encrusted monument thrust up like a gnarled fist. "Get in!" Yeroen cried. "I'll hold Smith long enough for the three of you to get through!"

"Four," Milo muttered, shouldering the rucksack. "There's four of us."

"Stigma, put up an obscuring spell as soon as you get through," Yeroen directed. "Pick a direction—the more random the better so Smith can't tell so easily which way you might have gone—and go. Go now!"

The battle was coming fast. Evidently, Kayn had managed to get ahead of the others who were now left to pursue him instead of blocking him. "I'll go first," Stigma said, "and Milo, you and Raster follow. Analisa comes right behind you to take your back. Agreed?"

They didn't wait for agreement. They tumbled into action in the order Stigma had given. Milo squirmed in between the uprights into the core, the emptiness feeling uncanny, since Stigma had gone only a couple of seconds ahead of him. He felt a heavy blast from the rear, at the opening he'd just left. Fearing for Analisa, he turned and ran out.

...and into blazing sunshine. Stigma reached out a hand to pull him the rest of the way through, and in seconds Analisa stumbled out blinking and shielding her eyes from the bright sun.

"Kayn was right there!" she cried. "He projected some sort of spell—something I've never seen—to catch me, and Yeroen caught it in a billowing net and threw it back at him! I could see the others coming up just as I dove through."

"Let's not wait to see how it came out," Stigma said.

"Thank you, Yeroen," Milo said back at the vacant passage. "And good luck." He looked around. It was familiar. He was back on the hill beside the academy at Rykirk. Stigma was already hurrying down the slope toward the gate in the wall that surrounded the weathered monument.

At the gate Analisa placed her open palm on the rusted lock, and the grated door swung open, creaking. The school was just down the hill. Students were milling around in a break between classes. They all stopped, staring in astonishment at the three drenched figures striding down from that off-limits place. As they came in among the students, Milo saw the headmaster hurrying their way.

"Halt!" Trevorthorne ordered. "You can't be up there!"

"I'm turning him into a toad," Analisa muttered.

"No," Milo said, stopping her. "He's just a silly old guy."

"That may be, but I don't feel like dealing with him just now," Stigma said. "Join hands. Time for some temporary invisibility."

They did, and although Milo didn't notice any change—he could see himself and his companions just fine—Trevorthorne's face went slack-jawed and the students nearby took a collective intake of breath. Trevorthorne stopped dead in his tracks, looking this way and that as Milo and his friends passed right by him.

"Let's go to the kitchens," Milo said, directing their steps. "Kayn hasn't broken through yet, and it may be a long time before we get anything to eat."

The cook recognized Milo right away. "Oh my! Look at you!" she exclaimed, and the three of them became aware of their wet, muddy, and disheveled state. "And you especially, young lady!" the cook said to Stigma, whose only bit of clothing, the smock from Milo, was a sodden wreck of mud and melted sap that barely covered her. "First, I expect you're as hungry as ever"—this addressed to Milo with a wink—"and then I'll see if I can't find a proper dress for you," she said, addressing Stigma.

As she bustled away, Stigma gave Milo a sheepish smile. "Last time I met her, she didn't criticize my dress. Of course, she couldn't see me and I was here to steal food. I guess she treated you better."

Milo nodded, Raster jumped down out of Milo's rucksack as he unslung it from his shoulder, and Analisa looked nervous. "Can we afford the time?" she asked. "Kayn..."

"Milo's right," Stigma answered. "I'm so hungry I could eat a—"

—broken off by Raster's turning over a large, empty pot that clanged and rolled across the floor. Milo quickly scooped him up. "Behave. We've got to make a good impression if you want something to eat." He put the cat back down as the cook came back with a tray of food from the morning's breakfast. Analisa forgot her concern and all three of them—four, that is—fell on the tray. Raster's manners were not up to his father's standards as he grabbed the nearest piece of meat, jumped off the table, and took it underneath.

"Oh that cat!" the cook exclaimed. "Such a gentleman!"

"That's your dad she's talking about," Milo told Raster under his breath. "So try to live up to his example."

"And where, may I ask, young man, did you come up with such pretty young ladies for companions? They're not local girls."

"Oh...just friends who ahh...just arrived," Milo told her.

"Yes," Stigma said, taking over. "We were all traveling together, but we got separated. We found Milo again, this morning."

"That's right," Analisa put in, shooting the other two a wicked glance. "He's like a brother."

The cook laughed, obviously not taken in but understanding the ways of young people. "I think I'd better see about that dress I mentioned," she said, and left them alone again.

"She's right," Stigma said. "I can't go around wearing this. I'm almost naked."

"You should be used to that, I'd think," Analisa commented with a bit of tartness.

Stigma gave her a look. "Costume doesn't count unless someone can see it, don't you think?" and she gave Analisa's tattered and mud-smeared clothing a glance over.

Milo's attention was back to Raster, who was poking around another stack of pots after gobbling his breakfast. Milo reminded himself that the young cat had never seen a real kitchen before.

The cook returned with a loose white blouse and a sturdy dark blue skirt. She also held out a light blue bodice embroidered with simple daisies in white and yellow.

"My niece left this here, but that was a while back before she...well, I don't think she's likely to be getting into it again. Looks like you could, though."

Stigma held it up for size and she and Analisa went off to the pantry where the cook said she could try it on. While they were gone, the cook turned to Milo.

"Did you get into the gate last night? My man didn't know if you were in your room or not when he locked the door. Old Trevorthorne was in a snit about keeping you away from there, that's for sure."

"It worked, thanks. I got in and found out what I needed to know. You can't imagine how much I appreciate your help and all you've done for me...for us."

The cook looked flattered. "You're a fine young man," she said. "Not like so many of the stuck-ups here. I'm happy we could help out."

The two girls came back. Not only did the dress fit, it looked stunning on Stigma. She held out the drape of the skirt and spun around, clearly pleased with the unaccustomed sensation of the twirling skirt. Milo clapped his hands and grinned. Even Analisa looked happy with Stigma's transformation.

"Oh yes," the cook said smugly. "That's a very big improvement over the way you came in."

"Thank you," Stigma said.

"You're welcome," answered the cook.

All of them laughed, and then Milo noticed that Raster had vanished. He went looking for him and found him high up on a shelf behind the ovens, with a sausage he had pulled down from the hook where it had been hanging to cure. He was licking his chops.

"Raster?" Milo scolded. "You can't do that."

"Oh, but it's good! Here, try some."

Milo grabbed the cat and the cat snatched the sausage as Milo carried him back to the table where the others were.

They had company. An angry Trevorthorne, with the groundskeeper—the cook's husband—and a couple of faculty members in tow.

"What's the meaning of this!" he shouted, either at the cook, at the girls, or just at. "And you!" he added, turning hotly on Milo and the cat.

"Headmaster." Milo nodded a calm acknowledgement. It reminded him how many times he had been scolded like this by the principal and various exasperated teachers at home.

"What are you doing here? Where have you been? Did you try to force your way into the...the..." He broke off, remembering that he didn't want to tell Milo what was behind the wall on top of the hill.

"We had some breakfast," Milo said. "Thank you for the hospitality of the school, and the kindness your staff has shown me since my arrival here."

"And these?" the headmaster demanded, gesturing to indicate

Analisa and Stigma, as if they were speechless and inanimate objects. "Where did you get to when I saw you just now, out on the commons?"

"These are my friends, and now that they're here, we'll be on our way. We don't want to disturb the peace of your school any further."

"Just one minute there, young man!" Trevorthorne ordered. "You've got some explaining to do!" He grabbed at the sausage that dangled from Raster's claws, the cat snatching it back.

"We really don't have time for that now, and I don't expect you want to see what may come to look for us," Milo explained, his tone civil. "You see, it's just like what you expected from thistledowners like us. We've gone and poked our noses into places better left alone, and I'm afraid we've really stirred up a hornets' nest. Only it isn't hornets, it's much worse. If we don't leave here soon, there's going to be...well, I suggest you get all the students and everybody else behind closed doors until this all blows over. It could be dangerous if anyone were to be caught outside. Not to mention what your students would have to tell their parents about what they've seen and been exposed to when they go home. As headmaster, I expect they'd hold you responsible."

Milo held Treverthorne's eye until the headmaster flinched. Trevorthorne twisted first one, then the other, nervous shoulder.

"Do you have any idea about what you've got up there on that hill?" Analisa injected into the dialog. Milo hoped silently that she wasn't about to infest the man with boils or something. "Milo might be no older than your students here, but the school hasn't seen his like in centuries, if ever."

"We just barely escaped with our lives," Stigma put in. "Unfortunately for you, when we escaped, we landed here, and it'll be pretty obvious to our pursuers where we went when they come looking for us. If we aren't here anymore, they probably won't waste time to start tracking us down. Even though they have a taste for human flesh, boiled, roasted, or just plain raw. All this succulent young meat here will tempt them."

By now Trevorthorne and his teachers were very uneasy. The headmaster tried to look dubious, but the twitching of his facial muscles gave him away. He wasn't likely to prevent their leaving any longer.

So they left.

Milo let Raster decide which direction they should go. The more random and unplanned, according to Stigma's logic, the less trace it would leave for Kayn to follow. Stigma also cast an obscuring spell to hide the traces their presence had left. Raster's choice led them more or less in an easterly direction, at right angles to the direction Milo had come from when he first arrived at Rykirk. They soon discovered that Raster was following his nose. In a dale below the school was the village of Rykirk, and the village meant kitchens. Raster had followed the scent of his next meal.

"I'm not sure this is such a good idea," Milo said. "Isn't Kayn going to suspect we'd go to the village? Might it put the people here in danger?"

Raster thought a visit to the village—and its kitchens—was an excellent idea, but the other two shared Milo's misgivings. Just then, Milo noticed Raster's ears turn and focus. "What is it?" he asked the cat.

"An interesting sound," Raster replied. "And a very odd scent."

Just then Milo heard the sound, too. A tintinnabulation accompanied by a creak and a bump. Then he, too, caught the scent.

"Oxen," he said. "I wonder...could it be..."

...and a green two-wheeled cart hove into sight, pulled by two huge beasts. "It is!" Milo exclaimed. "It's Einter! And that's Senster, the white one, and Dexter, his brother!"

Einter's wagon was clunking and jarring up the hill toward them, following the road out of the village. They walked to meet it.

"Hey!" Einter called in greeting. "Lookit! What brings yuh here, young'un?"

"Same thing that took me into Korrigan Forest. I could ask the same of you?"

"Oh, just makin' the rounds like I do. I'd welcome yuh onboard, but it looks like we're goin' opposite places."

"Oh, not really. We just need to get away from where we've been, and fast."

Einter gave him his squint-eyed look of appraisal. "There's fast, and sometimes there's slow. Sometimes slow turns out to be faster. I'm guessin' that you want fast so's yuh can avoid somebody."

"That explains a long story in a short way," Milo replied.

"Then climb aboard. Go into the box where yuh won't be seen."

Milo turned to his friends. "This is my friend who helped me before. What do you think?"

"Won't Kayn find us right away if we don't get as far away as fast as we can?" Analisa asked.

"Or would that be exactly what he would expect us to do?" Stigma suggested. "Maybe your friend is right. Maybe slow would be a better plan than fast."

Einter had climbed down from the bench, stretched out his back, and began gathering twigs and grass from the side of the road.

"Try this out," he said, twisting and tying the plants into small bundles. "We haven't been proper introduced, but I can pretty well see yer friend here's a witch. I just bet she kin turn these dollies"—and he held up the first one he'd tied into a rough human form—"into decoys to put yer pursuer off track." He reached out and pulled a hair off Milo's head.

"Ouch!" Milo said, flinching. Einter wrapped the hair into the small bundle.

"I see what you mean!" Analisa exclaimed. "And I'll send them off in another direction. Why didn't I think of that?"

" 'Cause yer too young to be that dishonest," Einter chuckled.

21

A Will, a Way

Analisa sent the three decoys off to create a false trail. "I'll send them out over the sea," she told her friends. "That way, when they fail, they'll fall into the water and be lost. That should win us some time while Kayn tries to figure out where and how he lost us."

"Why wouldn't he just search out Einter's wagon?" Milo asked. They were inside it now as it rolled and clunked over every rock and pothole in the road, moving at the usual ponderous rate of the two oxen pulling it.

"Stigma hid our trail with her obscuring magic," Analisa said. "We're as hidden from Kayn's magical detection as she is when she's invisible."

"Not to mention what your friend up on the box did," Stigma added. "He's not just your normal itinerant tinker."

"He's...well, I can't tell what he is," Analisa said. "He seems like he's got his own sorcery, but he's completely opaque. As if he was really an ordinary tinker. I can't read anything from him at all."

"Me neither," Stigma agreed.

"Whatever, but he's helped me in all sorts of ways, even when I didn't know he was helping. He knows stuff," Milo told them.

The three of them spent an entire, boring day shut inside the cart, jarred and rattled until they were so bruised by the springless knocking about that they could hardly sit down at all. Einter had pointed out that since they were trying to escape the notice of the most dangerous, powerful, and unscrupulous wizard of the age, sore backsides were a small price to pay.

"Maybe Yeroen and the others succeeded in subduing him," Milo suggested.

"Uhn-uh. No way," Analisa insisted.

"I agree," Stigma said. "The best they can do is to slow him down. I just hope he's in such a hurry to chase us that he won't have time to really turn his anger onto them."

Milo winced. He was trying to ignore his own fear for his friends and feeling guilty about leaving them behind to face what he had unleashed. His thoughts moved from them back to Bori. "What...how did Bori..." Milo started, fishing for a way to put the question that had stayed in his mind since the battle on the barrow.

"Bori was a paragon of cats," Analisa said.

"Yes, with a special mission," Stigma agreed.

"He's my dad," Raster put in proudly.

"I mean, how was he able to fight Kayn? He transformed himself," Milo said. "I had no idea that he could do a thing like that."

"I believe he was a descendent of Count Abracadabracus' cat," Analisa speculated. "I've heard that his cat had remarkable abilities. Some people in the Kingdom of Odalese think the cats in that town are from that bloodline, and have some of those powers."

Milo remembered the bronze lions that guarded the steps of the town hall. "Bori told me once that the town is protected by the bronze lions there, but he said he'd never met them wandering around."

"Maybe it's the real, flesh-and-blood cats, not the statues," Stigma suggested.

"When Bori transformed, those lions are what he looked like," Milo stated.

"Does that mean that I'm a really bad dude?" Raster asked, proudly excited.

"Maybe," Milo told him, "but don't let it go to your head. You already seem to think you're a lot bigger than you really are. And a pain-in-th'-butt sometimes. Remember, though. It's supposed to be a secret and not something that you can brag about." He gave the young cat a friendly pat to make his point. Raster lifted his tail into the air in acknowledgement, and purred, proud of his anticipated reputation.

At sundown, Einter pulled the cart off the road to camp under the shelter of some gigantic cottonwood trees alongside a stream. Milo helped him unhitch and water Senster and Dexter as he had in the old days, while the two girls collected fire wood. Raster went on a prowl. "I hope he doesn't bring back a bear," Milo commented.

"Takes after his pa in looks," Einter noted. Milo was silent. Einter patted Milo's shoulder. "Yeh haven't told me yer story, but I can guess a bunch. That yer in trouble's prutty clear, but that yer doin' what yuh can do about it is just as clear. Maybe yuh'd best fill me in, so I know what we're dealin' with?"

Milo sketched out the general details, getting more specific as he reached the relevant and most recent events. Einter nodded.

"Yuh sure got a bad one, an' no doubt about it," he said when Milo had brought their escape from Kayn up to the point when they had run into Einter on the road. "So, where're yeh plannin' to get on to?"

"Do you know about the Crane King and the Glass Tower?"

Einter nodded. "Travelin' as I do, I hear all sorts of stories. Yes, I know somethin' about that. That where yer headed?"

Milo nodded.

"Know how to get there?"

"I was there once."

"That's good. Might make it easier the second time. Or not. I reckon I ought to take you there to be sure."

"You know how to get there?" Milo asked, surprised. By now, Milo realized that the Crane Castle and the Glass Tower were hidden, and considered by most to be mythical. That he had been there was an exceedingly unlikely event.

"Yep. Lots of folks know the stories, but not too many can find the place, hidden as it is. So happens, I make semi-regular stops there. They always have a few pots for me to patch up. We can get there in, oh, say by Yule."

"I need to get there quicker than that."

"No, not really. Yule's about right. Yuh won't find it any sooner anyway, try as yuh might. Yule's the time most likely to get in. That's how it works. Timing. All about timing. Didn't yer teacher there in the wood tell yeh that?"

"Yes, he did," Milo admitted.

"Then stay with yer lessons."

While Einter was building the fire, Milo went through formal introductions. He realized that he hadn't done it when they first met on the road. Then Einter took them out into the woods to collect the ingredients he wanted for dinner while the fire burned down to embers. He made supper over the coals in a big dutch oven, and the two women were clearly surprised at how good it was, complete with fresh biscuits.

As they sat down with their plates of food, Milo noticed Analisa take something out of her pocket. A wooden spoon. He recognized it. It was the spoon he had whittled for her in the forest before he got to the Crane Castle. She glanced at him, and gave him a quick, shy smile.

By the time they were finished with dinner, Milo had told them where they were going and that Einter would take them there. The two women were clearly unhappy with the timeframe, and Analisa told him so.

"That's because yer young. Young folks—the ones that have more time left than us older ones—they're the ones always in a hurry. Milo, yuh tell 'em what I told you about Yule an' all."

Milo did that.

"But...but we've got to get there as soon as possible!" Analisa insisted.

"Then I'll get yuh there. By Yule," Einter said steadfastly, reminding Milo of his oxen.

"The Crane Castle only opens for special visitors an' special times, like fer Yule," Einter went on, continuing his ponderous form of logic. "That would be you three and Raster. Try to get there any sooner an' yuh won't find it. I expect the same goes for yer wizard feller, Kayn. Maybe he's a hotshot sorcerer an' all, but he's got to follow the same protocol like anybody else, an' I expect he knows it. I expect he knows he'll need you to get in, too. So he needs yuh more then ever."

Without explaining, he moved on with his knowing squint. "So yeh caught the Fish, didn't yuh?"

"What fish?" Analisa asked. Milo hadn't told that part of the story, and he was surprised that Einter knew about it. "What's fishing got to do with it? There's got to be a way to get there, if that's where we've got to go, before Kayn can either find us, or get there first!"

"If yeh want to run off on yer own, I 'm not stoppin' yuh, an' best to yuh," Einter said good-naturedly, but with his heels dug in. "I'll be goin' that way anyway, so yuh can hook up with me at Yule in case yuh decide later that's what yuh want to do."

Milo knew there was no point arguing with Einter, but Analisa went on for a time before she gave up in frustration, and stormed off in a huff. Unperturbed, Einter put away his things and rolled out his bedroll under the trees. That left Milo and Stigma to stare into the glow of the coals by themselves.

"So..." Stigma spoke, opening conversation. "You've been there? To the Crane Castle?"

Milo watched the tiny flame dancers inside the furnace of embers. "Yes. It's how I found the Glass Tower. How did you do it, since that was the first clue?"

"I didn't. None of us did. We knew what the Glass Tower is supposed to be, but nobody knows how to actually go there. So we—I—used that to point us in the direction that would lead to the next clue."

"Really? That means I was so dumb that I thought I had to actually find it?"

"Milo, you never cease to amaze. If you're dumb, then it's a new kind of sorcery. Nobody actually *finds* the Crane Castle except in stories and legends. And the Glass Tower is more like a signal than it is an actual place."

"Well, I was at Crane Castle—Bori and I—and I met the Crane King, his wife, Ayuthaya, and his daughter. I also met Blai, who weaves the rainbow. She's Ayuthaya's sister. Besides, Einter's been there, too."

Stigma just shook her head. "The rest of us knew right away what the first clue was about, and each of us set out—not to go to the Glass Tower—but to look for leads that would tell us about how that first clue could point to the second. But then the Pilgrimage opened for the first time in—I don't know, but a long, long time. It was obvious then. The second clue had to be about the Pilgrimage."

"Blai showed me that. She spun sun beams into thread and tossed a ball of colored yarn across the sky that turned into a rainbow." Milo dug down to the bottom of his backpack and pulled out the ball of sun yarn Blai had given him. "When the butterflies appeared, she told me to follow them."

Stigma's jaw dropped. It took her several wordless moments to recover. She took the ball of yarn and studied it, then handed it back with a bewildered shake of her head. "From now on, anything you say, I'll just accept it without question. I admit, it was a real stretch for me when you said we had to go to the Crane Castle. I think—until what I just heard—that Analisa believed going to the Crane Castle made more sense than I did."

She shook her head again. "Anyway, we all set out to make the Pilgrimage, the way the lore dictated. And you showed up at the End of the Earth. By the way, nobody knew where that was, either. And you were with those three slinger players, and they fulfilled yet another prophecy."

"I just sort of happened to meet them, and we got to be friends," Milo explained.

"There's more to it than that. That's when I really started to watch you, Milo."

"What about back at the park in Kingdom of Odalese?" he asked. "You talked to me then, even if I couldn't see you."

"That was different. I just thought you were cute. I wished you could see me, too."

"I would have been embarrassed if I'd actually seen you...well, you know how I mean. I was embarrassed when I figured out that you had to be wearing...something...to be seen at all."

She laughed. "I think you're cute when you blush. Like now."

"That's just the firelight," he told her, but he felt his ears burning, and that wasn't because of the fire.

"Tell me this," she said, serious again. "Why do we need to go back there? To the Crane Castle?"

"It's where this ends. It's what I saw at the lake in the cavern."

"We all saw things in the cavern. You saw how this ends?"

"No. I saw the Crane Castle and I knew that that's where this leads."

"We all saw different things in the lake. We all saw what our own parts are. But it was you who put it all in play. Only when we all play our parts will the Hunt find its conclusion."

Milo thought for a moment, watching how the flame dancers had diminished as the fire died. "Is that why you said what you did about me and the Hunt?"

"Yes, but I didn't really understand what it meant when I met you on the way to Rykirk," she added. "Now I think I do. You know, don't you, that dealing with Kayn...well, I can't imagine how it can be done. Now I realize that you're really the only one of us who can. I don't know why that is, but after all you've told me..." She finished by shrugging.

"Do you think Kayn—he saw something in the lake, too—knows how all this works out? Which of us will succeed?"

"I don't know. I don't think that it's determined. I think he believes, with all he knows, that he *can* win."

Milo didn't—couldn't—know. He wished that somehow he could believe, right down in his bones, that the good guy—with him being the good guy—would win. But he didn't feel that way. All he felt was a huge hole full of anxieties. It was something he couldn't really look into, or it would devour him. So he hung onto his determination to do whatever he had to do next, and not look beyond that. Secretly, he was glad that it would take so long to travel to the Crane Castle, and at the same time he hated the delay, wishing for all this to be over and done.

Progress was slow. Senster and Dexter were not to be hurried, nor was Einter. "We'll be there, and not a bit sooner," was all Einter would say when asked how far they still had to go. Milo had to comfort himself with the fact that every night they camped in a place farther along than they had the night before. After all, he reminded himself, that was how he had made the pilgrimage: a day's walk at a time.

Analisa champed a lot more at the bit. She made herself a broom out of willow switches and used it to reconnoiter, presumably looking for any sign of where they were going and who they might meet on the way. Stigma resigned herself to the pace, but remained quietly alert, as if on guard all the time. Raster was on the great adventure of his life and Milo admired that, even though it made him feel old whenever he noticed that he was indulging the young cat's exuberance.

Sometimes it was Stigma who would go out to scout, leaving Analisa behind as the guard. Milo suspected that on those occasions, Stigma needed to get away to release tension and be alone for a while. He envied them both, since he was always under the eye of one or the other of them, without reprieve. Even Einter, from his nonchalant way of dealing with any and everything, always kept tabs on Milo. It was a slow simmer that never let up.

One day, when Stigma was gone and it was Analisa's turn to walk with him as the cart rumbled along, she opened a topic pointblank. "You like her, don't you?"

It was a question—another question—that Milo dreaded and tried not to think about. But the way Analisa asked it, with uncharacteristic gentleness, demanded that he address it as honestly as he could.

So he did. "I...I can't think about that. Of course I do. But...if I let myself think about how I feel, it's too much. I thought about you a lot when I was with...when I was at the Barrow, but I couldn't do anything about that, either."

"When you were with the Keeper?" she asked.

The question set him aback. "The what?" he stammered.

"The Keeper. That's what you mean, isn't it?"

"Yeah, I guess so." He did a quick mental check to equate the term with Culebrant, and found that it fit. "I didn't know what had happened to you. All I could do was to hope you were okay."

Her eyes flashed. "You could have"—she stopped herself. "I'm sorry, Milo. I made it pretty clear that my business is my own. I guess if you'd come looking for me, I'd have bitten your head off. Besides, now I know what it was you were dealing with. That, and you wouldn't have escaped the Stone Knights if you'd come looking for me."

By now they had outdistanced the ox cart. Analisa sat down on the trunk of a fallen tree to wait for Einter to catch up. She patted a place on the log beside her. "Sit down, Milo. It's time we had a talk."

He sat, feeling very uncomfortable.

"You see, Milo, I like you. I liked you right away, and that made me mad, because we were competitors. At least, I thought I had to beat you to win, and I believed I *had* to win. Things are different now. I found out some things I didn't know back then: I didn't know that Aulaires is my aunt, the sister of my father who I never really knew. I realize now that she's actually been trying to help me, only I couldn't see it. And the Hunt. I thought it was a winner/loser sort of thing, but I've learned that it isn't like that at all. It's like...what you get out of it. Not that you finish ahead of the others, or that you do it better than anyone else. You always tried to help and be friends, and I rejected that because I couldn't trust you if I had to beat you. It shows that you had the right idea about the Hunt from the very beginning, and I've only just realized what it's all about. We aren't competing against each other at all. We're competing *together*. If there was a single winner declared, you deserve to be it."

Milo didn't know what to say, so he said nothing. He just watched Raster, who was poking through the weeds, looking for the sort of things that interest cats.

"I think that the prize at the end of the Hunt isn't really about being a better witch or wizard than the other contestants, it's about how you do what you do," she continued, looking off past the horizon as if she could read the meanings she needed from there. She plucked a dry grass stalk and twirled it in front of her face. "It's about finding your own way, but that doesn't mean that you have to beat others out in order to do it. Now, the way this Hunt is working out is pretty awful, because of Smith—Kayn, you call him. He's just the opposite of what the Hunt is about, and he's twisted it into something very ugly. First, he tricked us all into thinking he had a clue and off we went like a bunch of chickens. We went to the Valley of the Stone Knights to confront a terrible and unnecessary danger, and that should never have happened. We didn't look for other clues. We just saw others going and followed in a rush not to be left behind. You're the only one who took a different route. You, with no magical ability—I mean, you have it, but not the way the rest of us do, by training and being taught by a mentor—and you got to the Great Barrow following real clues instead of chasing the next contestant. You did it in your own way, relying on raw talent.

"Before, I would have either looked down on you the same way Count Yeroen did, or I would have done exactly what I did. I kept thinking that you were very clever and were disguising your real ability as a way to fool the rest of us. Now I understand that you have something even more important. And Smith is trying to use that against you. That makes me really, really angry."

Raster had come near, and Analisa used the grass stalk to whip back and forth while he tried to catch it. Milo thought she might be finished—the cart was rolling up the hill and had almost reached them—and was about to reply in a sort of rebuttal, when she continued.

"Stigma was the only one who understood," she said. "She thinks you're cute too, just like I do, but she saw who you were instead of what she expected you to be. Maybe that's because she spent so long being invisible, ignored and unseen by others. Anyway, what I wanted to tell you is, if you care about her, she deserves it, and I don't."

The tight line of her mouth told Milo how much this admission hurt her. "I don't think it's like that," Milo said firmly. "I don't think that you're wrong and she's right. I think each of us got caught up in this thing in our own ways. Each one of us has done the best we could, just like you say the Hunt is supposed to work. It's not about where you are when you start, or where you go along the way. It's about where you are at the end. Don't you see? Analisa, I haven't had any idea about what I was doing, all the way from the very first. I know you told me not to ever say that again, but you see now that it was the simple truth instead of a strategy to beat you or anyone else. What's important to me is that I've got your help now, and you really can't imagine how much that means. And from Stigma, and Einter, and all the others. But I also know that I've got to finish this before I think about anything else. I've got no guarantee that I can do it. I don't want you, or Stigma, or anybody else to get hurt. It's bad enough already…" he said, watching Raster snatch at Analisa's grass stalk.

Analisa looked into his eyes. "I think I understand. You still understand all this better than I do. Friends, then?"

"Friends," Milo said, and extended his hand for a shake.

She took his hand and bent quickly forward, grabbed his head in her two hands, and gave him a kiss, full on the mouth. She jumped up and was catching up with the cart as it lumbered past before he could gasp in surprise.

It was Yule Eve. The weather was cold. Thin, dry snow blew in skittering puffs to catch against the edges of older, rotted drifts that rimmed the roots of trees and bare rock. Milo had no idea where they were, or if they were any closer to the Crane Castle or the Glass Tower than they had been on the first day of the journey. The oxen steamed lazily in the damp, morning air and trudged along at their regular, imperturbable pace.

Analisa had gone aloft to look for a trace of their goal, but had returned after only a short time. "Can't see a thing," she said through chattering teeth. She rubbed her wool-mitted hands together, and pulled the scarf she was wearing more closely around her neck. "The clouds are just too thick and too low."

"Keep yer eye on that ridge ahead up there," Einter called from his seat on the box. "If we get a break in the cloud so the sun can shine through, yer ought to get a sight of the Glass Tower just about there."

"How does he know that stuff?" Analisa asked her friends.

Milo told Stigma and Analisa—Raster was rolled up into a cozy ball in the blankets inside the cart—about Einter's friends, Dame Renee with her cards, and Samuel, the Ogmanian librarian.

"There it is," Stigma asserted. "If he's linked with people like that, he's just not your average tradesman."

Milo decided to climb up on the box alongside Einter. If the man was really what Stigma had suggested he was, perhaps he could tell Milo something that had been bothering him for a long time.

"Einter? Do you know anything about the Stone Kinghts?"

Einter shrugged. "Oh, I've heard of 'em all right. Old legends. My Pap told me that his pap—my granpappy—told him somethin' about 'em. Said they was an elite guard that paid a terrible price to save the Oak King back in the Elemental Wars."

He stopped talking to stick his pinky in his ear and give it a good scratch. "Those was terrible times, I guess, with everybody fightin' everybody else. For all their good intentions, the Oak King's Guard got mixed up in the squabble an' the price they paid was to be isolated up there in the Valley of the Stone Knights, turned into stone but still fightin' anybody what showed up. It's what happens when trust is lost."

Milo climbed down from the box to walk by himself, considering what Einter had told him. What had happened to the other contestants, then, was sort of the same fate that had befallen the Stone Knights: lies and mistrust had lured them into a fatal trap.

Sure enough, an hour later the clouds began to lift and the sun stabbed through with a single ray against the ridge ahead. A flash of reflected light revealed the tall, still distant needle of crystal.

"The Glass Tower," Stigma whispered in wonder.

"What do you think?" Analisa ventured. "Should I take a flight to see what might be around it?"

"That might be a mistake," Stigma said. "If Kayn is around watching for us, he might see you and you wouldn't see him. I think I better go invisible and scout out who might be around."

It was agreed, and Stigma was off, leaving behind her pile of clothes. Milo shivered just thinking about how she could endure the weather, even if she said that her magic protected her.

Milo was studying the terrain, trying to figure out where the Crane Castle might lie in relation to the Tower. "What do you think, Einter?" he asked. He was testing directions from his memory, but it seemed so very long ago since he had been there that it was like viewing the memories of a different person. "Is the Crane Castle in the valley on the other side of the ridge?"

"Could be. That is, if it lets yuh find it. Then it *could* be on the other side of that ridge there."

Milo was trying to remember himself from back then. He had been so young, so innocent! He was overcome by an upswell of compassion, and the desire to protect that Milo-that-had-been from all the hurt that was to come.

"'Member what Renee told yuh," Einter admonished, as if reading Milo's thoughts. "Nobel Purpose. Beware not to let pity or hate, or let fear corrupt yer image of that card."

They pushed on until early afternoon. Cloud and ground fog had obscured the ridge, but by the slope and rockiness of the road, they had to be nearing the pass. Stigma reappeared from the cart, dressed in the clothes she had left there.

"Nothing. I saw the Glass Tower, but it looks abandoned. No one anywhere to be seen, or any sign that anyone has been there in a century."

"There'll be snow soon," Milo commented. "Fresh snow could either reveal our tracks if we walk over it, or hide them if we make them before it falls. What do you think, Einter? Should we push on as fast as we can to get onto the other side of the ridge before it starts?"

"The brothers won't go any faster than they're likely to go. But it might not be a bad plan for the three of you to arrive at the Castle before me. Raster can stay on with me, an' we'll get there when we get there."

Milo nodded in agreement, hiding the sudden spike of energy that shot through him. Fear, anticipation, and an odd sort of eagerness that the moment had, at last, arrived. He hauled his rucksack out of the cart, packed with the few things he owned without really knowing why he should. He felt his chest, checking the lump of the cross beneath his shirt. Analisa and Stigma watched him without comment, or question. "Okay," he told them. "Let's rock and roll."

22

Rock 'n Roll

"What did you mean?" Analisa asked as they set off, with Milo in the lead. "Rock and...?"

"Roll," Milo completed. "It's nothing. Just a saying where I come from. It means, 'Let's get down to business,' or 'Let's do this thing!' You'd say it when you finally start off to do something that's been hanging over you that you dread. Like now."

They moved quickly along the rocky, snow-rimmed trail, avoiding making any unnecessary noise but still choosing speed over stealth.

"Kayn'll sense us well before he can hear us," Stigma had pointed out. "He's much too skilled a wizard to let anyone sneak up on him."

Milo had considered trying to find Kayn using Dreaming, but decided that acting right away, now that he knew, more or less, how close they were to Crane Castle, was more important than the delay it would cause going into Dreaming. Besides, he felt too keyed up to achieve the degree of focus it took to enter that state.

They crossed the ridge and began to drop down into the valley beyond. The woods rapidly thickened and became gloomier. The snow turned into dripping dampness and the sharp edge of frost felt heavy and clinging.

Although there were no clear landmarks that he could recognize as the slope eased into flat ground and became more and more marshy, a kind of familiarity reassured Milo that he was headed in the right direction. "We're almost there," he said softly. "Stay together now and stay sharp."

This last was hardly necessary. The three of them were almost huddled together, trying to peer in every direction at once as they walked along.

Evening mists had begun to rise and make white patches among the spooky shapes of the cypress and willows that surrounded them. The ground was squishy beneath their feet. "There!" Milo said suddenly. They stopped. Only a short distance away, through the shredded mist, they saw the outlines of battlements fragmented by the tendrils of fog that drifted and shifted their forms. "It's the castle."

Vague outlines turned into solid reality as they moved closer, and details appeared to reveal a formidable castle wall. They began circling until they came to a postern with a tower above a shut gate. Its heavy oaken timbers were mossy and dark with age. Wrought iron bolts studded it, announcing its thick strength. They crossed the bridge that protected it, and found the outline of a smaller, human-sized door set in the larger gate. It had a closed peek-through and an iron knocker. Milo gave it several raps. The harsh sound was startling in the muffled silence, and the three of them waited nervously in anticipation.

A scrape announced the opening of the peek-through and an eye looked out. "Who seeks entry?" a hostile voice demanded.

"Travelers," Milo replied. "Seeking the hospitality of Yule."

The peek-through slammed shut. More sounds from inside. Iron hinges groaned and the door squealed as it opened. A porter, recognizable from the same squinty eye, looked them over.

"Travelers, huh?" he commented, more to himself than in greeting. "Well, come in then. We don't get many travelers here. You'll have to wait while I fetch the seneschal."

"You mean Cedric?" Milo asked coyly.

The porter gave him a curious look, but said nothing as he retreated deeper into the castle.

"Who's Cedric?" Stigma asked.

"The seneschal. I met him when I was here before. I was hoping that by using his name, I might get the porter to be a little more welcoming. I guess not."

They took seats on the stone bench along the sides of the passage. It was intensely cold, as if it had never been warm. Luckily, they didn't wait long before footsteps clattered on cobbles and Cedric, with the porter in tow, came under the arch of the gate.

"Young Milo?" he asked with surprise. "Is that you?"

"Yes, Sir, it is," Milo answered. "Here with two friends to ask for Yule hospitality."

"Why, of course!" Cedric welcomed, and turned to the porter. "Go tell the King and Queen that we have guests. Tell them that it's Milo, the Catcher of the Salmon, with two friends."

The porter had just scurried away when a new knock came at the door. Cedric opened the peek-through to see who was there. "Why, it's Einter, the Tinker!" he exclaimed and began unbarring the whole gate. Milo lent a hand to slide back the heavy oak beam that barred the double gate.

"The greetin's of Yule to yuh!" Einter exclaimed and gave the oxen a snap with his whip to move them into the opened gate.

"Welcome to you, Friend!" Cedric greeted and helped to tug on the other side of the oxen's yoke. The cart creaked and clattered into and through the gate, passing all the way into the courtyard beyond. Cedric and Milo reclosed the gate and set the beam back into its brackets.

"Milo! Stigma and Analisa! Glad to see yuh!" Einter exclaimed. "How'd yuh come to be here?"

"Just arrived," Cedric told him. "We haven't even had a chance for introductions yet, though I see you know them. Milo we know from a...an earlier occasion."

Milo felt uneasy. How did Einter get here so fast?

"Come!" Cedric told them. "Come all you guests to the King's Great Hall. I'll send the porter back to take care of your oxen. You must be chilled to the bone on a raw day like this."

"Nothin' a jug of ale can't cure," Einter grinned and fell in beside Cedric, leaving Milo and the two women to follow behind.

"Where's Raster?" Milo asked Einter, but he either didn't hear the question, or ignored it as he fell into conversation with Cedric about the weather, the condition of the roads, and the health of the castle's inhabitants.

"Something's not right," Milo whispered to his companions. "I've never seen Einter touch his oxen with his whip."

"Doesn't Einter always yoke Senster on the left and Dexter on the right?" Analisa whispered back.

"That's right!" Stigma agreed. "But they're not that way now."

"And where's Raster?" Milo hissed. "He should be here."

"What do we do?" Analisa asked.

They were climbing stairs out of the courtyard that led to tall doors in a high vaulted stone building. Cedric threw open one of the doors and Milo recognized the Great Hall. It gave off a sigh of cold, musty air. It was dim inside. Milo could see the shapes of people rushing about, clearing and straightening, and setting a fire alight in the enormous fireplace, as large as a whole room, at one side of the Hall. Just as the flames took and light began to seep into the Hall, Alerik and his wife Ayuthaya came down a low set of steps where the King's dais was at the rear of the Hall. He shuffled painfully, supported on Ayuthaya's arm.

"Einter! Milo! Welcome!" he called in a thin, weak voice that was, none-the-less, glad, despite his decrepitude. More people were filtering into the hall and servants were lighting banks of candles, bringing the Hall into life.

The company arrived before the king and queen. "Yule greetings," Milo offered. "These are my friends and traveling companions," he said. "Stigma and Analisa."

"Welcome, ladies," Alerik offered with a gesture that passed for the bow he couldn't make. As the introduction continued, Milo sneaked a sidewise glance at Einter. He was looking away and paying no attention to Milo or any of the others, as if looking for something in the rafters. No, Milo decided. He would not know where Raster was. People flowed into the Great Hall now, finding places at the tables that were being set by servants. The fire was blazing up and beginning to bite into the massive Yule log that formed the center of the fire. Warmth rolled into the Hall and the glow from the fire and the banks of candles drove the miserable darkness back into the recesses of the high, beamed ceiling.

"Come, friends!" Alerik said, shuffling painfully back up toward the dais where he took his place. Ayuthaya took a blanket from a hand maiden to wrap around her husband's waist and legs, gently arranging it to warm and support him as he sat.

Now Erisa came dashing in. She wrapped her arms around Milo to hug him as she kissed both his cheeks. "Oh, Milo!" she almost squealed. "What a wonderful surprise! And Einter!" She stood on tiptoes to buss his cheeks, too.

"I...I'm glad to be back," Milo said, somehow unsettled to see her kissing Einter. He wanted to speak with Analisa and Stigma privately, but there was no way. Instead, he introduced them to Erisa. "She's the King and Queen's daughter," he said, feeling clumsy. "She was...very helpful to me when I came my first time."

"Then thank you so much for your care of Milo," Analisa said, taking Erisa's hand in hers in the most earnest way. Too earnest, Milo noted. Behind Erisa's back, Milo rolled his eyes at Stigma, who grinned at Analisa's performance.

"Er...Erisa?" Milo said to the princess quietly. "Is there...could we get away for a moment? I don't want to make a scene of it, but I...we"—and he indicated Stigma and Analisa—"need to speak with you privately."

Erisa's expression showed that she had gone on alert. "Yes. I can do that. I'll tell them that the three of you would like to freshen up a bit."

As she went to her father to whisper in his ear, Milo exchanged glances with his companions.

"Of course," Alerik told Erisa. "But please be brief. As soon as everyone arrives, we should hold...the service."

Einter was watching them very carefully now, looking directly at them for the first time since his arrival. As soon as Erisa had led them out of the hall and into a quiet corner, Milo spoke up.

"Something's not right," he said, speaking to Erisa but glancing to his two companions for confirmation.

"No. It's not," Stigma agreed as Erisa looked puzzled. "That's not Einter. I know he *looks* like Einter, but we know him. We traveled with him to come here, and something's not right about who is in the Hall with your parents."

"He doesn't feel right," Analisa added. "Einter is...I can't describe it...unreadable. This person gives off an aura of...discord."

"I think I know who it is," Stigma offered.

"Yeah," Milo agreed. "I do, too."

"What do you mean?" Erisa questioned. "Of course it's Einter. He comes at least once a year. We all look forward to his visits. He brings us word of what's happening out there"—her words carried a special stress of significance—"and we don't see many people from outside. You're the only one in...a long time, Milo."

"Well, we know Einter, too, and that person isn't him," Milo insisted.

"Who is it, then?" Erisa demanded.

"It's...it's someone who's been hunting us," Milo explained. "A very dangerous person. He must have seen us and Einter, who really is on his way here, but the real Einter couldn't possibly have arrived yet. I think he's disguised himself as Einter, knowing that you would let him in."

"Milo, not just anybody can come here," Erisa stated. "In fact, only very special people can come here. We're under an...enchantment, that separates us from the rest of the world. From outside, we don't even exist, except for those special people who...who the enchantment allows in."

"Like Einter?" Milo questioned.

"Well, Einter is...an exception. He's unaffected by the enchantment, and maybe, from any enchantment. So he can come and go as he likes, just as if we were part of the regular world."

"What about my two friends here?" Milo asked. "Stigma and Analisa?"

Erisa looked at them and shook her head. "They couldn't get here normally, but because they came with you, they could arrive."

"Then, if someone came just as I was coming, couldn't he get in as well?" Milo pressed, continuing his progression of logic.

"I...well, I guess so."

"Then we brought a terrible person into Crane Castle with us," Milo told her. "You—and we—are in very serious danger. The man disguised as Einter is actually a very powerful wizard who wants something, something I've come here to bring. He'll hurt anybody that gets in his way. What can we do? We've got to let your father know about the treachery, and the danger!"

"It's too late for that." Lady Ayuthaya stepped into sight from around the corner that had hidden the young people. "You're right, Milo. That isn't Einter. And you're right, too, young lady,"—turning to Analisa. "He doesn't have Einter's aura, and I know whose aura it is. Erisa, daughter dear, that man is Kayn."

Erisa blanched. "Kayn?" she barely whispered. "Father's banished brother?"

"Yes," Ayuthaya answered. She held up her hand to stop the questions erupting from all four. "Say nothing. We must go back in. The ceremony must proceed. It's the ultimate priority."

Erisa nodded, if only slightly recovered from the shock. The four of them filed back into the Hall behind the Queen.

The Hall was filling with the other residents of the castle. Alerik sat alone at the table on the dais. "Where is Einter?" Ayuthaya asked him, her alarm showing only to the four who shared her secret.

"Oh, he stepped away as well. I dare say he hardly seems himself tonight," Alerik commented innocently.

As they took their seats, and as Erisa left by way of a side door, Milo saw the porter hurrying into the Hall to whisper into Cedric's ear. Cedric sent him away and came immediately up to the King's table.

"My Lord, a very strange thing. Einter has just arrived at the gate."

"What? Why, he's here! He's..."

"Bring him in," Ayuthaya said. "Bring him straight away and seat him for the service."

"But...but..." Alerik sputtered. "He's already...he was just...he just stepped away for a moment..."

"Prepare the service," Ayuthaya said. I've sent for Blai. We're going to need her."

"What's going on?" Alerik demanded, confused.

"Your brother has returned. We need to be ready, and we must find out what he intends. But first, we must carry out the service, as we are obliged to do." She squeezed Alerik's hand, reassuring him.

"What 'service' are they talking about?" Analisa whispered to Milo.

"I think I know," Stigma answered. "From the stories."

"I know, too—this time," Milo added. "From what I saw in the Well of Revelation."

The porter came back into the Hall, with Einter—and Raster—following.

"The greetings of Yule to yuh, one and all!" Einter called out. Alerik sat in stunned silence, his jaw open. It was Ayuthaya who stood, opening her arms in greeting.

"Einter! Old friend! Come forward and share our Yule table!"

"An' I see yeh've met the young folks. Hey Milo! Analisa, Stigma!"

Raster's tail went straight up as he scampered through the Hall, under tables, between legs, and in two jumps bounded up the dais onto the table in front of Milo, still moving so fast that he skidded into the place setting, which Milo was barely able to catch before it sailed off the edge.

"Hiya, Boss!" he said, with a meow. "Wait 'til I tell you what me and Einter did!"

"Einter?" Alerik asked shakily. "How did you..." he turned toward the rear of the Hall, where the first Einter had gone moments before, then back to face the new Einter, the real Einter, striding down the aisle between tables.

"Come and be seated," Ayuthaya said again, motioning Einter to the vacant place between her and her husband. Milo and his companions were on Alerik's other side. She gripped Alerik's hand again, in warning to say no more.

Alerik's confusion was tangible, and murmurs from the others in attendance showed the assembly's confusion as they noted these inconsistencies. Einter arrived at the table and the greetings of old friends was repeated. Milo tried to catch Einter's eye, but only when their greetings were complete did Einter give him a quick and secret wink. Then he settled into his place.

"Einter and I"—began Raster, but Milo stopped him.

"Tell me, but quickly. Don't let anyone else hear you speak. Now, what happened? How did you two get here so quickly?"

"That's what I wanted to tell you," insisted the cat. "We were traveling along, you know, the old slow way that those dumb old oxen go. I wanted to catch up with you guys, 'cause I didn't want to miss the excitement. Then, all of a sudden, Einter says, 'It's about time they got there,' or something like that. Then he said I should get there, too. He said that Senster and Dexter knew the way and could get there in their own good time, and he just picked me up, and in just a couple of steps we were standing in front of that big door, knocking! I haven't missed anything yet, have I?"

"Yes, and no," Milo told him. "At least, not the important thing. Now be still, listen, and watch. If you see anything I don't, you let me know right away, okay?"

Doors on the side of the Hall opened, and a page carrying a crossbow came in. A moaning sigh rose from the crowd as the page made his way down the corridor of tables to the dais. Alerik hung his head and Ayuthaya sat stoically upright, her face neutral. The page lifted the bow above his bowed head before the King, then turned to pass back out of the Hall, taking the door opposite his entrance.

Three young women came through the same door as the page. They were dressed all in white, their heads bowed and shrouded, as if in mourning.

"What's going on?" Analisa whispered to Milo.

Milo knew, remembering the same ceremony from his first visit when he had been as baffled as Analisa was now. "Just watch," he whispered back, locking his whole attention on what was happening.

Erisa came next, dressed in a matching white gown, except her veil was scarlet. She bore the great platter as she had the first time, but that time it had held the Salmon, and Milo had focused his whole attention on that. This time, he concentrated on the platter itself. It was empty. Erisa carried it gravely, but Milo could see that she wobbled somewhat, her own focus distracted by the events that had preceded the service.

Milo turned toward Alerik, who stared with intensity at his daughter as she approached.

"Pardon, Lord Alerik," Milo said.

The Hall went silent, anticipation tangible. The swish of Erisa's satins could be heard throughout the Hall.

"Whom does the Grail serve?"

The sudden inhale pressed from every throat in the Hall broke the silence as if everyone there had suddenly surfaced from drowning. Alerik's jaw dropped, his eyes wide with surprise. Einter, at his side, caught Milo's eye and winked. Milo waited steadfastly for Alerik's answer, then repeated, "Whom does the Grail serve?"

Raster dug his claws into Milo's thigh. "Look!" he hissed and Milo glanced upward. Erisa, turning to look the same way, gasped and stumbled. High in the rafters of the Hall stood Kayn with the crossbow he had taken from the young page. The bow arms vibrated with the release of the bolt now hurtling straight at Alerik's chest. Without thought, Milo surged to his feet, projecting the shield that Culebrant had guided him to make into the bolt's trajectory.

The edge of the shield caught the bolt's flight and it ricocheted away. Milo moved into Dreaming to slow time. He saw Kayn, eyes fierce with anticipated victory. Milo knew that in Kayn's mind this was the instant he had seen in the Mirror of Reflection: the bolt piercing his brother's chest to finalize the murder he had attempted so long ago.

Milo also saw the way the bolt, deflected from Kayn's aim, wobbled onto a new course toward Erisa, who, stumbling, dropped the platter. Milo reached out to save her as the platter, like Milo's shield an instant earlier, fell into its path.

The bolt struck it squarely in the center. The plate split into two parts, one to the right and one to the left. Milo reached Erisa, jerking himself out of Dreaming in order to help her. As he pulled her away, the deflected bolt passed so closely that its fletching sliced the back of his outstretched hand. The two halves of the broken platter clattered to the floor.

Milo switched back into Dreaming, but this time much more deeply than he had ever gone. Kayn, crossbow spent and useless in his hand, stood in the rafters. It was the moment Milo had seen in the Mirror, only this time he dropped through its surface into the Other Side.

What he saw was the Hall in the Crane Castle, with Alerik and Erisa and all those around them, but they seemed ethereal as if made of no more than smoke. Beyond them the Castle's walls were just as insubstantial and there was another world, one much more profound. Milo thrust his hand into his pocket to grasp the Dragon Cross. The two worlds solidified.

"King!" he shouted. "What ails you?"

He reached out to Alerik. The old bolt lodged in Alerik's hip shone with a putrid glow. Milo grasped it and wrenched it free. Alerik contorted in agony and black blood jetted from the rotten wound.

Milo turned toward Kayn. He held the old bolt in his right hand, the Cross in his left. Kayn released a burst of fire to destroy Milo, but the Cross absorbed it, draining it away to an impotent trickle.

"You are done, wizard," Milo told Kayn.

Kayn's face contorted in fury. Milo snapped the old bolt and dropped it to the floor. Kayn gathered himself for another attack, drawing all the power he commanded. But Milo looked beyond him to a much greater threat on the way: the huge and elemental colossus, the dragon Heronsuge.

Heronsuge was coming. Kayn glanced back. Would the dragon devour Kayn and perhaps Milo as well? Milo held the Cross high, as much to the advance of the dragon as to Kayn. "Your plan is finished. Ruined. You have nothing left."

Kayn cringed. Although he was unable to see beyond the Hall—Milo was the only one there able to do that—he sensed the onrushing power and his rage gave way to broken capitulation, his magic spent.

The instant was past. Milo pulled away from the depths of the state he had entered and surfaced into the Rule. He stood firmly in Alerik's Hall. Only Milo knew what had transpired. Alerik braced himself against the table, gasping. Ayuthaya rushed to Alerik's side and Erisa rose from the floor, straightening her dress but otherwise unharmed. Pandemonium filled the Hall as everyone came to their feet in shock, joy, astonishment, fright, or shear release. Milo stooped to retrieve his shield, which still rotated on it edge, not yet at rest. He placed it on the table, concave side up, before Alerik, then picked up the two parts of the broken plate to lay them into the shallow cup of the shield. The two parts nestled in the shield perfectly, finding the shape of their broken fit. Two drops of Milo's blood from the cut fell onto the center of the plate and soaked into the crack.

"King, whom does the Grail serve?" he asked for the third time.

Bedlam took the hall again. Milo gazed around. Raster hopped back up on the table from where he had been thrown when Milo jumped up. Einter was missing. Just as Milo was beginning to fear that the Einter he had believed to be Einter was also some sort of impostor, he saw the tinker striding forward from the back of the Hall, pulling Kayn along by his ear as if he were a naughty five-year-old.

Alerik, pale and shaken, smiled and stood up straight, the old wound rapidly closing and healed. Ayuthaya hugged him, tears of joy streaming down her face. She came to where Milo stood. "Thank you, Milo," she said, and kissed his cheek. Erisa hugged him and kissed his other cheek. Einter arrived with the captive Kayn and faced Alerik. At the sight of the wizard, the onlookers shrank away.

"Here he is," Einter announced. "What do yuh want t' do with 'em?"

"Einter!" Erisa squealed. "Be careful!"

"Oh, this one's not nearly so bad as he thinks he is. Why, my pappy told me that his pappy—my granpappy—told him that it was his, that is our, great-great-great-sompthin' or other granpappy that caught this one when he an' Alerik was young themselves, an' this one had just killed a lark with a stone from his slingshot. My granpappy what-ever-back-then grabbed him up just like this"—Einter demonstrated by giving Kayn's ear a tug, making him squirm—"an' he took him over his knee an' gave him a good solid whackin'. Not good enough, though, I'm afraid."

Just then the main doors of the Hall opened again. This time it was Culebrant—Heronsuge in his form as The Keeper—who strode into the company.

"I am Culebrant, the Keeper. This young man, Milo, has served as my apprentice to learn all he needed to know to perform the service that you, Alerik, as Guardian of the Grail, have waited for these long years. In my original form, I am the Elemental known as Heronsuge, the Guardian of the Path. Milo has returned the Dragon Cross to take its rightful place at the center of the Grail, thereby restoring it to its fullness and its purpose for uniting the manifest and the magical realms."

He turned to Milo. "Milo, hand me the Dragon Cross." Milo held out the Cross. It seemed to pulsate in his palm like a beating heart as he gave it to the Keeper.

"The Quest is complete," Culebrant announced, taking the Cross in his fingers and holding it up by the edges for all to see. "With this, *All* shall be healed." He laid it down onto the center of the platter. Milo noticed that there was a recess there, and the Cross fit it precisely. It fit so closely, in fact, that the Cross seemed to merge into the material of the platter to become part of the whole. Furthermore, the crack where the plate had been broken was erased.

"The Grail is whole," Culebrant pronounced. "The Fisher King and his land are healed. Healed, and fertile once more, the blight that has lain upon it and the world is purged."

He turned to address Alerik. "What will you do with this one?" he said, holding a hand to indicate Kayn, who cringed away.

"I forgive him," Alerik said. "The suffering that he brought on me, my land, and my people is ended. The Grail is at last whole. What was done, is done. He is my brother."

"This is good," Culebrant said. He turned to Kayn. "With the healing of your brother's words and the deeds of this young man"—he gestured to Milo—"your crimes are absolved and your wizardly powers made null.

The purity of Milo's intentions and his steadfast heart have succeeded in restoring the Grail. Your powers, based in corruption, deceit, and treachery are dissolved. You must live on as an ordinary man. If you choose, you may use your remaining years in atonement, or you may end your days nursing your spite and living as a petty thief. That's entirely up to you, as it is for everyman."

Culebrant now lifted up the Grail. To Milo's astonishment, his shield, which he had used as a receptacle of the broken parts, was now so firmly welded to the bottom of the platter that it was part of the legendary artifact. He could see the four-part design of The Dragon on its underside.

"You who are the guests of the Crane Castle"—and he looked to Milo, Stigma, Analisa, Einter, and Kayn, who was rubbing at the ear that Einter had, at last, released—"have your own choices to make. You may decide to stay on to live in Crane Castle or return to your birth-realms. By sunrise, Crane Castle will take its place within the Rule. It shall no longer float in the limbo in between. Milo, you are now the Grail Knight, and have the right to remain in the Grail Castle, but you shall be the Grail Knight regardless of where you go. You should know that your noble friend, Boriboreau, and his family reside with me. In time, a new star will appear in the sky of the Western Sisters for him. My advice to you is to consider what you believe to be your proper destiny. Your duty is to serve the Grail, but how you achieve that is your decision. Whatever you decide, go in peace, and with honor."

With that, Culebrant turned and walked out of the Great Hall, through the doors, and out into the night.

It was much later before the celebrating crowd settled down enough for Alerik to call for the dinner to be served. Milo was amazed at how vigorous he was, and how well he walked, with only the slightest hitch to his step. He couldn't seem to tear his eyes away from Ayuthaya, who herself seemed to have shed the look of centuries from her eyes. Milo wanted to take Erisa aside, to ask her about so much that he still didn't understand, but Alerik was as devoted to her as he was to his wife, hugging her and keeping her near his side as he greeted personally everyone in the room.

Milo turned to Einter instead. "Einter? How long has it been since Kayn shot Alerik?"

"Oh, in our way of thinkin', it's been...oh, centuries. But here in the castle, they've lived in the limbo of Time. There's no way to tell the difference between ten years an' ten centuries. "Course, time will start running for Alerik and all the rest of the folks here since the clock's going again."

"When did the Cross get separated from the platter?"

"I reckon I'm not the one to answer that question. Yeh'll have to ask that of somebody else."

The kitchen staff at last served the dinner, with piles of food on every table and dishes of every conceivable sort. Milo had never seen so much food, nor had he tasted food so delicious. Alerik served Milo himself, putting more on his plate even after Milo couldn't eat another bite. Alerik, on the other hand, ate like he had not eaten in all the time of his suffering.

The general celebration went on and on. The hubbub became a sort of buffer around Milo, who felt himself isolated in his own thoughts. It was almost like Dreaming, where he could see everything around him, but couldn't enter into it. There was so much for him to think about and consider, and every new thought seemed to lead to a hundred more.

Who could answer his questions? He had known what questions to ask in order to heal the King and restore the Grail, but not the answers. So far, he hadn't received any response to those questions. Who did the Grail serve? And what was it, really? He looked around at the celebrants, wondering who could tell him. Alerik and Ayuthaya would know, but he could hardly interrupt them in their moment of joy and release from the long, torturous enchantment. Erisa had joined Stigma, Analisa, and the other young people who were all dancing. Einter was stomping his feet and clapping his hands to the music, a huge flagon of ale before him. Only Kayn—demoted now from wizard to common thief—sat alone, looking as if he preferred to fade into the woodwork.

Of all the people here, Kayn—now just Smith—should know, if he would talk to Milo at all. Milo picked up Raster, who had stuck to him like glue the whole evening—very unlike the young cat—and went to where Smith sat.

"May I ask you something?" Milo asked the doused sorcerer. Smith glared up at him, but the ferocity of the look he gave Milo didn't quite make it, and even that seemed to fizzle like a candle flame that was burning out.

"I suppose you can," he said in a voice so subdued that Milo could hardly hear it.

"How old are you?" Milo asked, deciding to start at another of his questions to see if Smith was really willing to answer.

"Very, very old. Up until now, my magic has preserved me. I suppose it won't anymore." He seemed to shrivel a little as he said it.

"The Grail...it was already broken when the crossbow bolt hit it, wasn't it?"Milo asked, seeking verification for what he suspected was true.

"Yes. It had been repaired, and convincingly so, but it was broken long ago, back when the Dragon Cross was taken. I learned the lore of its breaking after I had shot my...shot the Crane King. I was banished for that, and so began my long quest for the Grail. I learned the lore of the Dragon Cross and how it had been taken, by the remnant of the Fallen after the War of the Elementals. In removing the Cross, they broke the Grail. It was the Crane Clan who became the Grail Kings and the keepers of the partially repaired Grail. Eventually, I learned where the Cross had been hidden but my own actions had inadvertently cut me off from getting to that place at the End of the Earth. I knew if I could gain possession of the Cross, I could reunite the pieces of the Grail and restore its full power, which I would then control. The Grail would belong to me and the whole world would be at my feet."

Some of the old, malevolent fury came back to him as he said this, and he seemed to forget that he was speaking to Milo. The instant he came back into reality, though, it faded.

"What does the question, 'Whom does the Grail serve,' mean," Milo asked. "And why do you want it so bad?"

Smith gave him a taunting look, and sneered. "If you don't know, you won't learn it from me." He turned a look of acid on Milo, but even this seemed to Milo a pitiful thing.

"You!" Smith spat. "You thought you were stalking me, you fool. I was leading you! After I figured out who you were and what you had—by pure, dumb luck after all my work of learning the lore of the Grail and the location of the hidden Cross—I realized that it was you who had to bring it back to Crane Castle. I saw how I could take the restored Grail from you then and finish the task of becoming Grail King. All I had to do was to see that you succeeded. You could never have done it without me. All I needed to keep up with your whereabouts was to possess something of yours. So I went back to the Kingdom of Odalese where you started and I got this." He flipped a coin into the air for Milo to catch. It was the coin with the buffalo on the reverse side that Milo had traded to the lady at the coin shop.

"I found that, the silly little medallion with the image of Count Abracadabracus and that mythical beast on it, and I could follow you wherever you went. I didn't even have to follow you, because I knew where you would show up if I pointed you in the right direction." He was obviously quite pleased with his cleverness.

Milo looked at the coin, front and back. What should he make of the claims that Smith was making? Was Milo really nothing but the discredited sorcerer's stalking horse?

Did it matter? What could Smith's claim mean since the whole affair had worked out the way it had? He put the coin into his pocket. "Thanks for the info," Milo said, turning away to leave Smith in the ruins of his own conspiracies. "Live in peace."

Just then Blai arrived. Erisa broke away from the dancing to join her, and the two of them went to Alerik and Ayuthaya. Stigma and Analisa came over to Milo and Raster.

"What's going on?" Analisa asked. Milo shrugged.

"What will they do now?" Stigma asked, more as an open speculation than for information.

"Maybe Einter can tell us," Raster suggested, and they joined the tinker where he sat, taking it all in.

"Oh, I expect everything's going to change," he mused. "One thing's sure, though. We'll be leavin' soon. Got to get you younguns back to K of O. You'll be wantin' to see what's become of the Hunt, won't yuh?"

"There's lots of stuff I don't understand yet," Milo stated.

"Then yeh ought to ask Blai," Einter suggested. "She'll know about as much as anybody, I'd say."

"What?" Analisa asked. "I thought you knew what was going on," she told Milo, rather accusingly.

"No. You're overestimating what I know again," Milo reminded her.

"But...you knew just what to ask, and when to ask it."

"Yeah, from what I saw in the Mirror of Revelation," he told her. "But that's all I knew. I didn't know what would happen to get me here and I didn't—*don't* know what happens next. I think I understand what it is the Mirror shows you when you look into it. It shows you what's in your own mind that you aren't letting yourself understand. I sort of knew what went wrong the first time I was here. I knew I'd done something, or *not* done something, that I should have done, but I hadn't really faced up to it."

"What about Smith?" Analisa pointed out. "He must have seen

himself killing his brother, but it didn't work out that way. Was the Mirror lying?"

"I think I understand that, too," Milo answered. "You have to be open to your own truth before the Mirror can show it to you. Kayn had been set on murdering Alerik for so long, nothing else could come into his mind, so his own closed thoughts warped what the Mirror could show him. He couldn't see anything else. He believed that killing Alerik was the one and only thing that would reward his ambitions. If he hadn't shut every other option out of his mind, he probably would have seen something else. So, ultimately, what you see is what you are. Kayn was so fixed on evil, he couldn't see any other choice."

"I saw..." Stigma began, then stopped. "What I saw, I'm not sure about yet. I don't know what it means. We all need to travel back together, though. When do we need to leave?" This last, she asked Einter.

"Right soon." He set down the mug he'd been drinking from and wiped the foam out of his mustache. "I'll go see if th' boys have gotten here yet."

As he ambled away, Blai came their way. "Milo? You've done now what I knew you could do. But...there's one more thing you could do if you're willing to take it on."

Milo, thinking of all that had happened that had started with just this sort of request, shifted unhappily, but said, "If I can, yes, sure."

"My niece, Erisa, has spent her whole life trapped here in this castle through its enchantment. She dreams about seeing the outer world and wants to go with the four of you. Alerik and Ayuthaya, although they're sorry to let her go, have agreed that she should. Will you take her?"

"That's it!" Stigma whispered.

"She's the Grail Maiden and will be Grail Queen someday," Blai continued. "Alerik will die someday as every mortal does and Ayuthaya and I will leave this world. All will change after that and Erisa must discover a new way to serve the Grail on her own. The best way for her to learn would be to go into the world to find out what it's like."

Milo spoke then. "Blai? I need to ask you...What is the Grail and whom does it serve?"

Blai smiled. "The Grail is a Power. The power of what has been within the innermost part of noble hearts and the promise of what can be. That's all. And that's *All*. Although Heronsuge—you know him as Culebrant—has returned to retrieve the repaired Grail to take it back to its proper resting place in the Garden at the Hub of the World, the power of the Grail remains, embedded in each of us. Every person who is drawn to take up the Quest must seek, and find it on his or her own, just as you have, Milo. Who does it serve? It serves us all."

"Okay. I think I understand," Milo answered. "But...what I need to know is how all this came about? When did the Grail get broken and how was the Dragon Cross separated from it?"

"That's an old, old tale," Blai answered. "It goes back to the War of Elementals, when the Fallen rebelled against the First Born, Anzu's children. The Grail was taken from the Hub and the Fallen possessed it. They intended to use it just as Kayn did. The war was fought over it. The Oak Clan, fighting on the side of the First Born, had recovered it from the Fallen, but they got trapped in what you call the Valley of the Stone Knights. The plate was broken in the struggle, but the Oak King escaped with the pieces. He put the two halves of the plate into the keeping of the Crane King, one of his most loyal supporters, but he took the Dragon Cross with him. No one knew where he had taken it, but by keeping it apart from the other pieces left it less likely to fall into the wrong hands.

"Generations passed. The Oak King's capital at the End of the Earth had long been abandoned and remembered only as the terminus of the Pilgrimage. Even the memory of the Dragon Cross faded from knowledge. The Crane Clan and the Fisher Kings guarded the Grail in its repaired state, though its powers were only a shadow of what it had been before it was broken and the key, the Dragon Cross, removed. Until you came. So you see, what you did tied the ancient past and all that transpired since into the present."

Milo let this sink in, sort of like a deep drink of water after a long thirst. When it felt complete, he said, "Sure. I'll...we'll"—looking to his companions—"be happy to have Erisa travel with us. All I can promise, though, is that we can travel together, at least as far as the Kingdom of Odalese. After that..."

Blai broke in. "Of course. You can't promise the future, and I'm not suggesting that you be her guardian. She must learn to make her own way if she's to accomplish her own Quest. Thank you for accepting her."

23

Thomas Jefferson Takes Milo Home

It took about a week for Einter, Senster, and Dexter to get Stigma, Analisa, Erisa, Milo, and Raster to The Kingdom of Odalese. Smith didn't come with them. As soon as they left Crane Castle, he slipped away almost without anyone's notice into the pre-dawn mist.

Erisa had brought Milo a gift, sort of. She gave him his old clothes, neatly laundered and folded, that he'd left behind at Crane Castle when Erisa and Ayuthaya had rigged him out more suitably for traveling as a pilgrim. Even the dollar bill that the lady at the coin shop hadn't wanted had been laundered, ironed, and folded. He decided that he would wear his old clothes when he arrived at K of O so he'd have something clean.

Blai left with them to see her niece off before taking on her own way back to the Glass Tower. Her way divided from theirs just as the sun began to rise. She said her goodbyes to each of them, finishing with Erisa.

"I would like to send you my blessing," she told her niece, then turned to Milo. "Milo, what did you do with that ball of rainbow yarn I gave you?"

"I still have it," Milo replied. "I never knew what to use it for."

"May I have it back?"

Milo dug in his backpack, rummaging down to the bottom to pull it out. Blai took it, glanced to see the rim of the sun sparking on the horizon, and threw the ball high in a rainbow that arced in the winter sky.

"Someday, when you're ready to return, remember this rainbow," she told Erisa. "I'll know and I'll send you its twin to lead you home again. You may bring a guest with you at that time," Blai added, and glanced at Stigma. Milo saw something unspoken pass between them, then Blai went her way, leaving her niece to travel with her new companions into a world that she had never seen before.

She had certainly imagined it, though, but as they actually traveled into it, Erisa admitted that there was much more to it than she had imagined. Milo understood. He recalled the first day when he had found himself in a place he'd only imagined before—The Kingdom of Odalese—and how much more exciting and baffling it had been than the way he'd imagined it.

It seemed like such a long time ago that he'd been to the Kingdom of Odalese and begun his adventures. In fact, Milo could hardly think about that time at all without starting the thought with, "Once upon a time..."

Despite her eagerness to see the world, Erisa was anxious about her new adventure and how she would cope with it. Milo certainly identified with that. She also missed her parents, her old friends, and her home, Crane Castle and the grim comforts its familiarity had given. Perhaps in sympathy, Milo was having bouts with homesickness himself, thinking about his mom, Gracie (his cat), and even his school.

Stigma and Analisa took Erisa under their wings, and Raster was a great distraction to Milo, so the traveling, while uneventful, was a comfort, too. The routine of moving, of covering ground a day at a time as he had done for most of the months since all this had started, soothed him. The forests of the valley gave way to hilly terrain, and that descended into a wide plain where an increasing number of people lived. Einter seemed to be well known at every farm they came to, and welcomed in every village. The hospitality that came with this recognition meant a comfortable journey and ample provisions, a luxury that Milo had rarely enjoyed. Milo thought about the hard times his travel had brought him, and now those trials seemed lifted. He spent the hours they walked to the rumble and clank of Einter's cart thinking about his adventures, musing on the Dragon Cross, and all that Culebrant had taught him. He thought about Deryl, Beryl, and Teryl and how they might be doing in their new lives. He wondered what would become of Ayuthaya and Blai, King Alerik, and the people of Crane Castle, but most of all, he thought about Bori.

He recalled with great detail how he had made Boriboreau's acquaintance, fighting back tears whenever he did this, but determined to honor his friend by remembering all he could. He went over their travels together and how Bori had eaten Milo's share of the Wise Salmon, and how that wisdom had served them both thereafter. And he considered Bori's surprising powers and the way he had stood up to Kayn in an act of savage defiance.

Every time he thought about Bori, he found himself fingering the Jefferson nickel in his pocket, studying its two sides absently as he had the Dragon Cross. He didn't know why. Was it because Kayn had used it as a tool to track Milo and Bori? The thing—just a small, unimportant thing—that had brought them to the moment of Bori's showdown with the wizard? Something so small with such consequences. What Culebrant called Destiny.

At last, the journey ended, as all journeys must. They reached The Kingdom of Odalese. Although Milo had never actually seen the approach to the city from the perspective of a traveler on the ground, he recognized the landscape around it, the River Dulcy, the town walls, and the attractive jumble of roofs that mounted up the slopes of the hill where the Kingdom stood, with the ruins of the old castle at the top. With every step his excitement mounted, though he couldn't really say why.

It was a chilly but clear day, right at noon, when they came through the city gate. Einter's cart clanked and creaked on the cobblestones, and Senster and Dexter lumped amiably along as they always did. Stigma stopped them. "Look!" she cried, pointing straight up at the sky.

Something incredible was happening.

Milo had never seen anything like it before: an icy rainbow, but not an arch like normal rainbows with their ends anchored to the ground. This one was a huge ring around the sun at zenith. In each of the four directions—north, south, east, and west—were bright spots like extra suns. And above all that, the clear blue sky.

"Wow!" Milo exclaimed.

"What is it?" Analisa asked.

"That's a halo," Erisa said. "It's a gift for Milo from Aunt Blai."

Everyone in the street was looking up now. Activities came to a standstill and people inside the houses and shops came out to stare as well when they noticed what was happening.

As Milo stared at Blai's gift, he became aware of someone standing at his side, staring up as well. He glanced.

It was Tinburkin. "That's a compelling recommendation from one of your more influential friends, wouldn't you say?" he commented to Milo without taking his eyes off the sky.

"Wha...?" Milo started. "What do you mean?"

Tinburkin looked at him with a friendly twinkle in his eye, winked, and answered. "Couldn't be a more signature endorsement, I think. The Rainbow Weaver throwing a special sign in your honor? I expect the Council will recognize that as a vote of confidence."

He turned away from Milo to extend a hand to Einter, standing with his oxen just behind Milo in the street. "Einter," he greeted. "Hope you've had an interesting journey."

"Ey, that it was."

"You know each other?" Milo asked in surprise, though he didn't know why he should be surprised. After all, Einter seemed to know everyone. Einter nodded, and Tinburkin grinned.

"Nary a dull moment with this young 'un around," Einter answered, nodding to indicate Milo.

Tinburkin turned to greet Analisa and Stigma. Tinburkin grinned at Stigma, looking her over. "Nice to *see* you," he commented, then turned to Erisa "And this then would be the Grail Maiden?"

"I'm Erisa. I'm happy to make your acquaintance," she said.

Tinburkin turned another wink at Milo. "Another reason for the Council to pay attention."

"What Council?" Milo demanded. What are you talking about?"

"The Council of the Hunt. You remember Barenton? The Magic Scavenger Hunt chairperson? That's the council he presides over. They're in session to assess the success of the 77th Hunt and its participants. You three are the final contestants to arrive, marking its end."

"Are there...how many are..." Milo asked, wary of an answer that would show how many victims were lost in the battle with Kayn and the detour into the Valley of the Stone Knights, and expecting the worst.

"All thirteen are now accounted for," Tinburkin reported. "Even the ones who were...detained in the episode with the Stone Knights. I found them all to be retrievable when the Council sent me out to bring them in."

"And Count Yeroen?" Milo asked. "And Aulaires? Lute? Sarakka? They're okay, too?"

"All here. Each has been interviewed by the Council and they have provided their full testimonies concerning their experiences during the Hunt. Only you three are still to appear."

While this conversation had been going on, the halo around the sun faded, turning the sky back to its normal, winter sky blue. The street of sky gawkers had re-formed around Milo and his companions.

"It's the boy," Milo heard someone in the crowd explain. "Oh, the Thirteenth!" her companion answered. Another voice said, "He's the one who fought the dragon!"

"What sort of stories are they telling?" Milo asked Tinburkin, upset at the inaccuracy.

"We shouldn't keep the Council waiting any longer," Tinburkin said without comment. "Come along, I'll take you all to the Courthouse."

The crowd parted for them, ox cart and all, as Tinburkin led them up the street until they arrived at the town square in front of the Courthouse. Milo looked up the stairs flanked by the two bronze lions.

"Me 'n Erisa 'll wait here for yuh," Einter assured them. He held a card out to Milo. "Dame Renee told me to give yuh this." Milo recognized the card she called The Wanderer. "Just to remind yuh to stay humble."

Tinburkin took Stigma, Analisa, Milo, and of course Raster into the Courthouse and up to the third floor. He sat them on a wooden bench outside the Council Chambers, then went inside. Soon he returned to call in Stigma. She was inside for a very long time. When she came out at last, she looked flustered, and gave no more than a tight smile before she hurried away.

Analisa went next. By now, Milo was beginning to feel nervous, despite himself. Raster, who had come with them, but had gone exploring, came back and hopped up on the bench beside Milo. "Hey Boss!" he greeted. "Have you seen 'em yet?"

"No, not yet," Milo replied, and gave the cat a pat.

"What's taking so long?"

"I've no idea."

"Well, I'll go see," Raster said, and before Milo could stop him, he jumped down and dashed away down the hall.

Moments ticked slowly away, mounting up into a longer and longer time. Raster came back. "They're really grilling Analisa in there!" he reported. "She's in tears. I thought about scratching a few of them, but decided I'd better tell you first."

"That was a good idea. But Analisa? In tears? What in the world are they asking her?"

"Oh, stuff like where she was at such-and-such a time when so-and-so was going on, or why she did this or what happened next. Stuff like that."

"And it made her cry?"

"Yeah. I think that's because of how they asked. One question after another, real intense like. And detailed. For every answer she's giving them, they ask ten more. I think maybe she's getting confused."

That made Milo feel even more like he was waiting to be called into the assistant principal's office (that had happened to him more than once).

"Raster? How did you get in? I saw you go down the hall instead of into the door there."

"Oh, that's because I went a different way," Raster said, obviously pleased with his own ingenuity. "Down the hall there's an open office. You go in there and out the open window. Then you walk the ledge that goes around the corner of the building. That takes you to the open window of the Council Chamber. I hopped down inside and hid under the table to watch for a while. You want me to take you there?"

"No, I think I'll just wait here," Milo answered.

"You think they're going to get to you today? It'll be suppertime soon."

"I don't know, but I guess I'll have to sit here until they call me. Why don't you go down and find Einter and Erisa? They'll see you get your supper."

That struck Raster as a good idea and he left. Milo was alone again. The butterflies he felt were getting more and more agitated. If the Council was as severe as they apparently were with Stigma and Analisa, it seemed hardly fair. On the other hand, after the adventures Milo had had, fair was not something he was wont to quibble about. What, he told himself, could these people's questions mean to him after all he had been through? Why question his friends like that? He knew what he had done and what he had experienced. How dare they question that? What could they possibly do that mattered to him?

Analisa came out. She wiped at her nose with her sleeve and her eyes were red. "Don't let them bother you," she warned quickly, and gave Milo a kiss on the cheek before she hurried away.

Tinburkin came out. "Your turn," he told Milo. "Go in there and be who you are."

Milo felt the butterflies surge into a swirling mass. He took a deep breath, the way Culebrant had taught him, and let them fly away. Then he went in.

"Be seated," Barenton said, his white beard wagging.

Milo took the chair that faced the half circle of cloaked judges sitting in high-backed chairs behind a formal table. Tinburkin took a place off to one side. Milo looked the judges over one by one, recognizing the Mayor of Kingdom, but none of the rest.

"You are the Thirteenth," Barenton stated.

Milo said nothing since it sounded more like an affirmed identity than a question.

"Why did you decide to be the thirteenth contestant when you could have been the twelfth?" asked the Mayor.

"I didn't choose to be the thirteenth," Milo answered. "I just let Analisa go ahead of me. Besides, why is that important?"

The judges glanced at each other. "We will be the ones to ask the questions," Barenton said in mild rebuke. "You just answer."

The questions came, one after the other. The judges seemed to know everything that had happened already: who he had met and what he had or they had done. It seemed to Milo that they were only checking his answers against theirs. Nor could he detect any order to the questions. They weren't starting at the beginning and proceeding to the end. The questions came in random order, jumping all over the place. It really was confusing. To keep from getting all balled up, he began practicing the breathing methods from Culebrant, focusing on one thing at a time without feeling rushed. Basically, he let his mind go open, almost like he'd do to go into Dreaming.

"Why did you choose to travel with the slinger players?" one judge would ask.

"They were fun to travel with," Milo would answer. Question closed. No wondering why they asked that or what they might want to know next. Open mind.

"How were you able to interpret the script on the Dragon Cross?" the next question would be.

"I didn't. The librarian in Inverdissen did." No more information. Answer complete. Mind open.

"Why did you go to Rykirk?"

"Because I was hungry."

Milo could have expanded any or all his answers, but decided there was no point. If they wanted to know more, they could ask.

On and on it went. It got dark outside and someone came in unobtrusively to light the brackets of candles. Thinking of home, Milo considered what magic it was to simply flip a switch to have all the light you wanted.

He was hungry. And tired. Besides, this was boring. He decided he'd had enough. "Listen," he said, breaking off the next question without bothering to answer it. "This has gone on long enough. I'm sure you are all as ready to get your dinners as I am. We're just going over things you already know. After what happened when I left the End of the Earth, I realized I'd gotten myself into something—I'm sure you all understand the meaning of that better than I do—that was much more than random puzzles I was inept at deciphering anyway. Since then I've had a number of...adventures that you've been asking me about over and over, though I've got no idea what you're trying to get me to tell you. If I knew that, I'd be happy to tell you, because I've got no reason, absolutely none, to hide any of it. Admittedly, I don't understand a lot of it. It seems there's no one who understands my questions, or can give me the answers. But as I see it, I've done what I did, and now I'm really not interested in sitting here any longer. So I think we should stop. The interview is over."

He stood up, ignoring the surprised faces of the judges, and as he turned away, Raster dashed from under the table to rub against his leg. Milo scooped him up and went to the door.

"Does this mean we can have supper now?" the cat asked hopefully.

"Yeah. It's time for supper."

Milo turned back to the judges. "Oh, by the way, I couldn't have done any of the things I did—I wouldn't even have survived to be here today—without the help of Boriboreau, this cat's father. He was my loyal friend. He asked no more than a meal, if we could even find one. He was a wise and reliable counselor who was always there with the right advice at just the right time. He was the bravest and truest, and at the end the fiercest, warrior when the need arose. If you want to award someone with something, put up a monument in your square to your most distinguished native son, Boriboreau."

With that, he left. Tinburkin gave him a wink.

He found his friends with the whole group of contestants waiting at the corner restaurant. Einter, Erisa, Analisa, and Stigma. Count Yeroen was there with Aulaires, Lute, and Sarakka, and even the others, who had been captured by the Stone Knights. Tivik, Ali-Sembek, Braenach, Weidan, Vianna, and Obeah Reah. They were all sitting at tables pulled loosely together and cluttered with wine glasses and the remains of their dinners. They stood to greet him as he came in, slapping him on the shoulder, shaking his hand, or—if they were the female ones—giving him a kiss on the cheek. He blushed, but this time it wasn't attributable to the effect that Aulaires' costume had on him. The company had hardly taken up their places again when Tinburkin came out of the courthouse and joined them.

"Well," he said, raising the cup that Einter filled and handed him, "here's to the conclusion of the 77th Magical Scavenger Hunt, and to its Thirteenth Contestant. May we remember it for as long as the Hunt is celebrated and its contestants come to seek its rewards."

All raised their cups to the toast. Stigma put one into Milo's hand and Erisa poured Raster a saucer of gravy.

"So." Yeroen said. "It's done, then?"

"The judges agreed," Tinburkin said. He glanced back and forth as he elaborated. "Not, of course, to declare a winner, because by now you all understand that that's not the point of the Hunt. The Hunt is a Quest, and a quest is not a thing that can be won or lost, but a thing that must be performed. The judges agreed to pronounce this Hunt to be the last of the Old Cycle. Subsequent Hunts will be commemorative of this one, but in a new numbering system."

"Why?" Milo asked. "Why would this one change everything?"

"Because all of the Hunts up until now have been predicated on problems left over from the Age of the Elementals," Tinburkin explained. "But with the Pilgrimage reopened, the Portals explored, the Grail restored, and the Crane King relieved, the core issues of the past are resolved. Now the Hunt must turn its attention to exploring the possibilities of a New Age and the mysteries of a Restored Grail. You see, Milo, that's what you accomplished. You vindicated the prophecy of the Thirteenth."

"And what is that?" Milo insisted. "What is it about being thirteenth? I don't get it."

"Because in all this time," Count Yeroen put in, "you were the first to be the thirteenth and final contestant. There have been twelve many times, and as many as seventeen, I believe."

Tinburkin nodded. "Yes, that was in the 46th Hunt."

"Thirteen can be a lucky number," Yeroen continued, "or a bad thing that signifies destruction."

"It's the number of this card," Obeah Reah said, holding up a card very similar to the ones Milo had seen Dame Renee use. The one she was holding up was ominous, with the image of a cloaked death figure holding a scythe. "The Thirteenth card is called the Grim Reaper, and is greatly feared because it can signify death and destruction. But it can also signify the destruction of the old, giving way to new beginnings."

"Because I'm a witch," Analisa put in, "people would expect me to bring on the negative meaning of thirteen, Death. Which could have over-taken any of us during the pursuit of this Hunt. Or it could have meant bad luck for the next decade, until the next Hunt takes place."

"But you changed that when you let Analisa go ahead of you," Tinburkin told Milo. "You see, perhaps the most important thing you did, considering all the amazing things that you accomplished, was your first action. You usurped the place of the Thirteenth for yourself. That was an awesome act of Power."

"Well, I didn't have any idea of what I was doing," Milo grumped.

"Which is the very reason it held such Power," Einter explained.

"Yuh did it out of spontaneous decency instead of calculatin' yer magical advantage. The paradox is what's kept the Old Order of the Hunt from doin' just what yuh did. True magic's from the heart, not with the head."

"It's why each of us," Aulaires said, glancing around the group for confirmation, "each of us in our own ways told the judges that you are our superior."

"Which they already realized, but which they had to document with a thorough deposition," Tinburkin explained.

Milo considered all this. Maybe he should have felt pride, but instead he felt weary. He thought instead of how much help he had gotten from so many others. And mostly, he thought of Bori. After that, there wasn't much room for vanity.

"What will you do now, Milo?" Erisa asked softly, and perhaps with unexpressed hope.

"I...don't really know," he answered earnestly. "I really haven't given it much thought. I think, most of all, I'd like to be just me, without all this important stuff and the expectations of other people hanging over me."

"May I quote you on that?"

It was the reporter from the *Odalese Observer*, who popped out from behind a stack of tables where she had been eavesdropping, scribbling madly into her notebook.

"What?" Milo asked in surprise.

"What you just said," the reported repeated. "That you plan to live as an obscure burger. Maybe you'd like for the City Council to award you a little farmstead on the edge of town where you can pursue your wizardly studies?"

"No. That's not it at all," Milo insisted. "I just want to go home and be just me, Milo." He had nervously begun to twiddle with the nickel in his pocket, and he now tapped its edge on the table top.

"Is that the magical medallion of Count Abracadabracus I've heard about?" the reporter asked.

"No," Milo answered. "That's the portrait of Thomas—

"—Jefferson," he said.

"Very good, Milo!" Ms. Mayfield, his history teacher said. "And I thought you were daydreaming again instead of listening."

Milo blinked. He was in sixth period history class, and the square at The Kingdom of Odalese had vanished. He was staring at the nickel with Jefferson's picture in three-quarter profile. He flipped it over. There was the image of a buffalo—an American bison—on the reverse.

"Jefferson sent Lewis and Clark to explore the extent of the newly acquired Louisiana Purchase and to search for a passage to the Pacific Ocean," he told his teacher.

"That's right, Milo," she verified. "Does anyone know the name of the Native American guide who led Lewis and Clark across the continent?"

Milo did, but he didn't volunteer what he knew. Someone else in the class answered that one. Milo was considering the long journeys that Thomas Jefferson had instigated.

The bell rang. Milo looked forward to seeing his own cat, Gracie, and his mom when he went home.

Readers Guide

1. This book features magic and mythical events. What is magic? What is imagination?

2. How does the tension between the familiar and the fantastic play during the course of the story?

3. How do the opinions of Milo's teachers define him and his abilities?

4. Bori, a cat, is a main character in the story. Although he speaks, does he still seem to be a cat?

5. Milo repeatedly states that he doesn't have a clue about what he should do. What does this reveal about him?

6. What is the significance of the number "thirteen" to the story?

7. Milo, who is fifteen, meets several adult men who become teachers and mentors to him. What about the adult women he meets? How is he affected by them?

8. Milo develops friendships with several girls his age. How does he relate to them?

9. Stars and constellations appear frequently during the development of the plot. What purpose do they serve?

10. Tinburkin pops up at odd times throughout the story. What is his role?

11. Milo is admonished to seek his own way. Does listening to the advice and information that others give him compromise his integrity?

12. The Grail is a well-known symbol in Western literature, especially the King Arthur stories. What is the meaning of the Grail Question?

13. The Grail Ceremony appears in Chapter 4 and is repeated in Chapter 20. In what ways is the second one different from the first one?

14. What does Blai's spinning of light into yarn and Milo's observations about the rainbow tell the reader about Milo and his quest?

15. What is a pilgrimage? Must it always have a religious reason?

16. Does the story that Deryl, Teryl, and Beryl tell seem a digression, or does it amplify the plot?

17. What is slinger? What role does it have to the narration?

18. Unfair play and vindictiveness arise during the slinger games in contrast to the game's idealism and sportsmanship. How does this foreshadow events to come?

19. Einter is an enigmatic figure. What do you think he represents?

20. Renee is a card reader. How do her oracular warnings prepare the reader for what is to come?

21. How does Milo's dream conversation with the oak tree prepare him—and the reader—for future events?

22. How does Musail mislead Milo?

23. The story becomes more complex as the myths, legends, astronomy, and techniques Culebrant teaches Milo weave together. How does this challenge the reader's attention?

24. Culebrant warps time so Milo can accumulate all he must know to solve the mystery of the Dragon Cross. Why must Milo learn these skills?

25. Culebrant impresses on Milo that he must make strategic choices that Milo feels are harsh and disturbing. What do you think?

26. There is a huge shift in the story when Milo enters the Barrow. What are these changes?

27. Each of the people who enter the Barrow has a piece of the puzzle to contribute. What does each one offer?

28. Kayn Smith projects a mirror image of the ideals of the Magical Scavenger Hunt. In what way does this expand the perspective of the quest?

29. Bori also undergoes a transformation. What previous clues suggest the possibility for this transformation?

30. How does Count Yeroen's alteration in his attitude toward Milo tell the reader how Milo's status has been reevaluated?

31. As Milo, Analisa, and Stigma travel with Einter to the Crane Castle, Analisa makes a confession to Milo. How does this signal her—and his—growing maturity?

32. By the end of the story did your concept of magic shift?

33. What other discussion questions can you think of asking?

CPSIA information can be obtained
at www.ICGtesting.com
Printed in the USA
LVOW12s0236290817

546778LV00006B/362/P